•online
@ offline•

•online @ offline•

moinak dutta

LIFI PUBLICATIONS PVT. LTD.
NEW DELHI

Published by:
LiFi Publications Pvt. Ltd.
211, 2nd Floor, Gagandeep
12, Rajendra Place, New Delhi–110 008, India
Phone : (011) 2574 1000
E-mail : info@lifipublications.com
Web : www.lifipublications.com

ISBN 13: 978-93-82536-25-3 ISBN 10: 93-82536-25-6

First published in 2014

Cataloging in Publication Data—DK
[Courtesy: D.K. Agencies (P) Ltd. <docinfo@dkagencies.com>]

Dutta, Moinak, 1977–
Online @ offline / Moinak Dutta.
p. cm.
Novel.
ISBN 9789382536253

1. Indic fiction (English) I. Title. II. Online at offline.

DDC 823.92 23

Printed in India by D.K. Fine Art Press (P) Ltd., Delhi–52

To

a candletree...

Acknowledgements

No one can do anything all alone. I have a real big list of people continuously egging me on, criticising me, constructing and deconstructing me. However, to put each and every one by name would take up quite a few pages. So I am trying to be brief and yet holistic.

- First, my mother, who despite being absent in the offline world, is always connected 'online' with me with her abundant memories.
- My father and wife, for putting up with me, every single moment at home. My in-laws, for being so hospitable. My nine year old kid, for all the time jumping onto the screen of my computer, and passing his innocent and curious remarks on my write-ups.
- All at LiFi
- My colleagues at work.
- My friends and relatives.
- Professors and monks of RKMRC, Narendrapur.
- And last but not the least, a dream within…

1

Just as Moni reached the last row of her excel sheet scrutiny, the cellphone rang. Anoushka calling.

'Oh no! Not now!' Moni hemmed and hawed before taking the call, then barked, 'No Anu, no booze tonight.'

Anoushka did not reply, and for a second or two it seemed like there was nobody at the other end. All Moni heard was a soft mewing sound, as if a feline had called her.

'Hey! What's up?' Moni asked gently this time.

'Moni... I'm ditched again! The *sonovabitch* Sandy has just quit me!' Anoushka broke into sobs.

'Oh ho... That's really unfortunate... Not again!' Moni offered in exasperation. Anoushka cried profusely, throwing her choicest expletives at Sandy alias Sandipan.

Sandy was Anu's fourth date in the past six months and going by her statistics, it had always been *about to* happen. Anu had never dated a man for more than a month and a half. The longest date was the second one with an insurance agent which lasted exactly a month and twenty five days. Knowing all this, Moni was not at all startled by Anu's most recent break-up. In fact, she was quite pleased. At least for some days now, there would be no all-nighter phone calls nor outbursts of feverish qualms at odd hours and allied paranormal symptoms of the dreaded disease called 'love'.

But, you know, sometimes, it is necessary to keep your own psychoanalysis at bay, especially when you are in the middle of a tough excel sheet scrutiny, trying to converse with your best friend and roommate who has just announced a turbulent break-up. So Moni kept mum and waited for Anu to regain her calm. Actually, Moni knew only too well how to handle this situation.

She sprinkled the oft tried medicine: 'Okay… Don't you worry sweetie… I'll be back early tonight and on the way I'll definitely bring the right potion for you.' That, Moni knew, sealed the deal, at least, temporarily.

Moni wrapped up for the day at eight, and after some quick grocery shopping, reached the front door of their third floor shared flat on Bardhaman Road, at nine o'clock. The door was unlocked, which meant that Anu was home. Moni got out of her shoes and headed straight to her flatmate's room. The flat had two bedrooms with an attached W.C. each and a common living room area. On entering Anu's room, Moni was shocked to see Anoushka Agarwal, yes, her flatmate of four and a half years, in the thick of… Ahem… Physical exercise! It was such a curious sight! Anu was jumping as if trying to cross an imaginary line. So engrossed was Anu in her task, that she hardly noticed Moni staring at her from the sidelines.

Anoushka had never been a fitness freak. In fact, she hated aerobics. But now, with Anu vigorously jumping up and down, Moni watched the big beads of sweat dance and settle on Anu's rotund face. She was wearing a green tee and blue tracks, her boobs moving around awkwardly without support. *Sagging like an old hag's*, thought Moni, now crying out aloud, 'Hey! What are you doing, you nut?'

Anu looked at her and flashed a peculiar kind of smile which reminded Moni of the brow less Mona Lisa (was it a smile or a sob?)

'I'm having a *time travel*... Wanna join me?' Anu said, panting.

'Time travel? What's that?'

For a moment, Moni thought the jumping girl was not Anu. But how could she not be? The creature, that plump structure lacking any womanly curves could be none other than Anu. There was only one kind of animal in the world that struck a close resemblance with her mate. How could she carry on jumping like that? The girl had once confessed that she was such a bad athlete and that even if she was allowed to run alone, she would come second. And here she was, jumping like a possessed kangaroo.

Anu stopped her aerobics and asked Moni, with a wink, 'Can't get that? You fool!'

'Na...' Moni said, confused.

'Well, my dear, you'll have to be a li'l bit imaginative,' so saying, Anu moved closer to Moni and looked into her eyes.

Anu's eyes were bloodshot, and at once, Moni realised everything. The jumping, the time travel, everything was clear as daylight. 'So, you're on grass again!' Moni shouted, like she were rebuking an errant subordinate.

Her yell had no immediate effect on Anu, who only went to her bedside table, picked up a red sketch pen and kneeling down on the white marble floor, started to draw a straight line.

After drawing a line of at least four feet long, she jumped over to the other side, and like a true professor standing on a podium in front of an august audience, started to deliver a solemn lecture, 'Students, let us presume for the moment, at least hypothetically, that the line drawn on the floor is the *Marriage Line*. Those who are on the right side of it are, presumably married and those who are on the left, are unmarried. Now, if we jump over the line, we can easily traverse a great deal of time… I mean, going from the married state to the state of being a bachelor and vice versa… Isn't it?' Anu asked like a seasoned orator or a hardcore thespian personality.

Moni was dumbfounded by this sudden performance by Anu the orator, at a presumed lectern, and the high content verbosity of the creature's lecture delivery, that she just kept on staring at Anu like an idiot.

'So, friends, by jumping over the line we are actually traversing time—We are having a Time travel! And the moment I am crossing the line, my velocity is equal to that of light. Isn't that awesome?' so saying, Anu bent forward, as if to accept the standing ovation of an audience, as professionals do, in huge halls before an audience. Pitifully, there was no one there else except for Moni. And Moni was so shocked, she was paralysed.

Anu now looked exhausted, and asked for water. Moni came back with a jug, knowing fully well how thirsty grass makes people, especially those who jabber too much when on it.

Anu gulped a jug full of water. Thirst taken care of, Anu sobered up slightly. Even before Moni could guess her next antics, Anu expressed her hunger in a sing-song, 'Hey! I am a hungry hippo... I am a hungry hungry hippo... Am a hungry hungry hippo...'

Hunger could be terrible for any grass smoker and given the normal appetite of Anu, Moni quickly made a mental note that after dope, her hunger would inflate exponentially. She simply asked Anu to stay in her room and went out to buy some rotis and chicken curry from the nearby dhaba, locking her flatmate from the outside.

When Moni returned twenty minutes later, Anu had slept off in her tee and tracks. Moni undressed Anu, pulled her to the bathroom and poured a bucketful of water over her. Anu woke up shivering, like a fevered patient. Her eyes shot a bewildered look, like in a nightmare.

Moni took her by hand to the living room and switched on the TV. Anu sat down like a doll on the sofa and started watching a reality show involving dancing divas from all over the world. Moni gave her the night robes and went to the bathroom to freshen up.

At dinner again, Anu broke all previous records by stomaching fifteen rotis and at least ten medium sized chicken pieces along with two bowls of soup. Moni said nothing for she knew her words would not register anywhere in Anu's brain.

After dinner, Anu fell asleep and Moni went to her room. She left her bedroom door ajar and opened her laptop, while in bed and going straight to her blog page.

She had a habit of posting lines or scribbling on the page almost every night. Sometimes she did that late into the night. Sometimes she scribbled something at night and erased it the next morning. It was her own way of purging herself of the daily grudges. Living in a city with no one around and a demanding job was exasperating. She had no family whatsoever, unlike Anu, who had a wealthy father to pay for all her eccentricities.

Anu's family lived in North Bengal and she was here pursuing her post grad in Education at the Shahid Khudiram Shikshangan or Alipore campus of Calcutta University. Moni's job, on the other hand, was all about facts and figures. She was the sales manager of the Blitz, a shopping mall on Alipore road, barely a few minutes from their flat in Bardhaman Road. She actually never wanted to be in the retail sector, but soon after college, she had to look for a job as her uncle, who had brought her up, was retired and her aunt and cousin brother began to question everything she did like the way she talked, dressed, her attitude, her eagerness to study further, her habit of scribbling, her silence... Everything. She could have tolerated all that. But one day, she experienced the creepy side of living with a man with long fingers and nails full of dirt. Some long male fingers had left their agonising imprint in her mental memory since living at her uncle's. She had left their place at Shibpur, Howrah three years ago and till date long fingernails sent shudders down her spine. She wanted an independent life and a life without long filthy male fingers around. So she moved out of Howrah and after a hard struggle of three years, she got the job of a manager of the mall. She was proud that despite all odds, she had managed to carve a niche for herself.

She found a decent accommodation in a decent locality. This life had made her forget her previous life at her uncle's home and all evil memories associated with it. She was now blogging prolifically in her free time. Her blog had nearly fifty posts, almost all of them were poems—if lines with some rhythm, pattern or thematic semblance could be forgiven for poetry. One day, she would publish them like all the great poets and authors who launched their books and became famous, she thought, hopeful of her scribbles. Her photos and interviews would be published in top magazines and journals. All these, were her dreams. To make it big, 'to make it large,' as a liquor commercial put it.

Thinking about liquor, she realised she had brought home a bottle of Smirnoff which had been forgotten in her bag in the living room. With some sanity restored in the house, she thought it apt to have a glass of vodka and try writing something worthwhile.

After two quick swigs, Moni lit up a cigarette and thought about typing her mind on the square sleek keypad. From her bedroom window pane, the half moon was visible, a slightly blurred white mass shining in a clear October sky. Few stars also gave company to the imperfect moon. Moni rested her head on her folded left arm and looked at the moon, as her right hand's nimble fingers touched blithely the soft plastic keys of the luminous machine in an otherwise dark room. Her creamy satin negligee left her smooth waxed thighs open to the nip in the midnight air. She shivered slightly, feeling soft and light like a fairy of some wonderland. Smirnoff rarely failed to deliver desired results. She fell into a deep sleep.

2

'Wake up you nerd!'

Moni half opened her eyes to catch the silhouette of Anoushka close to her face with toothpaste foam dangling from her mouth.

'*Ouf*! How many times have I warned you against showing off your filthy toothpaste face to me early in the morning?' Moni yelled, irritated, remembering the past night's dopey antics of her flatmate.

'I am sorry for whatever I was on, last night... But you know what? Today I'm off from university!'

'So?' Monideepa asked, wiping her eyes in the pillow, still groggy.

'So, you need not worry about housekeeping!' Anu replied, rushing to the basin to wash her face.

Moni alighted from the bed and went to the bathroom. Meanwhile, Anu prepared breakfast with crisp butter breads and omelets.

Moni was very pleased to see the arrangements for breakfast at the table. She began gorging on bread. It was already eight thirty and she had to reach office by 10:00 a.m. sharp. Management hawks from *Bengaluru* were going to visit their mall today. She would have to be ready with the month's sales figures, all spruced up. Besides, the hawks would be holding a briefing at the end of their visit which may spell out the company's future retail plans for Kolkata in general, and their outlet in particular.

'I'll be a little late today and there is no need to cook my dinner tonight,' Moni said pretending to read the day's newspaper.

Anu who was sitting in her chair, stood up and coming behind her, embraced her. 'O Moni! I am so sorry! I will never ever trouble you, I promise!' Anu murmured as she started planting kisses on Moni's cheeks.

Moni smiled. She could not retain her wrath or disdain when confronted with such heavy cajoling, which was Anu's hallmark.

'I am six years younger than you and so you have a duty to pardon me, haven't you?' Anu asked still wrapping her arms around Moni's neck.

'Ya… And you have all the responsibilities to commit nuisance… Right?'

'Haven't I apologised?'

'You know what you did last night?' Moni asked Anu pulling her to the red streak on the floor of Anu's room, still glowing like a child's whimsical artwork.

'What's that?' Anu asked as she looked at the line standing right over it, arms akimbo, trying to mentally retrace the forgotten path.

'Well… You called it the Marriage line last night!'

'Marriage… What?'

'Line, dear,'

'O ho… Ha ha ha,' Anu laughed, flashing her excellent canine structure.

Moni reached the mall at ten-ten. She wore white silk pants with elaborate black floral patterns with a high neck black blouse. On Anu's insistence, she wore wooden earrings with intricate carvings. Anu, being a university student, was well informed about couture. Moni usually went by her own dictums whenever she had to dress herself up for occasions. It saved her from all the trial before mirrors and serious brain racking.

'You are looking elegantly beautiful, Madam!' Anu had exclaimed earlier when Moni was standing straight in black stilettos, as she cast a final look in the mirror before descending to the hurly-burly of the city.

Moni knew she was attractive with her dusky face of dreamy eyes and long lashes. At twenty-nine, she was still in her best shape. However, on closer scrutinising her face, she could see wrinkles spread out evenly across the forehead—signs of a troubled childhood. Fortunately, those wrinkles were only visible to her and she was sure that her man—if there was one in the world—would discover those little cobwebs on her forehead, easily.

The management hawks swooped down exactly at twelve. There were three of them. One fat middle-aged man with a big butt that resembled an upside down handi, checked and rechecked all documents and folders on her machine. The other two, middle aged but thin, compared to the 'handi butt,' only inspected the floors, looking for holes in the general upkeep, maintenance and stacking and displaying system. As the display and stacking system were not directly in her area of work, Moni remained glued to the 'handi-butt' whose ID announced that he was some H. B. Bhatia. Moni, as she always did while observing any man, carefully surveyed Bhatia's fingers. *Fingers reveal a lot of things...* Moni thought as she looked at Bhatia's fingers. They were not long. Nor were they filthy or long with dirt stuffed in them like thin black lines. This pleased Moni.

Mr. Bhatia, meanwhile, had brought out a small notepad to take down the aggregate sales figures of the month from the Excel sheet. As he arrived at the last row of the sheet, Monideepa suddenly realised that the Value Added Tax collection column of the row had been left blank! She remembered the probable cause of her mistake. It had been Anu, for sure. Only yesterday, when working at that column, Anoushka had called her to announce her break-up news, disorienting her completely.

'What's this Miss Banerjee? You missed the VAT?' Handi-butt Bhatia looked up. His eyebrows took the shape of a corrugated tin section.

'O sir! It was a terrible mistake...' Moni fumbled. She prayed to God to save her from further embarrassment.

And God heard her prayers for sure!

Like a bolt from the blue, in came a girl in her early twenties wearing a dangerously low cut white *kurti*—short kurta and low-waist blue jeans. She dashed into the office and hugged Moni crying out:

'O Moni! You donno how happy am I today!'

Moni had never expected to see Anu in her office. She was so perplexed she could not even speak. But Anu was wearing her usual devil-may-care mood. She turned around, looked at H.B. and at once, dropped herself to pretend to touch his feet and get blessings as young family members do from their elders to show pure respect in desi style. The lethal cocktail of Western attire, deep cleavage and desi tradition, was probably too much for H.B. He just smiled clumsily, as if he was a gatecrasher of sorts.

'My younger sis,' Moni did the intro, realising the palpable effect of 'Anu' storm.

'O... Well, well...' H.B. mumbled, still scanning the desi-Western hybrid.

Moni also reorganised mentally her earlier calculations about Anu's physical attributes and appearance. Anu may have been a little rotund and loony, but she was definitely an eye-catcher when dressed for the occasion.

H.B. passed the rest of his scrutiny in a completely jovial manner, as if he had come all the way from Bengaluru for a picnic. Anu remained throughout the process, cracking all sorts of jokes and showing skin, very nonchalantly. H.B. was so much impressed by the smart bubbly girl that he even gave away his card to Anu promising help in the future, if need be, before he departed.

They had a good laugh on returning home and celebrated the encounter with H.B. with two cans of Budweiser and chicken momos and chili sauce.

'But why on earth, did you suddenly arrive at the office?' Moni asked curiously.

'Well... I wanted to see you there working and slaving... You know I am a masochist,' Anu replied pouring the last few drops of the bitter liquid down her throat.

'You're a crap!' Moni murmured.

That night, Moni stayed awake sitting by Anu till she dropped off to sleep, gently stroking her hair. The moon had brightened, compared to yesterday. With Anu sleeping like a log, Moni slowly walked to her bedroom, turned on her laptop and went to her blog page.

Last night, she had written an incomplete poem which should have saved automatically as a draft. But today to her dismay, she not only found the incomplete poem published on her page, but also additional comments from some visitor named *Silent Assassin*, as by mistake, she hit the publish button instead of preview. The name looked somewhat familiar. She tried to recall where she had seen the name, but in vain. The comment was equally strange: *'Life is full of hiccups and incidents and accidents with diverse emotional associations.'*

Moni clicked on Silent Assassin to link to the commenter's blog page. She found lots of snaps of nature: mountains and streams and flowers and similar stuff. Interestingly, all snaps were tagged with details like location of shoot, type of camera and even technical data like the shutter speed, aperture, focal length, make and model numbers of lens used etc.! So this 'Silent Assassin' was a nature photographer, deduced Moni.

A particular photo of the stupas taken at Ladakh's Shey valley, arrested Moni's attention. She started reading the caption info for every photo. In Ladakh, especially Shey valley, there were a lot of Stupas where lamas were buried. She also learned a new word—*Juley*. In Ladakhi, Juley meant hello.

But, how did this Silent Assassin end up on her blog page out of the several hundred thousands from all over the world wide web? Did this person have any prior knowledge of her?

Moni searched his profile page only to end up with the name *SA* posted in the name box and 'tramp' in the occupation box. There was no way to get back to the person ... no contact details, no email ID. She made a mental note of the blog page address of Silent Assassin.

After thinking hard for a while, Moni typed slowly but steadily, with the object of completing the unfinished poem in the edit box. The poem was titled 'Cobalt moon'. Moni typed:

O Cobalt moon,
Colour me in your hue,
Colour me the way you are,
So happy and true;
O cobalt moon,
Teaser of the night,
Colour me the way you are,
So shiny and bright;

O cobalt moon,
Queen of the night,
Colour me the way you are,
So smooth and white;

Colour me blue,
Colour me white,
Colour me to live,
Colour me like a bride;

Colour me silver,
Colour me pale,

Colour me to survive,
All the storms and the gale;

O cobalt moon,
Why can't I borrow?
Your paintbrush and palette
And colours of sorrow?

✦ ✦ ✦

3

Educational Psychology was Anoushka's favourite paper. She never missed a single lecture in that subject. Last month though, thanks to her dangerous fling with Sandy, she had skipped quite a few classes. At least twice, she had bunked lectures to go out with Sandy to a resort near Amtala and do what couples without a social licence did. On both occasions, the couple had played bed games, perfecting their romp in fun and frolic. She rode on Sandy like a warrior; Sandy also played like an expert in the field. He was calm, unlike previous others who were hyperactive and hyper-excited even before the real game began, and when it was actually time to perform, they were out of breath. *Poor fellas*!

But the same calm Sandy, 'the real McCoy' in her life, suddenly broke up with her. He said he did not enjoy their sexual misadventures anymore. That was only day before yesterday. Sandy had taken her to a hotel on Russell Street and after a good amount of boozing, she had passed out. Late in the evening, Sandy woke her up and dropped her home by cab. On the way, he had quickly said he was pissed off with the affair and wanted to close their chapter forever. Anu had stayed silent, trying to recuperate from the awkward sensation of a jarring head and a ringing ear, the after effects of heavy boozing. Plus, the words did not register fully in her brain then. Only after she had called him several times, from the unanswered phone calls, did she realise that she had been dumped. Her real McCoy had turned out to be a real fake. That *fling* had ended in a whimper. A game with a null and void ending. She got out of the flat that evening in a furious search of grass and came back home with two sacks full.

All her adventures had been like closely guarded secrets with Anu. There was hardly a chance for her dad to know about them and Monideepa, though a bit authoritative at times, showed no interest to butting in her friend's business. Sometimes Anu would question herself. Were her adventures really fun? Physical pleasure no doubt, but did they lead her anywhere new? Was it just another show of street-smartness before friends, and flaunting boyfriends? It was like a big ever expanding spiral which gradually collapsed in a tiny dot. One day she would also become a dot... A tiny black botch on a white paper into which a big spiral (of life) culminates. Somewhere she had seen a diagram like that—an illusory figure. What was the name of that figure? *Archimedean Spiral*?

Anu was now sitting in the last row of the gallery of the education department, almost touching the ceiling, lost in thoughts. Through the side windows of the hall, portions of the busy road could be seen, dotted with trees and buildings of different shapes and sizes.

Just then, a tall man with long curly hair entered the hall in a white cotton shirt and jeans. His face was long, sporting two very sharp eyes. Something about him was magnetic. Or she was sitting in an attractive direction.

Sushmita, who sat beside Anu, gushed, 'Our new Psycho teacher... Isn't he suauve?'

'Incorrect! He's IAB,' Anu quipped.

'IAB? What's that?' Sush asked quizzically.

'Indian Antonio Banderas,' Anu replied mischievously.

Sush started to laugh, a little violently as usual, jerking the upper part of her torso as if in a fit.

That was too much for IAB who asked Anu to stand up.

Anu stood up faithfully.

'What's the matter with you?' he boomed.

IAB had started to walk up the steps towards them, with hands in his pockets, in a leisurely manner, the way his Hollywood parallel often approached his screen heroines. The nearer he came, the more Anu started scanning him. From his left wrist was hanging loosely the Longines elegantes, with all its lustre and glory. His shirt pocket had a Parker Matte Black. Wasn't it dandy to own pens like that *with a dual ink system, a 0.5 mm pencil and a PDA stylus, all packed in one!* Anu thought with awe.

From his shirt pocket, Anu's gaze dropped to his waist. *The belt was pure leather...* Hidesign? She wondered and then lowered her gaze further to, well, the *danger zone* when she heard IAB cough hoarsely. He was probably demanding her attention, or eye contact (or both).

'So? Haven't seen me earlier, I guess?' IAB asked softly. His voice had a certain suppleness which only erudition could lend to a man.

'Ya... Sir! Actually, I have missed your earlier classes...'

'Then you should be all the more attentive to your lessons... Now sit down and please don't talk too much... It is a bit disorienting.' IAB lumbered back to his platform, without changing his gait.

Anu kept on standing.

'Haven't I told you to take your seat?'

Anu's eyes moistened.

IAB shook his curls as if he was sorry for himself and began retracing his steps towards Anu.

'I'm sorry Sir! Really!' Anu muttered.

'It is perfectly all right and... You know something, I like obedient pupils like you.' IAB flashed a smile, a real smile with no pretence.

The whole class broke into laughter.

Anu smiled, wiping her eyes with the end of her dupatta.

For the rest of the lesson, Anu kept on staring at the teacher on the sly. Wasn't he handsome? What could be his age? Thirty? Thirty one? Thirty two? Thirty three? *Was he married?*

Anoushka Agarwal was in a reverie, to say the least. The first thing she did after class was to ask Sush the real name of IAB, as she realised that a nom de plume would only worsen her stares and romantic renderings of him, but a real name was a real name, irreplaceable.

'O... He has a bit of a lengthy name, I heard.'

'Tell me?'

'Professor Ved Prakash Bhattacharya.'

'Oh ho! I nearly made that out! He's VPB instead of IAB!' said Anoushka, gathering her wits with every bit of muscle.

Sush laughed.

Meanwhile, Moni was having a hard time at the Blitz. Entering office today, the first thing she received was a fax from Bengaluru, directing her in no-nonsense terms, to dispose of the non-stick inferior quality cookware that had been lying around like ancient artefacts in the stock room, beneath cakes of dust. Actually, the cookware had arrived in their outlet of Blitz from Chennai, three months back. Most of them looked shabby and were of no use. There was actually no non-stick equipment as they did not have the mandatory Teflon coating, unlike cookware of the same category from other reputed brands. Moni knew that they were dumped on her outlet by the management honchos who meted out discriminatory treatment towards Kolkata. To them, the Kolkata business was slow and the shoppers there, too price conscious. So, the low grade items which failed to make a cut elsewhere were dumped there.

Last year, almost the same thing had happened with a pile of toiletries, imported from a Middle Eastern country. Moni had saved the situation by conducting 'reduction sales' of the products. But the same trick had already been applied to the non-stick items. Only last month, the price of wares had been halved and still, they stuck around unsold. Whenever, a shopper lay his or her hand on them, the floor manager Kevin would run, almost salivating, with the prospect of sliding at least one item off the shelf. But soon, his throat ran dry as the prospective buyer moved on to some other item. At least once, a tawa and handi were sold and billed, only to be returned later, with a lot of post-purchase grudge and sniggering.

Moni was helpless. With Diwali around the corner, dress materials and consumer durables were moving off the shelves with a terrible rapidity and reinforcements coming in quite quickly. More and more spaces were being filled by shirts and kurtis and jeans and tees and banyans and kids' wear and DVDs and CDs and music systems and coffee machines and toasters and microwaves and other small things like the metal and earthen diyas, lamps, perfume canisters, etc. The non-stick ware had already been taken off the shelves and thrown to the basement stockroom to gather more dust and cobwebs. Unwittingly, the management wanted them to be sold at any cost, now that they were thrown to dust.

What to do? Moni undid her hairclip and started to scratch her head, sitting at her table, looking at the month's sales figures, glowing like an intricate pattern on her desktop. She imagined H.B. coming down right here to her office and throwing her out, bag and baggage.

At twenty nine, with little income, it was very difficult for a single woman in a city to find two things in life—*a promising job and a husband!* She was on the wrong side of the Marriage Line and did not even take grass! Hence, time travel for her, unlike Anu, was too distant a proposition.

So, to save her job and herself, she would move away the unholy tawas and handis and pans and pots. *Only a blitzkrieg could save the situation this time*, chuckled Moni.

They would have to throw away the cookware indiscriminately, without thinking about the outcome. Besides, the management wanted them to be disposed of, right? What better way to dispose of anything than give away as freebies? With the festive season on, the Kolkata public would love the freebies, for sure!

Moni called Kevin, the floor manager, the stockroom-in-charge, and the accounts clerk for a brief meeting in her office.

4

After taking four consecutive classes, Ved retired to his room at the end of the third floor corridor of the university's main building. The room was chiefly occupied by a small table, a couch, a water dispenser and three small wooden bookcases. There was only one window in the room facing the main road. Come October, and the afternoon sun would peep into the small room. He liked this naturally sun-lit room. The slanted column of sunbeam created a beautiful spectacle in the office. Tiny suspended air particles could be perceived as easily floating in the air, enlivened by the reddish light of a setting sun. Ved closed the door and put down the books on the table. Then he walked straight to the window. It was his favourite spot. From here, he could see far and wide, the neighbouring area, from the sprawling National Library campus to further up the zoo. It was almost like having an aerial view.

He brought out his pack of cigarettes and lit up one. It was a quarter past four in the afternoon. He would have to leave the university soon and get to Ballygunge Circular road to pick up Sonai, his twelve year old daughter from school. Joining the university, he found it quite a pleasing thing to take and drop Sonai at school and then while going back home pick her up again. Earlier when he had been posted at the Diamond Harbour College, there was no scope of accompanying Sonai everyday to her school. Nowadays, coming to school, sitting by his side at the front seat of the car, Sonai would keep on rambling different things. All her rambles were related to computer games. At twelve, she was quite a game addict. Her addiction was so much that she even called Ved '47', the agent code for a protagonist of a popular but very violent computer game. Ved sometimes regretted having introduced her to such violent games. Sadly, he also loved those games. They were so engrossing!

On their way back home, Sonai would, sometimes sing rhymes she learnt at school. And how much Ved loved his daughter's company! He loved to see her grow up every day, becoming a lady on her own. Her words, her wails, her little hankerings—everything made his life colourful and helped him to forget the pangs of losing the woman who gave birth to his little princess. Sometimes, when Sonai would sit by his side and sleep off, resting her head on his shoulder, he would at once, be reminded of Mayurika. Ved would then just keep on caressing her soft brown curls of hair and drops of tears would roll down his cheeks like warm droplets of pent-up anguish and pain. In fact, after the sudden death of Mayurika two years back, he had taken it upon himself to give as much time to Sonai as possible, despite the fact that at home there were quite a few other members to take care of her too. His dad and mom were there, as also Padma-di and other servants.

Who would have ever thought that Mayurika would die so young? Appendicitis of a rare and critical kind took her away forever. It was discovered a little too late. Mayurika had actually suppressed her pain and discomfort too long. She talked about her severe abdominal pain when she could not bear it any longer. That's the way she was—the silent bearer of pains and burdens. Mayurika lived and died silently, trying to please everyone in and around the family but never sought her own comforts. Whenever Ved would ask her to take a break from managing the daily household chores, and her social service towards a few street children, she had just smiled and hugged him.

'May I come in, Sir?'

Ved's deep reminiscence was broken by a soft feminine voice at the door.

'Ya, come'n in.'

The same naughty girl in yellow salwar who Ved had rebuked a little while ago at the class for laughing and gossiping with her friend, entered slowly with a file held up to her bosom. The girl's face, especially her eyes, held mischief. A quick look at her revealed a certain waywardness, common to girls who came from affluence. Ved rubbed the cigarette on the ashtray at the table and was about to ask the student for the reason behind her visit, when the gutsy girl remarked, 'I heard smoking in educational institutions had been banned... Am I wrong, Sir?'

The remark surprised Ved too much. He looked up to meet the eyes of the girl. They were still mischievous. There was a twinkle in her bright, witty eyes.

Ved gestured for her to sit across the table and sank in his own chair.

'Ya, it was an offence for sure. But I am a bit uncertain about the disciplinary action taken against the violators.... Any idea?' Ved asked staring straight into the girl's eyes.

'No, Sir... Actually, it is Kohlberg's theory which brought me here.'

'On moral development?'

'Ya'

'Well ... I have some time at my disposal right now, to give you a long discourse on the topic. But as you have asked, there are three sequential levels, according to Lawrence Kohlberg, of moral development, namely a) pre conventional, b) conventional and c) post conventional. Interestingly, he further divided these three into two stages each ...'

Anoushka brought out her writing book and took down obediently, whatever she heard from Ved, spreading herself and her notes across his glass top table.

Ved looked at his watch. It was four twenty five and he had to be running to Sonai. The school would break at four-thirty and even if he would fly his car like those in the F1 circuit, he would still be some fifteen to twenty minutes late.

So he stood up making a lot of noise by pushing the chair back on the floor deliberately, to make the young yellow salwar look up.

'I'm sorry, miss...'

'I'm Anoushka, Sir...Ya, I remember, you've got important things to do... Thank you sir, for being so generous! But before you leave, can you please give me your contact number?'

'Why?' Ved asked, surprised by Miss Attitude's overtly socialising tendency.

'In case, I need any academic help,' Miss Attitude stressed on the word academic which was a bit intentional and that made Ved really curious.

'Okay… I can give my landline number.'

'Haven't you got any personal number?'

What was the girl up to? Ved thought and lied.

'Well… My cell got stolen and I haven't bought a new one yet.'

'That's unfortunate.'

'But you can have my email ID, if it helps you anyway.'

'Surely.'

Ved gave out his official email account. There was another personal email ID which he did not give. He gave the email ID instead of the phone number to avoid intrusions which might have been beyond his control. In case of emails, there were numerous ways to avoid unwanted emails like marking them as spam.

'Can I send my queries to you if need be?'

You are a game, Ved thought and reverted, 'O ya, you're welcome but as you know, I've a real urgency to leave, so bye for now…'

Saying this, Ved almost jumped on the leather bag kept on the table and ran out of the door, clutching it, without even being bothered about the fact that Anoushka was still there in the room.

Anu was pretty amused by the hurried exit of the professor as if he had wet his pants and was running to the loo. She smiled within herself and got out of the room and pulling the door, closed it from outside.

Walking across the corridor, Anu casually looked out of the glass casements and she saw a scene taking place right at the main gate of the university—a white Honda City dashed out of the gate with terrible speed and banged right into the busy road and swerved left, screeching on the macadamized road, like Hollywood cops do chasing some car lifter, thereby sending into disarray all the other vehicles on the road. *That's sheer machismo*! Anu thought as she got a slight glimpse of a white shirt at the steering of the white Honda.

Parking the car just beside the footpath, Ved rushed out of the car and started to run almost to the blue gate of the missionary school with a high walled enclosure.

'Where can I find Sanhita Bhattacharya of class seven, section A?' Ved asked a uniformed man at the entrance.

'Turn right and you'll get those pupils whose pick-ups haven't arrived yet.'

Ved walked into the enclosure and saw some children playing merrily inside. His eyes began searching for Sonai. Where was she? He found her sitting at a bench, head rested on her folded up, lifted knees, a forlorn figure.

'I'm so sorry dear.'

'You're late 47,' Sonai replied in a mock-grave tone.

'Actually an unexpected assignment held me up, Diana.'

'Then face the task, take me to an eatery… I'm hungry.'

'Okay.'

Ved enjoyed this little game of imagining himself to be the protagonist of a computer game, 47, while talking with Sonai, who, similarly, loved taking on the role of the female voice-over which instructed and delivered different assignments to the hero of the game. Physically, there was a similarity between Ved and the hero. Both were tall and fair complexioned. Only his head was not clean-shaven like the virtual hero's. But he knew he could shave his curls any day that Sonai alias Diana wished.

A few minutes' drive from the school gate brought them to a coffee shop. The red and pink facade of the eatery with trees and all that, made it an ideal place for 47 and his instructor to have a little talk on their next assignment. The setting sun lent a red hue to the sky which reflected everything—the road, the trees, the glass doors, the faces of people walking hastily across the road…

5

Moni's plan of giving away cookware as freebies, to every customer buying items billed worth over and above two thousand rupees at a time, was greatly appreciated by everyone. Kevin had made the rough calculation that even if ten customers spent the desired amount per day and if it continued for the next twenty days, then they would be disposing two hundred pieces of junk, a big relief. Besides, as per calculations, two thousand rupees on the bill meant at least, a fifteen to twenty percent profit margin, which would easily make up for (if not overshoot) the procurement cost of those obsolete items. Going by past sales records, they would overshoot and probably make considerable profits. Still, their plan would be reviewed after a few days to check the rate of disposal and assess the stock in hand.

Having drawn up such an excellent strategy, Moni felt good, accomplished. She went to the 'Ladies' changing room and scrubbed her face clean and then applied a moisturiser. After staring at her glowing face in the mirror reflection, she realised there was a light blackening around her eyes. She went straight to the toiletry section and picked up a newly launched under-eye-roll-on cleanser of an international brand. She also picked up a facewash, body lotion and few other things. Strolling about, she eventually landed in the apparel section. Kevin was there. He came rushing, thinking that Moni probably had something to tell him. But Moni simply smiled and waved her hand, assuring him there was nothing official behind her taking a walk around. Kevin went back and following him with her eyes, Moni saw him lean against a column of glass, and starting to chat to a sales girl with blunt facial features but invigorating body. *A disappointing front on an excellent chassis,* thought Moni, as she moved on.

Buoyed by her novel strategy to save her job and life for at least the time being, Moni wanted to do something expansive. After a lot of thinking she decided to visit a bookshop after leaving the office a bit early. She thought it to be great to buy a few books for herself. Only the other day, she read a review of a fiction which had won critical fame recently.

Wait a minute! What about buying a present for Anu? A surprise gift? What would she like to have? *Book, booze or bra?*

Moni reached the bookshop on Sarat Bose Road at nine. Entering the shop, she found it almost empty of customers. The cashier was dozing off on the counter before a switched-on monitor. The books were stacked all right, but not always under proper headers. Had she been the manager, she would have asked the salesgirls to order them by genre in their designated shelves. The display should be loud and clear at any shopping centre. Down the passage, she reached the end of the left flank of shelves for 'Contemporary English Fiction' as per the headers. The opposite flank was the section allotted to books on photography. A man in a white round neck tee and beige chinos was standing there browsing quite intently, a fat book on photography. His head was bent over the book, standing tall, with thick, curly hair almost hiding his face. The passage between the two flanks was a bit narrow, and Moni tried to pass through sideways. Alas, her back brushed against him and the fat book fell from his hand straight onto the floor bringing a big 'thud' in the otherwise quiet and empty shop.

'O ho… I'm sorry… Please don't mind,' Moni murmured, drooping to pick up the book. *Wasn't it heavy?*

'A few kilos perhaps, this book of yours,' Moni said smiling, handing over the book to the curly haired man, evidently trying to ease off.

'Ya it is, but worth carrying the weight, considering its content.' The man answered. His face was longish and muscular and his eyes were brilliant, almost sparkling. His curls gave his face a mystic look, like that of a musician or writer. 'Hello… I'm Ved,' said the man extending his right hand while holding the book in his left one.

'Hi! I'm Moni,' Moni shook his hand. Moni, out of custom, inspected the man's fingers. They were long without nails. The fingers were long, a bit disturbingly long, but they were good. They were not creepy. They looked clean. Moni smiled.

Ved turned back to the books and began leafing through other books on photography.

Moni got busy reading the titles. Whenever she went to a big bookshop she would get a bit confused. The images of so many books with interesting glossy cover pages puzzled her. She suffered from optical illusions caused by similar looking book jackets placed side by side. After severe indecision over *should I take it or shouldn't I,* Moni finally settled for two books, one by an upcoming Indian female author and another by an Afghanistan born American.

By the time she reached the billing counter, Ved was already paying up. Moni waited for her turn behind him.

'It's two thousand fifty nine only, sir,' the cashier informed Ved.

Ved then produced his card, signed on the bill and went out of the front door with two big red plastic carry bags.

Moni stood before the counter, gazing at the leisurely walk of the man, now out of the shop, towards a sleek white car parked a short distance away from the glass door.

'Five hundred and twenty only, madam,' the cashier announced, forcing Moni to divert her gaze from Ved and look inside her purse instead, for the books she had placed on the counter.

After at least five consecutive door bell rings, Anoushka finally opened the door. Her eyes were sleepy, hair dishevelled.

'Came home and slept off?' Moni asked as she entered the living area.

'Ya... Actually listening to songs and dozed off,' Anu replied in a sleepy voice.

'Okay, bring the soup and chapattis out of the freezer and put them in the oven... I'm freshening up quickly,' Moni ran to her room.

After dinner, while washing the dishes and other utensils in the sink, Moni asked Anu to open the bag she usually takes to the office.

'Wow! Body lotion, face wash, under-eye-roll-on, satin lingerie... Got a hike or something?' Anu asked quite surprised.

'There are books as well,' Moni replied from the kitchen.

'Na... I am not in books...' Anu replied playing with a tube of moisturiser in her hand.

'What's this? Suave... Advanced skin therapy?'

'Well, it's an American import... A good product from Unilever,' Moni said coming to the living room.

'Can I use it sometimes?' Anu asked.

'Take it.' Moni replied promptly.

'What?'

'I said take it.'

Anu came rushing and lunged at Moni, showering her with kisses and hugs, a childish surge of love, affection and gratitude all mixed up. Moni could not hold her balance and fell on the sofa with Anu all over her.

'Okay okay... Now tell me, you nut, how are you going with your studies?' Moni asked giggling, knowing studies or anything related to it, would be a sure shot spirit squasher, and embrace snapper, averting her death by suffocation.

It worked. Anoushka let Moni off, standing up, visibly downcast with reference to her least favourite issue.

'It's okay... I mean, exam part two is miles away,' Anu said playing with the moisturiser tube, sort of pressing it.

'But Anu... Your parents have sent you down here, far away from your home, to study and ...'

'Ya, I know, I know...' Anu replied walking away to her bedroom.

Moni smiled. She went up to the table and started cleansing its top with a blue liquid from a bottle. Then, she switched off the lights and fans in the dining area and living room, locked the front door and went back to her room.

Back in her own room, Anu pressed her face into the pillow and started crying.

How could Moni know that no one back home was worried about her studies? Her dad, Ramakant Agarwal had a lot of things to do: his timber mill, his furniture shop, his real estate business and his women. Her mom, Laksmi Agarwal was an illiterate to boot with, a strange rustic personality, who never tried to rein in her husband from inappropriate wealth and women. She was too happy with her household work, her pujas, her sarees and gold, her gardening etc. How could she tell Moni that her dad was infamous in Siliguri for his band of killers and conmen, who almost every month had cases registered against their names at the local police station for activities ranging from kidnapping, intimidation, and blackmail to smuggling of contraband items? How could she tell how much she hated receiving cheques of whopping amounts sent to her for her studies and general upkeep by her checkered father and yet simply could not forego them as the comfort of a fashionable, luxurious life was good! For the last four and half years, after coming to Kolkata, she never went back home during the long vacations, barring once, when her dad himself, had come down to fetch her, for his own reasons. He had wanted some of his ill-gotten wealth to be transferred to his daughter's account at a bank in Siliguri which required her signatures and other paperwork and her physical presence. She went, did whatever her dad wanted her to do like a puppet and came back on the earliest flight.

Now that some of his ills had been transferred to her name, she had become part of his evil, and there was no way out. I breed evil, she thought. Dumping money into her account was an intelligent ploy developed by her dad to keep her within his clutches, the way he manipulated everyone around including her mom, the meek and docile Laksmi Agarwal, the political leaders, the goons, the police and the administration. Tax evasion was of course another reason.

There was no one who really cared for her in this world, save Moni. Four years of shared existence with her in this flat in Kolkata had brought them closer to each other. She had become a true friend and someone to look forward to, at the end of day. Moni had literally no one in the world, as far as she knew. Yet, she remained so happy and blessed with her work and book reading and stuff like that. She had no boyfriend and no flings. Was she a saint? How could a woman with such an attractive face and body be a saint? Saint or no saint, Moni was her only friend, philosopher and guide in this big city of smoke and noise, masks and pretence.

Thinking all these thoughts, Anu got up and wiped her face. Suddenly she remembered the moisturiser and started to apply it, dabbing dollops of the advanced skin therapy on her face with cotton.

Anoushka was preparing to sleep when her cell started ringing. She looked at the screen and allowed the phone to ring for a few more seconds and then pressed the green button yawning out loud, pretending to be sleepy.

'Boliye...'

'Guddi *beti...*'

That was Laksmi Agarwal from Siliguri, Anoushka's mom.

Anoushka lay down on the bed with the phone stuck to her right ear.

'How are you doing?' Laksmi Agarwal asked, customarily.

'Good.' Anu replied with reluctance.

'How are your studies?' Laksmi asked treading cautiously.

'So so... How are you?' Anu asked, yawning.

'I'm okay... But your papa... He's not well,' said Laksmi Agarwal.

'How can he be well, tell me? Sitting on so many people's curses?!' exclaimed Anu raising her voice, almost unknowing.

'He's your father... Don't talk like that about him.'

'I don't want to spend a single alphabet on him... You raised the issue... Okay... Take care, good night!' Anu barked, suddenly becoming spiteful.

'Guddi... He loves you... He wants you to come back here and...'

Laksmi could have talked a bit more but Anu cut her short abruptly saying,'I know everything mom... Bye bye...'

'Guddi... Don't cut the line please...' Laksmi implored as her voice quavered.

'Mom... I don't want to hurt you, but as I've told you a million times earlier, please don't put me off by raising issues which I don't like.' Anu talked sternly.

'Thik hai... It's okay. I will not... Ever ask you to come back... But can't you be here for Diwali at least?' Laksmi asked.

'I could have gone there but you know I've got exams… I want to lead a life away from what you're in… I understand, my pop is your husband and you're bound to stick to him… And tolerate his ways… But I've made my choice…' Anu stated trying to be calm.

'Fine… As you wish… I wish you get the life you actually want… I'll never ask you again to come back here… But remember, your papa has funded your whims even… He deserves some kind of gratitude at least… If not your fondness,' Laksmi reminded.

'Of course! I'm grateful to you all! Haven't I told that? Okay! I'm going to send you and papa a long proclamation… Will that do?' Anu shouted hoarsely and punched the red button to disconnect the call.

Throwing the cell on the bed, Anu sobbed loudly pressing her face on the bed. 'God! Give me a break!' she shouted, rinsing her face with fresh sobs until she flushed red.

6

'Sunday is a fun day!' Sonai announced when Ved took her in his arms from her bed. It was eight in the morning. A perfect October Sunday with bright sunshine playing at Sonai's first floor room glass windows and an east facing balcony. A marvellous sight. Ved's father had built this spacious double-storied house in Mandirtala, Howrah, some twenty years back. Then, the locality was not as congested as now. The second Hooghly bridge connector had changed the area altogether. It had now become a hub of buses and cars and other transport vehicles. A lot of shops and restaurants had mushroomed all over the place. Even two nationalised and three private banks had set up their branches right where the bridge connector met the main road.

Ved took Sonai to the basin, washed her face and brushed her hair. Every Sunday, he did this. On weekdays, however, Padma-di took care of Sonai's morning rituals as Ved would be busy with his own daily preparations. But the day being Sunday, Ved had the whole day for his lovely daughter.

'Tum'ro is Diwali, you know that, Diana?' Ved asked as both sat at the breakfast table. Actually, Sonai was sitting on the lap of her granny, Debjani, who was trying to put pieces of chicken sandwich into Sonai's already puffed up and loaded mouth.

'O Granny!'

'Be a good girl Sonu, and eat that up and then dad will bring you a wonderful Diwali present.' Debjani Bhattacharya tried her best to make her granddaughter eat.

'Ma, her mouth is already full of food,' Ved said smiling.

'Oh! You and your daughter... You will make me mad... Now do all the feeding yourself, taking all your sweet time... I have a lot of things to do...' Debjani limped towards the kitchen. She could not walk fast with her arthritis and other allied ailments.

'What present 47?' Sonai asked as she came and sat on Ved's lap.

'Anything, Diana... Perhaps a laptop for you like 47's?'

'No... Diana doesn't use laptop... She uses a desktop.'

'Can't Diana consider PS3, taking into account the gaming aspect of the mission?' Ved asked in a mock serious tone.

'Diana is not into any game, stupid,' Sonai snapped back.

'Okay a desktop, then... Final?'

'Final 47.'

Actually Ved wanted always to buy Sonai a computer as she often played games, and painted and wrote her mind on his laptop. She needed one of her own. A desktop with good sound and video card and ample memory would actually be a better gaming machine than his laptop with limited multimedia components. He could even ask the vendor to attach gaming consoles like joystick, steering wheels etc.

'What you two are conspiring?'

Ved's father, retired barrister of high court, Biswanath Bhattacharya came to the dining room with a folded newspaper in hand and a pipe in his mouth. He didn't smoke anymore but took a pipe between his lips, as a sort of old habit.

'We're going out right after breakfast to take care of an urgent assignment that has cropped up all of a sudden,' Sonai talked like a serious agent of sorts, getting ready for a deadly mission.

'Assignment? Good, but will that be over before lunchtime dear? Your grandpa doesn't want to miss the Sunday lunch with you.'

'That's for 47 to decide,' saying this, Sonai jumped down from Ved's lap and started running towards the lawn as she spotted Bhajan *da*, the gardener, at the garden pruning trees with his long scissors.

'We'll go to Chadni and come back,' Ved replied.

'Hmm… Ved, I need to have a little talk with you regarding Sonai.'

'*Bolo* baba… Tell me dear,' Ved waited with all ears.

'Well, as you are busy with your own work… And we two are growing old and feeble, so I thought, we could send Sonai to a convent somewhere in North Bengal or better still, to Shimla or Ooty?'

'No, baba… I don't want to send her anywhere… I want her to be in front of my eyes,' Ved muttered with his head dropped as his chin rested on his throat.

'Okay as you wish… But then…'

'Then?'

'Well… Sonai needs someone who will take care of her like a mother does.'

'A mother is a mother... No one can imbibe motherliness, it comes from within, only from a biological mother.'

Ved looked up to the ceiling and replied as if talking to himself. Biswanath looked at his son's eyes for a while and strolled back to his study with his hands clasped at his back and head dropped.

Ved and Sonai reached a shop at Chadni at nine thirty. The shop had just opened and so there was no customer. Ved handed over the bespectacled middle aged man sitting on a revolving chair with a red tilak on his forehead, a paper slip containing the requirements or the configuration of the machine. The man seemed to be the owner or the manager of the shop. He barked and a youngish fellow with a stray beard appeared from nowhere and took the paper slip from the manager. He went to another counter or station and started typing up an invoice.

The vendor at Chadni agreed to send a hardware person to do all the set up and installation at their place within two days after Diwali. Ved and Sonai came out of the shop and got into the car. While Sonai was fastening her seat belt, Ved asked,'What to do now?'

'It's so bright and sunny, 47.'

'Ya and so?'

'Why can't we do a little survey at the Victoria?'

'You mean a reconnaissance of sorts?'

'Ya... A recce.'

'That'll be brilliant.'

Ved turned to catch the road towards the memorial.

'Sunshine on my shoulders makes me happy...' Sonai burst into a song impromptu, looking out of the glass window as shops

and high rises started to recede. Ved pushed a *John Denver* CD into the car audio system and then put his left hand on Sonai's tiny head to play with her brown curls. Sonai giggled the way she always did whenever 47 became a bit playful.

Ved thought he heard the sweetest giggle in the whole world.

✦ ✦ ✦

7

There was no way of waking up Anu before nine in the morning on Sundays. Anu would just lie in bed clutching at her pillows, even if one were to beat drums or blow the shrillest whistle in her ears. So Moni took it upon herself to wake up and do the housework like sweeping the rooms or preparing the Sunday breakfast. The jerk alias Anu would get out of bed at exactly nine thirty on a Sunday morning, and sleepwalk to the basin. This notorious sleepwalk had even caused her minor accidents, like, once, when she squeezed half a tube of pain relief balm on her toothbrush and brushed her teeth for at least fifteen minutes, before realising she was using pain relieving cream instead of toothpaste! On another occasion, she had peed into a bucket full of soap soaked clothes mistaking it for the pot. Luckily, the clothes were hers.

So when this Sunday, Moni woke up and found Anu standing in the balcony with her hair neatly combed and face creamed and cleansed, the first thing she did was look at the wall clock, wondering if she had overslept. Shockingly, it was only seven! Seeing Moni all woken up, Anu rushed to the kitchen and brought a cup of tea with biscuits.

'Is everything okay?' Moni asked completely dumbstruck by Anu's unnatural behaviour.

'Ya! Why?' Anu asked smilingly.

'No… I thought you are unwell… Waking up so early on a Sunday morning,' Moni replied.

Anu guffawed.'What's the plan for Diwali this year?' Anu asked as Moni and she settled down on the living room couch.

Last year, they created such a hullabaloo at the flat with some of Anu's 'work hard, party harder' friends having a 'blast' with blaring music, grass and vodka, that the other residents had complained both to the residents' society and the police. Hence, this time around, there would not be any partying at home.

'What to do?' Moni asked confusedly.

'Hey what about going out somewhere?'

'Where?'

'To a pub.'

'Pub?'

Moni did not like pubs. Pubs were full of strangers with varied drunken behaviour.

'Yah!' Anu exclaimed with newfound energy. Liquid or smoke intoxicating agent of any kind made her hyper.

'But you can't go grassy in a pub,' Moni said thoughtfully.

'So what? Liquid stuff can keep you grounded.'

'Grounded?'

At once, there was a flashback from the last year's Diwali when Anu was lying half naked on the floor and jerking her body, twisting and turning in all contortions, uttering like a possessed woman, 'I'm a snake woman, I can bite you from behind' in a tone as eerie as the song 'The devil woman'.

'What about some Diwali shopping today?' Moni asked, changing the topic.

'Have office today, na?' Anu asked twisting her eyebrows.

'O no… It's not that what you're thinking… We could go to some other place, not Blitz…'

'What about a visit to Floatel for dinner after shopping?'

'Okay… So meet me at Blitz at seven in the evening.'

Moni left for office at two thirty. Anu, with nothing else to do watched TV the whole afternoon. At around five, Sush called to inform Anu that they would have to sit for a selection test soon after the vacation. Sush also informed Anu that the paper on psychology would be tentatively the toughest one to handle, as was revealed by a small probe into the statistical records of students' previous performance.

'Statistics are bullshit,' Anu said trying to work up against the exam blues that threatened.

'Still … God knows what your Antonio Banderas will have in store for us.' Sush sounded pretty serious.

'Come'n, don't fret over the paper,' Anu snorted but within her heart, she was probably sinking.

The conversation with Sush made Anu realise her own academic under preparedness for the first time that year. What would happen if she got plucked? Her parents would be unhappy, especially her father, who would be baying for her blood, over his discontent for her ways of life in the City of Joy, Kolkata. Didn't Ramakant always grumble that she had gone to dogs?

Suddenly she remembered that she still had Ved Prakash Bhattacharya, VPB's email ID. What if she sent the professor a query requesting for a shortlist of important questions on psychology paper? Anu hurriedly dialled Moni, and asked for permission to use her laptop for a while, *to send an important mail to someone.*

Moni consented immediately.

Anu went to Moni's room, switched on the computer and logged on to send an email to VPB.

The body of the letter was simple and straight:

Hello Sir,

I am in a fix. Don't know how to handle the mammoth syllabus of psychology. Please help me out or I would fail in the selection.

Yours truly,

Anoushka Agarwal,

PGII, Education

Having written such a brief and precise letter to the most handsome teacher of the department, Anu glowed with pleasure; as if the whole burden of the exam had lessened. She started to hum a tune. If just sending a request for a shortlist of important questions could bring about such a change in her mood, what would happen when she got the shortlist itself?! Would she then break out in a song, like a saxophone, flouting the pollution control board's 65 decibel mark? Anu thought and broke into a laughter.

There was no surety of a reply from Banderas, though! Still, an effort was good enough. Out of simple curiosity and the need to distract herself, Anu moused over the history of websites visited by Moni and found a blog page visited by her friend quite frequently. *Curiosity is the mother of discoveries,* she thought. Piqued with some more curiosity over the next few minutes, Anu was hooked. She discovered quite a few things about her geek flatmate. Not only did she discover Moni's excellent hand at poetry, but she also noticed how someone called *SA* had posted comments of appreciation on Moni's poetry. One comment beneath the Cobalt Moon poem was interesting.

'Can anyone borrow sorrow?' *SA* had posted earlier that day.

'So, my geek mate is not a saint!' Anu murmured.

'Okay, I will have to be a bit watchful,' Anu thought when she logged out finally.

Coming to the Floatel and sitting snug on the yellow cushions of a black wrought iron chair with a spiral backrest at The Bridge, the top deck open air restaurant, Moni yawned a bit loudly. Because of Anu's excessive shopping, they had virtually ransacked every apparel store in all of Lindsay and Park streets. Anu had bought three salwars and two jeans for herself and two sarees for Moni, despite Moni's requests to exclude expensive gifts. Finding jeans with a thirty six inch waistline was a Herculean task. The sarees bought for Moni had to be reciprocated. So Moni bought another pair of jeans for Anu and a silver coin. Buying silver or gold before Diwali is considered to be lucky. The Bridge's open air deck dining hall had an advantageous view of the river, flooded by reflections of light. Every time a rocket cracker would go up into the sky and burst into several balls and patterns of light, the reflections on the black waters of the river would be awesome. Moni was capturing the sight in her mind's camera. She would definitely pen all this too.

Anu had a menu card. After some deliberation, she ordered *prawn masala circuit house* and *jalpuri lajawab* which translated as prawn served with coconut rice and pomfret fish marinated with spices and chargrilled. Anu wanted to have some drink but Moni stopped her saying that then there would be no Big Ben tomorrow. The Big Ben is one of the prime English pubs in the city that they were destined to check out on Diwali night.

Coming back home by cab, Moni looked out of the window and saw simmering lights of the decked up buildings fleeting by. Anu was not saying anything. But her snores could be heard, surpassing the din and bustle of the city around them.

8

The décor of the Big Ben was unique. This English pub was opened in the city as a part of Kenilworth Hotel's ambitious plans some ten years ago. The entrance to the pub was comparatively less fashioned. There was a glass swing door which led to a portico. The two walls of the portico carried pictures and pamphlets of the city of London in general, and British wine makers specifically. On the left wall, there was a celebrity write-up section where one found signatures of different celebs who had visited the pub at some point of time or other. Anu stood before the write-up board and exclaimed, 'Gee! Moni come and look!'

Moni was then actually in Baker Street, a small but neat in house bakery of the Kenilworth, right opposite the pub. She rushed in hearing Anu but was dumbfounded by Anu's high pitched exclamation which was fatally against civil deportment. Luckily, it was only three in the afternoon, and barring a few young snooker enthusiasts and bar tenders, there was virtually no one to object to her cries.

'What?' Moni asked rising and then twisting her eyebrows to indicate her surprise and irritation at the same time.

'Can you recognise this?' Anu pointed to a black scribble thick enough to resemble a stroke of a paintbrush in an erratic manner.

'No.'

'It's Shahrukh Khan's autograph, stupid!'

'Shahrukh Khan's really?' Moni was surprised for sure.

'Well... Will you kindly move from ogling at the autograph to something gastronomic?' Moni asked with desperation.

'O yeah!'

Anoushka made the mental journey back from SRK to TBB.

They chose to sit on a sofa on the right, near the entrance. It was a vantage point. From there, they could see the whole pub, every nook and corner of it. They could see the main counter with glasses hanging downwards from the clips, the waiters dressed in black jackets and white shirts running to and fro, The miniature replica of Big Ben made of wood standing proudly in the middle, the small platform meant for live bands to perform with psychedelic light arrangements fitted in different locations of the ceiling and big black speakers resembling ghostly black boxes sitting at the corners of the dance floor.

A waiter approached them. His breast pocket had a metal tab with Big Ben inscribed on it in a stylised font.

Anu started with draught beer pitchers while Moni stuck to her favourite—vodka. Peanuts and breadsticks were served as suitable snacks and garnishes. Moni was only halfway through her glass when Anu was one pitcher down and asking for another one. Moni looked around. Guests were coming in ones and twos and gradually the place was filling up. Most of them were gentlemen of various sizes and clothing ensemble. Some were the corporate types with their black jackets and shoes on and sombre faces. Two ladies entered with a lot of flourish, in brown hair, glittering sarees and black spaghetti straps. Anu was not looking at anybody. She was happy with her pitchers. Suddenly, there was an announcement. The overhead lights dimmed. Some Filipino girls appeared on the platform in skimpy clothes and the music started to play with psychedelic lights rotating in all directions, creating a brain maze.

'Can anyone really borrow sorrow?' Anu asked, keen to start a conversation.

Moni was taken by surprise with the eerie query.

'Pardon me, I read your Cobalt moon yesterday,' confessed Anu.

Moni quickly remembered that the jackass had asked for permission the other day to use her laptop to email someone. 'Sent the mail?' Moni asked.

'Ya... But tell me, Moni, is there any way to share sorrows?' Anu's face looked tired. Her eyes were half closed.

The jerk is on a high, Moni thought and decided to keep mum.

'Hello, you! Please answer me,' Anu seemed desperate.

'Well. Once you share your sorrows with someone, you feel lighter,' Moni replied hesitatingly. Never had she seen Anu so grave like.

'Hmm... Then I have a story to tell you... (hic)... Pardon my indisposition...'

Anu started rolling her third pitcher in her two hands.

'You know... When you hate being a member of your family, you have little option to share your buckets of wails and tears... (hic)... To start with, I hate my dad... And you know why… He's a smuggler with a lot of ill gotten wealth…(hic)… And I hate my mom as well…'

'It is okay, Anu, there are probs in everyone's life,' said Moni to pacify her.

'What okay? You know why I hate my mom… Because she's such a meek woman!'

'Isn't the song lovely?' Moni asked trying to deviate.

'Look Moni! You're my best friend, aren't you?'

'Ya… Of course!'

'Then… Will you please share my woes a bit?' Anu said clumsily, ordering another pitcher. Moni had taken in one and a half pegs and decided to quit there. *Even after staying with someone for nearly five years there are still untold stories to be shared,* Moni thought and waited with all patience to hear Anu's story.

After the sixth pitcher and halfway through her story, Anu stopped drinking. She had to, for she had rested her head on the back of the sofa and started snoring with her mouth wide open. Moni knew she possibly could not drag or pull or lift Anu out of the pub. There was only one option. Somehow she had to be woken up. Moni splashed water on Anu's face. But she merely half opened her eyes and tried to mumble something. Luckily, an attendant came to Moni's rescue. With his help, Moni dragged Anu towards the door of the pub. As they were coming out of the pub, a little girl, came running from the direction of Alcove, a family restaurant and lounge, housed in the same wing of the hotel, as the pub was. The girl could not stop and collided straight with Moni and fell on the floor instantly. Moni, signalled the attendant to hold Anu for a while and dropped to her knees to pull the girl up.

'O ho! I'm sorry!… O my God! You got cuts!'

There were a few bruises on the girl's left arm and blood was oozing out from one of them.

'It's okay,' said the girl standing up, grimacing.

'Oh no! Let me get you the first aid…' Moni looked around. The door of Alclove opened just then and a tall man with long hair emerged.

'Hello Diana! What's up?'

'Just had an ugly collision…' The girl said matter-of-factly.

'I'm so sorry… Actually I was in a hurry,' Moni said hurriedly to work up some excuse of sorts.

'O it is okay… Diana is a brave girl.' The man patted the shoulder of the girl who smiled clutching the man's hand.

'Excuse me… I think I've seen you somewhere!' Moni said looking for the first time at the man's face.

'Me? Where?'

'Let me think… O yes! I met you at the bookshop a few days ago… Your photography book fell as I brushed against you… Remember?' Moni asked as gleefully as if she was the female Columbus discovering the Americas.

'O yes! So? You have a tendency to run into people literally,' the man laughed heartily.

Moni flashed an embarrassing smile.

'Hello I'm Ved again, and this is my only daughter Sanhita alias Sonai…' The man extended his right hand.

Moni stretched out her hand too.

'I'm Diana,' the girl said.

'Diana?' Moni was curious.

'O it is a long story… You're in a rush? Aren't you?' Ved asked.

'Ya... Actually... My friend is so boozed out she can't even move... I was going out to fetch a taxi, after waking her up,' Moni said directing her eyes to the portion of the busy Russell Street, visible from the lawn of the hotel.

'Need help? Really? We've got a car to drop you home.'

'Yes we do help distressed people... We are actually in missions like that always,' said Diana alias Sanhita alias Sonai.

Moni's eyes were brimming with gratitude.

Anu was snoring hard when Moni pulled her outside. Ved took Anu's right arm on his shoulder and Moni took her left arm. Together, they pushed Anu into the back seat of a white Honda parked near the main entrance. Diana alias Sonai stood with the door opened. The jerk only opened her eyes for a brief moment, uttering something inaudible. Moni sat with Anu at the back. Sonai sat beside her father strapped in seat belts.

Ved turned the ignition on and asked, 'Where does your friend stay?'

'Bardhaman Road... Actually we stay together.'

Ved looked back and then steered the Honda out into the Russell Street.

'Your friend is a boozer then?' Ved asked.

'Ya... Sort of.'

'And you?' Sonai asked suddenly.

Ved chuckled and pressed his finger on her lips.

Moni smiled and looking at the girl, said, 'I do sometimes but not a heavy drinker.'

'Are you students?' Ved asked without looking back.

'Me? No, I am working at Blitz, a shopping mall at Alipore. My friend is a student of Kolkata University, Alipore campus. But how come you know that?'

'Just a guess,' Ved smiled and looked at sleeping Anu. His eyebrows contorted as if he was hard in thought. A ponderous figure, deciphering the secrets of nature, one might assume.

'Does your mall have James Bond's Night fire?' Sonai asked.

'Night fire? A game I suppose? Well, that should be in our mall... In fact we've opened a games and stationary section only recently... But it has good collections, I can assure you,' Moni said smilingly.

It took twenty minutes roughly to reach Bardhaman Road. Moni and Ved again pulled Anu out and took her to the elevator.

'Should I go up with you?' Ved asked.

'No... Thank you for your help... Anyway I'm Monideepa and my sleeping mate is Anoushka. Can I have your number please?' Moni asked as she pressed the key to the elevator.

'It is 26671___ the landline that is,' supplied Sonai who was standing just beside her father.

Moni waved her hand in adieu. Her other hand was under Anu's arm, holding the jerk's big stature. Anu was still snoring with her head tilted downward.

The elevator's door closed. Ved was still looking, kind of observing minutely, Anu's fully inebriated state.

At night, when the crackers and the fireworks got a bit infrequent, Moni opened her laptop. Anu was snoring hard, as if she was getting the sleep of a lifetime. Moni kept her bedroom door ajar just in case Anu needed help. Earlier, trapped in a similar intoxicated state, Anu had fallen off the bed twice and still slept heartily, without a groan. Anu had other allied issues like calling out sharply someone's name or waking up suddenly and crying horrifically. All these previous experiences caused Moni to leave her door open. From the glass window, the occasional fireworks ascended the dark sky.

Moni went to the mail box. Anu had sent emails through her own ID, it seemed. Moni went to her blog page and was surprised to see *SA*'s comment under her poem. It was so similar to what Anu asked her at the Big Ben. So it became clear to Moni that Anu had opened her blog page and seen the comment as well. Just then a ping sounded and the G-chat box opened. *SA* was there! Was he following her, on the net?

'Hello CT!'

'Juley!' Moni wrote, remembering the Ladakhi equivalent of hello.

'Happy Diwali… So you've seen the pics.'

'Ya, they were excellent, especially those of the stupas.'

'Really? They're called Chortan in Tibet… Went there a few years ago… So, how's life for u?' *SA* wrote.

'Fine… Cruising along the ocean called life… But tell me one thing… Are u following me? On the net… I mean…'

'Ya… Sort of… Any probs?' *SA* asked.

'Na… Not really… And as far as your comment on my poem is concerned, yes, one can borrow sorrow if the lender is willing,' Moni typed hastily.

'Really? Interesting…' *SA* wrote.

Moni turned her green dot grey to escape attention. She was not really willing to get into any further conversation with a stranger.

'Gone off? Well, burn your midnight oil to compose a few more lines…' *SA* wrote.

Moni did not respond.

'Okay then... Bye bye...'

The green dot against *SA's* name turned grey with a cross mark. He went offline.

Great! Finally gone out! Moni was relieved.

This internet is a curious place. Here one can live a different life than one has in the real world. Moni thought. She was Monideepa in real and *Candletree (CT)* in the virtual. Likewise *SA* is virtual and he must have a real identity as well. Because of the internet and the world wide web, one can actually live two lives... That's great! Living two lives simultaneously... Or even more, if one created several virtual identities... O what a technological marvel, this internet! Providing people with multiple lives... With more allied complexities... More friends and foes... Real foes and virtual friends or vice versa...Only the other day, she was reading somewhere, that a young man in Germany had decided to live Virtual for one whole year... He would not go out... He would earn virtual money by doing virtual jobs and then he would spend them virtually to get his daily supply of groceries and other things... What an idea!

9

The next morning, Moni told Anu how she had to be physically pulled and dragged and brought home last night in a helpful soul's car.

'Who's that helpful soul? *SA*?' Anu asked winking.

'What do you think? You? You'll pass out and all I will have to do is take your big buttocks on my shoulder and run across the road?' Moni cried aloud, pissed off.

'I'm sorry,' Anu was coming to her with arms outstretched.

O shit, she is going to kill me with her obnoxious embrace! Moni thought and jumped back, causing Anu to go off-balance and stumble and fall with a heavy thud on the floor.

The seismic wave consequent of the mighty fall touched everything in the living room. The TV stand shook, one of the pictures hanging on the wall fell shooting shards of glass everywhere... The metal pot containing flowers on the centre table shook for a while before gaining stability.

'See? Now I'll have to redo all these things before going out to office!' Moni cried out terribly upset.

Anu stood up and collected a broom and started to sweep the shards of glass.

Moni went to the bathroom.

The hazards of living with a freak were the prime thoughts with which Moni came to Blitz. But it got erased as soon as she got a call from Bengaluru at noon. It was H.B.

'Hello! Ms. Banerjee!'

'Hi, Mr. Bhatia.'

'You don't know what you have done! The sales figures of your outlet this month is the best in the eastern region! The management is considering a legitimate hike in your remuneration… so be prepared.'

'Thanks!'

'Congratulations!'

The call from H.B. made Moni feel extraordinarily good. At lunch, she thought of calling Anu. She had been rude to her in the morning. She could have dealt with her softly after all that she had heard from Anu last evening at the Big Ben, that she was not particularly on talking terms with her dad, that her dad has a business which is not clean, that her mom is a meek and docile woman who spends most of her time in the prayer room, and all other issues at home.

'Hello Anu?'

'Ya… Shoot…'

'Sorry dear… You know, one can't keep cool always… By the way, which shade of lipstick is your favourite?'

'Peach red… Why? Penance eh?'

'Just thought to give you one to pair up with your red salwar.'

'Really? You're a madcap.'

'So are you!'

'Err... Can I put a request forward?' Anu asked cautiously.

'Ya, surely.'

'Well, I need to check my email account...'

'Do it then! If it is still charging, plug it to the board...'

'Thanks.'

After the call, Moni thought of dialling the number with 2667 exchange code. Was Sonai having a siesta? Have her bruises healed up?

Moni looked at her watch. It was two thirty. She stood up from her chair, shut down her desktop and got out of her chamber. She would have to find peach red lipstick for Anu.

The cosmetics section was strategically located in the stationary section due to space cramp.

Moni reached for the shelf with lipsticks and lip glosses lined up alluringly. The flashy banners of exotic women with the most ravishing lips highlighted the section. The sales girl, in charge of the section, stood up from her stool and started dusting the tubes and the packets with a brush quite ostensibly. Moni picked up three variants of peach-red lipstick.

'Hey! You never told me you got Quantum of Solace as well?' Someone cried out from behind.

Moni turned around to see little Sonai standing with three packs of games in her hand. An elderly man in blue shirt and grey trousers was standing by her side.

'Hello! Sonai! You're here?'

'You said you people got games and so, I thought... By the way, meet my grandpa,' Sonai tugged the elderly man's trousers.

'Namaskar,' the man joined his palms together.

Moni drooped down to touch his feet.

'No no... It's okay,' the grandpa stopped Moni from touching his feet.

'This granddaughter of mine is a games maniac... And my son is particularly responsible for that,' her grandpa said smiling.

'So you're on a game hunt?' Moni asked.

'Ya... And *dadu*, this is Moni, if you want to know her name'

'Sorry... I've forgotten to introduce myself... I'm Monideepa Banerjee, the sales manager of this mall.'

'Well... I'm Biswanath Bhattacharya, grandpa of Sonai, as you can understand.' The elderly man smiled at Moni absentmindedly.

Moni took a quick glance at the man's face and fingers and then turning to Sonai, she asked:

'So you've come all the way to Blitz to get the games?'

'I can go anywhere for my assignment,' came the reply from Sonai who had started reading the info regarding the games at the back cover of the packets.

'Okay... How's your arm?' Moni asked on the sly, as she accompanied Sonai and her grandpa to the cash counter.

'It is fine... See?' Sonai showed her left arm. The bruises had almost healed, barring one, which was strapped by a pink adhesive medical band.

'Your mom definitely got angry yesterday when you returned home with cuts?' Moni asked Sonai while the grandfather was paying the bills, some distance away.

'Mom? Diana has no mom,' Sonai replied effortlessly.

'No Mom? O, I'm so sorry!' Moni did not know how to react properly in such a delicate situation.

'*Chalo*... Let's go Sonai. Say bye-bye to Aunty,' the grand father called out.

Sonai waved her hand to Moni and started following her grandpa out of the glass door.

Moni stood motionless and still. She suddenly felt that her eyes were itching. She rushed to the ladies' room.

After having lunch with roti and sabzi, Anu opened her inbox in Moni's computer to find an email from Prof. VPB. The mail read:

Hi Anoushka,

There's no need really, to fret over a mere selection test. As far as the educational psychology paper is concerned, do only what you are taught in the class, for instance—Piaget's theory or theory of cognitive development of a child, Thurston's multiple factor theory and the Stanford-Binet scale of intelligence from the Intelligence and Creativity section, classical and operant conditioning from the Teaching and Learning Process section, and of course, the introductory chapter about the definition and concept of educational psychology.

That's it.

All the best,

Prof. V.P. Bhattacharya,

P.S.: You've done Kohlberg's theory of moral development, I guess. But it seems you're still in the first stage of the level iii of Kohlberg.

After reading the mail, Anu at once, clicked the reply button to send a *'Thank you Sir'* typed in the boldest font. Soon after that, she switched off the laptop and called Sush.

'Hello Sush! Can you lend me your educational psychology notes tum'ro? I'll just get them photocopied'

Anu then leapt out of her bed and did a jig. VPB had answered her request. But, what's that he had written in the post script? First stage of level iii? What's that?

Anu opened her copy in which she had put down what VPB dictated to her, before the vacation, about the theory. There it is… level three, which meant—post conventional level… but where's the first stage?

Anu called Sush again.

'Hi Sush! Tell me the name of the two stages of level iii of Kohlberg's theory of Moral development'

'Hey! What's up? Cramming hard, you ass?' Sushmita was genuinely surprised.

'Why not, you dumbo? Exam is knocking at our door… Now please move your ass and find the damn thing out of your reading desk.'

Sush searched for a few minutes putting Anu on hold. Finally, Sush spoke excitedly, 'Hey! Now listen… Kohlberg has divided the phases of moral development…'

'Into three levels… I know that… Now move to the last one and tell me the two stages of it, you ass.'

'O ho… I'm getting to that… Wait a minute… Here you are: (i) defiance against the rigidity of conventional moral beliefs and (ii)…'

'Didn't I tell you to stick to the first stage of level iii? Okay I got it… bye-bye.' Anu slammed the phone.

So? Banderas was thinking that whatever she was doing, she was just trying to prove her defiance to the conventional moral ideas?

When Moni returned in the evening with the peach red lipsticks and showed them to Anu, she just took them and put them on her bedside table and returned to a bunch of papers, apparently studying them. This subdued reaction surprised Moni greatly.

'Hey! What has happened?' Moni asked.

'Nothing… Only to attend to studies… Day after tum'ro onwards, I have to face the exam gallows,' Anu replied keeping her eyes on the papers strewn all over her bed.

'Good! Great! So our jerk is mugging hard after a long time, eh?' Moni said and went away to change her clothes.

Anu came to the table to have her dinner at ten and went back to her room again, without any usual jabbering. Moni watched TV for a while and then went back to her room.

The laptop was plugged to the bedside board. She switched it on and logged on to her blog page.

She was thinking of little Sonai… Her beautiful lustrous eyes… Her candid smile… Her mock serious tone of speech… her matter-of-fact demeanour… Her motherlessness.

She was reminded of her own long lost mother… Her indistinct face… Blurred… And somehow, the face of Sonai gradually got superimposed on her mother's blurred face to make it distinctly one…

As if in a trance, Moni started to type on her new post:

<u>Mother</u>

For ten days and ten months she bore me,

It pained and ached
As I had been nourished by her blood;

Now that she is not here,
Stars and the planets of the dark sky,
Tell her—
I am fine,
Though far away from her…

After posting the lines, Moni started to cry, after a long time, pressing her face on the pillow, till the pillow got salt soaked in tears.

Ping!

SA came online with his green dot.

Moni was in no mood to talk. So, she did not respond.

'Hello! CT! Yes, you're right! Mothers are irreplaceable…' SA wrote.

Moni felt like turning her green dot grey with a cross in the middle. But she stayed on to reread her latest blog post—Mother—and she wept again, closing her eyes.

'Mother is like the beautiful sunny morning after a dark stormy night,' SA wrote again.

Moni did not respond.

'Hey! Why are you silent?' SA wrote for the third time.

'Ya… Reminded of my long lost mom by a little girl today…'

'A little girl?'

'Ya… A little girl who came to the mall where I work and suddenly, while conversing with me, told me that she has no mother…'

'May I know which mall do you work in?'

'Ya… Blitz at Alipore… Why?'

'Just curious,' SA wrote.

'You don't know how beautiful the girl is... Her face resembles an angel...'

'Really? Does she look like an angel?'

'Ya... She has her dad though and grandpa... In fact it was her grandpa who brought her to the mall...'

'You know her Papa?'

'Ya met him twice actually... A good helpful guy with long hair'

'O...'

SA suddenly went offline.

Moni stayed on to read her post several times and to cry even more.

✦ ✦ ✦

10

Usually, the first work day after Diwali vacation in the university went on at a leisurely pace. Teachers often failed to turn up on the first day. Students also scarcely attended classes. However, with the Part II selection test round the corner, PG II classes saw attendance of students. Rounding up his lecture with a few suggestive outlines for the ensuing exam, Ved was actually hurrying towards his room, when he heard a familiar voice from behind, 'Excuse me Sir!' Anoushka Agarwal hopped up beside him.

'Yes!'

'I am working hard on your tips Sir, but...'

'Okay follow me to my room,' Ved lifted the latch of the door and walked in, followed by Anu.

Sitting down on his chair, Ved heaved a sigh.

'Tired of speaking at length in the class, aren't you?' Anu asked.

'Ya... Part of the job.'

'If you are really tired, I can come another time...'

'Na... It's all right... Actually I need to tell you something...'

'Yes Sir!'

Anu struck an 'all attention' pose.

'Sit down, please.' Ved showed her the chair.

Anu sat down erect.

'Well… Psychology is not the only paper you'll have to sit for in the exams.' Ved said.

'Ya… Sir, I m working on other papers as well…'

'Really? That's good!'

'Yes Sir… But Sir, why did you write in that postscript that I am still in the first stage of level iii of moral development?' The unpretentious girl asked suddenly.

'Because of your age… Primarily.'

'And?'

'Your demeanour… Secondarily.'

'O… Is it bad?'

'The question of ethical judgments doesn't arise here, I guess. Kohlberg was just trying to classify different age groups into different psychological stages of moral development and mind you, each and every stage is logically important for the proper growth and development of moral structure'

'I see.'

'So if you're in the first stage of level three, it doesn't matter much… What matters instead, is to grow up to the next stage, i.e. the stage vi or the stage of formation of universal principles.'

'Like? Sir?'

'Well… In this stage, the individual develops true moral consciousness of his or her own. This is the stage, in which, the individual formulates his or her own moral principles on the basis of universal views and is mostly guided by his or her, enlightened conscience.'

'Can it be attained?'

'Of course! Why not? Every individual seeking upliftment of soul can attain that.'

'Can I attain it?' Anoushka Agarwal asked with utter seriousness.

'Ya, you can… Everybody can.'

'Thank you Sir, for being so subjective.'

'Thanks to you as well for being so candid… And by the way, you know, your face resembles my daughter's…'

'Daughter! Your daughter, Sir?'

'Ya… I have only one offspring, Sanhita Bhattacharya, and she's in class seven.'

'Oh!' Anu fumbled for the right words.

Ved smiled briefly before returning to some books on the table.

Coming out of VPB's room, Anu felt tizzy.

So Banderas is married… Married and burdened by a family… O ho… Wrong calculations.

Monideepa was checking some accounts with the clerk in the evening, when suddenly the office boy entered.

'Bolo…' Moni said, without looking up from the files.

'Madamji… A little girl is looking for you…'

'Little girl? Send her in…'

Sonai entered. Her eyes were puffed up, a bit red. She was wearing a beautiful white skirt and pink tee with the image of an angel embroidered on it.

'Hello Sonai! What a pleasant surprise! Who brought you here?'

'My dad… He's waiting outside… But tell me first, what should Diana do with a defunct game that does not even get installed properly?'

'Really? Which one?' Moni got up from her seat as Sonai showed her the *Quantum of Solace* CD bought by her only yesterday.

'It is not running?' Sonai pursed her lips.

'And you know, those at the counter are not going to replace it!' Sonai said fuming.

'Really? Let me see,' Moni took the disc from Sonai and went out of her chamber. Ved was waiting just outside the chamber. Seeing Moni, Ved said, 'I'm so sorry to disturb you… But you know, this girl doesn't listen to my words… I asked her to buy new ones, if they are not replacing it…'

'No! As a matter of fact, it should be replaced if it is not working! That's the standard practice,' Moni uttered as she rushed to the stationary section with the CD in her hand.

Soon, she returned with a new one and handing it over to Sonai, asked Ved, 'But, have you got the cash memo or the payment bill with you right now?'

'Oho! We haven't brought it… Actually she was in such a hurry. Just gone back home from school and came out again, skipping her evening food,' Ved said apologetically.

Sonai was ogling at the new packet, all her attention on it.

'Okay, that's no big deal… Wait a minute please…'

Moni instructed someone to bring snacks like biscuits and chocolates even before Ved could disapprove.

Moni signalled the cashier to make a bill of the biscuits and chocolates and even the new game under her account.

Ved was hesitant to walk away without paying, but Moni held his hand firmly, and said, 'Repaying a debt I already owe.'

Ved flushed.

Sonai giggled as Moni bent down to plant a kiss on her rosy cheeks.

The father-daughter duo entered the car and as the glass was rolled up, Sonai waved and blew a kiss to Moni. Moni smiled and waved back, standing at the entrance of Blitz.

As soon as Moni returned home, Anu caught her arms and pulled her to her bedroom.

'What happened?' asked Moni.

'I've an important thing to discuss with you... Right now.'

Moni sat on the bed and started to remove her earrings.

'Tell me, does defiance against conventional moral ideas indicate degeneration of any kind?' Anu asked.

'What a question!' Moni stood up.

'Na, Moni! Please! Answer me...'

Anu seemed desperate. 'I don't know what you're talking about... Is it anything related to your studies?'

'Not really... Generally speaking.'

'Well, defiance against conventional ideas can sometimes bring about discoveries... You know, looking at things from a totally different perspective... Hey! Wait a minute! Are you into some new rebel students' union?' Moni looked genuinely worried. Already, she was bothered by Anu's hyper-eccentricities, and now if ideas of rebellion got into her, then she would surely have to call the police next.

'Na na... Nothing of that... Only thinking,' Anu rebuffed.

Post dinner, when Moni visited her blog on GooglePlus, she expected *SA* to ping her like usual. But he did not appear. Moni scoured the web for sometime, highly alert and conscious, awaiting ping. But when the clock struck twelve and there was still no *SA* around, she thought of logging out. Puzzled, Moni mused, 'Why did I open it in the first place? I had nothing to write tonight, at least there were no such thoughts. *Did I open it and log on just to get into a chat with SA? Is SA becoming a habit of sorts for me?'*

With thoughts like these, Moni logged off and logged in again and the moment she did, a chat box opened and a message appeared: *SA misses CT.*

Moni looked at the online list of contacts. *SA* had a grey dot.

Who was this SA? What did he want?

Suddenly Moni started thinking about Sonai. Was the new game working? Had she played it? The beautiful face of the girl emerged before her, followed by that of Ved. Few other scenes started to appear one after another like a slide show—the father and daughter duo getting into the white car, window rolled up, the girl blowing a kiss…

'Why am I thinking all these thoughts? Am I lonely? Am I feeling tired? Do I need someone to love and be loved in return?' Moni wondered with her eyes closed, lying on the sleepless bed, as the night got deeper and darker.

Another night descended on the city with its late October fog, dew and chills. The honks of passing cars were sporadic. The lights of bedrooms and living rooms and balconies of the nearby buildings switched off one by one, making the skyscrapers look like towering ghosts. Someone was trudging along the footpath below, singing loudly, possibly drunkenly:

Tere bina jiya jaye na… bin tere, tere bin…
(Can't live without you… Without you… Sans you…)

The wayfarer's song, though not melodious, rung with a certain pathos, travelling far and wide, filling the lanes and by lanes and the ears of Moni and others itching to get to the kingdom of sleep.

In the adjacent room, Anu was trying not to sleep. The next day onwards, she had exams, and after mugging all evening until dinner, she was standing at the window of her dark bedroom, smoking. The song of the drunkard also reached her ears and she peeped out to catch the shadow of a limping man on the pavement below. Stray dogs barked as they followed him. The man took no notice of the dogs barking or the honking cars gliding past. He simply walked as if he had been walking down the ages to find his loved one, through the city's numerous lanes and bylanes and streets and roads which formed a big and complex web. The yellow streetlight posts stood like black guards on both sides of the fairly empty road. The conical light beams from the posts created a pattern of alternate light and darkness on the road. Anu exhaled her tenth ring of smoke. The ring floated around in the night's thick air before disappearing forever.

The October night was chillier at Mandirtala than at Bardhaman Road, probably because of the lower density of population, buildings and vehicles. Ved often told little Sonai an old bedtime story that made her close her eyes:

> A prince was once fighting it out with the dacoits in the middle of a vast ground with no sign of human existence around on a moonlit night to save his young love carried in a palanquin by six attendants. The prince fought a deadly battle, swinging his steely

dazzling sword like a master swordsman, forcing the dacoits to beat a retreat. But the combat left the prince with ghastly wounds and blood oozed out from his body like fountains of red. When his young love descended from the palanquin with weeping eyes, she saw the prince writhing in indescribable pain. She tore her clothes and tied up the wounds and carried him through the darkest night and densest jungle. As the attendants carried the palanquin running their fastest, the young royal woman prayed to God all the time, with her prince's head rested upon her soft lap. Tears rolled down her eyes and fell upon the prince's face and the prince, still paining and aching, smiled at his beloved.

The moon peeping behind the silk curtains of the palanquin fell upon the prince's blood smeared face, making it all the more beautiful. The young girl kept on wiping the blood from the wounds of the prince and cried as her tears fell on the face of the prince. She prayed to God as she cried. By the time dawn broke, the palanquin reached the vicinity of the king's palace. When the palanquin was finally made to descend on the ground at the palace gate, the attendants discovered lifeless bodies of the prince and his love, lying side by side with faces lit up by the rays of a sun just born.

By the time Ved ended the story, Sonai was fast asleep, her happily rested tiny head laid on her father's arm. Ved would keep on looking at her calm face for hours before he would finally doze off.

Tonight, Ved was looking at Sonai's face, a bit drowsily, when suddenly the face of Monideepa emerged from nowhere. He almost woke up, wiped his eyes and looked around. Then he slowly walked to his room, almost tiptoeing, and came back to Sonai's room with his laptop. He logged on to the blog site of name *CT* and clicked on the profile photo of the woman to make it bigger. Ved looked at *CT's* photo and looked at Sonai's face and discovered, for the first time, why he liked to follow the sales manager of Blitz, almost everywhere—both offline and online, because just on the right hand corner of Moni's upper lip was a small black mole, resembling Sonai's black mole on her upper lip on the left. After staring at Moni's photo for a while, he logged on to his page and signed in as Silent Assassin. Actually, he wanted his profile name to be *Silently Assassinated*, after the death of Mayurika, but Sonai had wanted him to be like the virtual hero of the game—bold, manly, well dressed and devoid of tears. So *SA* stood for Silent Assassin to everyone on his blog page. Even if for him, *SA* was always Silently Assassinated.

Now, an accidental meeting with the sales manager of the Blitz had changed everything. For the last few days, he could not even sleep at the end of the day, without chatting with *CT* alias Moni. It had become a habit—a little more than a harmless habit, something very much akin to clandestine fondness and even deeper than that after Moni had hugged and kissed Sonai today, Ved thought. Sonai also mingled quite easily with Moni, without her usual reservations, which only cemented his obsession with the woman of dusky complexion.

Thinking all these thoughts, Ved wrote in the chat box: *SA* misses *CT*. It took a whole day of mental deliberations for him to write that simple line with three words and soon after entering those words, he went offline. He did not know what Offline Monideepa or Online *CT* would think of him—a fanatic, a womaniser or a pervert?

He was also getting tired of already playing these offline online roles. Ved and *SA* should unite and that unification had to happen before Moni.

Ved does not know what would happen if the unification of his two identities happened before Moni. *Would she abhor him and think of him as a sex starved widower? Would she think that he had plotted and tricked her into some game? But… Could a woman who had such strong feeling of loneliness as expressed in her poems be cruel to another victim of the same disease? Could one loner be insensitive to another?*

It was half past one at night, when Ved alias *SA* logged in.

To his dismay, he found the green dot glowing beside *CT's* profile photo with black mole on the left upper lip clearly visible.

Ved keyed in after a moment's hesitation: *Hi there!*

His typed letters glowed against the white of the chat box. The green dot against *CT* was still there. Every moment, he expected *CT* to type a reply. He waited and waited. The clock was ticking away. Exactly seven minutes later, there was the ping… The most desired sound that made Ved's heart beat faster. *CT* had replied: *Juley! Not slept yet?*

Only expecting u… Ved wrote with unashamed earnestness.

Really? Why?

Coz u have become a habit with me…

A habit? Strange!

Ya! A habit which is hard to brush aside... But why are u awake? Ved sought.

Burning midnight oil... CT wrote back.

Ved laughed and sent an emoticon of a smiling face that glowed wonderfully animatedly, all yellow with clear black outlines.

Am I responsible, in any way, for this strange habit of yours? CT wrote.

Ved thought for a while, remembering a real life face with sharp brows and dark eyes with long eyelashes and the black mole on the upper lip. He remembered how Moni had brushed past him at the bookstore causing the book in his hand to fall with a thud on the wooden floor, the first time they met.

Singularly... Ved wrote.

Why do u think so?

SA: Coz women only are empowered to captivate men... It has been happening down the ages, for centuries...

CT: Really?

Ved typed as *SA: Ya... Really... Women are the most devoted kind of species...*

CT: And most lethal too... Moni added promptly.

Ved laughed and typed: *That's a saying, isn't it?*

CT: Yes... A saying... Now tell me your story...

SA: What do you want to hear?

CT: About your habits...

SA: Well... It's a long story; to cut it short, I have an interesting chemistry between heart and brain... They usually do not collide with each other. In fact, they conjugate to bring before me greater realities like the blessedness of being a human, the most fascinating species in this world...

CT: Great! U r a poet, I guess... A photographer-poet?

SA: Maybe… But that's not the issue… After reading ur blogs and chatting with you, I, for the first time, am facing a collision between heart and brain… My brain orders me not to disturb u… But my heart wants to chat with u…

CT: Really? That's an infatuation, I think… By the way, how old are u?

SA: Older than u by seven or eight years… Any other questions?

CT: Ya… Do u live in this city of Kolkata?

SA: Not really… In an adjacent city…

CT: Howrah?

SA: Ya…

CT: What's ur profession? A photographer?

SA: Ya, sort of…

CT: What do u mean by 'sort of'? A part time photographer?

SA: Ya…

CT: And ur full time engagement?

SA: Interacting with people…

CT: O a counselor? Therapist?

SA: Ya…

CT: Good! Now Mr. Therapist, tell your story, the shorter version of a long one, u intended to share with me, tonight…

SA:Well… Once one goes through the ugly twists and turns of life, one's soft interior gets hardened and one becomes gradually indifferent… A stoic… Now this stoicism makes one all the more hardened… That's me…

CT: O… A stoic photographer-cum-poet-cum-therapist? That's too many bundled words!

SA: Ya…

CT: Now, Mr. Therapist-photographer-poet, if I decline to continue my net friendship with u from now on, what u will do? Should u leave ur habit of chatting with me as well?

SA: I'll be pissed off, certainly! But I know, u can't do that to me… U have also grown within u the habit of interacting with me… Isn't it?

CT: Ur photos were excellent and ur ways of interacting with people are also quite exhilarating…

SA: Thanks… But the more you will get to know me, I'm sure, you will find me a brooding kind of a fellow with a peculiar kind of indifference and insensitivity…

CT: An insensitive person can't make a good poet or a photographer, I guess… So… It may be the case that your self-appraisal is wrong or wrongly presented to me by you…

SA: Hey! U r a great articulator of words! I like that!

CT.: What?

SA: The way u analyse people…

CT: Really?

SA: Ya… And I think it will be immensely profitable for me to keep my net-friendship with u… But I am uncertain if it is the other way round…

CT: Well… I like ur photographic skills… Ur ways of talking…

SA: Thanks…

CT: Welcome… Now… As we are already well past the first half of the night, should we end it here?

SA: O surely! Sorry if I've held u up!

CT: Na na… It's okay… Good night!

SA: Good morning, I guess!

CT: Ya… Good morning!

Ved switched off the machine. The screen glowed in a blue tinge for a while before becoming black, and the room plunged into darkness.

✦ ✦ ✦

11

It was the last day of the selection test and educational psychology was the paper she would soon tide over. As Anu's exam started at twelve, she left only at eleven thirty. It took barely fifteen minutes to reach the campus even as the bus or cab moved at snail's pace, considering the short distance. It was only ten in the morning. Anu mentally revised the tenets of Kohlberg and Thurston and Piaget and Thorndike for a few minutes. Then she went to the bathroom and unscrewed the shower knob completely. As soon as the water jet fell on her, she felt like singing aloud. Today, the selection test would be over and for the next few days, she could take leave from cramming her notes. The final exam would be in February next year… Next year… Yeah… A lot of time to have some fun before plunging into theories again.

Anu felt extraordinarily happy thinking about what she should do coming home after exam. Should she buy for herself a potion and spend the evening watching a horror movie and sipping the medicine? Or should she go out with Sush and others to a night club and shake a leg? Exam blues are hard to shrug off and after Part I last year, she had to party hard for three consecutive nights to rid herself of those unnerving sensations. A selection test did not demand that much partying though. One night's blast would be enough to throw away all the cerebral stuff.

The happy thoughts of partying made Anu do a jig under the shower as she burst out singing: *Let's go party tonight…*

The soap bubbles also danced along with her body.

Suddenly, Anu remembered that the exam was not over yet and that thought made her hasten up. Emerging from the bathroom after half an hour, she rushed to her room and started dressing up. She paired up her black Levis jeans with a pink kurti and folded her hair into a high bun. Then, she slapped a light foundation on her face and put on black earrings—two glittering hoops intersecting each other. Then, she pushed open Moni's bedroom door to find her sitting on her bed, her laptop flap opened and screen blinked. Moni was definitely absent minded.

'Won't you go to office today?' Anu asked.

'Ya! I'll have to!' Moni jumped out of bed, shrugging off her blank stare.

'Are you okay?' Anu asked, as she took a bite of buttered bread from the table.

'Ya! Absolutely fine!' Moni replied flashing a smile and running to the bathroom. Anu rushed to the door.

'Anu!' Moni peeped out of the bathroom.

'Ya?'

'Best of luck for your exam,' Moni smiled and said.

'Thanks dear!' Anu smiled back.

'Close the door,' Anu said, hurrying out of the flat, slamming the door.

Moni came out of the bathroom in a towel and hastily closed the door. As she crossed her bedroom door, she definitely heard the known sound of a 'ping' from her notebook. A glance at the screen indicated that someone had just posted an entry to the chat box for there was a known orange bar blinking at the bottom of the screen. Moni rushed in, adjusting the towel over her bosom to prevent it from falling. *SA* had left a message:

'Are u not there?'

Moni had made *CT* invisible by choosing the grey dot option.

She kept the notebook logged on, nevertheless.

Then she picked up her cellphone and dialled Kevin.

'Kevin... I'll reach office in the second half... Just manage a bit... Got some emergency back home...'

'Okay, boss... But there's a minor issue with the guys at the grocery section...' he cautioned. The grocery section had been a 'trouble area' since its inception. The sales personnel there were mostly on a contractual service and lesser paid than in other sections. Repeated requests to the management to settle the issue once and for all had not yielded any positive results. Moni simply could not understand why the management behaved with such negligence towards the section that was the distinctive 'bread earner' of the mall, despite odds of competition and the global market slowdown.

'What happened?' Moni asked, as she started massaging her arms and legs sitting on the bed with body oil.

'The sales girls are demanding a hike... They are on hold...'

'On hold? What do you mean by that? Not at their respective counters?'

'Ya they are… But they are largely reluctant… Just idling…' Kevin's voice trembled a bit.

Moni was suddenly reminded of a sales girl with whom Kevin was busy chatting the other day. That girl with *great chassis* had been transferred to the grocery section a few days back.

'Kevin… What's the name of that girl with plump features recently transferred to the grocery section?' Moni asked.

'Oh… That's Rohini…' Kevin replied quickly.

'Yes! Well, I was just thinking of taking her back to her original counter…'

'Apparel section, ma'am?' Kevin sounded pretty enthusiastic as if he himself was getting a hike for some reason.

'Ya… She's good at that I think'

'That's great! Should I inform her?' Kevin was definitely elated.

'No, I'll prefer to do that myself… Meanwhile, just ask the girls to be a little patient… Okay?'

'Okay, ma'am!'

Moni heaved a sigh, as she threw the phone on the bed and started to massage her arms.

She hummed a song by a group called 'The Cranberries'.

In your head, in your head, they are fighting… With their guns and their bombs…

Moni tried to recall the song as she stopped humming midway. She opened the music folder and started scanning the playlists by her eyes.

Aha! Got it! *Zombie*… There it is!

So it was *Zombie* playing aloud in the notebook on a repeat mode as Moni went to the shower.

The notebook still logged on to the web had posts entered in the chat box which became orange every time a post was submitted. The posts were sent from *SA:*

Are you not there still?... Hello!... Gone off?... Hey!... Please be online... Today is twentieth of October, u know... Today is the day when I lost my most dear one... Today is my day of the gravest grief... hello!... Don't u know?... Today I need u more... Please... Forgive me if I'm crossing the line ... Today... A few years back someone with a face like yours left me forever without even thinking what a miserable thing I would be without her... She just went away, leaving me all the more lonely, all the more insecure, all the more agonised... Please do reply, if you care... Reply even if u don't care for me... Please... Bye bye...

Moni came out of the bathroom after half an hour. Entering the bedroom, she saw the orange glow at the bottom of the screen and leaned forward to click on the chat box.

She read and reread the lines several times, which confused her. Why was *SA* stalking her this way? Was the guy mad? Was he a pervert? What was he? Wait a minute! He had mentioned that he lost someone with a face like hers! Strange! Did she know him? Where had he seen her face? On her blog page? Did mere resemblance with someone else's face or features merit such infatuation? This was strange! Curious! Baffling!

Moni logged out and switched off the machine. She would have to hurry to office.

The first look at the question paper made Anu inordinately happy. Thurston, Kohlberg and Piaget were all there. The short questions were tricky though. Four hours of serious slogging, and Anu was almost sure that she had scraped through. Had Sush not craned her neck to ask for help every two minutes, Anu would have fared even better. But, overall, the performance was electric. Actually, it was far better than Anu's own expectations. So, coming out of the hall, at the end of the exam, Anu felt really pleased. Joy crept through her heart and she thought it apt to meet Prof. VPB, to convey her sincerest gratitude. VPB was in his room, smoking as usual. His tall silhouette against the open window was draped in the sunset yellow hue. Anu walked in.

'Hello Sir!'

'Yes?'

'Thanks a lot for your help Sir!'

'You're welcome…'

VPB sounded unusually sombre. He had not even looked at Anu when he talked. His eyes were always on the rear window, as if he was looking for something in the street below. He talked over his shoulders very reluctantly, as if he was not willing to talk to anyone. Anu felt herself guilty of intruding on VPB's privacy. She stood there for sometime to elicit some response from VPB, but he was standing still like a statue, at the window, almost ignoring Anu's presence. So, Anu stepped back a few paces and finally uttered, 'I'm sorry, Sir… Just came to pay my sincerest gratitude…'

'It's okay…' VPB replied in a flat monotone.

'Bye bye Sir!'

'Bye… And Anoushka!'

VPB suddenly turned around. Anu stopped and looked at his face. VPB's face looked particularly colourless, faded like a weary old man's.

'Yes, Sir!'

'As I told you the other day... The stage of formation of universal principles... It's hard to get into... It requires one to undergo a lot of inner turmoil, before one settles down... It requires one to be a fighter and a dreamer... You see what I mean?' VPB spoke disjointedly, struggling to find proper expression for his thoughts.

Anu nodded half-heartedly, uncertain of what the professor's words actually meant. VPB was looking at Anu, though his stare had a peculiar absentmindedness.

'Yea Sir! May I go now?'

'O sure!' VPB nodded.

Anu came out, and strolled across the verandah to the staircase. Sush was chatting happily with some other classmates, quite animatedly shaking her ponytail, leaning against the brick railing.

'Hi Anu! Where have you gone to?' Sush asked smiling.

'To the toilet,' Anu lied.

'You owe me a treat for the service you rendered today... Wish to go to the canteen?' Sush gushed.

'Not really... I'll have to hurry home... Keep your treat pending.'

'Okay,' Sush went back to the post exam discussions.

Anu climbed down the broad stairs. *Formation of universal principles requires inner turmoil and dreams....* What was that? Why had VPB looked so worried and clumsy? Was he in any trouble? *I should have stayed a little longer and asked him the reason, but, would that be proper? What if it offended him? Was his daughter all right? Should I mail VPB on reaching home?* Anu thought, as she trudged downstairs lethargically.

Reaching the ground floor, Anu took the left corridor to reach the second gate of the university. The path that bent like a sickle from the corridor to the second front gate ran through the car park of the staff of the university. Anu looked out searching for a white Honda. She found it parked under the shade of a Gulmohar tree, with all its whiteness singularly conspicuous, flanked by a yellow sedan and a grey SUV. She felt like going near the car to touch its doorknob, as if to get a feel of the person who owned it. She walked towards the car. There was no one at the car park. Anu looked through the window to have a look at the interior of the car.

White towels on the seats… Water bottle in the bottle holder near the gear shaft… Piles of CDs on the dashboard top, a book… What's the title? *The Upanishad*! My goodness!… CDs of songs… CDs of games… Games?… *Hitman 2* computer game cover with distinctive enough picture of a bald man with red tie… Hitman 2 computer game? VPB plays games and reads the *Upanishad*? Goodness me!

'Hello. What are you doing here?'

Anu turned back hearing a gruff voice from behind. One of the security guards showed up, glaring with inquisition.

'Just passing by… Don't worry, I'm not a carjacker!' Anu said clearing her throat and flashing a smile.

12

Staring at the black water of the river, sitting on a secluded step on the bank, Ved felt like a sage—contemplative, oblivious and purged.

Every year on this day, the twentieth of October, Ved would visit the river bank in the evenings alone, and sit by the sooty waters of the Ganges, which had been flowing in this part of the country for years, for centuries. The nip in the air caused him to shiver. He was still wearing his white full sleeve shirt and beige trousers. He had come here straight from the university. The sky which was reddish earlier had gradually changed its hue to acquire its present blackness. The stars had spread across the sky the way they had exactly a few years ago on the same date, when Mayurika died. Both of his parents knew that Ved would return home late that night. The night of Ved's mourning alone. He would just sit here by the river until eleven, when the last boat of the ferry service would draw home with tired looking handfuls of passengers from Kolkata. He would wait till the boat was taken to shore and anchored and the boatmen would tie fat ropes with the big vertical logs on the bank, ghostly columns submerged in water. Then he would see the boatmen lighting up their bidis in the dark and walking across the muddy bank to match steps. At the step, they would stop and wash hands and their faces and gargle and spit. Then they would walk past him, talking all the way within them. Once every year, Ved would stay back at the river step, listen to fragments of their usual talk—mostly related to their day's earnings and individual share.

After the departure of the boatmen, the step would become desolate. The mist would cover most of the river; only some distant glittering light could be seen from the second Hooghly bridge still populated with fleeting cars. Ved would finally stand up, wriggle his toes to get rid of the uneasy numbness from sitting for long, and head towards the car parked nearby.

Ved lit up a cigarette, walking towards his car, leaving behind the sooty waters—cool and sombre. It was eleven thirty. The twentieth day of October was at its legitimate end, giving way for the twenty first. Ved took the Foreshore road. The road with godowns and warehouses on both sides looked ghostly. Sonai had fallen asleep, Ved thought and stepped on the pedal. Fifteen minutes later, when Ved reached Mandirtala, the four point crossing was largely empty. Barring a few cabs with windows rolled up, there was hardly any vehicle at sight. All the shops were closed. A few stray dogs were sleeping, coiled up, under the yellow vapour lamp stand. Ved took the road towards the girls' school till he reached their white double storied house. After parking the car in the garage, Ved rang the doorbell twice. Padma-di opened the door with sleepy eyes. Ved slipped out of his shoes and started walking towards the living area. The living area opened to the dining and the kitchen. Debjani was wiping the dining table with a cloth but her eyes were fixed on the TV.

'Has Sonai slept off?' Ved asked as he took up the remote from the couch.

'Sleep? Don't you know your daughter? All day she was in front of her computer, playing games and all that... I am only waiting for her vacation to be over,' Debjani said, looking tired.

'Has she dined?' Ved asked as he walked briskly towards the staircase.

'Yes... Ate after grumbling a bit... Still on the computer perhaps.'

Ved took to the stairs.

Sonai's bedroom door was half-closed with the curtains drawn. The blue night lamp was on. Sonai was sleeping, covered by a quilt.

Ved walked in tiptoed. A big rag doll with a torn off nose was lying just beside Sonai. A few books were also strewn on the bed. Ved took them up and placed them beside the computer. Just then, he noticed the yellow LED indicator of the UPS glowing. Ved pressed the grey button for a few seconds to switch off the UPS. The monitor was still warm, which meant it had not been switched off much earlier. Ved took a sudden turn towards Sonai and his eyes met the batting eyelids of Sonai, who had been silently watching her dad from her bed, under the pretence of having fallen asleep.

'You naughty!' Ved jumped on the bed.

'Ha ha ha ...' Sonai giggled.

Soon the father and the daughter were embroiled in a mock fight, punctuated with giggles and shrieks.

'Grandma said that you played games all day today?' Ved asked.

'Ya... Played games online!'

'Online?'

'Yeap!'

'How come?'

Ved was surprised to know that his daughter had learnt to connect the machine to the World Wide Web.

'Simple! Your username and password were saved... I just chose the right options by clicking on...' Sonai said yawning.

'Really? That's incredible!' Ved muttered in disbelief.

'Now get changed and have your dinner... I'm feeling sleepy,' Sonai said as she turned her back.

13

Actually Sonai wanted to avoid questions from her dad. She could not lie to her dad. She could not tell the truth either, at least now, with the entire issue so delicately poised. Soon after her dad went out at as early as eight in the morning, Sonai hooked on to the web. She had all the intention of playing games online. She had collected addresses of some sites which feature latest versions of different games. She opened the browser and as soon as she typed triple w on the bar, the dropdown menu came up with names of at least four frequently visited sites. Two of them were names of two hugely popular search engines and the other two were pretty curious blog pages bearing names like *CT* and *SA*.

She first clicked on *SA* and had soon found it to be the blog page of her dad's, as it carried the unmistakable photographs of landscapes and nature taken by her dad at different times in different locations. She had seen them all before in her dad's fat photo albums kept in his bedroom cupboard. She knew that most of them were taken by her dad quite a few years ago, because after the death of her mom, he had never touched his Nikon. It had been wrapped up in old newspapers and cotton and perched high on the top shelf of his cupboard. Under one particular photograph of a Buddhist stupa in the blog page, she found a comment left by someone called *CT*. Curious, she clicked on *CT*'s blog and what did she discover? Hey! It was the blog page of that woman at the Blitz! That woman who had planted a kiss on her cheeks, that woman who pulled her up as she fell at the entrance of Alclove, that woman who exchanged the faulty disc of the game with a new one in no time along with biscuits and chocolates!

She minutely scanned each and every part of this frequently visited blog. The blog page had an attractive leafy design with a black and white profile photo of the owner. Diana alias Sonai looked at the display picture of the owner of the page. A longish face with sharp nose and shoulder length hair looked almost perfect. The supple lips frozen in a half-smile only accentuated the simplicity of the woman with inherent beauty. The eyes with lustrous brows were definitely dreamy. The face was turned sideways a bit so that only one earlobe was visible. The earlobe had a small stud, silvery and simple. Diana knows that the real face was more elegant and sharp than the one on screen. The centre of the page had poems. So Moni was a poetess! Diana thought. She wrote lines as beautiful as those on her face. Diana started to read the lines. On one poem, her eyes froze. The title of the piece was 'Mother'. Diana read, uttering each word carefully, sort of pronouncing them distinctly…

Stars and planets of the dark sky,
Tell her
I'm fine
Though far away from her…

Diana read and reread those lines till she felt a sharp pain in her heart as if someone was slowly putting a needle into her bosom. Her eyes started twitching at first. But she knew that she was about to cry. Her mouth widened and she put her palms on her mouth to make the groan inaudible. She felt hot. She felt singed. Several moments passed as Diana, little Diana, cried so as to become little Sonai. In her foggy eyes, the photo of Moni gradually turned into the face of another woman of whom she had only indistinct memories.

However, Sonai recovered to become Diana again, wiping back her tears with the help of her arm. *So SA visits CT both online and offline!* Diana thought. They chat perhaps, for at least twice, Diana had observed on the sly *SA* responding to pings from *CT* late at night as he sat on her bed with his laptop. They chatted! *But what do they chat about?* Couldn't their chat records be discovered? As they chatted on Gtalk, Gmail accounts, if opened, could lead to a clue, Diana thought. She opened the login page of Gmail. In the username space she typed Silent Assassin and on the password tab she wrote hitman and clicked. The page did not open, as the password error flashed in bold red letters. She backspaced to try another password. It was also not correct. She tried another, this time conceiving something related to her own name.

Thus, she tried several times using names of all family members, their nicknames, residence phone number, cell phone numbers, dates of birth of her dad and her own. But still the password could not be traced. Diana grew impatient. She would have to know the chat records; she would have to find out what was going on between the two—*SA* and *CT*, her dad and Moni. Diana scratched her tiny head to dig out a possible match. What could it be? Suddenly an idea came to her. As Silent Assassin is a name or rather an epithet associated with Hitman, she thought of using words or phrases or numbers related to the game.

She started negating those which were too small like '47', the agent code of Hitman. She then moved on to the names of different stages of the game. *Anathema* was the first stage. So she typed Anathema with bated breath, and *Hurrah*! It opened! The page started loading with a blue progress bar widening rapidly on the top. There were so many chats between the two! Some were pretty lengthy—comprising twenty to thirty lines even!

Suddenly there was a *ping*. *CT* wrote: *Good morning!*

Sonai was surprised. For a moment, she thought of disconnecting the modem. But then, she was too curious to leave the virtual mystery world. She typed in the blank space of the chat box:

SA: Good morning!

CT: Busy with work I suppose…

Sonai felt the thrill of impersonating her dad in the virtual world to someone known to her, in a very good game of hide and seek—*online hide and seek*, she thought and typed:

SA: Ya… a bit of office work…

CT: Sorry to intrude then…

SA: No! No! Its okay… In fact I'm enjoying it!

Sonai wrote hastily.

CT: Enjoying it? Really?

SA: Ya! It is good to have someone to chat with… Someone who really cares for me.

CT alias Moni wrote back:

How do you know that I do really care for you?

Sonai felt like jabbering a lot of things, but soon she was reminded of the fact that she was impersonating her dad, and if Moni comes to know that, she would definitely tell everything to dad and she would be branded as an imposter. Chances are that it would cause her dad to take unprecedented steps like throwing away the computer and the modem and the packets of games. Moreover, she wanted to know how far *SA* and *CT* had progressed. So, she took some time to type a suitable answer which prompted *CT* to write again:

CT: Tell me, how do you know?

Sonai bit her lips and smiled before hitting the alphabets:

SA: Because the first thing you do in the morning is to get online and greet me!

CT remained silent.

Sonai thought now it was her turn to poke Moni a bit. So she continued typing.

SA: You miss me, don't you?

The green dot against *CT's* name suddenly became grey. Moni went offline.

This reaction was not at all expected by Sonai. She stayed online for a few more minutes, hoping with every passing moment that the green dot would glow again. But it remained grey, till Padma-di came upstairs and took her to the bathroom. With Diwali vacation still on, Sonai had all morning to probe and devise plans to get to the bottom of the *SA—CT conundrum.* So she bathed and had her breakfast in a very quiet manner, which was so unlikely of her that her granny asked twice if she was all right. She just nodded. After breakfast, she went straight to her bedroom upstairs and got online and opened Gtalk. The grey dot was still there. Moni was offline. Sonai clicked on the profile name of Moni. A box opened and there was a statement: *CT* is offline but you can send messages to *CT*.

Sonai was tense. She started writing her mind and even before she could realise, she wrote quite a few lines and was about to hit 'Enter', when she realised that she had to impersonate *SA* So she quickly modified the message in order to make it look like a message from *SA*. Then she hit the 'l' like cursor to post the message and logged out almost immediately. Her heart was throbbing. She was sweating even on the chilly morning of twentieth day of October.

Shutting down the computer, she walked across to her dad's bedroom to stand before a six by five inches portrait of her mother. She looked at the face bent sideways with a candid smile. She kept on looking at the photograph with a fresh garland of white Rajnigandha flowers upon it. She moved her right palm on the photo as if to touch the beautiful face with a strong sense of yearning and murmured:

'Mama... I'm sorry Mama for what I've done today... But... I think you'll forgive me... I need you Mama but I know you can never come back from the sky... So... I took it upon me to find someone like you... Bless me Mama...'

Drops of salty water ran down the little flushed cheeks of little Sonai as she kept on mumbling words and wishes, stroking the photograph of the woman who had brought her to this world.

'What are you doing there?'

Debjani called out suddenly from behind, almost startling Sonai, who quickly wiped her tears and turning back to her granny, rushed towards her with open arms.

14

If a habitual drunkard asks for a bottle of milk instead of a bottle of whiskey, what would you think? That the guy had gone mad, of course! Moni felt the same when Anu called her in the evening and asked her to bring home a computer game called Hitman.

'Are you okay?' Moni asked her on a serious note of doubt and suspicion, knowing fully well that Anu's selection test had ended that day.

'Ya! Of course!' Anu yelled over the phone that could be, in all probability, a demonstration of the deafening shrillness of her vocal pipe.

'Shout again!' Moni quipped, suppressing her smile.

'Why? You a saint?' Anu reverted more shrilly.

'A bit louder dear…' Moni egged on.

'Why? You stuupeed?' Anu shouted.

'Only thinking if you can break glass by shouting over the phone… Kept the phone near a glass jar on my table!' Moni answered and laughed out.

'You moron! I'll kill you!' Anu kept yelling as Moni cut the line off and laughed again.

Moni reached home at eight. The moment she entered their living room, Anu came rushing and took from her hand the plastic carry bag containing vegetables and chicken.

'Got the game?' Anu asked as she started to unpack the chicken and vegetables in the kitchen.

'Ya... But why on earth have you suddenly become interested in games?' Moni asked, as she came to the kitchen door and watched Anu washing the vegetables.

'Why? Can't grown ups play games?' Anu replied without looking. Her hands were busy under the tap rinsing tomatoes and cucumbers and cabbages and potatoes.

'Should I cleanse the chicken?' Anu asked Moni who looked absent minded, staring blankly at the sink.

'Yes... I'll marinate it soon,' Moni said as she walked away to her room.

Switching on the light, Moni took a look at her room. The bedside table was neatly organised. Her books and creams and lotions were arranged meticulously on the table. Her notebook in computer was there too with the battery charger cable fitted. The bed cover was smoothened out, and a small quilt placed on the bed, folded. The mosquito repellent lent an aroma to the room. Moni felt very comfortable. She pulled the hairband out and carefully opened the safety pin that held the *pallu,* broad hem of her saree pleated to her blouse. She hummed as she folded the saree and put it into the wardrobe. Then she unhooked her blouse and took a towel.

'What should I mix with the chicken?' Anu shouted from kitchen.

'You need not do anything... Don't fiddle with the chicken Anu! Let me get freshened up,' Moni answered shouting back as she went to the bathroom.

Anu heard Moni's voice and she decided to obey Moni, principally because she had no idea how to marinate the chicken. There was another reason and that was the sudden discovery of a cellophane wrapped game disc lying on the living room couch.

Anu rushed to the packet and tore open the disc and went straight to Moni's room to load the disc onto Moni's laptop.

The machine screen became dark for a second or two as the game opened after being installed. There was the common storyline narration at the beginning which was followed by some initial animation video clips. Anu skipped them all by pressing the escape button to get to the 'play' section of the game. The first stage of the game was called *Anathema* in which the protagonist of the game i.e., the agent coded 47, clad in black suit and a red tie, was assigned to find out a clergyman who was abducted by a warlord. Anu quickly went through the tutorial section to get an overview of the movement and maneuvers of the on-screen hero of the game. Soon she became the agent herself as she started to control the movements of the on-screen agent by clicking on the mouse pad and pressing different keys. Her eyes had all the keenness of an agile secret operative and her face seemed stony, reflecting the strong resolve befitting any undercover agent. Off-screen and real Anu turned on-screen and virtual secret agent '47'. Off-screen, plump faced Anu became on-screen superhero—the smart, quick, dishy and bold Hitman, walking lazily in the beautiful compound of a deserted chapel to get into a shack full of weapons of the most dreadful kind.

Soon the agent as controlled by Anu's fingertips found out his choicest weapon—the 'Ballers', bearing the insignia of the agent on its handlebar. Anu pressed certain option buttons to get more weapons for her hero. After gathering quite a few guns and sniper-rifles and knives, Anu rolled her fingers on the keys to get the agent to move towards the chapel entrance. Once within the chapel, Anu found a box left for her operative. She clicked on to make agent '47' pick up a letter from the box.

'What does the letter say?'

Someone asked suddenly from behind. Anu was startled out of her wits to see Moni standing just behind her, drooping almost over her shoulder, with her wet hair hanging loosely in the front.

'Oh! It was you! Well... The letter says that the priest is abducted,' Anu said flashing a smile trying to eliminate her surprised frown.

'Been watching you play for the last five minutes...' Moni answered, getting closer to the bedside table to pick up a tube of moisturiser.

Anu's eyes were glued to the screen.

'I'm going to the kitchen to make the chicken ready,' Moni said as she walked out of the room.

Anu made no answer. She just nodded. Her hero would soon leave the chapel in search of the old clergyman.

Opening the refrigerator, Moni found a torn packet of sliced bread stacked on the mid-shelf. Anu must have left it in the morning. What about making something with the bread? Moni put on her apron and started slicing the chicken into small pieces while the oil was left on the pan. Then she poured pieces of the chicken into the pan and simmered them brown. Where's the cornflower? Moni opened the cabinet to bring out a glass jar half-filled with white powdery substance. She poured the powdery thing into a bowl and added water to it to make a paste. She would use the cornflower paste as a sort of binder to hold the chicken pieces and bread together. On the other oven, she placed another pan and started to fry pieces of onion, carrot and capsicum. Having done that, she transferred the fried chicken pieces onto the other pan containing onion, capsicum etc. and stirred them together.

She felt curiously satiated in her efforts of preparing something in the kitchen. This sense of satisfaction, Moni observed, was somewhat similar to what she usually felt while composing a few lines of poetry. Thinking about poetry, Moni suddenly remembered the message she got in the morning from *SA*.

Was he online? Has he left any other message?

Anu finished the first stage of the game—the Gontranno sanctuary in no time. It was fairly easy to pass through. Anu could have lumbered on to the next stage of the engrossing game, had she not heard Moni calling her to the table. It was ten thirty. Anu pressed the quit button. The screen darkened, only to reveal the trademark of the game occupying the whole screen.

Hitman 2: Silent Assassin

It read.

Silent Assassin or *SA* in short… What an epithet! Anu thought, as she closed down the windows.

'Check out my chicken gold coin, buddy!' Moni was all exuberance, as she saw Anu coming to the table.

'C.G.C? What a name!' Anu said and quickly put a piece into her mouth.

Moni smiled at Anu's habit of using random abbreviations, for everything like C.G.C for Chicken Gold Coin.

'Wow! It's fantabulous!' Anu uttered, closing her eyes to savour every bit of the C.G.C.

Moni pushed a bowl of chicken balls with cornflower coating towards Anu and sprinkled soya sauce and tomato puree over them.

Anu started gorging like someone who had starved the whole season.

'How was the game?' Moni asked conversationally.

'It was simply mind blowing, you know... There you have an agent called '47' alias Silent Assassin or *SA* on a mission to hunt down an old priest abducted by some Italian gang leader and...'

Anu jabbered on excitedly.

'Really? Silent Assassin or *SA*, you said, is the name of the agent?' Moni asked looking thoughtful.

'Ya! Why?' Anu asked.

'Nothing... Carry on,' Moni said absentmindedly.

'Where was I? Oh... Yes! Now the agent can be equipped with arms and ammunitions as per your choice... Definitely, the more your agent progresses, the more you earn weapons for him, quite naturally.' Anu then moved on with her immaculate description of the game, to the minute technical details which sounded like Geek's Hebrew to Moni.

After dinner, Anu went to her bedroom.

Moni asked if she would love to play the game at night. Anu declined. She said that she was in need of a good night's sleep, especially after the lack of it for the past few days, courtesy, the selection test.

So instead, Moni opened the flap of her computer notebook to log on. She had lots of queries.

Why is today the day of grief for SA? Who left SA forever and why?

Gtalk took some time to open. Those few seconds seemed like hours to Moni.

Finally, when she connected to the chat box, she was disappointed.

SA was offline.

Moni typed: *May I have the pleasure of knowing why today is your saddest day in life?*

After that, she went to her own blog page *CT's* poems.

And on the compose tab, started to do what she felt like doing whenever she had the occasion to stare at the white page. She wrote, feverishly, with her jabber-fingers running to and fro on the keypad, like someone possessed.

Golden mean?
Middle age?
Midsummer Night's Dream?

Have you ever witnessed
The strange fusion of childish whims
And superannuated lethargy?
Quietness dotted by flood of foolish blood?
Aging with agelessness?
Rhymes with reasons?

Have you ever
Woken up with a young heart and fading brain?

Have you?
Ever?
Caught in the middle?
Of a Riddle?

Have you?
Haven't you?

Having scribbled some lines and posted them, Moni simply stared at her poem absentmindedly, as if in a trance.

She would have gone on staring at her newborn baby on the blog for hours had Anoushka not opened the door with a bang and screamed, 'Hey! Got the nappy? I'm leaking!'

Moni almost jumped out of the bed startled by the sudden shrill scream of Anu in her half dress. Her heart was thumping. Her lips quavered for a while, ultimately giving way to laughter.

'O! Anu! You're such a darn thing! Look up my cupboard.'

Anu ran to the cupboard and rummaged a packet and rushed out yelling, 'Thankeeeu'.

Moni logged out, switched off the light and lay down on the mattress, straight with her hands under her head, staring up at the white ceiling upon which the light from the opposite apartment somehow managed to draw curious patterns, as it came through the window glass and iron bars.

15

Ved drove the car lazily down the bridge, following the left hand side, signalling with his hand all the time for every vehicle to pass by him. It was only ten in the morning and the traffic on the broad and shiny flyover was quick. Everyone was in a mad rush, barring a certain white Honda. After the selection test, Ved had only two or three classes to take and he was in no real hurry. Just when he drove down the flyover and stopped at a traffic post before making a right turn to catch the Alipore road, a taxi came up beside him and the cabbie rolled down the glass and yelled, 'Are you counting pebbles on the road?'

'No! Actually counting the lamp posts,' Ved replied smiling.

Had it been any other busy day, Ved would have stepped on the paddle and whizzed past all those ancient boxes with yellow paint on the road. But this morning was different. He slept late last night and woke up late. Last night, Sonai kept him awake. A strange statement from little Sonai, last night, made Ved realise that his little daughter is no longer little.

Ved actually was so much surprised by the statement of Sonai that he simply stared at her like an idiot. The statement was still ringing in his ears.

Ved had gone to Sonai's room last night to plant a goodnight kiss on her forehead. As soon as Ved's lips had touched her supple forehead, she opened her eyes and muttered:

'Isn't it time for *SA* to resettle?'

Ved looked into Sonai's eyes. There was no hint of mischief in them. They were still and poignant.

'Why? Doesn't Hitman claim that women make men go astray?'

'Does it really? Then I make you go astray, don't I?'

Sonai's eyes were fixed still on Ved's.

'Oh no! Never!' Ved croaked.

Sonai sat up on her bed. Her face was flushed. Ved felt worked up inside with severity of anticipation.

'It is far more difficult to live a motherless life than a wifeless one.'

Sonai finally uttered, choked with emotion as if she would cry.

Ved at once held his daughter in a tight embrace, trying to soothe her. But, surprisingly, Ved himself felt very troubled inside. His eyes twitched. He felt a strong upsurge of emotions. His cheeks were trembling. He hastened to the toilet. Standing in front of the wash basin, Ved kept splashing water on his face for several minutes. When he somehow managed to cleanse his emotions in the wash basin, he turned around to find Sonai standing right behind him with a towel in her hand. Her face was half lit by the light of the bathroom. Ved did not even look into Sonai's eyes. He felt ashamed. He took the towel from his daughter's hand and wiped his face in a tumultuous manner, as if he was going to rub the skin off his face. Having done that, he strolled along to the switchboard, plugged in the mosquito repellent and made a quiet exit.

The road that ran straight from the National library campus to the university was flanked on both sides by huge billboards. Ved's eyes spotted one with the line:

'Marriages are made in Heaven, with a little help from us!'

The line was painted in red upon a huge billboard announcing the launch of the latest matrimonial service of the city.

Ved smiled as he swerved the car left, to enter the university campus which would soon be populated with the teachers and the taught.

Exiting the elevator on the third floor, Ved started walking to the Head of the Department's office. The office door was shut. He pushed in and entered. The leather chair of Dr. Nita Ramani was empty. Ved looked at his watch. It was eleven. The ever dutiful Department Head did not turn up late anytime. Ved never saw her coming late to the office or to any seminar or even to any party. Her severe sense of punctuality had earned her the nickname 'bell'. Ved always felt that that was a wrong way to interpret someone's virtue.

'Hello Ved!' a soft voice called from behind.

Dr. Ramani paddled into her office. Owing to arthritis, Dr. Ramani moved slowly, time and again placing her palm on her knees as if holding them. Sometimes, she grimaced while doing so, like she did the moment she came and slowly, very carefully, sat down on the chair. Ved looked at Dr. Ramani. She must have been very beautiful in her younger days. Her eyes were sharp and yet had a calmness to them. Age had started making impressions upon her face with different contours appearing distinctly on her forehead, under eye-region and neck. Her white hair cropped and shiny, made her look all the more charismatic.

'Where's the register?' Ved asked.

'Why? I think you need not sign today,' Dr. Ramani mumbled, as she opened a file and looked up.

'Why?' Ved asked perplexed.

'Today is your off-day, I presume,' Ramani smiled as she looked at Ved's face.

'Oh ho! Is it Wednesday today?' Ved asked, feeling stupid.

'Yes, son,' Ramani's smile broadened to become a grin.

'I'm so sorry!' Ved smiled not knowing what he should do.

'Go back home and take your daughter out for a lunch!' Dr. Ramani said in a kind voice.

'Yeah!' Ved replied as he brought out the car key from his pocket.

'Bye bye ma'am,' Ved said as he turned towards the door.

'Ved!' Dr. Ramani interrupted.

'Yes!' Ved turned his head resting his right hand on the copper door knob.

'Have you decided to lead life like this throughout?'

Dr. Ramani asked, slowly but clearly, pronouncing each and every word in a careful manner.

Ved's eyebrows got twisted.

'I'm of your mom's age and I have the little prerogative to give you the right direction, haven't I?' Dr. Ramani asked looking at Ved's perspiring face.

Ved stood still. His chin was rested on the upper portion of his chest. He looked down at the tiled floor. The floor tiles looked like a bigger version of a crossword puzzle, only to be filled up with right alphabets.

'I know you've got problems... It's hard to shrug off memories... But think about your kid... She needs someone... to give her all the love and care of a mother... The positive aspect of your daughter is that she had lost her mom so early that she could possibly, even forget all the pangs of being motherless if she gets someone right now. The more she'll grow, the more she'll feel lonely... For a child's proper upbringing, a mother is more needed than a father, at least psychologically...'

Dr. Ramani spoke earnestly. Ved was surprised to hear all those words from a person who never appeared so informal and candid than ever before.

'Well... I know the issue is very very subjective... But...you know,' for the first time Dr. Ramani's voice trembled a bit. But she soon took control of her voice undulations and continued in a wistful strain.

'You know... I kind of look upon you as my son... Whom I lost...'

Ved looked up to see a pained face of an old mother with white hair. Dr. Ramani's son died in a road accident few years back, Ved remembered.

Ved nodded both ways, not knowing how to show acceptance or denial in an emotionally supercharged scenario like that.

Coming out of the office, brooding heavily, Ved strolled towards his room at the end of the corridor. Why was, suddenly, everyone asking him to open his mind and remarry? Was there something really missing in him that prompted Sonai or Dr. Ramani to spell the same for him? Was he getting weird leading a widower's life? Did he look like a haggard with no wife to take care of him?

The first thing he did on entering his room, was to take a long and critical look at his clothes on the small rectangular wash basin mirror. He shaved customarily. His newly bought purple shirt looked quite smart when paired with black trousers. His hair was neatly combed with a middle partition. The curls looked perfect… Only… Only there were some streaks of white in some of them… Covered by the younger ones—black and shiny. 'I'm definitely ageing…'

Ved thought and smiled. Suddenly the long dreamy eyes of the manager of Blitz appeared before him as if she was smiling from the mirror. Ved kept on looking at the face blessed with a heavenly smile. Ved plunged into a reverie in the beautiful afternoon of late October. However, his reverie was interrupted.

'Sorry to disturb you sir!' a known voice was heard.

Ved swung his head towards the door. There stood Anoushka Agarwal with the upper half of her body visibly into the room through the half open door, leaning forward.

'Yes?' Ved asked surprised seeing the part one student still in the university even after the selection test.

'May I?' Anoushka asked for the permission to enter her teacher's room.

'You're already in, I suppose,' Ved said as he walked back to his table.

'What's matter? Kohlberg or Thorndike?' Ved asked suppressing his smile.

'It's *SA*… Sir!'

'Essay? What essay?' Ved asked still surprised.

'Not essay Sir! But... S and A in caps... And maybe italics...' Anuoskha said with an enigmatic smile.

Ved felt a sudden jerk within him. 'What *SA*?' he asked trying to face the girl with cool nonchalance.

'You play games? Don't you? Especially Hitman?' Anoushka asked.

'Ya,' Ved responded. His voice was trailing.

'And you use *SA* as your profile name in chat box, right?'

'Yes... But how do you know?' Ved asked with dilated pupils as if he was hearing a phantom spelling his doom.

He felt hot. His throat turned dry.

'You know someone called Candletree?' Anoushka asked excitedly.

'I don't know what you are talking about,' Ved spoke dryly.

'You don't know Candletree?' Anuoshka seemed persistent.

'No... Not really,' Ved retorted and searched for his cigarettes.

'O.'

Anuoshka's face became pale. Her eyebrows made a circuitous loop. She was thinking hard, putting the index finger of her left hand on her lips.

'Are you a junkie or something?' Ved asked, quite disturbed by the girl's whimsical and erratic attitude.

'Sorry Sir! I must be wrong!'

Anuoshka left the room abruptly, like the way she came.

Ved lit up a cigarette and took the first puff mouthful.

The next few puffs were taken quite hastily by Ved. Then he stamped the bud under his feet and called home.

'Hello...'

Debjani Bhattacharya's voice at the other end seemed tired.

Ved looked at his watch.

It was twelve twenty.

'Have you taken your lunch?' Ved asked.

'Lunch? Your daughter is still in front of the computer!' Debjani squealed.

'Really? Playing games still?' Ved asked in an indulgent manner.

'Games? Don't know... A few minutes ago, when I went upstairs to take her to bath, she said she was online and could not be offline for the next half an hour.'

'Online? Strange! Give her the phone,' Ved said, this time, not so indulgently.

'Okay. Hold on... You and your daughter! You'll make me mad one day!' Debjani grumbled all the way upstairs till she gave the phone to Sonai.

'Sonai!'

Ved said the moment he realised the phone was being handed over.

'Yes... Papa.'

'What are you doing online?' Ved asked.

'Online? Who told you?' Sonai seemed surprised.

'You told Granny that you were online?'

'Oh...Yes... I was... But now I'm offline'

'Don't download too many games... Playing games always is detrimental to one's health... N't you know?'

'I was not playing games or downloading them,' Sonai said.

'Then what were you doing online?'

'Chatting... Er ...trying to chat,' Sonai fumbled.

'Chatting? With whom? Why? How?'

Ved was too surprised to swallow the fact.

'Actually… I got online friends,' Sonai said softly.

'Online friends! My goodness! Who are they?'

Ved's surprise only heightened, his brows picking up undulations and jaw dropping further.

'Not many… In fact only one so far…'

'Really? May I know who that is?' Ved probed.

'Maybe someone you know,' Sonai replied as enigmatically as Anu had in his office.

'Come'n Diana! Don't be so evasive with your agent!' Ved said playfully.

'Why not? If the agent himself is secretive in certain cases,' Sonai said.

'Me? When? About what?' Ved said, his brows almost reaching his hairline and jaw dropping to meet the chest.

'You think! Bye bye!'

Sonai cut the line.

The toll plaza at the end of the second Hooghly Bridge was uncommonly less crowded. Ved slowed down when he reached the plaza gate. There were several channels. Ved took the one designated for cars. At the toll ticketing window, Ved could see the ticket vendor's right hand popping out. He pushed a ten rupee bill into the grimy hand and sped up.

'Hey! Your ticket!' the vendor shouted as he tried to throw a crumpled piece of printed slip into Ved's car through the right hand front window which had started to roll up.

'Keep it!' Ved shouted back as he took the lane to Mandirtala.

Ved was hurrying home. He would have to. His mind was filled with terrible anticipation.

Had Sonai chatted with CT? If so, what had she told her? What would Moni think about him?

The white Honda swerved through the gate. Ved alighted quickly and dashed indoors. Debjani Bhattacharya was watching the afternoon soap sitting on her bed with her legs stretched on the mattress.

'*Ki re*? How come you returned so quickly?' Debjani said the moment she saw her son entering the room.

'Today was my day off!' Ved said, smiling.

'That's what I thought in the morning... But then again, sometimes you go out even on your holidays... So...' Debjani replied smiling back.

'Where's Sonai?'

'She is upstairs... Sleeping...'

'Sleeping? Has she taken her lunch?'

'Yes... After talking to you she got up from computer and bathed and took her lunch without even bothering me! She even ate fish!' Debjani said.

Ved smiled.

Sonai eating fish is a rarity.

'Okay... Watch your favourite serial... I'm going upstairs...' Ved said as he went to the staircase.

The door was open. Ved entered his bedroom. Sonai was lying with her face turned sideways. Ved walked up.

'Sonai... Dear... Papa is back...' Ved murmured as he stroked his hand over Sonai's head.

Sonai did not move.

'Sonai...'

Ved repeated as he sat on the bed, right beside Sonai, waiting for a reply from her.

'Okay! Sleep... Let me get online and have a chat with *CT*... I need to know what your point of discussion was,' Ved deliberately descended from the bed and walked up to the computer.

'No... She might be busy!' Sonai shouted and jumped down from the bed to hold Ved's hands.

'Really? How do you know?' Ved asked.

'She works in a mall... Not in university,' Sonai said.

'Yeah... I know... But tell me, what did you tell her?' Ved asked in a careless manner in spite of being very tensed and worried inside.

'Nothing!'

'Nothing? Okay! Let me check the chat details... Just tell me your user id,' Ved said as he sat down on the chair facing the computer.

'Papa... I'm sorry,' Sonai came and stood beside Ved. Her eyes were glistening.

'Why? What happened?' Ved asked, curiously.

'I... I used your username and password to log on,' Sonai muttered. Her head was dropped as she stood there.

'My username? *SA*? Password? How, you cracked it?' Ved was so surprised that his voice trembled.

'I used trial and error method... And I remembered vaguely your finger movements on the keyboard...' Sonai spoke almost inaudibly.

'My goodness! You cracked it? O my God!' Ved shuddered and shouted.

'Anathema,' Sonai answered looking up half way.

'Anathema it is! But how the hell did you crack it?'

'Remembered vaguely your fingers moving on the keypad,' Sonai repeated.

'My God! You know what you've done?' Ved shouted agitatedly and stood up.

'What?' Sonai asked, looking guiltless, this time.

'You acted like an imposter! It's a crime!'

Ved was in rage. His face reddened with uncontrollable angst.

'What crime?' Sonai asked.

'You don't know the word crime? You plucky geek!'

Ved shouted and the very next moment he did a thing which he had never done to his dearest daughter. He slapped her on her face. The slap was so unexpected that little Sonai just stood there and rubbed her flushed cheek for a while, looking at her dad and then she cried aloud and ran downstairs. Ved tried to stop her but she just hopped down the stairs crying even more loudly, which brought Debjani out of her bedroom. Biswanath, Ved's father who was in the garden with Bhajan *da* came running also.

'What happened?' Biswanath asked as Sonai jumped into his arms. Debjani looked up at Ved with inquisitive eyes.

Ved was standing on the landing.

'Papa slapped me!' Sonai said weeping.

'What? How dare he?' Biswanath almost roared and handed Sonai to his wife who took her immediately and started to caress her and tried to console her with her soft words.

'Take her to your room,' Biswanath ordered.

Debjani walked towards her room, balancing Sonai on her hip, still looking at Ved with terrible grief written on her face as if she would cry.

Ved stood still on the landing.

'Why did you slap her? You idiot!' Biswanath roared again.

'I… I… Lost my cool,' Ved mumbled.

'Next time you hurt her, I swear, I will just throw you out of the house!' Biswanath threatened and rushed to the bedroom into which Debjani had taken Sonai.

Ved stood silent. His eyes blurred. He felt an indescribable pain. He sat down on the staircase, with his right palm covering his face.

After sometime, when Sonai's yells softened and sobered up downstairs, Ved stood up and went to his room. He pulled the curtain and lay down on the bed with his trousers and socks on. He closed his eyes but tears continued to leak from the corners of his eyelids, pressed so tightly.

Why did I slap her? Am I getting ill-tempered? I shouldn't have slapped her! Ved thought and the tears rolled down his cheeks even more, like small rivulets.

'Won't you eat?' Ved heard someone asking him.

He opened his soaked eyes.

There stood Sonai in her white frock, near the bed. She looked like a fairy, with loose strands of hair falling over her shoulder and the streams of sunlight filling up the translucent curtains, lighting up her face in an interesting, poetic manner. Her cheeks was puffed up. Her eyes had swelled. Ved sat up and opened his arms. Sonai lurched forward, pressing her face against Ved's chest.

'I'm sorry Papa… I will never be an imposter ever in future…' Sonai said.

Ved hugged her closely and choked up! 'It's okay… It's okay dear…' he said.

Sonai rubbed her face on her father's chest and spoke haltingly, 'I miss her.'

'Whom?' Ved asked in a low voice.

'Mama,' Sonai answered in a voice that trailed.

'I too,' Ved said.

For the next few minutes, the father and daughter remained silent. Sonai clung to Ved's chest like a baby. She was a baby. Ved patted Sonai's back trying to soothe her to sleep.

'Papa...' Sonai broke the silence.

'Yes ...' Ved responded dreamily.

'*CT* Moni is a poetess and a poetess can never be bad... Isn't it?' Sonai asked suddenly.

Ved was surprised by his little daughter's strange analysis.

'How do you know that she writes?' Ved asked.

'I know. Saw her blog page, her chats,' Sonai replied.

'But,' Ved stopped.

'Moni is good,' Sonai said, hiding her face into Ved's chest.

'Really? How do you know?'

'I know... She loves me... She loves you,' Sonai said straightforwardly.

'Really?' Ved took Sonai's face in his hand.

'Really?' Ved asked again looking at Sonai.

'Yes! I think I owe an apology to her, otherwise she might misinterpret the whole thing,' Sonai spoke thinking.

'Yes... You're right...'

Ved was surprised to hear Sonai speak like a grown up woman.

'You're getting older and wiser... A bit too fast,' Ved said smiling and kissed Sonai's puffed cheek.

'Pardon me?' Ved asked.

'Not fully!' Sonai replied with a sudden luster in her eyes.

'Okay… Tonight we'll have our dinner outside… Name a restaurant,' Ved said.

'I would love to go to Moni's place tonight and meet her!' Sonai said promptly.

'Moni's place? You mean Bardhaman Road?'

'Yeah! We need to go there… You and I… Agreed?' Sonai asked looking at Ved.

'But… Er… She might be out,' Ved hesitated.

'She usually returns in the evening… Agree to go?' Sonai was insistent.

'Let me think…'

Ved was still not sure what could be the outcome of such a visit.

'Don't worry… Just pretend to be angry with me… As if you pulled me up there to seek an apology from her,' Sonai said, as she winked.

'Diana O Diana! You're such a …'

Ved stopped to find out an appropriate epithet for his intelligent and impulsive daughter.

'Plucky geek?' Sonai asked, trying to fill in.

'No! Plucky contriver!' Ved yelled.

Moni was holding the weekly meeting with the floor managers when Anu called her.

Moni could have pressed the silent button of her cell but she took the call remembering Anu's strange behaviour in the morning when she played the computer game bought last night and time and again, came to Moni to ask strange queries like *Is Moni dating someone or not? Or, does Moni know the consequences of flings?* All these repeated queries had flabbergasted Moni so much that finally before leaving for office she had asked

Anu, sternly, not to interfere too much in her life. That final word had left a bitter taste for Moni, which she had hoped to overcome. So she pressed the green button in spite of having an important meeting.

'Hello!' Moni said, as she left her table and went to the washroom.

'Hi Moni! Congrats dear, for finally being a bait of a charmer!' Anu said.

'What the hell are you talking about? You nerd?' Moni barked, irritated by Anu's incoherent, abysmal and confusing statement.

'You know well!' insisted Anu, before disconnecting the line.

Moni looked at the screen of her cellphone and uttered curse words through clenched teeth.

Had Anu gone mad, finally? Moni thought.

16

Anu's fingers trembled when she tried to unlock the front door of their flat. She had gone out of the flat as early as ten and had waited at the university for Prof. VPB. She had not eaten a single piece of anything since the past night. Now, after coming back from the university, she was feeling hungry, tired and more than anything terribly dejected.

How could Prof. VPB and Moni keep on having a steady affair without even letting her know? How could Moni, in whom she had confided her every little secret, not even have cared to talk about her newfound love? Had she not always looked upon Moni as her dearest sister, friend and guide in this cold, hard city of concrete? *Why did Moni do that? How could she be so cruel and selfish? Had Moni taken her to be a competitor? How could Prof. VPB be so indifferent to her? Were both of them just having fun at her expense, thinking of her as a jerk?*

Last evening, when she was playing the game, she suddenly came across the acronym *SA* and had at once, realised that it could be related to Prof. Ved Prakash Bhattacharya as it was in his car, she saw the cover of the game. Moreover, she remembered how a guy with long curls brought her and Moni back from the Big Ben that evening when she poured more poison down her throat than she could possibly handle. So, *CT* alias Moni and VPB alias *SA* met after the incident and VPB helped his Moni out of a messy situation. She was the mess herself that night. She was still the mess in their life. Moni had categorically asked her not to interfere too much into her life, that morning. Probably, Moni had always felt so, but never blurted it out before.

I have no interest in staying between the two. I was a dumb ass to stay in between and force them to play hide and seek. I have been an idiot. I have been a real jerk!

Thinking all these, Anu called Moni and congratulated her.

Now the whole thing being as clear as daylight to her, she felt sorry for herself. What would she do now? Should she go back home? Should she throw a party welcoming VPB and Moni into their new life? But how could she do that? How can she cheat herself? How can she ward off the tingling pain in her heart whenever she chanced upon her hero, her first love, the *Indian Antonio Banderas?* How could she muster up the will to share her first love with a woman she always considered her elder sister?

She decided to leave. She opened Moni's laptop and started typing words. It took twenty minutes to finish off a long word document and place it right at the desktop. Having done that, she did not shut down the machine. She took it to the living room and placed it with its flap opened, on the glass table. She wanted Moni to read that letter the first thing on entering their flat.

'What will I do now?' Anu thought. It was only 3:00 p.m. and Moni would not return before seven. So still, she had four hours to think and decide. Should she pack bags and leave for the airport to catch the flight to Bagdogra? What would her parents think? Would they be pleased to see her after a long gap? But then, she would have to return to the city again for the final exam. She would again have to go to the university to face the sarcasm filled eyes of VPB. Should she quit her studies? Should she quit life?

The more she thought, the more she became restless, indecisive. Finally, she went out of the flat with a bag containing clothes and toothpaste and toiletries and two fat wads of money. Actually, she had in her cupboard three wads of notes, each, worth of two thousand rupees. She left two thousand rupees under the laptop for Moni for the expenses of the month which was ending. She mentioned details of her expenses owed and settled, including those of sanitary pads taken from Moni's cupboard last night in her letter to Moni.

Leaving the flat, Anu hailed a cab to Sush's home. It was near Naktala Fire Station, a half-hour ride from Bardhaman Road. When the cab reached Naktala Fire Station, it was already five thirty. The sun had almost set and the city sky was approaching dark.

Anu stood near the fire station, not sure which way she should move, for she had never been to Sush's place ever before. She remembered vaguely that Sush had once told her that she lived near Naktala Fire Station. But there were so many houses on both sides of the road, and it would take a real deal to find out exactly Sush's residence. Anu dug into her jeans pocket to dish out her cellphone. 'Holy crap!' she screamed. In her hurry and excitement, she had forgotten her cellphone!

'Now? What should I do? Should I keep on circling the neighbourhood in search of the house of a student of education department of the name Sushmita,' she wondered. She realised she would have to now rely heavily on physical descriptions of her friend, instead of more useful information like her father's name, address, or phone number!

Anu tried to recall Sush's cell number. It started with 983 as did all numbers of a cellphone service provider of the city. Suddenly, Anu realised that the only cell number of someone living in the city she could easily recall, barring her own, was that of Moni. Should she call Moni and tell her that she had decided to leave her forever? Oh no! That would be silly and another point of mockery and shame.

Clueless, Anu walked along the left-hand footpath, looking at the tall buildings on both sides. Most of the buildings were residence blocks having shops or garages on the ground floor. Anu walked. The footpath was not crowded, though a few people were always passing by. Most of the people were returning home. Anu saw children dancing their way home. She saw young professionals riding back home, looking grave with phone earplugs busily tucked in their ears. She saw autorickshaws running to and fro on the lane. She saw lovebirds walking lazily with their arms crossing each other's shoulders, like comrades. After a few minutes of walk, the perspective gradually changed. The tall residence blocks were replaced by smaller ones. The types of shops also changed. Earlier, they were glittering shops of food or electronic items. Now, there were small groceries and stationary shops with less vibrant lighting systems. In fact, in some side shops there were only lanterns and candlesticks, instead of electric lights. These shabby looking shops reminded Anu of her hometown. She walked on. A few yards away from where she stood, she found a liquor shop with a strong iron grill barrier upfront. A few lewd men in lungis were grouped together in front of the shop. Anu walked in and waited at the counter. A man wearing full sleeved woollens peered at her through the tiny hole in the middle of the iron grill. His eyes were clumsy. Seeing Anu, he grinned unpretentiously, revealing his paan-stained teeth.

'*Ki debo,* What will I give, Madam?'

The man asked grinning, his left hand hovering over his groin area visible through the wiremesh behind the Iron grill. The haggard looking people near the counter laughed out as if they had heard the cleverest joke of the year. Anu felt hot. Her ears were burning red.

'Whiskey,' Anu exhaled.

'Which one? A big one or a small one?' the obnoxious creature asked now clutching his balls.

'A big one,' Anu hissed.

Another roar of laughter around her.

Finally a bottle was handed to Anu wrapped in an old newspaper through the delivery hole. When Anu reached for the bottle into the hole, the man placed his left hand over her right hand. Anu concentrated on jerking the bottle and hand free of the hole with half a mind to dole out a mouthful of expletives. But she kept mum and threw some banknotes into the counter, before leaving the place.

With a bottle in her hand, she started looking for an ideal place to pour it down her belly. But the main road was full of traffic and lights and people. For a moment, Anu wanted a dark, depopulated place. She crossed the road and took the right flank as she noticed the right hand side of the road somewhat less congested. Her eyes popped out every time she saw a dark alley. She walked down twice those alleys only to reach someone's house. After sometime, walking down the footpath, Anu found a dark alley leading to marshy land.

'Hurrah!'

Anu cried out aloud and her cry was soon devoured by the shrubs and bushes of the swampy ground. Some distance away, Anu could see tiny drops of light peeping out of houses. Anu walked across carefully, taking her shoes in her hand, feeling each and every step. The grass was soft and moist. The adventure and thrill of being in unknown territory excited Anu greatly. She found a comparatively dry place. From her bag, she brought out a skirt and spread it on the earth. In the misty darkness, it was impossible for her to guess which skirt she had brought out and spread.

'It could be the one bought last year from the designer store at Park street... But who cares anyway?'

Anu thought as she unwound the bottle cap.

Ah!

The smell was delicious. Anu poured the liquid straight into her mouth. It tasted bitter and it burned.

'Damn! The bastard had given me a cheap thing!' Anu shouted and poured more to singe her throat.

A few more swigs later, Anu felt at ease within and without. The mosquitoes that made her slap herself several times in vain attempts to kill or mortally wound those tiny devils, suddenly became less frequent. The darkness coupled with the mist looming large over the place which had looked so eerie even a few moments ago, became a comfortable curtain shutting her out from the real world. She felt like being in clouds! She felt like being in a sea with waves rolling over and over till they disappeared. Anu definitely liked this cover of mist and darkness enveloping her. She felt it to be good to be in a wasteland, far away from the teeming population and din and bustle and sobs and cries and yells and so many other undesirable things. She felt contradictions in her bitter happiness—grim gaeity in her isolation. The freedom of being herself made her emotionally vulnerable.

'I want no father, no mother, no Moni, no VPB!' Anu shouted drowsily, articulating words with a very heavy lethargic droll of a tongue. Her head became weighty and she used her hands to hold it.

Suddenly, a little distance away, she thought, she saw someone standing wearing white robes.

'Padre Vittorio?' Anu asked, taking the shadowy creature for the Priest of the computer game Hitman.

'I have sinned, father!' Anu cried, looking at the whiteness in human shape.

With no response coming from the shadow, Anu stood up and started to run towards the phantasm. Suddenly, her feet got entangled in a shrub and she fell, face down.

'Father, forgive me...' Anu muttered. Her eyelids were as heavy as tonnes of stone. She could not keep them wide open. She closed her eyes. The darkness outside mingled with her darkness within.

It could have been a few seconds or minutes or hours that Anoushka lay there on the soft wet grass. Anu lost count of the time spent. She had felt the darkness for an infinite period of time.

Then suddenly, there was light. Strong and piercing rays of light blinded her. She felt as if the sun had come down to shine on her. She thought she was wide awake, standing in the midst of an unknown forest with long pine trees reaching the sky which had been just painted azure by the God. She was so enthralled by the calm beauty of the place that she felt within her an irresistible urge to explore it. So she started walking briskly, turning her eyes to each and every object. She walked faster and felt the yellow and worn out leaves crumbling beneath her busy feet. Then, she thought she heard a distant tumble of water flow somewhere. She ran in its direction, brushing past tall trees with algae grown over them. Soon, she arrived at a clearing. She saw a stream meandering through the woods and near it, sat a girl, dressed in a white gown with satin borders. The girl did not see Anu, for she was sitting near the stream, her back towards her. Anu walked towards the girl in white. The brown curls cascading down her shoulders looked very much familiar to Anu.

Anu called, 'Hey You!'

The girl turned around and the face of the girl left Anu speechless for a while. The girl's face strangely resembled Anu's. The same eyebrows, the same lips, the same complexion, the same eyes…

Anu thought she was looking herself in the mirror.

'Goodness me! You… You look like me!'

Anu shouted almost.

The lookalike smiled.'*I'm you,*' she said as she stood up.

Anu looked at her white long skirt and bare feet. 'You're me? What's that? A puzzle?' Anu asked, amazed.

'Yes... I'm you... Yourself.' The girl answered, with a benign smile.

'How that can be?'

'Why not? I am you... Your inner self...'

'Really?' Anu asked definitely thinking the girl (or herself?) to be a madcap.

Anu scrutinised the face. The girl's face was much more radiant than her own, hence, much younger.

'Hey! You look younger than me...' Anu exclaimed.

'That's because your inner self is younger than your physical age...' The girl in white answered.

'Okay... For a while if I take your claim to be true... Then, tell me, why are you here?' Anu asked, curiously.

'I want you to rediscover yourself...'

'Rediscover? Myself? How?' Anu was confused.

'Follow me...' so saying, the girl in white started walking towards the stream. She walked effortlessly, as if her feet were not touching the ground. She almost glided on the thin air that separated her bare feet from the earth and leaves below. Approaching the stream, the girl sat on a stone and stooped to draw water from the stream in her cupped right palm. Water was dripping from her palm, continuously. Then she slowly extended her cupped palm with water towards Anu.

'Drink... From my hand...' The white robed girl said.

Anu looked at her palm. The water in her folded palm looked brownish.

'Drink...'

The girl repeated, as if she had been waiting for ages to make Anu drink from her palm. Anu put her mouth to the palm so that the brownish liquid touched her lips. There was a strange aroma in the liquid. Anu thought she knew the sweet invigorating smell. She sipped. The liquid watery thing left a cool sensation in her mouth which gradually reached her throat and bosom and belly.

'It's lovely!' Anu said and sipped on till the liquid was no longer there and the palm went dry.

'Want some more of it?' The girl asked.

'Yes!' Anu said almost jumping to her toes.

'But you need not to pour water from your palm... I can have it myself,' saying this, Anu dropped her two palms together into the stream and cupped out the liquid. She drank it. The smell was sweet as ever and the cold sensation even more pleasant. She felt the water soothe her soul. She felt blessed. Anu cupped more water and poured into her mouth repeatedly till she felt satiated and bliss. The girl in white sat there on the stone and watched her drinking madly like someone who was dying for water.

'How do you feel?' The girl asked, as she kept on running her hand through her strands of brown hair.

'Fine!' Anu replied.

Actually, Anu was having a strange feeling. She felt as if she was in a very pleasant place with no cares or worries. Her mind was completely blank. She felt calm within and without. She felt that the world was a very happy place and human existence only enhances happiness. She felt that the trees, the leaves, the stream, the water, the silence, the sun rays—all were there only to please her, to make her live for long, to make her happy. Anu felt so happy that her jubilance gushed through her eyes. Tears of happiness rolled down her rosy cheeks.

'Who are you?' Anu murmured.

'I'm you... Your happy self,' the girl intoned.

'My happy self?' Anu asked, bewildered still.

'Yes... You are happy and my work is over,' the girl said.

'You came to make me happy?' Anu asked.

'Yes... To make you happy with the world... The real world,' the girl stood up and descended from the stone.

Anu walked towards her mirror self.

The girl took Anu's hands into hers and whispered:

'Don't look for happiness outside... Look within yourself and you'll find that...'

Anu looked into the girl's mesmerising eyes. They were deep and yet so emotive.

'What should I do? Please don't leave me...' Anu cried as she pressed her palms into the soft feathery palms of the alien dissembler.

'Your mind is what the world is... It's virtual and at the same time it influences the real... So be in the best of your mind... I'm sure you will... For you've taken the elixir of life... As far as your future... You have true passion for something watery and aromatic and intoxicating... Be a sommelier... That's your life...'

'A sommelier?' Anu asked feeling rather somnolent.

'Yes...' The girl said and she took away her palms from Anu's.

Anu tried to tighten her grip so as to hold her back, but the girl's hands slipped. The alien self of Anu walked straight into the stream and when she reached midstream, her body was already half-immersed in water. She walked still and her body got lowered and after sometime Anu saw the girl's brown hair floating and then, after few more minutes, was gone. The girl drowned in the water of the stream. Anu rushed down the water. The cool stream reached her knee. She waded through water till it reached her neck and she felt she had lost her touch with the bed of the stream. She lost control and slipped. The water shut her eyes out as it entered her through her mouth and nose. She panted, short of breath. She thought had she lost her senses, for the second time.

17

Moni reached home at seven. The front door was locked. Moni fumbled for the key in her bag and opened the door. Rudranarayan Chowdhury, the elderly ex-army neighbour, was just then coming out of his flat. Moni liked this elderly man, who had been living alone for many years now. Rudranarayan, Moni heard, had been left alone by his family. But this man, Moni noticed, had a unique character. He seemed happy always, as if he had been blessed with an eternal smile. His bonhomie with everyone, ladies and gentlemen, kids, doorkeepers and even with the maintenance staff made him more endearing. However, on rare occasions, his pent-up grief found release in alcohol, and he would drink more than usual. Moni would then hear him crying or singing aloud on one or two of his drunken occasions, standing in his balcony, taking big swigs. Seeing him, Moni flashed a friendly smile, like all residents did, expressing warmth for the eccentric man. Moni always felt that Rudranarayan was genuinely good. He was friendly, caring and carefree.

'Hola! Coming in dear, after a hard day's work?' Rudranarayan greeted Moni, with equal warmth.

'Yea... Uncle... But...' Moni began, wondering if she could ask him about Anu.

'Anoushka? The Butterfly? Is she not home?' Rudranarayan read Moni's mind instantaneously.

'Yea... It seems so... Anyway... Goodnight...'

'Goodnight dear...'

Rudranarayan walked towards the elevator.

Moni took off her shoes and switched on the light, entering the flat. The living area bore an undisturbed look. The couch cover was neat and spread as if no one had sat on it ever. Only her laptop was there on the table with the flap opened. The jerk had left it there!

Where had she gone? To a party?

Moni went to her bedroom.

'It is time to call Anu's mom and inform her about the growing eccentricities of her daughter,' Moni thought panicking, as she started to undress. *'Where has the idiot gone? To Sush's?'*

Changing into a comfortable linen suit, Moni dialled Anu's cellphone. The ring could be heard somewhere from within the flat itself! She had left her darn cellphone at home! Moni fumed from within.

She walked briskly to Anu's room. There it was glowing brightly on the bed! Moni picked up the phone and found Sush's number from the list of contacts.

'Hello Sush!'

'Hi Anu!'

'Sorry... I'm not Anu... Actually Anu has left the phone home... Is she at your place?' Moni asked.

'Anu? At our place? No! Why? What happened?'

'No... Nothing... Actually, it's already seven thirty... And she's not at home... Left her phone... Wondering where she has gone...' Moni murmured thoughtfully.

'Must be nearby... Don't worry...' Sush said unconvincingly.

'Okay... Sorry to disturb you.'

'Oh no! It is fine... Tell her to call me once she comes back.'

'Surely.' Moni dropped the phone.

She came to the living room and switched on the television and sat down on the couch. The laptop was there on the tea table. Moni leaned forward and was about to close the screen when she noticed the screen in standby mode. She pressed her finger on the mouse pad and the screen got illuminated. The desktop was absolutely clean! All the folders containing various software and documents were not there! Only there was one folder with the name 'Letter to Moni'.

Moni clicked it open. It was a word file.

It read:

Hello Moni!

Must have been surprised to see your desktop clean! Well, I did it to make this file conspicuous to you. Don't worry! All your files are kept in your documents folder.

Moni, I think, for all these years I have only been a source of perennial troubles to you.

Never did I actually help you in the household chores. I pay though for the expenses and that too sometimes becomes erratic.

I think you are too magnanimous to live with me and bear all those hassles. You usually do my laundry, arrange for my food and even physically move to and fro to keep our existence in this city smooth by depositing the monthly phone bills, electricity bills, maintenance charges, groceries etc; I can never repay the debts I owe to you. More than anything else, you had always been my friend, philosopher, guide and guardian. If you were not there I would have gone to the dogs, for sure.

I am exceedingly happy to find that you have finally found your match. Prof. V.P. Bhattacharya alias SA really needs a woman like you. In fact, my respect and admiration towards you has only doubled with your decision to get involved with a widower who has a little daughter. Prof. VPB teaches us Educational Psychology and I know him personally. He's definitely a man with an awesome, magnetic personality and very handsome features. All he needs is a woman who would be able to take care of his little daughter with all her motherliness. After living with you for all these years, I am doubtless certain that you will fill the void quite easily.

Living with you was supremely rewarding to me in many respects. I learnt a lot by watching you all the time. Don't think I am writing all these just to flatter you. I have no urgency to do that, really. You're the woman of the world and I am a misfit. I am an anachronism exemplified.

Now if an insane is allowed to live with a sane person for long time, then chances are there that the sane one will lose sanity. (It is just the classic case of one rotten apple ruining a whole basket of good apples!)

So, I have decided to leave you, which will make your life comfortable, I guess. (Sorry for interfering too much in your life already!)

But I'll miss you.

Love,

Anu

P.S. I've kept some money under the notebook. Please foot my pending bills for the month. (Thanks for the pads last night.)

Keep on writing poems. You have a flair for writing. I wish I could see you one day on the news as the winner of some grand prize (Booker or Pulitzer? You guess…)

Don't panic. I'll be fine. Don't call my parents. They will curse you!

Enjoy crossing over the Marriage line! (Remember one of my grassy lectures?)

Moni read the letter twice. Her head was spinning. What could she do? Call the police? Call Anu's parents?

Beads of sweat accumulated on Moni's forehead.

'Shit!' Moni mumbled. *'SA is a Prof? That too at Anu's University? Holy Virgin!'*

Moni scratched her head. Suddenly, she felt hot. She unhooked two buttons of her nightwear and leaned her head on the back of the couch. *How could Anu know all this?* Moni could think no more. Everything got jumbled in her head.

Suddenly, the door bell rang. Moni hastily buttoned herself up and rushed to the door. A man in beige trousers and purple shirt stood at the door with his head down.

'Not interested in any promos,' Moni said thinking the man with his face covered with long curls was a salesman. Moni's neighbour Rudranarayan must have been singing aloud, standing somewhere on the corridor, for Moni heard his booming voice filling up the corridor as soon as she opened the door. She, however, tried to concentrate on the man's face standing in front of her.

A small girl soon emerged from the back of the man.

'Sonai?' Moni screamed in surprise.

'What are you doing here?'

Sonai came forward with outstretched arms. Moni picked the angel up.

'Hello! I'm Ved... Ved Bhattacharya...' The man looked up.

Moni felt ripples down her spine.

'You?' Moni stood dumb.

'I'm Sonai's father, if you can recall... Can we go in?' the man said.

'Yeah, of course! Come'n in...' Moni fumbled and stood aside.

The man sat down on the couch.

'Water? Can I have a glass of water?'

Sonai asked, still clutching on to Moni's shoulder, not looking at Moni or her father.

Moni took Sonai to the kitchen and put the glass under the water purifier nozzle.

'My dad is angry with me…' Sonai said, almost whispering into Moni's ear.

'Why dear?' Moni asked as she put the glass near Sonai's mouth.

Sonai drank quickly.

'He'll tell you,' Sonai said in a hushed tone.

'Okay! Let's face the allegations then!' Moni said in a lighter vein, half smiling as she took Sonai to the living area

'Where's your flatmate? Anoushka Agarwal?' Ved asked.

'She's not at home,' Moni fumbled again.

'Well… First of all, I would like to express my sincerest apology on behalf of my daughter for sending you messages through the chat box… Actually, she kind of impersonated me, online, by hacking my password and chatted with you, without my knowledge which is very distressing for me… I'm really highly embarrassed by my daughter's pranks… And only today I discovered her playing an imposter behind my back and so I came… I can assure you never ever, will things like these happen in the future… In fact, I've come here with Sonai, only to make her confess the whole thing before you and to take a vow not to repeat those whimsical, silly things in the future…'

Ved talked straight with a few pauses, taking his breath in between and called his daughter in a sinister tone.

'Sonai!'

Sonai at once, got down from Moni's lap and standing before her, clasped her palms together and mumbled:

'I'm so sorry Moni Aunty! I'd never do that...'

Sonai could not complete her sentence. Her beautiful hazel eyes were full of tears. She started sobbing.

'Come'n Prof. Bhattacharya! Stop this nonsense!' Moni screamed, as she held Sonai's hands and pulled her towards her bosom. Sonai's groans only became louder.

Moni started patting her back and kissed her on her cheeks.

'Oh ho! Come'n Sonai! You're a brave girl! You're Diana! Aren't you dear? Don't cry... Please... For me... Look, if you cry, I'll also cry... I love you baby... I love you...'

Big drops of tears started rolling down Moni's cheeks which she wiped with the back of her palm.

Ved sat like a defeated worn out man, resting his drooping head on his folded arm.

'Look Mr. Bhattacharya... I'm in no mood to discuss these things with you right now... But, be rest assured, I've taken no offence to your little daughter's pranks...'

Ved looked up.

'Sorry.' He said and stood up.

'Sorry for disturbing you... And thanks...' Ved uttered slowly.

Sonai slowly went up to her dad.

'Thanks for what? I think it was not entirely your daughter's fault... I'm responsible as well... Didn't I chat with her? Anyway... I've a major issue here at my house and I need to hurry...' Moni said with uncommon coldness.

Ved looked at Moni with his eyes pinned on her. His eyes wore an exasperated expression—an expression befitting a tired man. 'O sure! We're going away…' Ved started walking towards the door with Sonai following him.

'Mr. Bhattacharya?' Moni called after him.

'Yes?' Both Ved and Sonai turned to look at her.

'I need a bit of help… Actually my flatmate, Anu is still not at home and she has left an awkward message for me… Look…'

Moni showed the letter on her desktop.

Ved and Sonai leaned on to the machine and read feverishly.

'My god!' Sonai screamed.

'Anoushka is such an idiot!' Ved shouted.

'That's not an issue… All of us are idiots in some way or the other, like in the real life or in the virtual one… Online idiots… Offline geniuses… Or the vice-versa… Aren't we?' Moni stated firmly looking straight into Ved's eyes.

Ved's eyes quivered. He looked away.

'What to do now?' Sonai asked giving alternate glances to Moni and her father.

'Get ready… We're going out… Get a photo of Anu… And any other proof of her identity like photo id etc.;' Ved said as he started pressing numbers on his cell.

'Photo? Maybe in her cell… I've got her cell phone… She left it here…' Moni said as she rushed to her room to get dressed up.

'Where are we going to?' Moni asked when the car took the Race Course road.

'Missing persons' squad… Lalbazar,' Ved replied looking at the lit up smooth macadamized road ahead.

The windshield had become a bit foggy. Cars were honking past fast. Traffic police could be seen standing at intersections wearing heavy overcoats, waving luminescent signal sticks of red and green colour. Sonai was sitting on Moni's lap, right beside Ved.

'Does she drink too often?' Ved asked without looking at Moni.

'Yea... Often...' Moni sighed.

'Hmmm... Frequents night clubs and bars?'

'Not clubs but bars...' Moni's reply was brief.

'Do you do the same?' Ved asked this time casting a momentary look at Moni.

'Not really' Moni answered.

Ved chuckled.

At the Police HQ, the In-charge of Missing Persons' squad was most helpful. Specific information was sent to all police stations across the city within an hour. Moni and Sonai sat at the corridor on a wooden bench. Ved ran to and fro, seemingly busy either talking to someone in uniform or jabbering on his cell. Sitting beside Moni for quite sometime, Sonai remained largely silent. Moni had twice called the gatekeeper of their apartment asking whether Anu had returned or not.

At about ten thirty at night, Ved appeared before Moni.

'Found any info?' Moni asked.

Sonai looked up at her dad.

'Not yet... Let's see...' Ved replied.

Sonai was wiping her eyes with her fingers.

'Feeling sleepy?' Ved asked as he put his hand upon her daughter's head.

'No! Don't touch me!' Sonai suddenly shrugged Ved's hand off.

Ved smiled.

Moni pulled Sonai by her hand, closer to her and asked softly, 'Aren't you hungry?'

Sonai looked at Moni and nodded smiling.

'Okay! Let me find some food for you two...'Ved said and was about to go out of the building.

'Mr. Bhattacharya!' Moni called.

'What?' Ved stopped.

'Is there any need for all of us to be here all through this wintry night? Sonai might catch a cold...' Moni said.

'Yes... Then?'

'Can't you ask the officer in charge to let us know if any info reaches them?'

'Surely!' Ved went to the officer's room.

He came back within ten minutes.

'The officer would let us know... Given him my cell number...' Ved said.

'You should have given them my number...' Moni said.

'I don't know it!' Ved retorted.

'Oh I'm sorry! Note it down...'

'What for?' Ved asked with a curious face.

'Who knows you might need it,' Moni replied suppressing her smile with a worked up grim look.

Ved looked at Moni who looked back at him. Moni bit her lower lip at one end and scanned the creature standing in front of her. His hair was ranging loosely over his shoulders. The purple shirt had already become a bit strained and crumpled in places. Moni looked at her watch. It was already five minutes past eleven.

'Okay! What about dropping me off at my place then?' Moni said.

'All right,' Ved brought out his car key.

By the time they returned to Bardhaman Road, Sonai had already fallen asleep and snoring, resting her head quite comfortably upon Moni's shoulder.

Ved kept the ignition on.

'Come down, won't you?' Moni asked.

'No! We'll have to reach home!'

'But Sonai is sleeping!' Moni snapped holding Sonai over her shoulder.

'No probs… Will just tie her up with the seat belt,' Ved said as he looked at Sonai's sleeping face.

'Mr. Bhattacharya… Will you mind staying back here at our flat with your daughter for the night?' Moni asked as she ran her hand over Sonai's back, sort of caressing her.

'Stay back? Here? At your flat?' Ved asked with incredulity.

'No! On the pavement! Mr. Silent Assassin!' Moni replied and cautiously descended from the car and started walking towards the elevator, balancing Sonai on her hip clutching her by her left arm.

Ved asked the gateman the way to the parking space.

18

Moni gently put Sonai on her bed and placed a quilt over her, after sliding her softest pillow under her tiny head. Then, she wiped her face and hands and feet with a wet towel and was thinking of applying cream on her lips, when she heard Ved's cell ringing.

She rushed out to see Ved talking to someone over the phone, sitting on the couch. Seeing Moni come out of her room, Ved signalled his hand and nodded his head twice sideways so as to make Moni understand that the phone call was not related to Anu. Moni went back to her room. She walked up to the bedside table and found a particular cream tube among a heap of tubes of cream and lotions. Suave–advanced skin therapy. Moni looked at the tube and felt like crying. Anu, the idiot, had not taken it!

Moni took out a dollop of the cream upon her fingers by pressing the white tube with sky blue label and carefully motioned her fingers on the dry lips of Sonai. Sonai moved her face away and murmured something sleepily, showing her displeasure at the touch of cold cream. Moni ran her fingers through the supple hair of Sonai who again returned to the calm of sleep. Moni went to the toilet.

'How many do you eat?' Moni asked Ved as she put bread slices into the toaster.

'Four,' Ved replied as he kept pressing buttons of his cell.

For the past few hours Ved had been continuously calling various police officers. Once, he called his dad and asked him to talk to someone.

The dinner was ready—bread slices and sabzi dal.

Ved ate silently, munching bread. Moni ate only two pieces of bread. She could not eat. For the first time in all those years she was having a dinner without Anu around.

After dinner, Ved asked for Moni's permission to light up a cigarette.

Moni shrugged.

'Sorry can't provide any night wear for you... Unless you agree to wear women's robes for a change tonight,' Moni offered, trying to bring in some laughter to the otherwise grim atmosphere.

Ved laughed, heartily, for the first time since evening.

Moni looked at Ved's impeccable teeth, his shaven face, and his white tinged glossy curls spread sparsely.

'Is there any real chance of getting her back?' Moni finally asked in a self-questioning manner.

'Why not? Especially when the Deputy Commissioner of Police himself is running round,' Ved said optimistically, exhaling through his nostrils.

'Deputy Commissioner of Police? Really?' Moni asked, astonished.

'Yes… He's a friend of mine… School mate from St. Xavier's,' Ved replied disjointedly.

Moni kept mum.

'Why don't you go and try to sleep?' Ved said looking at his cellphone screen.

'Me? No… You can go to my room and lie down beside Sonai,' Moni said.

'Is she sleeping hard?'

'Yes! Must be tired and hungry…'

'Yes… But she will not wake up… She sleeps sound,' Ved added as he looked at the half open door of Moni's room.

'Is it Anoushka's room?' Ved asked, pointing at the room with closed door beside Moni's room.

'Yes,' Moni sighed.

'May I go and lie there?' Ved suddenly stood up and asked.

'Why not?' Moni said.

'Okay,' Ved walked to the door and pushed it open.

'Don't worry… I'll stay awake by my phone… Go and take rest in your room… If Sonai moves a bit just pat her…' Ved said, as he entered the room adjacent to Moni's bedroom.

Moni nodded and walked into her room, dimly lit by a small bedside lamp. Sonai was sleeping. Moni looked at the sleeping angel. The light from the bedside lamp fell on her face, so calm and lucid. Did she look like her mother? Moni tried to guess the face of Sonai's mom. She might have been fair-complexioned with a sharp nose. Her lips might have been small.

It must have been really distressing for Sonai to lead a motherless life at such a tender age. Moni thought as she brushed aside the loose strands of hair falling over Sonai's eyes. Just then, she noticed a tiny piece of eyelash on Sonai's cheek. Moni plucked it with her fingers and keeping it on her palm, blew a whiff of air so as to make the eyelash fly. *God! Make this little angel happy...* Moni whispered. The more she looked at Sonai's face, the more her heart filled with pity. The innocent face of the girl pained her heart as she was constantly reminded of the angel's motherlessness. She felt a strong ache within, for the face of the sleeping child reminded her of her own sadness. She was reminded of her long forgotten anguish of losing her own mother at a very young age. She could recall how she was made to suffer because of being almost an orphan. She remembered her bygone days, her days of struggle to keep everyone happy at her uncle's home. She had been overcome by an indescribable grief. In her aggrieved state, she could detect a similarity between herself and little Sonai. She slowly lay down beside Sonai, under the same quilt. But even when she was trying to lie down on the bed beside Sonai, she was all the time very cautious of her slightest movement, for she feared that she might disturb Sonai's sleep. She might wake her up. The little movement of the quilt made Sonai wriggle her feet and then suddenly Sonai lifted her one leg on Moni and with one arm softly embraced her the way some people embrace a bolster while sleeping. Moni allowed herself to be embraced by Sonai in her sleep. Sonai's intimate presence only mellowed her further. She planted a gentle kiss upon her cheek and heaved a sigh. Just then she thought about Anu. Where had she gone? Had she run into any trouble? Within minutes, her mind became restless. She slowly pulled Sonai's leg up and placed it sideways and got down from the bed. A look at the table clock revealed that it was already two thirty the next day. *Was Anu all right? What would happen if she fell into some danger?* Moni felt thirsty. She poured water into a glass tumbler and drank it down in one go. Didn't Mr. Bhattacharya assure her saying he would stay awake the whole night? Was he awake or snoring? Moni walked to the adjacent room. The door was closed but the light was on inside, and the slice of light could be seen coming out through the gap between the door and the floor. Should I knock? Moni thought. Moni raised her hand to knock on the door. Just then the door opened and Ved rushed out. Seeing Moni at the door he was surprised, but after recovering flashed a warm smile saying, 'I think we got her! Just got a call from Lalbazar… She has been found… I'm out… Take care of Sonai,' Ved rushed towards the front door, fishing out the car key chain from his pocket.

'Hey! Mr. Bhattacharya! Wait a minute! Where is she? Is she okay?' Moni cried out.

Ved stopped at the door, looking back. 'She's absolutely fine! Don't worry… She's okay… I guess,' Ved replied with assurance.

'Can I have your cell number please?' Moni asked.

Ved smiled and blurted the number in one breath and opened the door. A whiff of cold air came in. Moni felt it warm and soothing, though.

'Drive carefully… Mr. Bhattacharya,' Moni said almost involuntarily.

Ved smiled and nodded before he ran towards the elevator. Moni stood at the door staring blankly for a while before she closed the door and sat down on the couch in the living room.

The news that Anu had been found relieved Moni greatly. The restlessness soon gave way to a sense of calm composure. She was even partially elated and all her dreadful thoughts which made her apprehensive including being seized by premonitions of the worst, had considerably weakened. Moni felt happy and secure. She put her legs on the table and hinged back her tired head on the backrest of the couch and closed her eyes. Sleep besieged her.

The smoked windscreen, the mild purr of the engine, the encapsulated silence and the vacant streets... Ved felt alienated from the outside world as he drove the machine down the known roads and streets and avenues of the known city with its well known landmarks and sleepy existence. Only the time of the day was a bit undiscovered or unexplored. Had he ever driven through the city streets in the wee hours of morning? Probably once, many years ago, he drove home early in the morning, before even the sun had risen, with a foggy mind and benumbed senses. That was the morning which followed the darkest night of his life—the night of Mayurika's departure forever, from this mortal world.

He felt the same this time around. The city sans its crowd and din and bustle, appeared lonely. But more than that, it looked ghostly, darkened and grave.

Ved drove. He felt as if he had been driving for ages, perhaps for centuries, perhaps his whole life had become a long drive without any destination. He felt as if he would be running to and fro through the cobwebs of roads and streets and flyovers. He felt himself like a withered leaf fallen from the tree and blown away by the strong wind. He was reminded at once of a screenshot of an award winning English movie in which a white feather of a bird was shown gliding away in wind from one place to another—from one roof top to someone's windowsill and from there to someone's garden and from the garden to someone's hat. From that hat it took off to glide further away before it finally came to a rest on the lap of the protagonist of the movie who was framed, sitting like a statue at a bus stop waiting for his bus to come.

Why am I driving down the lonely road? Ved thought. Do I need to do all these? Do I need to show that I care for both Moni and Anu? Do I need to do all these for my own happiness? Do I need to pull Anu out of the dungeon so that I could carve my way towards Moni with no offense taken by anyone? *Why am I doing it? Why?*

Running down the lonely road through serpentine streets, Ved finally stopped before a white three-storied building with blue borders. The building was well lit with almost all its windows appearing like white squares, serving a sweet contrast to other buildings beside it with dark windows, curtained and bleak.

Ved inched the car a few yards to keep the entrance to the building unblocked. Ved parked the car besides the iron railing of an empty bus stop. Descending from the car Ved gave a quick glance at the bus stop. Darkness had accumulated with all its might under the corrugated tin shed of the stop. Even in that darkness Ved could perceive some human shapes lying under the shed covered by quilts or something of that sort, like lumps of irregular lifeless bodies. They were the *Christs of Kolkata*. Ved strolled towards the portico.

Once inside the building, Ved went straight into a room with a fairly large wooden table placed at the centre. A man, in the official uniform of a law keeper was sitting at the table. His face could not be seen as his head was turned down which made his bald head distinctly shine under the light. Ved looked around. Four chairs, a wooden bench and a stool comprised the other pieces of furniture in the room. The table had all the papers and files of the world. Two telephone sets were placed quite precariously, with sufficient negligence, upon heaps of papers as if they were some paperweights of curious designs. Where was Anu?

The man in uniform was still in his sleepdom. Ved made a slight tap on the table with his knuckles.

The bald head moved a bit only to drop down further to reach the table top. Ved feared that it would hit the table with a bang. But it did not drop further. Probably its fall was prevented by the lower portion of the chin which acted as a fulcrum.

'Excuse me Sir!' Ved said out aloud.

The man's head at once moved up, almost sprang back to its straightened position and a pair of reddened eyes opened, which carried the singular expression of terrible irritation.

'Who's the fuck?' The man mouthed out the sentence as if he was spitting.

'Sorry to disturb you Sir, but, I think, I heard it right from Mr. Anuj Verma, the D.C.P., that a girl in her mid-twenties was found by you in an inebriated state somewhere near Garia… I want to take the girl into my custody…' Ved spoke in a flat tone with no undulations, as if his voice was mechanized.

The man's countenance changed quickly from its irritated look to some very amicable and genteel.

'Mr. Bhattacharya? Are you?' the duty officer said as he stood up and wiped his face with his right palm.

Ved read the nameplate pinned on the left side pocket of the officer's uniform. Debashish Samanta—it read.

'Sorry Debashish *babu,* for troubling you at this hour... ya, I'm Ved Bhattacharya, Anuj and I were classmates...' Ved smiled and said lightly.

'Just a minute...'

Mr. Samanta, the duty officer of the police station walked out of the room busily, pulling his trousers all the way.

A few minutes later, Mr. Samanta returned with Anoushka at his heels.

'My goodness! Prof *IAB*? Here?' Anu shrieked as if she had seen a phantasm.

'For you, dear lady,' Ved uttered slowly.

'Really?'

Anu looked. Her eyelids quivered briefly. However, soon she recovered, and hopped to the wooden bench. Ved stood where he was. Officer Samanta walked to his chair.

'Fill out the form, Sir,' Samanta said as he pulled out a printed form somewhere from the heaps of papers.

Ved moved towards the table, but his eyes were stuck on Anu who was sitting merrily on the bench swinging her legs all the time like a little girl as she looked around.

'Are you okay?' Ved asked some ten minutes later as he sat at the wheel. Anu was sitting beside him.

'Yeah... Absolutely.' Anu winked. Sitting beside Anu in the car with all windows rolled up, Ved for the first time smelt an odour of liquor with some very earthly smell emanating from his passenger of the immediate seat. From the corner of his eyes, Ved tried to look at Anu. Her jeans had green imprints all over them as if she had been rolling around in grassy fields. Her right elbow had a patch of mud still.

Ved smiled and turned on the ignition.

'Going home, aren't we?' Anu asked.

'Yes... Fasten your seat belt,' Ved spoke in a tone of mild command, which Anu obeyed immediately.

'I'm sorry for all the hassles,' Anu said, looking at the empty road through the windscreen.

'Okies... Want some music?' Ved asked.

Anu nodded.

The darkness of the night had begun to smooth out a bit. Somewhere, crows were cawing.

Ved selected a Kenny G track before he punched the play button.

'Will you mind if we stop somewhere and have a little chat before we go home? Actually it's only four in the morning and...' Ved broke off.

'Moni might be sleeping...' Anu added as if she was assigned the task of completing incomplete predication.

'Yes... My daughter is also with her... Sleeping,' Ved added.

'Really? So you two are already living together?' Anu said in a tone which mixed elements of surprise and ridicule.

Ved said nothing. He pushed the red button with a triangle sign, which made all the four indicators of the car blink in unison and stepped on the accelerator.

'Where are we going?' Anu asked.

'To Babughat... To bear witness to the sunrise...' Ved replied.

'Great!' Anu said.

'You're not feeling sleepy, I guess…' Ved said as he turned the wheel to catch the road towards the river.

'No… Just woken up…' Anu said happily.

19

'Will it be all right to be here at the ghat so early in the morning?'

Anu asked as Ved parked the car near a tea shop which had an old man sitting at a stool in front of a stove with aluminum pan over it.

'There are lots of early risers in this city who come to bathe here customarily, every morning, before sunrise,' said Ved, as he switched off the ignition, pulled the handbrake and prepared to get down.

Anu got out of the car. It was still considerably dark outside and human shapes of men and women were seen mingling with dark silhouettes.

A few shops selling flowers were abounding with customers. Ved started walking towards the tea shop. The owner of the shop, an old man with long white beard, smiled as soon as he saw Ved approaching. Ved went near the shop and sat down on a wooden bench with its peeled off veneer. The bench made a creaking sound as Anu sat on it, following Ved. The tea seller's face had wrinkles and crow's feet. Anu looked at the man's face closer and found a striking resemblance with the face of the famous philosopher poet of Bengal, Tagore. The Tagore lookalike tea seller handed a glass of water to Ved to drink. Ved appeared quite familiar with the man, his every move, every gesture, much like the way in which the tea seller appeared to be with him. The tea seller passed a glass of water with a small white flower petal floating at the brim to Anu, who thought the petal was an accident. She was about to ask the tea seller to change the content of the glass when the old man raised his white eyebrows and uttered softly, '*Nahi beti*... No dear... Drink it... It'll do good to your soul...'

Anu was perplexed with such an unwarranted response. Ved smiled looking at both of them and gave the man his empty glass back. The man took it and soon handed Ved a small earthen pot of tea. Anu looked at the steamy vapour rising up from the pot held in Ved's hand. The very image of hot vapour rising from the pot, tempted Anu to have the same in her own palms, in that chilly dawn of late October.

Surprisingly, the tea man held out another earthen pot with effusive hot vapours, to Anu.

She looked at the pot. 'Hey! There's no milk in it! I don't like tea without milk.' Anu said.

'You need that exactly at this hour,' the man warned.

This habit of the tea seller of dictating terms to her, unnerved Anu. With fresh determination she insisted, 'I would love to have tea with milk.'

The man raised his white eyebrows. His face was grave but there was a hint of smile in it as if he were mocking.

Ved stood up, brought out a few coins from his purse and placed them on a top of a glass jar, arranging them vertically one over another, making a small coin tower. Then he bent his head sideways and batted his eyelids as if gently asking Anu to accept the tea seller's milk-less tea.

Grimacing, Anu took the cup and gulped the liquid down in one go, before placing it with a thud on the bench and walked off.

Ved flashed a smile at the old man, expressing his helplessness and followed Anu.

'Start a new life!' the old man suddenly spoke out aloud, touching his wrinkled forehead with folded palms.

Ved smiled again. Anu did not smile. She looked back with her lips parted wide open in amazement.

'How obstinate!' Anu yelled as they moved away towards the ghat.

'He's just like that…' Ved said and soon he hopped down the concrete slabs of the river ghat.

The eastern sky was acquiring a pinkish tinge foretelling the arrival of the sun.

Ved stroked his palm over a portion of the step, sort of dusting it off and sat down.

Anu came down and sat beside Ved, without dusting. Both of them kept looking at the eastern sky waiting for the sun to rise. And it rose, finally, like an orange ball, harmless and sublime.

'Wow!' Anu gushed.

'One can live a life only to bear witness to such a grand occasion,' Ved whispered.

'Yea…' Anu replied, voice trailing off.

'And this moment which is real now, will soon become a thing of the past… A virtual thing…' Ved continued dreamily.

'Yea... And this moment will virtually be a moment to cherish for long...' Anu said.

'Yes... All of us have our moments of life which glide by only to become memories... Memories of happiness, unhappiness, anxieties, restlessness... Like those moments of the last night... Moments which became memories...' Ved said sighing.

Anu remained silent.

Ved looked at the orange ball at the sky which was slowly changing its shape and colour.

'So... How were your moments of last night? Had they become memories to cherish for long?' Ved asked.

'I think they are,' Anu said.

'That's good!' Ved said smiling.

Anu turned her face from the eastern sky to Ved and asked, 'How do you analyse a situation in which one decides to take a detour?'

Ved was surprised by what he thought was such an irrelevant and unexpected question.

'A detour? Of life?' he asked back.

'Yea... A detour of life!' Anu repeated with conviction.

'Well... If it is the call of your mind then go for it...' Ved said turning his face from Anu to the river which had been turned into a silvery ribbon from a black, slimy stream by the ascent of the sun.

'I think it is... I wish to become a sommelier!' Anu said, standing up.

Then, she hopped down the steps to reach the fringe of the ghat where the ripples of water played merrily with a soft murmur. Reaching the last step of the ghat, Anu sat down, squatting on her haunches, dipping her palms together into the river, and splashing water on her face. The cold water sent shivers down her spine. She was at once reminded of the last night's memories… Memories sweet and divine… Memories of her conversation with her self… Her destiny. She whispered softly, 'Elixir of life.'

Ved looked at the sun, the glistening river, the blue sky, the boats, the ghat, and the pious people dipping their heads in the cool water and shivering. Catching all these in the new born sun, after so many years, made him long to hold his camera again. His fingers itched after so many years to freeze the moment into frame. His shutter-bug self, lying dormant for so many years within him, now wriggled and wriggled quite violently to startle him.

'What about a detour of life for me as well?' Ved thought and smiled. 'The blue sky and the glowing sun… All I need at this precise moment is a camera…

'What would be the shutter speed?

1/250 Av.

What would be the ISO Speed?

200.

The flash should be off and the aperture value should be 10,' Ved thought as he stared at the scene.

Anu was standing still at the fringe, like a statue of some modern goddess in street-savvy attire. Against the sun, her back seemed black. Only her hair swayed in the breeze.

What about capturing Anu in frame? Her resplendent face would surely be extravagantly photogenic! Ved thought for a moment as he felt a sudden return of some long forgotten sensory pleasure of being an avid amateur nature photographer.

Ved's mind raced back a few years. He pictured himself, standing at a large window overlooking a vast expanse of a barley field with shades of bright green, citrus green, primrose yellow, copper yellow, bright yellow in a valley. He remembered how miserably he had suffered from AMS (Acute Mountain Sickness) and how he had to survive on aspirins, aerated drinks and ginger rich tea.

Ved thought and soon his eyes twitched. He thought he should light up a cigarette. He brought out a fag and lighted it. The smoke did not come easily. He inhaled hard. The smoke was till sparse.

'Hey! You've lighted up the wrong end!' Anu laughed as she saw Ved trying to take a puff from a fag with its filter burning.

'Oh ho!' Ved smiled despite consternation, throwing away the fag.

'Thinking something?' Anu asked.

Anu's face glistened. Tiny drops of water could be seen upon her eyelashes and eyebrows.

Ved smiled with an apparent unease.

'Moni called?'

'Not yet...'

'Your daughter? She must've called...'

'No, not yet... She's going to miss her school, I guess... I can't take her school today...'

'Why?' Anu asked innocently.

'We're all tired, aren't we? Having a sleepless night?' Ved sounded apoplectic.

'Sorry...' Anu said as she dropped down her eyes and stood still.

'Why did you do this? Why?' Ved asked, looking at Anu's wet face.

Anu stood without the slightest sign of any movement. Only her lower lip got swelled and her eyes pressed hard and closed.

Suddenly, she put her arms around Ved's neck and embraced him tightly. A few moments later, Ved could hear her sobbing, with a vehement shake, as if she would soon cry out loud. Ved could feel moisture gathering somewhere on his shoulder.

Ved put his right hand on Anu's head, touching her smooth hair.

'Don't be a child… You're grown up, aren't you?' Ved murmured.

Anu sobbed more and panted.

'Come'n… Let's go home… Moni is worried…' Anu laid her head on Ved's shoulder, though her embrace got loosened a bit.

'Moni loves you dearly… You never know how she had spent the last night…' Ved kept on stroking Anu's head as he muttered.

'I also have no one in this world except Moni…' Anu said feebly.

'Why not? You've got your mom and dad… Parents are one's best friends!' Ved retorted.

'Don't know…' Anu said as she hinged back to her normal position, pulling up her head from Ved's shoulder.

'Wipe your face…' Ved extended his handkerchief to Anu.

Anu took it smiling. Ved flashed back a smile that was as candid as the morning which had just cleared of all the wintry mist.

'Want to have a breakfast at Flury's?' Ved asked.

Anu nodded gleefully. Ved thought he saw a glimpse of his daughter, Sanhita, in Anu.

Just then, Sanhita called. 'Good morning Diana!' Ved hollered cheerfully into his cellphone.

'Good morning! My foot! Where are you, Dad? Forgotten me? I've got my school today and its already eight in the morning!' Sonai cried in her shrillest voice.

'Sorry Diana... 47 is a bit busy with a rescue mission... Calm down... What about skipping school today and having a day out with 47?' Ved replied soothingly.

'No way! Today is the last date of submission of contributions to the school magazine and I need to submit the painting...'

'Hmm...' Ved sighed.

'Bring me my uniform and satchel to Moni's place... I'll go to school from here!'

'But Sonai...'

Sonai snapped the line.

Ved kept on looking at the phone screen and was thinking of dialing up the number from which Sonai's call came.

'The breakfast at Flury's can wait... Let's go back...' Anu said.

'Are you sure?' Ved asked.

'Sure! I don't need your pity to survive!' Anu replied and jumped up a few steps and started walking briskly towards the car.

Ved shook his head and followed Anu, who did not even turn back once.

'Attention Deficit Syndrome?' Ved murmured, looking at Anu walk like a participant in a walking race.

20

Moni saw the man playing a metal musical instrument blowing through it and pressing keys with his white nimble fingers standing on a long and wide beach with golden hue spread miles and miles across. The blue sky taking the shape of a big spotless dome and the green sea at a distance, made the scene a perfect picture postcard of some alien country.

What is he playing? Moni tried to recall. Clarinet? Flute? Oh yes! It's a saxophone…

The white shirt, worn by the saxophonist was trembling in the breeze like a white flag. Every time, the man blew air into the silver pipe, his cheeks got inflated and no sooner had the air left his mouth to the pipe, the cheeks flattened. Moni kept on observing the man's beautifully clean and pure fingers moving effortlessly on the shiny silver key knobs as if they were there only to perform that singular task of weaving music. Moni thought. The ethereal music coming out of the instrument mingled with the breeze and spread far and wide as if reaching even the distant boats floating somewhere on the forever widening expanse of shiny water. The salty breeze from the sea brought melancholic happiness of some distant land, perhaps of the Mediterranean, perhaps of the idyllic plains of Egypt. Moni looked at the sky which appeared like the canvas of a master painter, full of brush strokes of varied thickness. Moni felt blessed. She thought she was only born to be a part of this wonderful, remorseless world of colours and rhythm. She kept on listening to the music and felt like living every moment of her life like never before. She felt as if she was drinking the airy form of happiness called music. This airy form gradually filled up the vacant lots of her heart. She felt intoxicated by the endless flow of music. She realised for the first time how music could transmute one into an airy shapeless form, a spirit. Moni spread both her arms sideways as if she was expecting them to be turned into wings in no time.

'Take me away, take me away,'

Moni kept on whispering, wishing every time to be in that alien land where from breeze came bearing happiness.

'Open your eyes…'

Someone said in a voice that reminded Moni of a voice too known.

'Oh my god! You!'

Moni almost shrieked seeing Ved standing there where the saxophonist stood a few minutes ago.

'You play saxophone? My god! Were you that man whom I longed forever to meet?'

Moni gushed and her voice trembled, almost choking up with a sudden surge of weird passion that only befits a woman who meets her long lost love by accident. Moni started sprinting towards Ved and the short distance between her and Ved seemed long, a bit too long, as if it would take the whole long day or a whole long year or a whole century to traverse. Her legs became heavy as if they were made of the heaviest kind of material.

'Stop there!' Ved said, as he stood his ground like a statue, wearing the same white shirt worn by the saxophonist a few minutes ago.

Then, Ved drew a line on the sand, stooping down on his knees, with his right index finger.

'This is the line of marriage.' Ved uttered as he stood up again, 'I am on this side of the line, and you are on the other side and unmarried. Now dare not cross the line to be on my side... It wouldn't suit you the best, to be on the same side of the line as a widower...'

Ved uttered slowly taking time to pronounce each and every syllable of every word distinctly as if he was trying hard to put forward some kind of grave moral lesson to some grave moral sinner.

'But... But... I... I wish to be with Sonai... She's lovely...allow me at least to have a little chat with her... She has such a beautiful face.' Moni muttered, not fully aware of what she was saying, as if in a drunken stupor.

'That is your solicitude, I understand...' Ved said strangely.

'Only solicitude? Goodness me! You found only solicitude?' Moni asked in a broken tone.

'Yes, solicitude, which is another name of pity... And I need no pity... Sonai doesn't need that as well...' Ved said.

'Okay as you wish...' Moni replied in a dejected voice. She could no longer talk as her throat became choked. She wanted to yell a lot of things that she never got to express. 'It is not solicitude, Mr. Bhattacharya! It is empathy... It takes a great deal to live life without a mother from one's nappy days!' Moni wanted to yell but failed.

Soon, a white horse arrived on the spot and Ved put his left leg on the saddle to climb the beast and soon ascended the magnificent beast. The beast first pulled its front legs backward with a mighty effort, which made the muscles of its legs conspicuous. Moni looked at the beast, its rider and the way it galloped across the sand. The rider's body swayed, matching the rhythm of the beast's movement. The front legs of the beast were pulled backward with more force, sending grains of sand shooting up while its rear legs acted as a support system to help the proper jump and landing. Moni kept on looking at the beast.

When the beast got the desired momentum, it seemed that the front and rear legs of the beast would collide with each other. It was wondrous to look at the beast in flight, with its legs meeting each other and its rider almost lying down on it with his head drooped to the level of the beast. Both the rider and the beast seemed one, galloping with great force. Their eyes were lit up with an indescribable excitement and energy. But apart from being a show of great energy, the spectacle was extraordinarily beautiful, just like a dream…

Am I dreaming? Moni thought for a while. Oh yes! I must be!

The next moment Moni felt a soft kiss on her cheek and she opened her eyes to see a little girl standing just beside her.

'You got no office today?' Sonai asked Moni.

'Oh, I'm so sorry!' Moni jerked into complete wakefulness and looked around to see her lying on the couch of their living room. She recognised the little girl as well. She also found for the first time, a tinge of her father in the girl's face, those glowing eyes they must be Ved's.

'Got any news of Anu?' Moni asked as she sat up and started looking for her cellphone.

'Yes… Anoushka has been found out… I called dad and he told me that he would be dropping your friend Anu soon… He would bring my satchel and school uniform here… Now I need to get bathed quickly… My school starts at ten thirty…'

'But… Then your dad will have to run home, bring your satchel and take you from here to school?'

'Yeah! Quite naturally!' Sonai replied promptly.

'Can I call your dad?' Moni asked.

'Why not? Let me dial him,' Sonai said.

Moni handed her the cell. 'Hello Dad! Moni wants to talk to you'

Sonai gave Moni the phone. Moni took the phone in her left hand and walked towards the balcony.

'Hello Mr. Bhattacharya... It's Moni here...'

'Good morning Moni.' The voice at the other end sounded weak.

'Are you okay?'

'Yes... Anu is by my side... We're returning...'

'Sonai wants to go to school...'

'Yes I know... She's got something to submit for the school magazine and today is the late date of submission,' Ved replied.

'Mr. Bhattacharya, may I suggest something?' Moni asked hesitantly.

'Sure...'

'Well... I think, it would be better if both Anu and you come here, have bath, take your lunch and have a good nap... Both of you need rest... I may take the trouble of carrying Sonai to school...'

'Thanks... But Moni... Sonai's satchel is at our place and her painting is there as well, so I need to bring them from there and if I can bring them from our house, I can drop her to school as well.'

'Just a minute please...' Moni put the call on hold and rushed back to the living. Sonai was sitting on the couch, fiddling with Moni's laptop.

'Sonai'

'Yes?'

Sonai looked up.

'Are you going to school today with the only object of submitting your painting? I mean, is there any other need? Do you really need books and copies today at school?' Moni asked.

'No... We will have no classes today... But I need the painting and the school uniform...'

'Okay... Let's see...' saying so, Moni made a phone call on her cell to Ved:

'Mr. Bhattacharya... I think I can arrange for Sonai's uniform and satchel... As far as the painting is concerned, let's see if we can replace it with something not less worthy than it... Don't worry... You need not hurry... But come back here... I will keep your lunch ready on the table... Now, will you please hand the phone over to Anu?'

Ved gave the phone to Anu who was sitting by his side in the car. Ved had parked the car under one of the several trees that line the two flanks of the Red Road.

'Good morning Anu...'

'Good morning...' replied Anu, out of some disoriented dream.

'Come back home sweetie... I've got chicken masala for you...' Moni said haltingly.

Anu remained silent. She felt a sudden pain in her bosom as if someone had placed a heavy stone on her that she could not throw away. She felt she could not take in the required amount of air in her lungs due to that heaviness upon her bosom. Quite involuntarily, Anu started rubbing her bosom with her right hand and her face wore a pained grimace.

Ved got alarmed. 'Are you okay?' he asked, seeing Anu rub her bosom almost violently and leaning her head at the headrest of the seat with a mild groan.

'Are you okay?' Moni asked, through the phone.

Anu had already dropped the phone on her lap and her whole body seemed to be losing its normal balance, as if she was fainting. Ved took back the phone hastily and uttered, 'Moni, I think Anu is feeling a bit unwell... I'll talk to you later on...'

'Wait a minute... Where are you?' Moni asked, her voice trembling.

'We're at the Red Road... I am going to splash water on her face... She's weak perhaps... Don't worry...' Ved tried to keep his voice as calm as possible.

'Can you keep the line on.... While you splash water and try to wake her up?' Moni asked desperately.

'Okay,' Ved pressed the loud speaker on and placed the cell on the dashboard phone holder.

Moni pressed her own cell to her left ear. She was perspiring. Sonai was standing in front of her, looking at her anxious, sweating face.

'Wake up Anu... Hey! Anu! Wake up!' Moni heard Ved's voice coming through the cell.

'Wake up dear...' Moni mumbled as if she was praying alongside. Her eyes were wet. Her face was wet.

Every moment passed was like eternity.

Ahhh... A soft feline sound broke the climactic point of mounting anxiety.

'Anu? Okay?' Moni heard Ved's voice which seemed a bit relieved.

'Where am I?' the soft voice asked.

'You're at the Red Road and we're going home,' Ved replied.

'Is she okay?' Moni asked immediately.

'Yes! The princess has just woken up!' Ved teased.

'Hello Anu?'

Anu picked up the phone.

'Yes dear... I'm okay... Don't worry... And... I love you...' Anu said in an intermittent fashion.

Moni pressed her lips together as her eyes got rid of two big drops of tears which fell straight on the floor, near her feet.

Sonai, who was monitoring the whole episode so much charged with emotive expressions of varied degrees, came closer to Moni and clasped her waist tightly in a hug, pressing her tiny head into Moni's belly.

'Come home… I need to go out to office… Okay?' Moni asked.

'Okay…' Anu cut the line.

'Now, Sonai, will you mind if you submit something other than your painting?' Moni asked as she pulled Sonai in her arms.

Sonai looked at Moni. Her eyes were full of curiosity as looking like two round balls.

'What?' Sonai asked insolently.

'Say, a poem?'

'A poem? But… I don't know how to write poems…' Sonai replied in an exasperated vein.

'So why? I am here *nah*? I can help you out!' Moni replied animatedly.

'Really? How?' Sonai asked.

'Okay… Get my laptop… Meanwhile let me arrange for your uniform and satchel…' Moni said as she started dialling numbers. Soon, she ordered someone to bring a new satchel and uniform of class seven of a well known school on Ballygunge Circular road.

The person at the other end of the phone was probably much too compliant, for Sonai noticed that Moni simply gave out instructions and hung up.

As soon as Moni stopped talking over phone, Sonai rushed to the table at the living room upon which the machine was kept.

Moni washed her face, went to the kitchen and started mincing onions.

Sonai came to the kitchen door with the machine in her arms.

'Open a blank document…' Moni ordered.

Sonai gently placed the machine on the dining table, sat on the chair and as soon she opened a blank page, she yelled:

'Done!'

'Now look at the page… And think…' Moni said as she started to marinate chicken pieces.

'Think what?' Sonai asked turning her head towards Moni.

'Think about anything you like most…'

'Games?'

'Games! Well… Can be… What do you want to write about games?' Moni asked as she smiled.

'Games excite me most…' Sonai said and turning back she started typing something.

Moni could hear clicking sounds of keys being pressed on the computer. She looked at the watch. It's nine fifteen already. She would have to really hurry. Kevin will surely bring the satchel and the school uniform before ten, Moni hoped as she hurriedly put the marinated chicken pieces into the kadai. Smoke came out from the hot kadai as soon as the chicken pieces were dropped.

'Sonai!' Moni called.

'Yes?'

'Have you written anything so far?'

'Yeah!'

'Read aloud...' Moni said as she started stirring the chicken and added ginger and garlic paste.

'Well... It's not about games...'

'Okay... Read it out to me, please...' Moni said.

Sonai cleared her throat and read:

'I got you,
As you got me;
One fine morning,
Near the open sea;
You smiled at me
And I smiled back;
Reminding me
Of the forgotten track;
I owe you
A lot of love, O Dear!
Don't go away
For that I fear;
Hug me fast,
Hug me tight;
I'll also hug you,
With all my might.'

Sonai stopped.

Moni stood dumb with the ladle in her hand and the chicken burning on the kadai.

'You wrote it? Now?' Moni said, as she slowly came to the table to have a look at the screen.

Sonai was sitting on the chair but she was not looking at the screen. Her face was bowed. Moni looked at the screen. She saw the alphabets typed neatly in a Word document. She placed her hand on Sonai's head. Sonai groaned, her body tossed and trembled. Moni took Sonai in her arms and kissed her on moist cheeks and forehead, running her fingers through her hair. Sonai cried. Moni could not hold herself back from hugging the little girl and Moni cried. She cried for long. She cried even after Sonai stopped crying. Moni cried quite hysterically, as if she was crying to compensate for all those years she did not cry. She cried as if she was holding back all those years, buckets of tears in her eyes. She cried, groaned and muttered words as if in a fit. Little Sonai was so surprised by this sudden and uncontrolled outburst that she too sobbed and at one point even began patting Moni, trying to soothe her in her own childish manner.

After a few minutes, Moni's groans became less frequent and she seemed to be regaining her composure.

'Will you not drop me to school?' Sonai asked.

'Oh dear! I'm so sorry! Forgive me!' Moni quickly wiped her face from the edge of her sleeve and pulled Sonai towards the bathroom.

21

'So… Sommelier? That's what you want to be?' Ved asked.

Anu nodded. She could not talk. Her mouth was full of triple chocolate passion. At Flury's, tasting triple chocolate passion comprised dark, milk and white chocolate mousse with cocoa and lemon torte was pure delight. Ved had brought her to Flury's despite her reluctance, which he knew was a mere facade, because he noticed how quickly Anu's face had blackened as soon as Ved had mentioned the alternative of going back to Bardhaman Road.

Ved was chewing cookies. Anu did not respond. She was savouring chocolate mousse with her eyes closed.

'We hope that there would not be another misadventure…' Ved said.

Anu's eyes popped open. She looked at Ved. Her brows were furrowed. 'What did you say? Misadventure?'

'Yes…' Ved replied coolly.

Anu smiled. The contour of her face went through a gradual transformation. From a hardened state it turned into something soft with a tinge of despondency.

She took out a napkin from the triangular table top napkin holder and wiped her lips removing traces of chocolate on them. Then she looked straight. Her eyes bore a certain stillness, as if her mind was far away from the Park Street upon which Flury's had been doing business as one of the premier confectioneries of the region for nearly hundred years.

'Misadventure is part of some people's lives even before they are born,' Anu finally uttered.

'Really? Can you please elaborate?' Ved asked casually as if he had missed the whole point. That Anu's voice was sombre and lugubrious, that she was in a state of brooding, was deliberately overlooked by Ved.

'I can... Surely, I can... But where are you trying to drive me to? Eh? Why are you doing all this?' Anu suddenly asked quite venomously. Her eyes were glistening. Her voice turned shrill and there was enough indication of inner turmoil in her demeanour. Her face froze. Her spine straightened.

Ved smiled innocuously.

'No no... Don't be so evasive... Answer me...' Anu insisted.

'Don't be so insistent...' Ved said and stood up.

'Where are you going?' Anu asked, grabbing Ved's hand.

'Not going anywhere, dear... Just wanted to have some truffle...'

'Oh! I'm sorry!' Anu loosened her hold.

Ved walked up to the glass case featuring several kinds of exotic confectionery items and bent down to take a distinct look at them.

Anu took out another napkin and started to roll it on the table with her fingers. She was still playing with the napkin, when Ved returned to the table.

'You know Origami?' Ved asked her.

'Not really,' Anu said and was about to discard the rolled up napkin when Ved took it up and started making various folds. Within a few minutes, it turned into a flower, a lotus.

'Wow!' Anu gushed.

'It was pretty simple… Learnt it at school…'

'Still remember? You've got a brilliant memory…' Anu said looking at the napkin-turned-lotus.

'It is all because of practice… I do it quite often for Sonai,' Ved said.

'What are the other things you do for your daughter?'

'I hug her and pat her back whenever she rests her head on my shoulder like you did this morning at the river step…' Ved said suddenly and smiled.

Anu stopped. Her whole body frame just stopped as if it had no life, as if it became a statue. Only her eyelids quivered involuntarily.

Ved's benign smile spread wide across his face. He patted Anu's left cheek with his right palm twice and then held her chin and gave it a little quick shake, the way usually elder ones cajole young ones.

Anu said nothing. She bent down her head and her body shrugged a bit.

Ved took up the napkin-lotus and unfolded it.

'Wipe your face…' Ved murmured.

Anu took it, with her face bowed still.

'Truffles are yummy!' Ved exclaimed as soon as two plates of truffles arrived.

Anu looked up. She appeared shy.

'Have a bite, dear… It'll just melt in your mouth…' Ved said, pushing a plate towards Anu.

Anu took up a piece of the delicate chocolate cake by her two fingers and dropped it into her mouth.

'How's that?' Ved asked.

'Fabulous!' Anu remarked.

Ved pushed the other plate at Anu.

Anu tackled both plates with full gusto and greed, joy and happiness.

Ved just kept watching her gorge. His face had all the peace of the world.

'If you really want to become a sommelier then you'll have to make a sacrifice of your taste buds,' Ved commented as Anu licked her fingers.

'I'm ready to do that...' Anu promptly answered.

'Really? You're supposed to avoid anything rich in flavour and content... For instance, spicy foods, chocolates, liquors...' Ved continued.

'Ready for the sacrifice...' Anu said, presently wiping her fingers with a napkin.

'Really?'

'Yeah! Really!' Anu asserted.

'Good!' Ved replied.

'Tell me one thing Prof, do you really think that I'm inconsistent in my thinking?' Anu asked.

'So far yes...' Ved replied.

'Hmmm'

Anu just made the sound and fell silent.

'But there's always time to start a new life... If one is passionate enough,' Ved said.

Anu said nothing. She looked over the white curtains of the glass window to see Park Street getting populated.

'I think... I have reached that third and the last stage...the formation of post-conventional ideas... You know... I think I'm just there... Slowly inching towards my goal... And with a certain belief...' Anu talked absentmindedly, as if she was musing within herself, completely oblivious to Ved's presence even.

Ved placed his chin upon his right palm and looked at Anu's side profile. 'It could have been a great shot....' Ved whispered thinking of capturing Anu's face sideways in a black and white frame with the glass window and street partially visible through the window and the glass table and the empty black chairs with red cushions.

'Hello! What are you looking at?' Anu asked, seeing Ved stare at her.

'Nothing!' Ved shrugged to come to terms with reality.

'Should we get up?' Anu asked.

'Yes! Of course!' Ved stood up hurriedly, looking at his watch.

'My goodness! It is already ten! Sonai must be cursing me! I'll have to call Moni...'

22

'Diana is so elated today!'

Sonai gushed soon after she jumped into the back seat of the cab, beside Moni. It was ten in the morning and the city roads were starting to get messy with vehicles of different shapes and sizes pouring onto them in a mad rush.

'Why dear?' Moni asked. The cab had overtaken a state bus with an ugly crumpled rear emitting thick black smoke clouds.

'Diana has got a poem and a new school uniform and satchel.' Sonai said as she tugged the skirt.

'Ohho… Ha ha ha' Moni laughed.

'Are you a V.P. or something?' Sonai asked playing with the zip of the side pocket of her brand new satchel.

'Why?'

'Only a V.P. can arrange for new things so quickly…' Sonai's voice had all the happiness.

'No dear… I just happen to be a manager with some people to boss over who are always obliged to be bossed,' Moni said thinking of Kevin. 'Kevin needs a hike, especially after the way he arranged for the school uniform and satchel and the water bottle even, in such a short notice,' Moni thought.

'You're a manager—poet?' Sonai asked.

'Ya, sort of...'

'Then my dad is a professor—photographer,' Sonai announced proudly.

'Yeah... *That* I know...' Moni replied.

'Seen those pics of Leh and Ladakh on his web page?' Sonai asked, staring at Moni with a kind of seriousness.

'Yes! The photographs are fabulous...'

'Ya... They are... But...' Sonai bit her lips.

'But?'

'But the thing is that he hasn't touched his camera for the last couple of years.'

'Really? Why?' Moni was curious.

'Don't know... He does not go out to take photos nowadays...,' Sonai replied thoughtfully.

Moni looked at the tiny eyes of the little girl.

'Do you feel bad that your dad is no longer taking photos?'

'Yes... To some extent... Because I know that he is not only reluctant to pursue his most favourite hobby, I fear, he is losing interest in everything... In his studies, in his job... Probably in his life...' Sonai uttered with a solemnity beyond her years.

Moni felt that she was having a conversation with an old lady with a very sensitive, agile and discerning mind.

Moni moved closer to Sonai, put her palm on her head and said, 'I think you're not fully correct in your appraisal... Your dad still pines to take photos... I know he buys books related to photography... And...'

'And?' Sonai asked.

'And he would love to be away with his camera if he gets a chance...'

'Really? How do ye know all these?'

'Because...' Moni was about to think and phrase up when Sonai stopped her by pressing her hand over Moni's mouth and yelled suddenly, 'Because you're his online friend who is getting into offline mode!'

Moni laughed, a bit embarrassed.

'I like your way of interpreting things and your sentences with technical jargon...' Moni said heartily.

'Tech jargon? Where?'

'Mode... Online... Offline,' Moni said smiling, as she tugged at Sonai closer.

Sonai smiled and closed her eyes, enjoying the cajoling.

'Your dad can never lose interest in life when he has such a cuddly doll like you at home,' Moni whispered.

'Is it so?' Sonai asked sleepily.

The cab came down Chetla bridge and at the Rashbehari crossing it hit the signal. Several cars stood bumper to bumper. Moni looked at the blue sky with white cloudlets floating through the window. Winter mornings in the city are awesome.

'Tell me, one thing, why do you write poems?' Sonai asked as if to start a conversation to kill the time at the signal with engines of cars purring all around and people shut in those cars waiting with impatience.

'Poetry is the expression of your feelings...' Moni said looking at a group of small school children crossing the road wearing sweaters and pullovers of many hues. Their faces were happy. Their manner was playful.

'What are feelings?' Sonai asked.

'Like the way you feel... For example, when I hugged you a few minutes ago, how do you feel?'

'Warm...' Sonai promptly replied.

'Right, now if you express that feeling saying *I feel warm when you hug me*—it is poetic...'

'I see...' Sonai became contemplative.

'Now tell me how do you feel?' Sonai asked.

'When?'

'When you hugged me, of course!' Sonai said.

'Peaceful... As if the world has no cares... As if I can hold on to you like that for eternity and there will be no discomfiture... As if I could die like that holding you in my arms,' words gushed from Moni's mouth effortlessly.

Sonai listened, motionless and awed by the sudden outpour and rhythm of her words.

Moni could have uttered more sonorous phrases had her cellphone not rung just then.

'Hello.'

'Hi, I'm Ved... Are you off to school?'

'Yeah we're... At Rashbehari right now...'

'But... Sonai's uniform and school bag? Is she going to school sans uniform?'

'No... We've got all we needed... Talk to her.'

Moni gave the phone to Sonai.

'Papa! You won't believe... I got a brand new uniform, satchel and pencil box and water bottle and...'

'Really? What about the books?' Sonai's father asked.

'We don't need books today... We need something to submit for the school magazine...'

'Oh yes yes! I remember... But your painting is at home dear!' Ved sounded nervous and astounded at the same time.

'I got a poem...'

'A poem?'

'Yeah dad! A poem... The first one written by me!'

'Really? You've written a poem? That's surprising!'

'That's surprising for me as well!' Sonai quipped.

'Okay! I would love to listen to that after school... Should I take you from school then?'

'I wish I could spend a little more time with Moni... She can pick me up from school, can't she?'

Saying this Sonai looked at Moni, covering the microphone of the cell with her fingers.

'Tell him, you're going to pick me up and drop me home. Please... Tell him...' Sonai spoke in a hushed tone, insistent.

Moni looked at her watch.

'When will your school break up?' Moni asked in a hushed voice.

'At four,' Sonai's eyes had all the eagerness.

'Please Moni...' Sonai pleaded folding her hands together.

'Okay...' Moni said as she took the cell from Sonai's hand.

'Hello, Mr. Bhattacharya!'

'Yes...'

'Will you mind if I pick up Sonai from school today, just for a change?'

'I won't, of course not. But... won't that put you in trouble?'

'Not at all... I would love to...'

'Okay. Then I'll be at the university... Will be waiting for you two there'

'Okay... Where's Anu, by the way?

'She's right beside me... Want to talk?'

'No... Isn't she feeling tired?'

'She is... We have had our breakfast and we are running back to your place...'

'Okay... Tell her that the keys are with the watchman...'

'Okay... And er... Thanks!' Ved said hesitantly.

'Thanks? For what?'

'For whatever you've done so far...'

'Thanks to you as well then,' Moni retorted.

'For what?' Ved asked.

'You know,' Moni said and snapped the line with a smile.

'Stop here, Uncle!' Sonai yelled as the cab took Ballygunge circular road and ran a few yards.

Moni saw a walled enclosure with a big blue iron gate on the left.

Sonai, who was sitting at the left back seat, hopped out of the cab in no time. Moni brought out her purse. By the time Moni got down from the cab and walked towards the gate, she found Sonai talking with a girl of her own size. School children dressed in uniforms of the same colour look identical. Many more of varied sizes were thronging at the gate. Some were holding on to their parents' hands, some had aged relatives by their side.

'Sonai!' Moni called.

'I'm here!' Sonai waved her hand.

Moni paced towards the gate.

'Meet Devakshi, my best friend,' Sonai said introducing a little girl with specs that made her look like a studious, nerdy type.

'Hello, I'm Moni.'

Moni extended her hand for a shake.

'Hi… I'm Devakshi Nanda, Class seven, section a…' The girl replied promptly.

'Let's go!' Sonai said as she pulled Devakshi by her hand.

Devakshi looked at Moni for a few seconds before she joined Sonai, running.

Moni waved her hand as she saw two tiny girls running through the corridor of the main building. Their hair swayed. Their satchels jumped from one side to another. Giggles echoed down the corridor. Moni kept on looking for a while, before she turned back towards the gate.

23

'Won't you come in?' Anu asked as she opened the door of the flat.

Ved looked at his watch. It is ten twenty and he needed to get to the university by twelve. He looked at his purple shirt. It was crumpled. He looked at his shoes. They were dusty. His beige trousers looked brownish.

'I need to get to the university by twelve and before that I'll have to take a bath and freshen up.'

'You can have a bath here and food and then go home to get into better clothes. Moni had left chicken masala for us, remember?' Anu said.

'Okay… I'll just have a bath and food and run back… Done?'

'Done!'

Ved entered.

Anu went straight to the dining place and started arranging the food.

'Why don't you fresh yourself up first?' Ved asked.

'I'll… Let me arrange the proper meal for my guest…' Anu chuckled.

Ved lay down on the couch.

Anu switched on the fan.

'Should you go to the bathroom first or I?' Anu asked.

'You go.'

'It'll take time for me to get rid of the sleepless nights' dirt from my body and clothes,' Anu said a bit poetically.

Ved smiled.

Anu smiled back like an enigma.

Soon she entered the bathroom. From the living room, Ved could hear the hissing sound of water falling on the floor and the soft humming of the bathroom singer's song the bathroom.

Ved looked overhead at the fan that spun tirelessly. The fast moving blades of the fan trapped his gaze in a maze. Ved recalled suddenly that he hadn't slept the last night. The very thought of having a sleepless night exhausted him. He thought it to be a good idea to have a nap. A short nap is good for health.

Anu emerged from the bathroom after forty five minutes. She changed into a black skirt and red V-neck tee and dabbed cologne over her shoulder and arms. She was feeling hungry. She would have to ask VPB to get freshened up.

Entering the living room, she found VPB asleep. His one leg was rested on the glass table, the other leg on the floor and his head tilted sideways on the armrest of the couch.

Anu looked at the face. It had calm. The beautiful hair looked untidy. Anu got nearer.

She saw the pen peeping out of Ved's shirt pocket. Mont Blanc?

'Hello! Wake up!' Anu said giving a mild push to Ved.

Ved jerked into wakefulness and stood up. 'Which class?' he asked.

'Class?'

Ved looked around.

'It's me Anu. You've fallen asleep at our place....'

'Oh ho I'm so sorry!'

Ved looked at his watch. It was eleven fifteen.

'My god! I'll have to be at the university by twelve!'

'Cool off! You've got ample time to get freshen up,' Ved nodded and walked to the bathroom.

'Moni has an excellent hand at cooking, hasn't she?' Anu asked, licking her fingers dry. Post bath, Ved also felt hungry. The only thing he wished desperately to do was to wash his dirty linens and get into fresh clothes. Anu offered Ved one of her tees that was oversized for him. In fact *two Veds* could easily get into that and still there would be considerable space left. Anu even offered him one of her pants. That would surely lead to *wardrobe malfunction,* as sudden slipping off pants from the waist would be called (by addicts of *haute couture*). So Ved declined to wear those. It was better to put up with the discomfort of wearing crumpled and slightly dirty clothes than oversized ones which made her look singularly ridiculous. Besides, there was always the peril of *wardrobe malfunction* lurking.

'Absolutely! The chicken masala was too delicious to miss. One could walk extra miles to have something like that,' Ved said, savouring the aftertaste of chicken masala.

'Only Moni is not present... She would have been extraordinarily pleased to hear this compliment from you.' Anu said.

'Hey! Are you digging?' Ved asked, sensing a mocking tone in Anu's voice.

'No no... I'm serious!' Anu replied shaking her head.

'Okay then let's call her... What's her number?' Ved asked as he walked up to the wash basin.

'You've got it in your cell, I suppose,' Anu said without looking.

'Oh yes!' Ved picked up his cell and went to the call register to dial Moni's number. Then, 'Hello... it's me, Ved'

... ...

'Yes...Your chicken masala was fabulous... Hope to have more of it soon.'

... ...

'Surely.'

Ved cut off the line.

Anu was in the living area. She was sitting on the couch, trying to read something from a magazine. Ved walked towards the couch.

'It's almost twelve... Won't you go to the university?' Anu asked without looking.

'No... I'm thinking about taking a rest here till four as Moni would be bringing Sonai here...'

'So you'll skip your classes today?' Anu asked with narrowed eyes. She was thinking.

'Yes! Any probs?'

'Nah! Nothing! You seem to be highly unpredictable... You change schedules too quickly, I guess... Anyway, I need to sleep.'

'Oh surely! Go to your room and sleep,' suggested Ved. 'And another thing, I change schedules only to accommodate others,' he added, smiling.

'Really? Why? Why for god's sake, you accommodate others when you know too well you can't be pleasing everybody by doing that?' Anu asked with a sudden rise of emotion called *borderline fury.*

Ved said nothing. He looked at Anu in black skirt and red tee. She's just a little girl, not older than Sonai. Ved thought and smiled.

'Hey! Why are you flashing that idiotic smile of yours?' Anu asked, this time her tone was simply full of dejection.

Ved picked up the *India Today* magazine left by Anu on the table. Ved got into the lead story, 'Why the economic slowdown hasn't caught India?'

Anu waited for an answer. With no response forthcoming, she broke the silence, 'But… how can I leave you here?'

'You can actually. Just switch on the TV and go to sleep.'

'Won't you sleep?'

'Yeah… Let's see…'

Anu switched on the television and handed Ved the remote before she went to her room and closed the door.

Ved surfed channels until he got *Nat Geo. 'On assignment. Nat Geo special,'* the voice over could be heard as the trademark yellow rectangle of *Nat Geo* got faded away. Ved sat up. His eyes were glued to the screen.

> *'Today we are going to show you ten best photographs out of ten lakh snaps being taken by our Nat Geo correspondents in a single year… Taken at different times and locations, spreading over the Arctic to the Amazon, west China to Egypt, Honduras to Seychelles, these photographs not only*

catch human life in the most struggling forms but also in the most joyous states... These photographs are not mere snaps, they carry the essential grit and tolerance our correspondents had to lug every moment... We rate them in accordance with the difficulty the photographers had to overcome to catch them, the overall composition, the peculiarities and yet their commonness, the play of mind of the photographer and his audience and above all, the emotive value... We start from the tenth one...'

Ved's body was bent forward. His eyes were transfixed.

'This snap was taken by our German correspondent B. Hoffman when he went to West China on assignment...' the voice over continued.

Gradually, a picture unfolded on the screen. It was an amazing picture of a man crossing a stream by hanging from a stout rope connecting two ledges of two mountains between which the stream flows. The man was hanging from a pulley. But the novelty of the picture was that the man had a calf hanging from another pulley right behind him and he was trying to pull the calf by his feet hinged to the second pulley. It must have required a savage amount of strength and stamina to pull oneself and the calf. The veins on the man's temple were visible. His face wore a strange grimace. His hands looked stretched and stressed. The hanging body of the man and that of calf, some twenty to thirty feet above the stream, cutting through a range of mountains, was beautifully captured.

Ved looked at the face of human struggle against the serene backdrop of green mountains and his heart was filled with wonder—peculiar and unsavoury—at human existence and the roughness of wild nature. The camera work was excellent catching each and every detail of the snap—from the puffed veins of the man's hands and face to the haplessness of the calf with his four legs dangling in the air and piteous eyes.

'What are you watching?'

Ved heard Anu's voice from behind. He looked back, craning his head. The black skirt and red tee had been replaced with a satin gown with three knots at the front. The knots rendered Anu's physicality all the more conspicuous by making the satin gown tightly fitted to her. Ved looked at Anu's eyes. They were a bit puffy. Was she crying?

'*Nat Geo*,' Ved replied and turned his eyes again to the TV.

'Could have taken a nap, I suppose,' Anu said, exhausted.

'I can't simply,' Ved reply was prompt and brief. His eyes were on the screen.

'Why?' Anu asked as she came from the back of the couch and stood by the armrest, looking at the TV with disinterest.

Ved pressed the rubber button of the volume control section of the remote.

The voice over of the TV program got louder.

'Now we move on to the ninth one which is another example of excellent camera work…'

The screen got reddish. One could see the silhouette of a baby river dolphin against the perspective of a fluorescent red colour. The colour of the water appeared red as sun rays came filtered through it. The shot had understandably been taken underwater. The face of the baby dolphin caught while floating resembled that of a new born baby with eyes closed.

'This is a picture of an Amazon river dolphin. We assigned it the ninth best position, because, probably, for the first time, it made us aware of the fact that even in the muddy, polluted waters of a river in Amazon, there are dolphins, still propagating their generations, despite all odds…'

The voice over continued with impeccable rise and fall of tones which only a voice over expert could deliver. Ved stared at the dolphin, the red water, the black shadows and the glow of the sun as visible through water—a kind of glow covered by something translucent.

'Great shot! Ain't it?' Ved asked, turning to Anu who had come and sat beside him on the couch.

'So, you're interested in wildlife photography?' Anu stated. Her face did not appear particularly happy. She appeared rather distracted.

'Yeah… Not only wildlife photography but photography in general,' Ved answered.

'Really?' Anu asked with a sudden show of interest in breaking into a long conversation.

'Yes! Of course! But the only thing is…' Ved stopped. He felt he was digressing.

'The only thing is?' Anu asked, her keenness becoming all the more pronounced.

Curiosity is any woman's birth right. Ved felt.

'I haven't touched my camera for a long time,' Ved sighed.

No sooner had he stated it than Ved felt that he would be dealt a volley of questions. Surprisingly, Anu did not ask any. She just kept on looking at Ved with intense eyes and her left hand playing with the loose ends of her shoulder-length hair.

Her lips were tightly closed, but Ved noticed a kind of curve in those lips that could have been a genuinely suppressed smile.

Ved got back to *Nat Geo.*

Suddenly, he felt Anu's hand on his back. The touch was gentle as if a very reluctant one.

'Yes?' Ved moved aside a bit and turned his body sideways to sit vis-à-vis Anu as he asked.

Anu moved away her hand. Anu's eyes were shining as if they wanted to tell a lot of untold stories.

Ved picked up the remote from the table and pressed the red button on the left hand top to put the TV on standby.

Anu was pressing her palms together, placing them on her lap.

'Yes? Want to say something?' Ved asked, in a mellowed voice as if he was trying to soothe an unruly and untamed cat.

'You love Moni, don't you?' Anu asked in a tone which had more conviction than query.

Ved laughed aloud which broke the comforting silence of the wintry noon.

'Hey! Answer me! You playboy!' Anu yelled with a start and held Ved's arms and shook him heavily. Her eyes had an unmistakable expression of pathos and angst.

Ved stopped laughing. He took hold of Anu's hands firmly and shoved them away.

'Anoushka Agarwal, I'm your teacher and don't you ever try to malign the teacher's responsibility towards his students by demanding any kind of reason or any kind of physical proximity.' Ved was sombre, to say the least.

But his sombreness did not deter Anu from breaking into another fit of yelling.

'Really? A teacher? Then, what business does a teacher really have to spend sleepless nights for a mere student and why the hell is he so keen on giving his student the august company that the student doesn't really demand? What are you trying to prove, you masochist? Are you an ascetic bent on serving humanity? Even if that is the case, then why do you act like a pretentious young man to emotionally trap an innocent, civil, decent woman like Moni? Why did you do this? Why? You loner?' Anu yelled like a madcap. Her head was swinging, making her hair fall loose on her forehead and even partially blocking her eyes.

Ved was aghast. 'What are you talking about?' Ved asked having trouble understanding Anu's accusations.

Anu was out of breath after her high decibel throat work.

'Playboy, Masochist, Ascetic, Loner… Fine! Four distinctive and remotely related epithets for one person! Great! Why don't you join creative writing?' Ved said flashing a sardonic smile.

Anu did not speak. She was eyeing the floor but her bosom still heaved, which meant, her heart was throbbing fast with the sudden rise of her tempo.

Ved stood up.

'I need to leave,' Ved said as he pulled his socks and ran his fingers through his hair combing.

Anu looked up. Her eyes were red, full of tears.

'Don't go away, please,' Anu said as she clutched Ved's trousers and pulled him towards her with a monstrous force, taking him unawares.

Ved lost his balance and fell on the satin gown. At once, Ved felt the softness of Anu's bosom touching his chest and the smell of cologne coming from her armpit and neck and her tresses of hair caressing his face.

Anu kissed Ved upon his lips and it tasted wild, full of lust. Anu her right arm round Ved's neck and with her legs coiled Ved's thighs as if she had been starving for centuries to make love.

Ved allowed Anu to kiss him despite knowing that this could really turn him on. He thought it to be Anu's way of expressing her gratitude towards him. He remembered the *Upanishad*, the most religious, philosophical and esoteric texts he had ever read. The several texts of the *Upanishad* were the only books Ved turned to, aside from photography journals, soon after Mayurika's death, to find the balm and protection for his pained, agonised, restless and remorseful soul. He recalled lines from an English rendition of *Chandogya Upanishad:*

> *'A man is a fire. Speech is his fuel; the breath his smoke; the tongue his flame; the eye his embers; the ear his sparks…*
>
> *A young woman is a fire. The loin clothes are her fuel; when one invites her, her smoke; the vagina her flame; what one does within, her embers; the pleasures her sparks…'*

The kiss was hard, full of saliva coming out of a young woman hot and fiery. Ved knew with his non-participation, the fire of the woman would die down, though it would leave her with a taste of purposelessness and disappointment.

Ved mentally retraced *Chandogya Upanishad's* pages and he could clearly see the lines written in black on pulpy white pages:

> *'The blissful one, leaving this body and entering the light beyond, appears in its own form. That is the highest*

person. Here he moves about, feasting, playing, or taking pleasure with women, chariots or kin, not remembering this appendage, the body.'

Anu's sweat covered face with closed eyes looked perfectly sensuous. Ved felt the soft left hand of the young woman gradually move down his back and spine. *Should I wait or start the process of drifting away?* Ved thought for a split second.

Do it now! Ved's conscience ordered against this young woman with great issues of attention-deficit who just wanted to live life meaningfully but was uncertain about the path to choose.

Hey you! Are you not seeking pleasure out of a helpless young mind with young body? Are you not deriving pleasure pretending to be a person with a lot of philanthropy? Stop it! Your body is just an accessory!

Ved first moved his lips away by applying mild force. Then he firmly placed his hands on Anu's shoulder and barked: 'Anoushka! I'm no Sandy! Are you listening? I'm not Sandipan!'

'Sandy? Who's that? I want you to be in me,' Anu groaned as if she was having everything in her fantasy.

'Get back to reality! Life is no fantasy! Okay?' Ved sounded as if he was serving an admonition and gave Anu a shake.

Anu opened her eyes. She looked at Ved with eyes that had hate and terrible frustration. Then, she laughed, showing her teeth, jerking her body. Her laughs were no mere laughs, they were full of hate too.

'You got erectile dysfunction, you priest! Run home and play games on your computer and read religious trash!' Anu laughed and scorned.

'Surely! I'll! But if Sandy comes back and tells you that he has got your compromising pictures in his cell, what will you do?' Ved said calmly with minimum voice undulations, knowing too well that he was just playing a gamble based on his readings of Anu's mind and her past life about which he got to know from her scrapbook only yesterday when he spent some time in her room alone.

'What! Sandy got my…' Anu jumped up with a bang and stood dumb, not knowing what to do or say. She just stared fixedly at Ved trying to find something in his eyes.

'You know Sandy?' Anu asked, bewildered.

Ved observed Anu's eyes and soon learnt he had achieved what he had wanted—to move Anu from lustful passion to something thought-provoking. Only he hoped that she would not become too panicky. Even if she becomes too anxious, then there are always ways and means to give her support to get back to something she likes, to pacify her. Ved thought.

'Yes… I got to know about him through your diary which I had chanced upon to read without your permission, last night…' Ved said in a confessional tone, wary of the fact that Anu was becoming too bothered and overtly anxious.

'O…' Anu said, thinking hard.

'I hope Sandy would do nothing to blackmail you… He's scared of you…' Ved stated yawning. He was feeling tired. After a sleepless night if one was to play mind games, then it would be very strenuous.

'So? It's all your imagination?' Anu asked looking confused.

'It was just a possibility I was thinking about… Based upon the glimpses of your misadventures which your diary showed me,' Ved said.

'I deem it improper and beyond civility to read someone's personal diary without her permission...' Anu said expressing her displeasure without being too hateful or angry.

'The fire has died down considerably.' Ved thought.

'Look Anu,' Ved said, clearing his throat, 'I think a few hours back you took a resolve to start something new... You claimed you wanted to be a master sommelier, right?'

'Yes!'

'I presume there will be no backing out from that resolve... and I guess you have the passion to be someone like Shatbhi Basu or Gaia Agnetti or Ami Shroff... They all took this wonderful art as their destiny because they all believed that their soul lies in mixology... I have read that Ami Shroff got into the trade after watching Tom Cruise in a movie called *Cocktail*... Now that movie was probably seen by a million others worldwide but surprisingly not every one of them felt ignited to be a mixologist... But Ami wanted to be a mixologist; why?' Ved asked.

Anu watched Ved. And for the first time, she realised why Prof. VPB was respected by everyone in the university. He had the voice befitting an influential orator and his eyes spoke his mind a beautiful, enriched and sublime mind, a mind with no clouds of doubts or confusions.

'Why?' Anu asked bemused.

'Because, Ami had that zing within her to be a sommelier... Everyone needs that zing... That emotional quotient to drive one towards his or her goal...' Ved continued with a kind of enthusiasm that was infectious.

'Take Shatbhi Basu... She took to mixing drinks when it was thought that women should not even go to bars, forget bar tending as a profession… Do you know how the zing drives one into something without even knowing where the boundaries or borders lie? For instance, some people driven by that ignited mind, travel miles to get to the place where they feel they will be properly fitted?'

Ved asked as if he was being flooded by some kind of zing himself, the uncontrollable, unchained sense of being freed from the limitations of space and time. Ved spoke as if he was floating away to a different state of being, completely ignorant of the fact that it was a wintry afternoon and that he was within the four walls of some kind of concrete coop in a city full of smoke and ashes and noises and all kinds of unsettling physical turbulence.

Anu listened to what she heard and felt invigorated and enthused.

'You're a great teacher, no doubt… A great motivator… but…' Anu said, choked up. She felt like crying, though she did not really understand why she felt like that. Am I feeling guilty of trying to provoke someone to sex? Anu thought.

'But… What?' Ved asked standing arms akimbo.

'But I am… Such a shit! Tell me one thing; you take me for a bad girl, don't you?' Anoushka asked suddenly. Her face was sweaty. Her nose was erect and her Adam's apple rolled up and down twice as if she was swallowing something hard to swallow.

Ved broke into laughter.

'You're not only a bad girl, you're the worst girl I've ever met, but this girl will be someone like Ami Shroff or Shatbhi Basu, I know that for sure… Now buckle up you silly! Wash your face and have a sound sleep… Sleep brings sanity…' Ved said cheerfully, all smiles.

Anu never expected that kind of answer from Ved. She felt humbled and at peace. She also wanted to hug Ved and cry on his shoulders like a baby.

Ved probably guessed her mind for he came forward, pulled her up and uttered in a voice which had all the elements of someone very indulgent and all knowing, 'Promise me you'll join the STIR Academy of Bartending soon.'

'STIR? What's that?' Anu asked like an inquisitive kid.

'The academy is run by Shatbhi in Mumbai… I'll check out the formalities and help you in every way to get to a suitable place to learn the art of mixology… And for the last time I'm asking you, are you fully sure that you'll learn it with all your heart and move on from there?' Ved asked. He seemed serious.

'Yeah!' Anu said with extended emphasis on the 'h' at the end.

'Great! You know something, only yesterday they found several chests of sparkling wine bottles dating back to eighteenth century under the Atlantic Ocean at a ship wreck site, and the most significant part of the story is, they retrieved some bottles and a bunch of super enthused sommeliers tasted the wine, they certified it to be the most beautiful thing that they ever tasted! Can you imagine?' Ved said with a sudden gusto. His eyes were popping out and his face wore a look of excitement.

Anu felt that the man in front of her was probably one of those sommeliers who tasted the wine.

'Can you imagine? Those sommeliers said that the wine was too good to be tasted and some marine geologists confirmed the fact that the particular place where the bottles were found, was actually a great place to store sparkling wine with the temperature consistently hovering around four degree centigrade and absolute darkness all around,' Ved said. His excitement had subsided a bit and his eyes were fixed to one corner of the room looking distracted.

'So?' Anu asked.

'So? So what? If our history and geography work together they give you rare opportunities to experience the strangest things…' Ved said.

Anu nodded not knowing fully, though, why she nodded in the first place.

'Probably those sommeliers with an extraordinary co-ordination between their tongues and noses and brains, found out exactly which kind of wine it was… Isn't that marvelous?' Ved asked still absent minded.

'Yes… It is…' Anu agreed.

'Now I want you to be just like them… Pushing your sensory perceptions to the extreme… Only then you'll feel life is worth living' Ved smiled and said.

Anu nodded. This time she felt she got into her brain what Prof. VPB was hinting at. Anu felt a kind of joy sweeping her from top to toe, or toe to top. Didn't matter which.

24

'Gosh! Sanhita! I can't believe it... You're writing poems these days!' Devakshi said after Sonai submitted the poem to the class teacher.

They were walking down the corridor of the first floor of the main building of the school with big arches and pillars which made the building so grand and majestic. Whenever Sonai walked down these corridors she felt so tiny, almost like a Lilliputian.

'Kind of liking poems of late,' Sonai said looking up to the ceiling of the corridor which was ably supported by big ancient iron beams placed side by side, one after another. The beams were painted red and the ceiling was white. Standing below the colossal structure and looking up, it look like being under a white sky crisscrossed by red lines.

'What are you looking at?' Devakshi asked, amused to see Sanhita walking slowly with her face turned up.

'The white ceiling and the red beams,' Sonai replied.

'Seen something like that in a computer game, I suppose?' Devakshi asked knowing fully well that her mate had only one thing in the world to be thoughtful about—computer games.

'Not really... Red lines across the white sky...' Sonai said distractedly.

'Hey! What's up? Are you all right?' Devakshi asked.

'Yeah,' Sonai said and looked down.

'First you write poem, then you look up to the ceiling and call it a white sky with red lines... I'm at loss really... What are you up to?' Devakshi said, nonplussed.

'Nothing...' Sonai answered briefly.

'Okay... Now that we have a break, why don't we go to the hall and have a chat there?' Devakshi proposed.

'The hall' is actually a seminar room which often lies vacant. Devakshi and Sanhita often come to this second floor room and sit on the leather front row seats to while their off periods away.

The seminar hall was empty as usual with rows of empty seats neatly arranged. The walls had big glass windows covered by long blue curtains. Sunlight filtered through the blue curtains gave the room a distinctive serene look. The silence was calming enough to break Sanhita into a self-possessed murmur of a kind.

'I feel like the happiest person on earth today... I got a poem and new school uniform and satchel as gifts... And I am so happy...' Sanhita murmured.

Devakshi sat beside Sanhita, her best mate and waited for more to come.

'You know something... Today is a special day for me as I feel I have got back what I lost a few years ago... It is like suddenly coming across your most treasured thing which you thought you lost forever...' Sanhita continued.

'What's that?' Devakshi asked her mate.

'Mother's love... Her smell... Her fond touch... Her smile...' Sanhita said.

'Hey girl! You've become a poetess!' Devakshi gushed.

'That's all because of her...' Sanhita said.

'Who?' Devakshi was curious.

'Moni ... Monideepa Banerjee ... She's a fairy ... a Godsent fairy... who has come to me to soothe me, to comfort me, to help me forget all those days of being motherless... So that I can live again without being troubled by the fact that I lost my mom...' Sonai said, her voice trembling.

'I always knew you're pained by your mom's death. But never imagined you're so much pained... I thought you're happy with your games and gadgets... Tell me, now that you know you got someone just like your mom, why are you so sad?' Devakshi asked, leaning towards Sanhita, her best mate, to hold her hands with her.

'Because I don't know what she thinks, what my dad thinks... All those adult people, grown-ups with developed brains and ideas... What they think...' Sonai alias Sanhita Bhattacharya uttered with sadness and seriousness.

'Is she the woman who has come today to school with you?' Devakshi asked.

'Yes, she is Moni... The person who taught me that when you express your mind by writing words in a rhyme, it is poetry, and before meeting Moni, I had no idea about writing anything of my own... and I can tell you it is a wonderful experience' Sanhita muttered, dreamily. She felt she had talked a lot and yet she wanted to talk more.

Devakshi sat there silently, holding on to her mate's palms which were sweaty.

'Hey! You're awesome!' Devakshi broke off suddenly and kissed Sanhita's cheeks.

'I'm so proud of you!' Devakshi said.

'Me too…' Sonai replied with eyes full of salt.

'You know something,' Devakshi said, 'the moment I saw your Moni, I felt she was your mom… She looked so much you… I thought I was looking at a grown-up Sanhita… She's so much you!'

'Really?' Sonai asked, smiling.

'Yeah! Buddy!'

Devakshi nodded in affirmation, making her glasses slip off the bridge of her tiny nose.

'Tell me,' Devakshi asked, moving a bit closer (as if she was going to get into something very secret the issues concerning the national nuclear arms deployment strategy, for example) 'How come Moni escorted you to school? Are you people living together?'

'No. That's a long story… Moni's roommate went missing, she is also dad's student and dad went out looking for her and Moni and I ended up giving each other company…' Sonai explained.

'Good …' Devakshi said.

'Yes, it was real good time we had, we two…' Sanhita stated.

'Cool!' Devakshi gushed, without indicating why she thougt it to be cool. 'Lets get up, it is time for our next session… the break is over, I think…' Sanhita said, as both of them heard the electric bell ringing.

'Yes… back to the mob!' Devakshi quipped.

Sanhita smiled lethargically, as they started strolling back to their class, leaving the hall vacant again.

25

'Do you think these woollens will boost sales?' Moni asked, running her fingers down the uneven hemline of a pullover, with few stitches missing. She had just picked it up from a pile of pullovers and sweaters and comforters in the stock room.

The sales girls were tagging them. Incessant clicking of staplers created some unholy music of its kind. Price tags with codes were being stapled to garments with strict accuracy. The girls were talking amongst themselves.

'They are better than last year's ... at least,' Kevin murmured, standing right beside Moni and looking at the woollens with optimism.

'Hmm ... Kevin, have you ever noticed our surroundings?' Moni asked suddenly.

Kevin was not sure what the manager was talking about. He knew that the best way to respond in circumstances like these was to nod non-committally, which he did.

'Last year there was no Monte Carlo at your back ... Got it?' Moni hissed and walked back to her office.

Reaching her room, Moni closed the door.

'What are they thinking? They can dump any darn thing here and we would just sell them and keep the figures moving?' Moni fumed from within. She took out her cell from her bag and sat down on her chair.

'Hello Sir, it's Moni here ...'she began.

'Boliye...' Bhatia responded somewhat illegibly. His mouth sounded preoccupied with food.

'Sorry Sir, to disturb you at lunch,' Moni said in her softest voice.

'It is okay dear... Carry on ... I'm always at your door,' Bhatia grinned.

'Sir, the woollens ... They are below par...'

'What do you mean by below par? They are imported items!' Bhatia stopped munching.

'Sir... They are shabby... with botches...'

'What have you to do with botches? Tell me? They come in boxes and there can be few botches and marks ... Look Monideepa ... You are there to sell, you're not in quality control... Selling is your area... Okay?' Bhatia sounded irritated.

'But Sir...'

'No ifs and buts... Just sell... We are contemplating starting a new reward scheme—the best sales manager of the country... And you know where you stand? Not within the first ten. And one thing, of late, I have noticed you're complaining a lot about the quality of products ... That'll not suffice for poor running of the show, you know... All centres get the same products ... And they sell ... Few complain...' Bhatia talked and stopped and talked as if his words were not coming smoothly.

'All get the same products? Really?' Moni asked with consternation.

'Yeah! Almost the same … Mostly the same…' Bhatia said.

'Okay sir… Bye…' Moni cut off the line trying hard to hide her dejection.

Then she stood up, pushed her chair back a little and walked to the glass window overlooking the street. Midday city came in view. Monte Carlo store across the street is doing brisk business. Moni watched happy faces coming out of the store with paper bags of different sizes. On the window sill there was a crystal memento. It had gathered dust.

Moni remembered it to be another small recognition of her efforts to sell off some junk.

Sell … Sell … Selling junk is your area. You're not in quality control … you just sell … Moni murmured within herself.

'But the market is getting steep…. It's growing … and it is competitive. You can survive only by selling avant-garde things … and not trash,' Moni thought.

What Bhatia and people like him were doing, was actually going backwards …. They were taking measures to cut the cost and maximise profit by compromising on the saleability of products … But that would backfire, be counterproductive … Blitz is not downsizing … Is it? Moni questioned herself.

Overlooking a window, Moni saw cars honking and whizzing past, pedestrians running to and fro like atoms in random movement, peddlers shouting trade cries, street urchins playing with empty cardboard boxes and plastic disposables and so many images … converging in singular distaste. The city was ruthlessly fast, and mindlessly busy.

'What am I doing here? Selling items of self-gratification and false propaganda and allurement? Am I a wrong person at a wrong place or just another being, trying to practice survival strategy? But that's reality—the offline life with real situations and real troubles. No poetry, no scribbles, no trance ... only big, ugly dreams which were always associated with materials,' Moni thought despondently.

'Madam...' Kevin entered.

Moni looked up. Kevin held some woollens in his hand.

'What? Now don't tell me you've discovered rat holes in them?' Moni flippantly uttered.

'Actually yes! There are a few holes in them ... Not as big as rat holes though...' Kevin spread out the woollens for Moni.

There were few holes in some of them which looked like a stitch defect as it happens sometimes when woollens are woven on machine.

'Machine slips I guess,' Moni said, rubbing her nails on the tiny holes.

'What should we do with these?' Kevin asked.

'What should we do?' Moni almost repeated what Kevin said in an absent minded manner.

Kevin waited. Moni bit her lips and thought for a while.

'Okay... Put them back into the boxes'

Kevin nodded and went away.

Moni picked up the cell and called Bhatia.

'Now what?' Bhatia seemed irritated.

'Sir... Now we have discovered rat holes in some of the woollens ... What should we do? Send them back?'

'Rat holes? Are you serious?' Bhatia asked.

'Yes Sir.'

'Okay ... How many of them are defective?'

'Haven't counted them so far. They are quite a few I presume,' Moni said feeling tired.

'Okay … let's see what we can do. I'll get back to you shortly…' Bhatia was contemplative, as he snapped the line.

Moni picked up the intercom and called Kevin.

'Kevin, how many of the items are really with some kind of defects?'

'Quite a few ma'am.'

'How many exactly Kevin? I want the number!' Moni was restless.

'Then we'll have to unpack the cartons ma'am and run a check.'

'Then do it … quick!'

After several minutes, Kevin hopped into the room with a piece of paper in hand.

'How many?' Moni asked straightaway Her face had a kind of suppressed firmness.

'Well … There are twenty pieces with botches… five with machine holes and fifteen others with stitch defects,' Kevin looked up from the paper in his hand.

'That means forty pieces … Out of … Errr… How many?' Moni asked absentmindedly.

'Two hundred ma'am …' Kevin answered.

'Grand! We're dealing with an importer who has just set a benchmark of shipping defective items … Isn't it? Unprecedented really? Eh?' Moni flashed a sarcastic smile.

Kevin just looked down as if he was the importer. Just then Moni's cellphone rang. Bhatia was calling.

'Yes Sir!' Moni said and waited.

'Is there anybody around?' Bhatia asked the first thing as soon he heard Moni as if he was going to discuss some kind of clandestine affair, a classified info, for example.

'No one really... Go ahead,' Moni said as she signalled Kevin to leave her alone for a while.

'Tell me, how many are found to be not up to the mark?' Bhatia asked, still hushed up.

'Forty out of two hundred,' Moni answered matter-of-factly.

'Okay... That's not alarming...'

'What?' Moni interrupted. 'What do you mean? 20% of the lot is defective! Isn't that enough?'

'20%? Oh yes! 20%. Hmm. But you know that hardly matters when we get Monte Carlo and Benetton without tags ... if you ever try to get them through designated ways with tags and all, they would cost you a fortune, my dear ... So, we have taken the cheaper way out as we always do to rein in the cost in this sluggish economy... And so, we overlook minor glitches, by keeping things in broader perspective, you know ... do one thing, sell them in-house,' Bhatia huffed and puffed after talking at a stretch.

'What's that? In-house selling?' Moni asked naively.

'Simple! Just give them away to forty of your most enterprising personnel, preferably on an auspicious day, like on the eve of some kind of festival ... like ... let me think... yes! On the eve of the Christmas! And ... you know ... you've got ways to get back the money spent on them by taking some financially stringent options on the salary day afterwards, on any month in the same calendar year. Got it?' Bhatia jabbered like a kind of boast.

Moni felt a hot lead entering her head through her temple.

'Sir... I have a query...' Moni asked trying to be sane.

'Yes... Dear...' Bhatia was overly zealous.

'Why can't we ask the importer to do the same thing for us?' Moni asked.

Bhatia probably never expected a query like that. So he kept silent for a while and then coughed twice and finally cut off with a perfunctory 'Let's see'.

26

'You look distressed,' that was the first thing Dr. Ramani said, on seeing Ved enter her room in the late hours. It was four and the university was becoming depopulated. Corridors were getting empty. Canteens were being deserted. Classrooms were being closed for the day. Students could be heard running down the stairs with their happy feet, making brisk sounds—all going home.

'Yes I'm ...' Ved replied and sat down.

'Is your daughter all right?'

'Yes, she is ...' Ved said and tried to smile.

But he realised he could not smile the way he wanted. He was tired. He was sleepy.

'Are you in love?' Dr. Ramani asked suddenly. Her eyes were fixed on Ved's. There was a glimpse of a smile on her lips.

Ved smiled. He just smiled though he wanted to tell a lot of things. He realised that his mind was in a disarray and he needed a kind of self appraisal. So he got up, blithely.

'Sorry for the leave, something unforeseen came up and I had to take a day off... Mark the leave as C.L,' Ved said as he started walking to the door.

'Going home?' Dr. Ramani asked.

'Yes I'll ... but before that I'll go to my room... need to collect some books...' Ved answered.

Reaching the end of the corridor, Ved pressed the latch downwards of the brown door with dusty façade and rusty nails and knobs. Entering the room, he felt comfortable, away from the emptiness of the corridor and Dr. Ramani's piercing questioning eyes. He let his eyes roam freely in the nooks and corners of his room. The tiny room was filled with books. There were wooden racks on the wall with books. Books were there on his table and there was the small cupboard at one corner with books and papers. Amidst books, Ved was soothed. He felt a kind of insularity from the world. He felt good realising there was no one to intrude on his solitude or thoughts.

He walked to his table and patted on the chair softly to dust it off. Then he sat down and threw his head backwards, facing the white ceiling. The ceiling was blank, empty. He felt restless, got up and walked to his favourite spot, the window. Through it, he saw the familiar trees of the campus, three eucalyptus trees standing side by side. Their leaves rustled in a breeze coming from an unknown source. Ved felt restless still. He looked at the fragmented sky of the city—blue and bright as it should be in winter. He recalled suddenly the voice over of the *Nat Geo special*. He recalled the snaps of the river dolphins and the man pulling an animal over a river hanging precariously from a rope with his struggling and pained face. He imagined himself to be that photographer travelling all the way to Amazon to capture the river dolphins on film or the man fighting against all odds in one unknown corner of China.

Hey! I can do it even here! Ved thought. Surely I can! Objects of photography are everywhere ... one only needs a pair of good eyes.

Ved remembered Anu's face at the Flury's. He could exactly recall how Anu stood at the river step with the rays of the new born sun sweeping the whole world. He remembered Moni and Sonai sitting in the corridor of the police headquarters on a long wooden bench. He remembered how Sonai dozed off on Moni's lap and how Moni ran her fingers through Sonai's hair.

Suddenly Ved was reminded of the fact that Moni was supposed to collect Sonai from her school. Has Moni reached the school? Ved thought as he looked at his watch. It was four fifteen. Ved pressed the keys of his cell.

'The subscriber you are calling is currently on another call. Please stay on line or call later,' a recorded voice declared.

Ved redialled after ten minutes and received the same response. He brought out a cigarette. The winter afternoon was dying fast. Soon, the evening would descend and the street lights would be switched on. Even if Moni reached the school now, she should be bringing Sonai here by five. Ved thought and taking a puff or two from the cigarette turned it off on the ashtray and stretched his legs and yawned. *I haven't slept for years.* Ved thought and closed his eyes, resting his head on the chair's back.

'Are you sure Monideepa Aunty will come here to take you home?' Devakshi asked Sonai.

All the children had gone home. Devakshi's grandpa would come soon.

'*Dada* is always late...' Devakshi grumbled.

'But that has given you an opportunity to stay with me after school hours... Isn't it?' Sonai asked.

Devakshi nodded her head.

Has Moni forgotten me? Sonai thought and felt really helpless.

'Don't worry dear ... she'll come for sure,' Devakshi said in a consolatory tone.

Sonai felt terrible. She did not feel like talking. They were sitting on the steps under the portico of the main building of the school from where anyone can see the front gate which was closed. Only a turnstile was kept open. Presently, an old man dressed in a white shirt and brown pair of trousers was seen entering through it.

'Grandpa! I'm here.' Devakshi called out.

'Sorry for being late again,' the old man grinned, and revealing toothless gums, brought out a bar of chocolate, dangling it suggestively with frail fingers.

Devakshi grabbed the bar and giggled.

'Is this your friend?' Devakshi's grandpa asked, looking at Sonai.

'Yeah! Her aunt is yet to turn up,' Devakshi explained.

'Is it so? Can I help you in anyway?' Grandpa asked.

Sonai looked up. Grandpa's smile had crow's feet. Age had spread its tentacles all over his face and body. His shirt did not conceal his aging either. But, his eyes still rocked gently with humour. Sonai had earlier noticed this strange quality of humour in the eyes of old people.

Both grandpa and Devakshi were looking at her. Devakshi's eyes were eager.

'No, there's no need for you to be troubled... Aunt would come soon...' Sonai said and even smiled to dissuade Devakshi and her grandpa from being overtly anxious.

'Are you sure?' Devakshi asked.

'Yeah! I'm fine. I'll wait here ... now you go home... I'll call you after reaching mine,' Sonai said.

'Okay then... Take the chocolate,' Devakshi smiled and handed Sanhita over the bar of chocolate in a red wrapping.

'Thank ya...' Sonai replied.

Devakshi waved her hand and started to walk towards the turnstile, holding on to her grandpa's hand.

Sonai looked at them. She watched the duo walking out of the gate merrily chatting. Sonai could hear their indistinct words. She sighed and looked around. The trees in the courtyard looked like sombre shadows. Sonai looked at the mosaic patterns on the steps and at her new tunic and satchel. She was immediately reminded of Moni.

What the hell was she doing? Sonai thought and felt angst rising. She looked at the empty car park and deserted courtyard with ghostly trees spreading dreadful shadows.

'Hello! Sanhita! Dad hasn't come yet dear?' Someone asked from behind. Sonai looked back and saw the teacher in charge of their class standing right behind her on the steps. Sonai looked at Miss Sehgal's oval face with golden-rimmed glasses. Miss Sehgal's eyes carried a worried look.

'Actually ma'am, my aunt is supposed to take me home today...' Sonai murmured as she stood up and dusted her back.

'You know her number?' Miss Sehgal asked.

'No ... not really.'

'Okay ... call your dad then. He's in the city ... isn't he?'

'Yes ... but.'

'What? Don't know your dad's number?'

'No ... I mean... yes ... I know his number ... But ma'am as you know, my aunt is supposed to come to take me home ... so...'

'Maybe she's busy ... Maybe she has got into some kind of unavoidable situation ... Come with me to the office...' Miss Sehgal took hold of Sonai's right arm and pulled her to the office.

Ved almost jerked into wakefulness, hearing his cell ringing and vibrating in his shirt pocket. He started almost and reached for his cell. A call came through from an unknown number. The room had become almost dark. Only a faint ray of light was coming through the window. Ved pressed the green button.

'Hello!'

'Hello! I'm Neha Sehgal, the teacher in charge of Sanhita Bhattacharya's class ... Am I talking to Mr. Bhattacharya?' A female voice asked.

'Yes! Of course! I'm Sanhita's dad!' Ved answered promptly.

'Well, Mr. Bhattacharya ... Your daughter is still at school as no one has turned up yet to take her home. Will you, Sir?' the female voice was terse.

'Yeah! Of course! I'll be reaching the school ... Well ... Within half an hour, max!' Ved blurted out quickly.

My goodness! It's five thirty ... my God! I'll have to run ...' Ved switched on the light and picked up the *Bhagwad Gita* from the table and the door keys from the drawer and ran towards the elevator.

Reaching the car, he jumped to the seat, clipped the seat belt and ignited the engine. Within a minute, he was out of the university and racing down the road. The cars running in front of him, appeared too slow. Ved thought of a computer game called 'Road rash' and stepped on the accelerator as his left hand shifted the gear shaft too quickly.

Reaching the gate of the school, Ved looked at his watch. It was five minutes to six. He had made it within twenty-five minutes. He parked the car beside the footpath and jumped out.

The ground floor office door was ajar and a white streak of light was coming out of the room, falling on the shiny tiles of the corridor.

Ved hastily walked towards the door. He saw Sonai sitting on a red couch. Her head was down. Beside her, Ved could see her water bottle and satchel.

'I'm so sorry!' Ved flashed an uneasy, embarrassed smile at Sonai and then at the woman with oval face and golden glasses.

'Your dad has come dear!' the woman, presumably the teacher, called aloud which prompted Sonai to stand up.

Ved looked at Sonai's eyes. They were red.

'Hey! Were you crying? Diana!' Ved tried to put up a cheerful face.

Sonai said nothing. She just picked up her satchel and water bottle and turned to the teacher saying: 'Thank you ma'am.'

The teacher smiled.

As they came out of the gate, Ved opened the left side front door of the car. Sonai walked into the car. Switching the engine on, Ved stooped towards Sonai and plugged her seat belt to its designated slot.

'Am I guilty anyway? Diana?' Ved asked trying hard to remove the dark cloud of despondency from his daughter's face.

'I'm no Diana and you're no 47!' Sonai uttered each word distinctly, solemnly.

Ved looked at his daughter's grave face for a while and looked out of the windshield for a next few moments before steering the vehicle.

27

'Mr. Bhatia, as I can understand I'm not in any kind of quality control, and in no position to suggest remedial measures concerning quality ... All I can say is that, I find it quite untenable to compete with stuff like that in an increasingly quality conscious set up,' Moni talked straight and felt good that finally she talked straight without being too bothered by the outcome.

Now that she had talked straight, she felt she had let go of a bit of venom that had been storing up within her from day one on the job.

There was, however, no immediate response from the other end. Bhatia might be processing her words hard.

'Okay Miss Banerjee! I think I've listened to you more often than I should. I can appreciate the way one can disguise one's incompetence in a jugglery of words.' Bhatia was stern.

'But sir, I was talking about a wrong perception of the paradigm,' Moni said a bit analytically but she was rebuffed, a bit insolently, by Bhatia.

'Yes! That's the point! We are actually trying to minimize the cost, especially in a market which is not bullish at present...

but I think I have no real need to hear from you about marketing strategies. We have enough people on our payroll quite outstanding marketing grey cells, working round-the-clock, to take care of all that... However, it seems, you want to project yourself in an excellent position which is good, and I have a suggestion: why don't you join some institution as a management guru?' Bhatia said with sarcasm, no doubt.

Moni felt miserable. But she tried to soothe her troubles, thinking it would be wrong on her part to stand in front of the canon and to ask for the firing. So she said nothing. She only hoped that her silence might have an effect on Bhatia. Bhatia was also exhausted by the quick exchange of words. He slammed the phone.

Moni felt definitely thirsty. She opened the water dispenser, filled a bottle to the brim and drank water, emptying the bottle down her throat. After that, she felt she had extinguished her rage.

Now what? What will I do to sustain myself? Moni thought and walked up to the window. Monte Carlo, across the street was full of neon lights. A bunch of youngsters, presumably, college students, were coming out of the store.

My God! Sonai! She's at school! Moni rushed to the table and dialled Ved's number.

'Hello! Moni here ... I'm so sorry ... Sonai? Has she come home?' Moni stammered.

'It is okay ... She's all right ... I've brought her home...' Ved replied in a tone which held no apparent sign of displeasure.

'Is it? That's good! I was actually caught in a meeting and there was a bit of tension in the meeting. And I forgot ... I'm so sorry and ashamed ...' Moni continued stammering.

'It is okay… I assure you… Sonai is fine … want to talk with her?' Ved asked.

'Yes! Please?'

Moni felt from the sounds that reached her through the line that the phone was handed over to someone. But that 'someone' was not responding, she was just holding it.

'Hello! Sonai? I'm so sorry dear!' Moni felt like crying.

There was no response.

'Hello Sonai! Talk to me dear! Please!' Moni implored.

Hearing nothing from the other end, Moni got terribly upset. The intimidation from Bhatia, the growing sense of distaste about the job, the creeping loneliness, Anu's improper and erratic disposition—all had already taken a heavy toll on her and she felt shaken by Sonai's non-responsive attitude. She broke into tears and sobbing all the way she just murmured, 'Sonai dear, you never know what I've gone through today… please dear don't do it to me… Don't end it like that… I don't know how you've taken it, but I can say that staying with you for a day or two had given me back a lot of things… Reminded me of my own childhood… And I'm sorry if I've hurt you, but I've done nothing deliberately… Forgive me dear…' Moni sobbed and stopped talking. She could not hold her tears back. They were just coming out of her eyes and she knew no way to put a plug to her leaking eyes.

'I'm all right…' Sonai said and added:

'I've no regrets as I got you… Do you hear me?'

Moni could not speak. She just smiled and wiped her face.

'Hey Moni! Are you not there?' Sonai asked.

'Yes dear…' Moni feebly answered.

'I miss you…' Sonai said.

'Me too…' Moni replied.

'I'll call you later. Dad is calling me… Need to eat.'

Sonai said.

'Okay… Have a good night's rest … You're tired,' Moni said.

'I'll… You ought to do the same… Bye bye'

Sonai cut the line off.

It was late in the evening when Moni came out of her office and gave necessary instructions to Kevin before she started walking down the footpath. There was a chill in the air. A light breeze was blowing. Moni wrapped her ears with her dupatta and waited for the auto at the stand. There was no auto. Moni waited. The mist mixed with the smoke coming out incessantly from the passing vehicles had created a kind of smog. The smog was not heavy but it would become denser for sure, with the descent of the night. The headlights of vehicles looked a bit smudged in the smog as if someone had been using the water paint brush over the whole scene. Moni looked around. No one was there at the stand. Are the autorickshaws observing a bandh today? Bandhs are like malignant diseases in this part of the country. They spread fast, catching you unawares.

Just then, like a god sent chariot, piercing the smog came an auto rickshaw with its yellow round headlamp jerking like that of a one-eyed monster. *Cyclops*… Moni thought and she waved her hand customarily. The auto stopped right in front of her. There was a single male occupant at the rear seat and the driver was there as usual holding onto the scooter like handle bar of the vehicle, peeping his head out, with questioning eyes. There was music too blaring loudly. FM radios are now part of the auto journey. You can never miss them. They are there always to entertain you even if you don't like to be entertained. Moni hopped into the rear seat. The male co-passenger moved a bit. From the corner of her eyes, Moni cast a sly look. The man looked shabby with a brown dusty bag on his lap. His eyes were cloudy a bit. Sitting in an auto back seat with a haggard looking man in a smoggy evening is the worst case scenario. The auto driver changed gears and the clumsy vehicle started to rumble forth. *Cyclops is in pain... Maybe he's aging.* Moni thought and smiled. A mild breeze blew into the rickshaw and it brought the unmistakable smell of country liquor from the co passenger to Moni's nose. My idea of the worst case scenario is going to be worsened further... Now you'll have to bear the arid and putrid smell of country liquor at the end of the crappiest day... Moni thought as she brought out her hanky and wiped her nose.

Just then a song started playing in the FM radio. The music that was the prelude of the song was curious, as if someone was playing a flute which was accompanied by a regular rhythm in some kind of electronic music synthesiser. Moni tried to listen to the song primarily to distract her mind from her physical surrounding which was causing her irritation. Moni listened intently:

'ise uljhi nazaro se hatti nahin,
daante se reshhmi dor katti nahin,'
(can't move my stare from those anxious eyes... can't tear silk ribbon by teeth even...)

Moni felt overpowered by the song, the lyrics and its music. She felt as if the song was for her, it was made for her, it was made to be sung by her and she sang along the song slowly, whisperingly. The more she sang, the more she felt she was the lovesick singer expressing her doubts and suspicions about love, about her helplessness at her growing sense of aging and yet her undiluted urge within to find someone to fall in love with and her fears of sleeping every night alone.

'Bardhaman Road ma'am?' The driver turned back with quizzical looks.

'Oh yes!' Moni smiled sheepishly.

She was embarrassed by her absentmindedness.

'Thank you,' Moni said to the driver of the auto.

The driver grinned, revealing betel-red dentures, though his smile carried a sense of bewilderment. The drunk co-passenger nodded and also showed his unclean teeth. Moni looked at the man and at once saw his long filthy fingers. Moni shuddered with a kind of sense of horror returning back to her with terrible rapidity. She knew why she always hated long filthy fingers of men. They simply pushed her back to an inglorious past. So she turned her look quickly from the man's fingers to the auto driver's face, which was full of curiosity.

'*Kiun*... Why ma'am?' The driver asked, quite innocently.

'For the song...' Moni said as she hopped down and paid the fare before moving to their apartment.

She was still humming the tune when she rang the bell. Anu opened the door. She looked fresh. Her hair was neatly tied in a bun and she was wearing a red kurti and a pair of white leggings.

'Don't rebuke me please!' Anu shouted the moment she saw Moni and hugged her.

Moni stood there at the door. Even before ringing the bell, Moni had thought for a while about how she should behave with Anu after her homecoming. She had thought that she would put up a cold face to Anu and would talk less with her and also thought about even creating a sort of wall between her and Anu. But seeing Anu after so many hours and that too in a neat and tidy condition, she felt happy. In fact, she was so happy to see Anu again that tears rolled down her cheeks. So she stood there at the threshold, with tears rolling down her cheeks and Anu embraced her whispering a million times,'I'm sorry for everything… I beg a hundred pardons… Forgive me please… Forgive me dear…'

Anu also cried, putting her head on Moni's shoulder.

Moni pulled Anu into the flat and closed the door and took her gently to the couch.

Anu was still clutching onto her. Had it been any other day, Moni would have just thrown Anu on the couch and gone to her bedroom to change her dress. But she was herself overcome with a strange kind of happiness mixed with melancholy. She was definitely feeling happy to find Anu by her side after almost two days. Now that Anu was right beside her, she felt relieved of all anxieties and yet she was sad within because the way Anu embraced her reminded her of Sonai and Sonai's absence seemed to arouse a little pain in her heart. Yesterday, she had spent the night with the girl who had been by her side this morning also. *'I've no regrets as I've got you…'* The girl's words rang in Moni's ears and her eyes moistened again.

Anu who had been all along cajoling and crying and seeking pardon was surprised to see Moni sitting there beside her with her eyes fixed somewhere on the ceiling. Anu had expected Moni would rebuke her and she was even anticipating an outburst of ill temper from her. In fact, Anu's self-castigating heart would have found a balm if Moni gave her a slap or two on the face. But the way Moni just sat there with a disoriented look, bothered Anu.

'Are you okay?' Anu asked worried.

'Yes… I'm,' Moni muttered looking at Anu and smiling weakly.

'I know how have I troubled you and put you into severe stress… Almost inhumanly, a bit too selfishly… But here I am, you see? Hale and hearty as ever…' Anu kept on talking.

'No it's okay…. I mean … everyone has the right to go … and come back … and probably to go away again,' Moni uttered, philosophically.

'Yes! You know not, what experiences I have had in the last fifty or sixty hours … I feel my mind is now genuinely enriched by those experiences … I learnt that life is good… It is just a matter of your mind to understand things and interpret them… Tell me, how do you feel if you find yourself somewhere and then rediscover yourself?' Anu asked in a voice that was hitherto unknown to Moni.

'Finding oneself?' Moni asked, dreamily.

'Yes! But that's a long story… I'll love to tell you all… What about running a talk-shop after dinner? Are you willing to hear all that? Really?' Anu asked with a lot of enthusiasm.

But soon, she realised that Moni had not even changed and freshened up after coming home and felt bad about her over-enthusiasm.

'No no… Get up dear… I shouldn't be holding you up… Get changed… I'm switching on the geyser…' saying this Anu almost ran towards the bathroom.

Moni stood up and walked across to her bedroom.

28

'That's not done, Sonai!' Ved said finally.

All the way from school to home, Sonai had barely talked. Reaching home even, she remained largely quiet. Even when Biswanath took her in his arms and kissed her and Debjani gave her a bag of goodies, she did not show any outward emotion. She just kept quiet, as if all of a sudden she had become dumb. This took everyone by surprise. Though Biswanath and Debjani said nothing, their enquiring looks were not missed by Ved, as if Ved was somehow guilty behind this sudden change of behaviour of their granddaughter.

'She's just a kid, mother, and you people need not be so worried about her every movement…' Ved said while having dinner with his parents.

Sonai had gone upstairs as she expressed her wish to retire early. Sonai had not even eaten much which made Debjani grumble a bit. Biswanath munched busily. He said nothing. Debjani looked at her husband and then turned to Ved and asked: 'Where you have been? To that woman's house who works at a mall?'

Ved was taken aback. He looked at his mother. Debjani stared back with enquiring eyes. Biswanath stopped munching, his eyes on his bowl of soup and vegetables, observed with a kind of sternness: 'I find it good that you have finally decided to move on with your life. But I don't think it is a very good idea to take all your decisions of life by yourself, especially when we are here still … and whoever you choose, we'll be happy to accept but she should also try to know us, our surroundings, our house.'

'What do you mean?' Ved asked, bewildered.

'Your father met that woman at the shopping mall where he once went with Sonai, and felt that you knew each other for quite some time. But, what pains us is the fact that as we have never really objected to any of your decisions, why are you doing this hide-n-seek with us?' Debjani asked.

Ved laughed. 'O Moni! She's… Well… Just a friend… And I don't think we will be seeing each other for months… Nothing has happened so far… And if really anything crops up, I will be the first person to inform you of that… Rest assured!' Ved said and stood up.

Both Debjani and Biswanath looked at Ved for a while before restoring their concentration on the dinner.

Ved climbed the stairs and when he reached Sonai's bed room door, he found it ajar and peeped in. Sonai was lying on the bed upside down wearing her Mickey mouse night dress and busy scribbling something on a piece of paper. She was so engrossed in her work, that she hardly noticed her dad entering the room. Ved tiptoed towards the bed. Sonai was definitely writing something. Ved inched forward and narrowed his eyes to get a clearer picture. What was she writing, so busily?

Ved, being stupidly curious, moved a few paces more towards the bed till his thighs touched the side wooden beams of the cot.

Goodness me! It looks like a poem!

Ved looked at the short line written one after another, in a vertical, column like structure.

It had a title as well!

Ved let his unabashed curiosity take over. 'I miss you…' it read. He continued reading:

I miss you,
Like the dry earth misses the rain,
I miss you,
Like moving meadows through the train,
I miss you,
Day in and day out,
I miss you…

Ved became so excited that he cheered on impromptu:

'Hey Diana! Good work!'

Sonai at once, turned and crumpled the paper into a roll instantly in her left palm. Her face showed embarrassment and surprise. Her lips quivered and she shouted out loud: 'Look! It's not fair to peep into someone's personal things…'

'But dear … You're not writing a diary entry … I suppose … I've read a little and it seems you're writing a poem! That surprises me really!' Ved gushed.

'Nnna … I can't let you see it!' Sonai shouted and tightened her grip further over the paper.

'Okay! Okay! Cool off! I'm not going to read it … if you're that unwilling … but please dear, don't crumple it that way …

It's your first poem, don't malign it!' Ved pleaded with all his tenderness.

'I'm not going to malign it. I'll keep it somewhere and, for your info, it is not my first poem! I wrote my first one only yesterday though, at Moni's place, on her computer. And even submitted it,' Sonai replied calmly.

'Really? Where have you submitted it?' Ved asked, bemused.

'Well ... it just happened at Moni's place ... I submitted it to the teacher in charge today at the school for the school mag,' Sonai informed bluntly as she kept on looking at her left palm, stealthily, which held her crumpled poem.

'Really? That's great! Awesome! But were you not supposed to submit a painting?' Ved asked.

'Yes! I was ... But I didn't have the painting with me at Moni's place and so when Moni asked me to write something for the magazine, I wrote the poem ... Pressing the keys of Moni's computer ... Sitting on her dining table while she worked at the kitchen and from there dictated to me and helped me to write a few lines...' Sonai said in a dreamy tone as she recollected the process of writing her first poem.

Ved thought he was staring down at a different Sonai, an unknown one with an unknown voice.

'Splendid! Most wondrous thing I've ever heard! I'm so proud of you girlie!' Ved exclaimed and planted a kiss on his daughter's forehead.

'I have told you earlier today I had written a poem and that I was going to submit it ... Remember?' Sonai asked.

'Really? Oh yes! I remember! I had called Moni in the morning to ask whether you had gone out for school and then you probably said something about your poem … Sorry, if I've become too much forgetful dear! By the way, who brought you the new tunic and satchel? Moni?' Ved asked.

'Yeah! She's the boss of her store, you know… She just called someone and placed the order over phone, and bingo! They were delivered right at her doorstep! Amazing, isn't it?' Sonai asked.

'Yes… Of course!' Ved replied, absentmindedly.

Sonai jumped down from the bed and went to the cupboard and opening it, kept the piece of paper and came back to the bed again.

'You haven't really noticed where exactly I've kept that poem, have you?' Sonai was mock serious.

'Of course not! Can I ever get an opportunity to see your first poem?' Ved asked cautiously.

'Let's see … I've got no copy … You might read it on print if they publish it in our school magazine … Otherwise … You can ask for a copy from Moni … I hope she has not deleted it from her computer … Now tell me, are you not going to sleep tonight?' Sonai asked as she dusted the pillow by her hand, sort of stroking it rapidly.

'Yes, I will … But will you not listen to the bedtime story?' Ved asked.

'That story of the prince and the princess dying together?' Sonai asked, though she did not look at Ved. She just ran her fingers on the stitch patterns woven on the bedsheet. Ved looked at the movement of Sonai's fingers on the stitch work.

'I understand fully your dislike towards the story … It was boring, meaningless and full of sadness … Wasn't it?' Ved asked.

'Yes … it was … and …' Sonai stopped suddenly.

'And what?' Ved asked.

'And it strangely reminded me of my mom and you…' Sonai answered haltingly.

'Really? Okay! Tonight I'm going to tell you the story of a film… a beautiful film called Mr. Destiny… I saw it many many years ago and I've forgotten the nuances but I think I have in my mind the basic storyline.'

Ved readied himself for the storytelling session. He knew what he was going to tell but was not sure of its effect. Either Sonai would accept the story or she would reject it outright. Whatever the outcome, I need to tell her the story. Ved thought and he looked at Sonai. There was eagerness no doubt, in her eyes.

'You know Michael Caine? Don't you?' Ved asked.

'Yes! I know … He played the role of Bruce Wayne's mentor-cum-butler in the film Batman,' Sonai said.

'Right! Now this Michael Caine is a strange man gifted with the supernatural, almost divine power to alter and fiddle with people's destinies, though very few people knew that. Now, this James Belushi … You know James Belushi?' Ved asked.

'Yeah! Of course! I know him … He was probably in Red October along with Arnold … Now get on with the story…' Sonai replied impatiently.

'Did he really act in Red October? Maybe. Anyway, this Belushi worked under a stinking rich man with obscene amounts of wealth and fortune, and always aspired to be the rich man himself, sort of replacing him, to own his cars, his gorgeous wife and the palatial mansion … Now, what happened, one night, while he was driving home, Belushi's old car broke down in front of a pub in a lonely street … James went into the pub with the object of making a call to a car breakdown service … The pub was empty, and poorly lit.

Suddenly, James found Michael Caine standing outside the parlour with a neat black suit and a bow … He smiled at James and beckoned him to the parlour. James went and Michael Caine gave him the telephone, so that he could call the break down service. James called the service and waited for the van to come to the parlour … And to while the time away, James and Michael broke into a conversation … Michael told James that he was Mr. Destiny and could change people's fates … James did not believe him, quite naturally … Then Michael, etched two luminescent drops in air and with the mere movement of his fingers made them to spin in the air, like two magically suspended marbles … The drops whirled for a while before coming to a stop.

Michael then told James that his destiny had been altered … He had now become what he aspired to … James shook his head in disbelief and went out … But soon, his doubts were cleared as he found himself impersonating his rich employer in every sense … He went to his employer's house where, quite surprisingly, he found himself in the family photograph, standing beside his employer's wife and children … Even the employer's wife came towards him and kissed him and took his arms as if he was her husband … James was puzzled and at the same time he savoured the happiness of being the man he wanted to become. James then wanted to go to his own house to meet his own family members … But going there, he found that no one recognised him…. He felt sad and purposeless and then he wanted to return to his own life …

To get back his family members … Though, he had all the wealth and fortune in the world and a stunningly beautiful woman as his wife … He wanted to get back his old life, with its incongruities, dilemmas and suffering. So he went back to Michael and asked him fervently to bring him back to his old life, to his family, to his simple house with a small lawn upfront and Michael smiled and spun the luminescent drops reverse… And…'

Ved stopped to gather breath.

'James became his true self again!' Sonai completed the sentence.

Ved was feeling thirsty after narrating the story.

He went up to get the bottle of water.

When he came back, he found Sonai lying on the bed with her head resting on the pillow.

But she was wide awake.

'So? Sonai? What is the moral of the story?' Ved asked.

'To be what you really deserve…' Sonai replied instantaneously.

'Yes! And never to dream about impersonating another…' Ved added.

'Are you still thinking about my little prank of impersonating you on the internet?' Sonai asked suddenly.

'No! Not at all!' Ved shook his head. 'The story, probably, tells us not to dream of easy success by falsehood or shortcut magic …. And more importantly, to be with one's family,' Ved added as an afterthought.

'Yes… And I wish I had met Mr. Destiny,' Sonai said with a yawn.

'What would you've wished for then?' Ved asked.

'That's a secret! Anyway, it was a real good story… I loved it…' Sonai said, as she turned to Ved who was sitting cross-legged on the cot and placed her left arm on Ved's leg.

'Goodnight Sweetie,' Ved said as he kissed Sonai on her forehead for the second time that night.

Ved waited at the bed till Sonai fell asleep. Then he put a cover on his sleeping child and walked away slowly to his room, closing the door behind.

Ved came to his room, switched on the light and went to his reading table to get hold of the *Gita*.

He knew he needed to read the book to calm his mind and put to rest all doubts and anxieties. Tonight had been strikingly different. Sonai gave him two definite answers. First, she told him that the story of the prince and the princess reminded her of her mother and dad and secondly she had said in unambiguous terms that she no longer enjoyed her role of playing 'the Diana' or for that matter, the role of Ved as 'agent 47'. Those two remarks carried deep import for him.

Sonai was trying to get rid of the make believe world in which she had been living so far. Ved thought. She is growing up fast and spreading her mind to understand the world around her… she was beginning to explore the world and the people in her own ways… Probably the encounter with Moni has caused this change of attitude… Sonai was going out of the online world to understand the offline world or it may be the other way round…

Ved thought further and he suddenly realised a strange thing… *If online world means the virtual world of the mind, then Sonai is going out of the offline or the real world to understand the online world or the mental space... Online-offline... The mental space and the real and physical one...*

Ved continued thinking as he opened the *Gita*. He opened chapter three of the book and read what Lord Krishna told Arjuna:

> *The senses are said to be greater than the body; but greater than the senses is the mind...*

Ved closed his eyes and plunged into thoughts, a singular idea concerning the real and the unreal, the mental and the physical, the online and the offline. He thought deeply, taking his mind even deeper every moment so that he could unleash his true mind into its truest form, without inhibitions, without constraints.

Online world or the so called virtual world of the mind is of more import than the offline world...but we need both to live... To sustain ourselves and to enrich ourselves... These two worlds never collide... they just collate... They gather perceptions and combine to make our lives even more beautiful... They work in unison... And yet they are separated by their own characteristics...

Sonai had the idea of mother imprinted in her mind and now she was searching for someone to fit the bill... Like I was searching for an idea of happiness, pasted in my mind... Like Anu is searching for her route to self discovery... Like Moni was scribbling lines on her blog page to fit the bill... We're all doing the same. Ved thought.

We are all constantly moving online to offline and vice versa... We are all experiencing the two worlds simultaneously, though we rarely think about the holy interaction of the two worlds... And even if we do, we do it in our lugubrious fashion which actually mars the positivism of life… We fail to understand that life has a duality—the 'online—offline duality'… The duality of living physical and psychological… Living in dreams and non dreams…

29

Moni looked at Anu and smiled. Anu was snoring, lying on Moni's bed, the pillow under her arms. Only a few minutes ago, Anu was jabbering in her own hyperactive way about her night of adventure in a wasteland. She had told her how she had bought a bottle of cheap whiskey from a roadside shanty and how she drank the bottle empty, sitting in a marshy place and how she dozed off and had the prolific 'dream in a dream,' in which she first walked through a forest and then near a dreamy stream met her own self, sitting like an angel who asked her to drink water from the stream and drinking water from the stream, she had realised she had drunk a kind of potion that made her even more sleepy and by that time, the angel-like-self just vanished into the stream. Then Anu told Moni how she and Professor VPB had gone to the river early in the morning to witness the sunrise, and how Anu had then noticed the gradual transformation of the sun from a dim yellow egg into a big and dazzling ball of fire.

Anu had enjoyed a day's worth roaming in her own way… Moni thought and she also felt an urge to go out one day, aimlessly, much like Anu. But she would do it not out of any false idea or belief. She would not go out thinking wrongly about herself or about anyone. She would do it as one would, bask in the happiness of being close to nature.

'Anu is just a child,' Moni thought, 'an impetuous one... with certain aberration in character caused by her oppressive home environment ... now that she has found energy and a goal to live for, she will happily cruise towards it.'

Moni looked at Anu's face and body spread awkwardly on her bed and smiled.

Then, she opened her computer. There was the word document on her screen prepared by Sonai. Without even opening the document, she could recollect what was written.

'I got you/As you got me...' were words the poem began with. She remembered the way little Sonai wrote those beautiful lines, with eyes fixed on the screen and brows twisted. Sonai's face glowing by the screen's bluish light, would forever be pasted in her mind. How could she forget the way Sonai read out those lines after writing them? How could she forget the night spent together with Sonai sleeping on her bed, exactly in the place now occupied by Anu? How could she forget the little girl's smiles and tears? How could she forget her embrace, so soft and so childlike?

Am I getting too attached to Sonai? Or is it just a mere part of my growing attachment with Ved? Or is it the case that I am actually falling in love with both of them? Am I getting too soft, seeing a widower and motherless child? Am I trying to fit myself into the position of someone's wife and another's mother?

Moni asked herself and she found no distinct answer, other than that she was genuinely in love with Sonai, a kind of motherly love. Prof. Ved had remained so far partially discovered to her, but one thing she had understood for sure; Ved possessed a beautiful mind—a mind full of duty and kindness. Anu had made a strange remark about Ved.

'He's a real man who knows where to stop and how to be in control of oneself.' Anu had said earlier while jabbering about her experience of going out with Ved. When Moni pressed her hard to explain her statement, she just smiled mysteriously. *What could that statement have meant? Had Anu in anyway, tried to get physical with her Prof.?* Given Anu's record, that could not possibly be ruled out. Hey! Why am I thinking all these? Am I suffering from any kind of jealousy? Do I really want to be alone with Ved and experiment a little bit to find how much control actually the man has over his baser instincts?

Moni thought and she was reminded of her dream in which she saw Ved playing a saxophone and then riding a horse. Both activities are very filmy. Moni smiled as she thought of her own inane, idiotic dream. Reclining on the head rest of the bed, putting a pillow at her back, Moni opened a blank word page and thought about writing something. What to write? What about writing a poem about a horse and a man?

Moni looked at Anu, snoring heavily now. *What about writing a story... About someone like Anu... Or about Anu and Ved... Or about Anu, Ved, Sonai and me?*

Hey! That would be great! Writing how we are getting slowly attached with each other, through the incidents... Through our tears of happiness and sorrow... Through the internet and even without it...

Moni kept on looking at the blank page. She felt a kind of energy building up within as if it would soon gush forth with all its intensity. Moni felt a shiver. She put her legs into the cover that was spread over Anu and placed the laptop on her legs and started typing.

After typing a few lines, she felt she should not write directly on the computer. She felt that Anu might see her work and create a hullabaloo. So, she deleted whatever she had written and took up a pen and paper.

She thought that she would first write a broad framework into which she would gradually add materials to enrich and modify it to a novel. But after writing a few lines, she felt helpless and thought of retiring to bed.

But the pen was still in her hand and she had the white writing pad waiting to be filled in with her words. Twice, she moved the pen over the white page without making any mark. Suddenly, she started scribbling:

I looked at her face,
And her piteous eyes,
Telling tales unsavory…

'Are you good?
Are you fine?'
I asked,
Trying to put my exorbitant self
Into her;

But…
Her piteous eyes said stories
—unheard, unknown, untold;

And she went away
Never looked back,
Leaving me stranded
With my expensive soul.

Moni's pen stopped. She looked at the lines and read them slowly and a deep sense of self-pity filled her mind. She thought of Sonai. She imagined her sleeping in her father's arms.

Moni also realised that novel writing was not actually her forte. She thought she would write poems only, because poems carried the strongest emotions while prose, even if they were emotionally charged, could never be like a poem. Then at once, she thought she was oversimplifying things. It could have been that her words held no prose quality. It might have been the case that she lacked the sense of reasoning or logical mind to concoct a story with a strong plot. She finally decided that she would mix prose with poetry. She would write a poem in prose to encompass the secrets of life and joy. She thought she would write a long poem someday about the basics of life, about human relationships, about her mind and the minds of others, about space and time and about timelessness.

30

'Have you seen *Cocktail*?' Anu asked the first thing in the morning, sipping a cup of tea on the living room couch. Moni had come out of the bathroom and was rinsing her wet hair with a towel.

Last night was a terrible one with divergent thoughts playing in her mind. She had felt an emotional rise and fall last night—from the peak of elation to the nadir of hopelessness and dejection. She thought about Anu, Sonai, Ved and herself. She even thought about plotting a story, though she ended up writing a few lines on Sonai instead. She pondered about the same sense of recklessness working in tandem with Anu and Sonai. She also thought about her own occupational status at the Blitz, about Bhatia and his sugar-coated bitter intimidation. All these thoughts made her weary. Finally, when she retired for the night, with Anu playing a nasal musical just beside her, she felt a kind of belonging. She felt Anu's presence by her last night was necessary, for that provided her with a sense of belonging which made her sleep the rest of the night peacefully.

So, coming out of the bathroom, when Moni heard that strange query from Anu, she was not at all displeased. She smiled, looking at Anu.

'Hey! Have I asked you something too difficult to answer, for instance, the basic Theory of Relativity?' Anu asked, irritated, seeing Moni standing in front of her with a stupefied look of a cow.

'No! Actually … I was lost in some thought. Yes! I've tasted many cocktails. I liked the Screwdriver and the Bloody Mary…' Moni answered.

'Ha ha ha … You're such a brooder!' Anu guffawed and added, 'I was talking about a movie… With Tom Cruise playing Brian Flanagan, a bartender, in a pub owned by some Coughlin, a curious kind of fellow, with his own set of strange rules… Haven't seen it?'

'No.' Moni said as she started walking to her room. She would have to get ready quickly to gulp down another kind of cocktail at Blitz, in all probability.

Anu followed Moni to her room.

'Well … Professor VPB had asked me to watch the movie to get into the idea of being a mixologist … And I spent last evening, watching Brian and Coughlin and now I know I've got a path to choose and follow…' Anu jabbered.

Moni opened the wardrobe and stared at the salwar suits and sarees, neatly arranged in columns and rows.

'What should I wear?' Moni thought.

'Hello! Are you not hearing me?' Anu asked.

'Yes dear… You've seen a film and you're going to choose and follow a path,' Moni reverted absentmindedly.

'Yes! And now that I've finally decided to do something with all the passion of my heart, I'm feeling definitely blessed!' Anu stated with a newly discovered optimism.

Moni recalled Anu's drowsy mumblings of the previous night and she felt she had already heard similar things from Anu, only the 'new path' thing was a bit unclear still.

'Which path you want to choose and follow, dear?' Moni finally asked, as she brought out a pink kurti and a white pair of flowing pajamas which narrowed at the heels.

'The path of a mixologist!' Anu gushed.

'Mixologist? What the crap is that?' Moni almost shouted, turning round to face Anu.

'A person who makes cocktails… A person who can tell the exact potion needed by someone at a particular evening… A person who can, by merely smelling the odour of a wine, possibly determine the very origin of the potion … its history… its geography…' Anu talked smoothly as if she would continue talking the whole day in a single breath.

Moni looked at her friend. What the heck was Anu doing with her life? 'Are you thinking of quitting your studies for that?' Moni asked alarmed.

'Not yet decided on that… I wish to do both… Studying at the university in daytime and working as an apprentice in a pub at the evening,' Anu said, thoughtfully.

'That's good … only that would demand extra efforts on your part… Not bad,' Moni said as she started putting on the kurti to get ready for work.

When Moni got down from the autorickshaw in front of Blitz, she felt an excitement within.

'Good morning, ma'am,' the security at the gate greeted her as he opened the glass door. Moni entered. The maintenance staff was vacuuming the floors.

'Ma'am … Good morning!' Kevin greeted.

'Yes Kevin, any news?' Moni asked as she pushed the door of her office.

'Bhatia Sahab called me to enquire about the woollens ... And few lights in the apparel section are not working ... Called the electrical maintenance contractor...' Kevin informed.

'Okay ... If the contractor is not sending anyone within one hour, call him again and remind him that we could scrap his AMC... What did Bhatia Sahab actually enquire about?' Moni asked as she put her bag on the table.

'Nothing that mattered. ...Asked if we are taking good care of those woollens at the stock room...' Kevin said before walking away.

Moni opened the upkeep balance file in her computer.

'There's still some residue of last year's dough ... We can actually utilise it in adding a touch of paint to the mall's façade ... What about vinyl boards? A pre-Christmas makeover could draw customers,' Moni thought.

Moni's cell rang. 'This Bhatia will make me insane...' Moni mumbled on seeing the caller id. 'Good morning Sir!' she said.

'Good morning Moni... How are you going?' Bhatia asked.

Moni tried to decipher the mood of her boss from the voice. It sounded okay.

'Decking up for Christmas Sir...' Moni said.

'Fine! Very good indeed! You've got unutilised amount still?' Bhatia asked, donning the mask of his infamous naïveté.

'Yes Sir... A paltry amount though.' Moni played safe.

'Good... Now listen to me... We've decided to partially buy your theory... We're not going to put those woollens on racks... We'll just keep them aside for a while ... We're having a discussion with another importer and hopefully we'll be getting new items with trendier and flashier looks by the end of this month ... So... There would be no sales drop in the woollens .... We'll be competing tooth and nail, you see!' Bhatia spoke incoherently, noncommittally.

'What do you mean? We'll be losing time ... Customers have already started flocking in search of woollens ... And moreover, what will be the fate of the faulty ones? We will just throw them out of the window?' Moni asked, feeling all the time, the cold old fury rearing its ugly head somewhere within.

'No no ... We'll just mix them up with the new ones! That's the trick!' Bhatia laughed.

'Fine! Grand! What an idea Sir ji!'

Moni exclaimed, working up a sense of wonder at her boss's innovative marketing ideas and at the same time, suppressing her impulse of bursting into laughter at the man's jittery endeavour to wrap up things by throwing the dirt under the carpet.

'I am here all the time to help you out ... And to make the most out of the situation ...' Bhatia blew his own trumpet.

Moni heaved another volley of praise before hanging up.

Thank god! No misgivings! Moni thought the moment Bhatia's call ended.

But why is he still not withdrawing those rat holed woollens? What's the compulsion? Why is he so soft about those woollens?

'I'll have to do a bit of cross-checking,' Moni thought.

But the very next moment she felt there was no need actually to get into any kind of probe because that would unearth, possibly, a filthy thing or two, about Bhatia, or about someone else, or about a whole group of office staff.

I am already fed up with the job and now if I nudge something to get more stench into my nose, then probably I would detest the job to the extreme and then what would I do? If I need to write my mind, if I am to continue with my poetry, I am to survive first in this world … Adjustments… Compromises… All are part of the survival strategy… Moni thought and felt upset. She just closed the upkeep balance sheet and shut down the computer.

I'm living a dog's life …

Moni took a notepad and played with her pen over it, not being sure how she would colour the white, virgin paper. But she knew she had an urge to write something …. She wanted to make the virgin paper pregnant with her thoughts, ideas, emotional eternity… She knew she had to write to salvage her wrecked mind, her drooping spirit, her detestation and so she started writing. She started the task of venturing into a field which attracted her always. She decided to write profusely to purge her mind. She started to write to relate to the real world she was in. She wanted to unify the virtual and the real through her words, because she knew words are one of the many tools available to decipher, interpret and get hold of the virtual. Words were real and yet they captured the unreal as they essentially come from mind—the unreal, abstract, unexplored, fathomless mind.

31

'The day is unusually bright and sunny,' Ved thought as he brought the car out of the garage. He then checked the fuel meter, the coolant and engine oil levels, and switched the fan on to drive out the staleness of the air in the car.

From the car, he could see Sonai coming out of the house, hopping merrily, down the driveway, flanked by Biswanath and Debjani. Biswanath was carrying the satchel while Debjani had in her hand the water bottle. Debjani was giving her customary words of useful advice on good conduct and discipline. Sonai barely paid any attention to her granny's useful bits of advice, though. Coming near the front door, Sonai tapped on the metal. Ved opened the door. Sonai hopped in. Biswanath put the satchel and the bottle on the rear seat.

'Bye bye…' Sonai said, waving to her grandparents.

'Bye… Eat your tiffin,' Debjani reminded.

Ved pressed the clutch and shifted the gear.

'You know something; I feel it would be a great day at school for me …' Sonai said as the car took the wide approach lane to the second Hooghly Bridge.

'Why?' Ved asked as he turned on the car stereo.

'I just feel it... A great day always begins this way... Bright and sunny and your loved ones by your side... And the soft breeze blowing, carrying the scent of flowers and the chirping of birds... Reminding you that you're not alone...' Sonai murmured.

Ved was moved by the spontaneous flow of the simple yet profoundly beautiful words from his daughter's vocabulary.

And there was Josh Groban playing *'Everyone needs to be loved and understood'* in the car stereo. Ved was ecstatic.

'Good! You know, I think, from today, I'll call you *my little poetess* instead of Diana... Will you not love it?' Ved asked.

'Quite okay with me!' Sonai giggled.

'Well... Will you comply with a request of mine?' Ved asked and at once he was surprised at the officialdom of his syntax.

'What?'

'Your first poem... I need a copy of that...' Ved stated.

'Why? Will you put it into a frame and hang it on the wall as a kind of prize?' Sonai asked, innocently relishing her father's adulation.

'Yes! Of course! Why not? If I could, I would love to make a gold plated replica of it,' Ved remarked happily.

'Oh dad! Come'n! You're overdoing!' Sonai flashed a smile, embarrassed by the exaggerated and probably overrated praise.

'No Dear! When you come to know that your kid has grown big and beautiful enough to have a mind of her own and when the kid is found diligently working on that mind, spreading every bit of it to something creative and sublime, you as a progenitor, only feel proud and your pride lets you indulge in all kinds of ridiculous excesses,' Ved said with a rise of emotion in his voice.

Sonai got rid of her seat belt and climbed up to Ved to kiss him on his cheeks.

'Hey! I'm driving!' Ved laughed.

Descending from the car at the school gate, Sonai stopped by the window.

'Dad, I want you to do something if it happens the way I think, it will ...' she said somewhat dryly.

'Can't get that... What?' Ved asked. He had noticed a change of attitude and talk in Sonai. The change was dramatic and too blatant.

'I might ask you to call Moni and let me have a little chat with her when we reach home at the end of the day... Will you mind?' Sonai asked, thoughtful.

'Well... No ... Not at all ...' Ved said and turned the ignition on.

'Good day!' Sonai said and turning back she walked through the turnstile. Ved looked at his little poetess for a while before turning the steering.

For Sonai, the first four classes held no value as she knew that just after the lunch break, Neha Sehgal, the teacher-in-charge, would come and formally announce whose entries were selected for the school magazine. So, quite naturally, Sonai was tensed and gripped with terrible anticipation the moment, Neha Sehgal entered the class after the break, wearing a white cotton saree and a black blouse, looking as elegant as ever. Miss Sehgal started the announcement, standing on the podium, pronouncing the names of the entrants as distinctly as possible. Every time someone's name was announced there was a clapping and the proud entrant would stand up straight. Every time a name was announced, Sonai felt the list would end with that and her name would not be featuring in the list. But Devakshi was continuously whispering in her left ear, sort of egging her on saying, 'Don't fret ... Your entry can never be rejected...'

Sonai just smiled feebly, trying her best to ward off the nervousness. But she felt that her heart was beating too fast and her tongue was running dry.

'Sanhita Bhattacharya!'

Miss Sehgal announced. For a moment, Sonai felt she heard it wrong. It might be someone else's name which sounded like hers. But everyone was staring at her and clapping. So Sonai stood up.

The teacher descended from the podium and started walking towards her.

'Why is she coming down?' Sonai thought.

The teacher walked up slowly to the place where she was standing. She could feel the whole class looking at her with anticipation. The teacher came closer and put her hand on her shoulder and smiled. The smile looked unpretentious. Sonai smiled back not knowing why she was smiling though.

'I have read your poem several times and I found it extraordinarily stirring... It was charged with a kind of emotion which anyone could relate easily, almost effortlessly... It was simple and yet strong enough to be selected for the magazine'. The teacher said.

Sonai was shaken. She did not even dream that her debut poem would be so much liked by anyone. It was written with all the suddenness of a heightened emotion. So, bereft of words,

Sonai just stood there, with her head bent down, feeling shy and at the same time unimaginably happy at her wondrous predicament.

'Good work! Keep it up!' The teacher said as she patted softly on Sonai's shoulder.

Sonai felt there was warmth and encouragement in that pat. She also had a strange sensation of the warmth spreading all over her body.

'Now, Sanhita is going to recite her poem so that the whole class can hear it…' The teacher declared suddenly and handed a copy of the poem to Sonai.

Sonai took the piece of paper in her trembling hands. She looked at the lines but they appeared blurred. Sonai realised the reason soon. She had tears welling up.

But the class was waiting. Miss Sehgal was looking at her expectantly.

'Come'n Sanhita… Read it loud!' Devakshi whispered and nudged her in the ribs.

Sonai was suddenly reminded of Moni's face, glistening, with beads of sweat on her forehead, standing in front of the gas stove in her kitchen. She remembered the keys of Moni's laptop shining brightly as if tempting her to press them, and she started reciting the poem. Reading aloud, Sonai, for the first time, felt the import of each word and each sentence. She discovered the rhyme and the reason hidden behind each line and each word and each syllable. Her voice rose up and down following the rise and the fall of the tempo of every line as a singer's voice does.

The class was enthralled. The class made no movement as if all of them were petrified. The silence was deafening, which was only broken by Sonai's voice soaring one moment and falling the next. Sonai felt she was not actually reciting, but someone else had taken over her voice and was reciting the poem. The voice was captivating for it carried every bit of her heart. Sonai felt happiness within. She felt sad as well.

'For whom was it written? Moni?' Devakshi asked as soon as the teacher left the class.

There was a melee in the classroom as everyone came and patted Sonai.

'How do you write it?' someone asked.

'Teach us! Teach us?' another asked.

Sonai looked at the curious faces of her classmates. They were so happy. They were so proud of her.

'You people go to your desk … We're going out for a stroll in the backyard for a while…' Devakshi said, almost ordering the crowd of mates.

'Hey … We're also her friends … She's not yours only…' Tiyasha, the monitor of the class, said.

'Okay, Tiyasha, may we have a little stroll outside? We'll be back soon,' Sonai asked Tiyasha.

'Okay… Five minutes,' Tiyasha said as she started pushing and shoving the girls to their desks.

32

'Give me your cell!' Sonai demanded boarding the car.

Ved stuck the seat belt around her and brought out the phone from his shirt pocket. Sonai started talking to someone over phone:

'You can't even imagine how my teacher appreciated my poem... I mean... Our poem... I was asked to stand and recite it to the whole class and when I did that, everyone was moved. The class was silent... Oh Moni, I owe this all to you!'

Sonai said aloud. She was visibly excited.

Ved was curious to know what had happened at the school. But Sonai was on phone and she was busy talking to Moni, as it seemed. So Ved suppressed his curiosity. He drove down the circular road. On the sly, he looked at Sonai's face. She was beaming. Ved watched her nodding her head, dancing eye brows, swinging her flock of hair, and making other several gestures as she talked over the phone and at once Ved realised how much space Moni had acquired in his daughter's soul. He looked at Sonai, as a kind of detached observer, almost a third party.

Presently, Sonai ended her call and put the cell on the niche just above the glove compartment.

'May I know what had transpired between you and Moni?' Ved asked as if he was an outsider, a third party.

'Oh Dad! You know… My poem, written at Moni's place, has been selected for the magazine and… I was asked by the teacher to recite the poem … You never know how very happy I am today!' Sonai shouted and giggled, as if she could not contain her happiness brimming over.

'That's wonderful! I'm so proud of you dear,' Ved smiled.

'And … You know… For the first time I realised… I like the thing … That poetry… It is much better than those Computer games, you see?' Sonai observed.

'True… Poetry is better than games in many respects … though the comparison is not a very common one…' Ved remarked.

Sonai's eyes were fixed on the windshield. But Ved knew that her mind was roaming.

'I'm loving it!' Sonai said suddenly.

'That's the only thing needed, dear, to love and enjoy the work.' Ved collaborated.

'Hey dad! Why can't you take up your camera again?' Sonai asked, this time moving her head towards Ved.

'Haven't felt the urge so far … My mind is occupied with other things, I presume…' Ved spoke, feeling helpless to properly justify his state of mind.

'Unwind your mind then! Get back to the thing that you always enjoyed,' Sonai said.

'Yeah! I'll see to it,' Ved remained non committal.

'You know dad... I've seen your snaps several times ... They are beautiful... They are lovely...,' Sonai muttered.

Ved pulled up the car near Race Course. The car stood still with its engine purring, facing the flyover to the bridge.

'What about not going home straightaway? What about going somewhere else where both you and I can spend a little time together in our own ways?' Ved asked, looking at his daughter.

'Well ... I wish to go to any place that's not crowded ... Can't we go somewhere with a lot of green grass around so that we can sit over there for some time?' Sonai asked.

'Got it!' Ved turned the car to change the lane and then sped up towards Kolkata maidan.

The vast expanse of green maidan looked awesome in the fading light. Far away, a few boys were playing cricket wearing white. They looked like white dots running on a green palette. Ved parked the car under an old banyan tree. The tree was old enough to have cracks on its old brownish black trunk, which was a few feet in diameter. Its branches were well spread out, but they were without sufficient foliage. So the branches looked bare almost.

Ved got rid of his socks and shoes and keeping them aside, he stretched his legs. Sonai also did the same and sat by her father.

'Isn't the place beautiful?' Sonai asked.

'Yes, definitely...' Ved answered as he bent backwards and tried to support his inclined upper torso by his two hands.

'Tell me dad... If you had your camera here, what picture you would have taken?' Sonai asked as she plucked a grass leaf and started chewing it.

'Camera? Picture? Well... I would have taken a picture of you sitting under the tree with your legs stretched as they are right now and to get that gigantic tree into the frame, I would have definitely stepped quite a few yards backward .... It would not be a close shot ... But a wide angle one, capturing the vastness of the field ... And the shot should have been taken after a light meter reading ... To adjust the aperture and the ISO... But I would not fiddle with the natural light in any case... Meaning, there would be no flash gun ...' Ved said and started thinking about other technical possibilities of the hypothetical photo.

'Dekho Baba. See dad. How much of photography is still left in you? I mean, if a man can talk so much about a photo not taken, then what would he do when he actually possessed a camera and tried to take a real photo?' Sonai asked.

'Real? Unreal? Hypothesis and the actual...' Ved murmured, inaudibly.

'Are you saying something?' Sonai asked.

'No ... Nothing ... Sonai, dear, do you seriously believe that I'm moving away from my own self?' Ved asked.

Sonai looked at her father's sad face. She felt that her father needed her support and love.

'You are the best dad one can have, but sometimes you just become too much sad, and then you don't even talk to me properly...' Sonai sighed.

'O no dear! I'm okay... Perfectly okay... You are my eyes dear, my ears, my heart...without you I would not have moved on, I would have stopped altogether, had you been not there...'

Ved spoke in a strain of some kind of trance, as if he was muttering all those to himself, as if he was self-appraising, as if he and only he was present there and Sonai was just his alter-ego.

Sonai just listened to her father's uninterrupted train of thoughts speeding through, breaking apart the darkness and mist setting in slowly on the maidan.

'I can't understand … If you're really so much happy with your readings of those religious texts, then why are you sad?' Sonai asked, puzzled.

'Because, I'm still human …' Ved replied almost spontaneously. But soon he realised that there was no point in talking all those things to Sonai. So, he stopped midway, and adding a smile asked her, 'Hey! Are you feeling hungry?'

'Of course, I am!' Sonai replied, instantly, as if she was waiting exactly for such a query.

'Okay then! Lets go somewhere to dine,' Ved said, as he picked up Sonai's socks and shoes.

'No… need to go home … to eat sitting on my granny's lap,' Sonai said as she ran towards the car, bare footed.

Looking at Sonai, Ved thought he had experienced an out of the world evening that brought him love, candidness, hope, joy, dreams and a lot of peace.

33

'Ma'am, won't you go home?' one of the girls from the counter, tapped on the door and peeping in, asked Moni.

Moni usually left Blitz by eight in the evening, if she was not hard pressed. Today, she had no specific work other than the routine checks of the accounts and the stockpile. She had finished that earlier on.

After that she just wrote. She conceived of a fantastical poem—a long poem in a conversational tone as if a real interaction was taking place between two human beings—male and female. They would be sitting in a wasteland perhaps, far from human habitation and talking their minds out. They would start with introductory queries like, 'how are you?' and then they would move on to more physical ones like, 'What is your favourite food or drink?' Then they would ask each other another set of questions like, 'Which colour do you like and why?' Questions and counter questions would be volleyed back and forth until they returned to, 'What is your idea of happiness?' or 'What do you do to relieve pain?'

The more they talked, the simpler their questions would get. At one point, they would ask each other about their own selves like, 'Who are you?' and 'Why are you here?' and 'What are your negative capabilities?'

These queries would dissect each other's souls until they laughed and cried and panted and dissolved into tears again, only to be wise enough to despise themselves. After severe self-castigation, they would find humility. Their humility would instigate sexual energy between them, and they would not feel like keeping any secret between them. With their minds exposed, they would now try to explore and understand each other's bodies. They would make love under the open sky. It would be a moonlit night and they would caress. Their communion would go through several stages. At first, gentle. Then, suddenly violent like in a kind of fight. After physical exertion, they would go on another kind of exploration. They would try to become one. They would hold on to each other tightly, as if to remain embraced forever.

This effort would make them look physically inseparable. But they would know for certain, that this game would be just a temporary thing, for they could never be joined together physically forever. So they would loosen the embrace and start the exploration of the mind again. At one point, their queries would not even be related to their own selves. They would think about life and their existence and the universe. The more they would think, the more their queries would dwindle. They would not ask questions to each other, but question themselves. This introspection would continue for some time and then they would lose the urge to talk. They would just lie side by side, looking at the night sky bedecked with stars and they would keep on looking at the black sky and gradually losing their all physical sensations. They would close their eyes and find a strange kind of illumination within. Their mind's eye would reveal the secrets of existence. They would feel their bodies weigh nothing.

Weightlessness would be followed with the feeling that they were not there on earth. They would forget where they had been lying. They would be without any physical sensation. This shut down state or physically comatose state would release their minds from their bodies. Leaving the garment of physicality, they would fly to outer space, to another planet in another galaxy, perhaps.

The counter girl was still standing at the door when Moni realised that she had been idiotically staring at her without answering her.

So she just nodded and stood up and started picking up the notepad on which she had jotted down the basic structure of her longish poem. She noticed that she had exhausted quite a few pages of the fat notepad already. She smiled at her effort. She then picked up her cellphone and the purse and put them into her bag. She looked around her cabin, thinking hard if she needed anything to take home. Finally, she switched off the light and went out.

'I would not get an auto at nine, so I better walk the distance that would give me some more time to think about the poem,' Moni thought and she started walking briskly.

'Why aren't you picking up the phone *dammit*?'

Someone yelled from behind and Moni turned to see a familiar silhouette coming towards her, piercing the November mist of the city.

It was Anu, thumping the pavement hard.

'Hey you! Here? What happened?' Moni asked puzzled.

'We have been waiting at home from seven thirty… I called you at least thrice… The cell rang… You never picked up… Then I thought you might be in some kind of danger… So I asked Melvin to bring me here,' Anu yelled.

'Oh… Is it so? Sorry… I was busy with some work…' Moni mumbled.

'It is okay, now that you are here… Let me introduce you to Melvin… Come here Melvin!' Anu asked someone to come.

Moni noticed a man of medium height descending from a white car and slowly walking up to her. When the man came near, Moni found him to be impeccably dressed in a deep blue suit and red tie. The man extended his hand. Moni shook hands with the man.

'Hi! I'm Moni… Monideepa Banerjee…'

'That I know. I'm Melvin de Souza.' The man smiled as he shook hands.

Moni noticed Melvin's hands were smooth and his fingers manicured.

'Met Melvin today at a pub and we've become friends…' Anu added.

'Oh that's great!' Moni said.

'Your mate is an extraordinary woman with a lot of impulsiveness,' Melvin remarked and smiled again.

'Come'n, Melvin! You know what I want!' Anu said as she patted the man's shoulder.

Melvin laughed.

'Now that you've found your mate… Can I leave or should I drop you home?' Melvin asked Anu.

'Oh yes! Surely! We could walk this short distance. Nice to meet you…' Moni said, almost preventing Anu to come up with any reply.

Melvin waved. Anu and Moni waved back.

Melvin got into the white car and whizzed away towards Hazra. No sooner had the car left the place than Moni pulled Anu by her hand signalling her to stop and her eyes danced. She asked: 'Again?' Anu just laughed the wildest laugh of hers, breaking the silence of the wintry night.

Then she shook her head in rapid succession and said, 'No no! You're making a mistake… I'm a changed woman now… I'm now treading to a definite goal… For I've learnt to live another life… I've made a detour of life…'

'Really? Let's see… How far your detour of life can take you…' Moni said almost challenging.

'You'll see, once I tell you the whole picture… Yesterday I told you only a part of it…' Anu said as she started walking in a manner that befits a jaywalker.

'You know something? Sonai called me from her dad's cell…' Moni remarked suddenly.

'Did Prof. VPB talk with you?' Anu asked.

'No… Sonai talked a lot… Actually, she called me to give thanks, as she felt I deserved that…' Moni replied.

'Why?' Anu asked promptly.

'Because Sonai wrote a poem at our place and that particular poem had been selected for her school magazine… so she was elated, naturally…' Moni explained.

'Good! It seems you're spreading your brand of poetry… Tell me, did the professor tell you anything?' Anu asked.

'No... Why? Do you expect him to tell me anything?' Moni quizzed.

'Not really... Anyway... If he calls again just tell him I've started the journey and I'm on the right course,' Anu stated enigmatically.

'On the right course? What's that?' Moni asked.

'I'll tell you... In due course,' Anu flashed a smile and jumped in the air.

'Don't do that to me! I want to hear the story tonight itself!' Moni voiced her utmost curiosity.

Anu was not listening to Moni for she was singing full-throated:

> *'Aye khuda...tujhko pata...tu rahulu kulu...kya tera pata...*
> *hum toh yahaan pe musafir hain...jo dhunte apni manzil ka pata...'*
>
> (Oh god... You know... Where do you live... Where you are...I am just a wanderer here... Who is searching for her destiny...)

Moni smiled, seeing her companion dance and sing like a kid in her own hours of fancy and imagination, reigning supreme.

Moni joined Anu singing, as she walked by her side putting her left arm over her shoulder like a comrade, a co-soldier, a mate, a soul nourisher and wanderer, living moments of life. Anu was surprised to see Moni singing in the street, breaking all shackles of her self-imposed reserve. But soon, she felt the vibes of friendship sent across by Moni and she accepted that with her heart, nerve and sinew.

They walked the short distance with longer strides, breaking the mist and chill of the night and both of them felt warm and invigorated.

34

After dinner, Ved followed Sonai to her bedroom. Sonai jumped on the bed, dusted the pillows and Ved sat down on the bed. Sonai, as usual, put her head on Ved's lap. Ved at once knew that he would have to tell Sonai another bedtime story so he started rummaging his head for a story.

'Dad!' Sonai called.

'Yes dear…' Ved said as he started stroking Sonai's forehead gently.

'Dad, I don't want to hear any story tonight… Just keep on running your fingers through my hair… And I will sleep off…' Sonai murmured with her eyes full of sleep already.

Ved abided by his daughter's wish. He ran his fingers gently through Sonai's soft tresses of hair.

'Remember… What I said listening to your story of Mr. Destiny?' Sonai asked, mumbling as if she was dreaming.

'Yes dear, you said if you had met Mr. Destiny, you would ask him something,' Ved said trying to recollect Sonai's words.

'Ya… I would just ask him not to change anything in my life… For I think I've got everything in life… You as dad…

Memories of my mom... My granny and grandpa... Moni... Devakshi... Sehgal ma'am... I've got everything and everyone,' Sonai said, with her eyes closed.

But Ved sensed a kind of pathos in Sonai's voice.

'What is it dear? What still makes you unhappy?' Ved asked with earnestness of a father.

'Nothing dad... Don't you worry...' Sonai said mumbling.

Ved said nothing. He just kept on stroking till Sonai stopped mumbling and fell asleep. After sometime, Ved put Sonai's head on the pillow, put a cover on her, and slowly went out of the room.

Coming to his room, he switched on the light and opened the cupboard. He wanted to see his camera. It was there on the top shelf, wrapped up in an old newspaper. Ved brought it down and removed the newspaper, cutting the strings by which it was bound to the camera. Then he took up the camera in his hand and by running his fingers over its body he wanted to feel its contours. The black body of the camera looked shiny as ever. Ved opened the lens cover and put his eye into the view finder. It was okay. Only he would have to buy new cells for it.

Scrutinising the camera, Ved found one or two scratch marks on its body and he remembered exactly how those scratches were made. Once it fell from his hand in soft mud near a river and on another occasion it got brushed into a tree trunk somewhere in Ladakh when he tried to climb up the tree with the camera hanging from his neck to get a better view of a valley.

He remembered his long treks for better shots, better compositions, and better light. He remembered how he had suffered from breathlessness once on arriving at Shey valley.

He remembered how he had to wait for the mountain bulls to come and graze, sitting on rocks as early as six in the morning, shivering to his bones. He recalled how he puked fourteen times a day, suffering from high-altitude sickness and how he thought quite foolishly that he would die puking.

'This camera bore witness to all that and more,' thought Ved. 'With it, I took a series of pictures of Mayurika, all black and white portraits. With it, I took the first ever snap of Sonai when she was barely three months old.'

Staring at the camera, Ved saw in his mind's eye several moments of the past glide by. He felt sad and yet happy. He felt a slight but definite pull towards the machine after a long time. He felt he could still go out with the camera to capture life in all its beauteous forms. This feeling gave him a certain joy.

He placed the camera back again into the cupboard and took a decision—a small insignificant decision as it may sound, but it was a decision taken after three years almost. He decided that he would buy rechargeable cells for the camera very soon.

Then he went to bed. He was feeling a thrill—a thrill of recovery, of hope and of subtle joy.

As soon as he closed his eyes, he saw the wonderful picture of Sonai sitting under a big banyan tree with her legs stretched out and smiling, yelling, 'Come'n Dad! Come'n!'

35

'You just approached Melvin and said *I wanna learn the tricks of your trade*... That's it?' Moni asked disbelievingly, when Anu told her about her sudden friendship with Melvin, the master sommelier of Big Ben.

It being a Saturday, Moni and Anu decided to have a long adda session after dinner, as they both felt the need for one, with so many things happening in their lives. So, they were on the bed at Moni's room, buried under the quilt and chatting.

'Yes! That was it!' Anu said.

'He was certainly taken aback by your oddity of behavior?' Moni asked laughing.

'Yes! Of course! He was so surprised that he just jumped and hopped a few yards as if he had met a kind of phantasm,' Anu said grinning naughtily.

'Hey you jerk! When will you recover?' Moni said.

'But I kept on insisting, sitting on the high stool near the counter, in a whispering fashion though, so as not to attract the attention of bartenders... And Melvin, poor Melvin... He had to bear it all without speaking much, for he had so much work to do… Like giving instructions related to mixology to his subordinates and keeping an eye on the perfect blends… Whenever he would come within a few yards of where I was sitting, he would hear me whispering all kinds of odd requests like how a *Mango minty maria* can be made… Or what was the secret behind the making of a *Sparkling peach*… And I was so obstinate that I would keep on repeating the same question over and over again, till he could come near me and tell me to note it all down quickly… And I noted it down on tissue papers… Using abbreviations invented by me then and there… So I learnt that 60 ml vodka is to be mixed with 90 ml of mango juice to make a glass of *Mango minty maria,* while for a Sparkling peach, you need to mix 90 ml of white wine with 10 ml of *Cointreau* and 50 ml of orange juice and you need the peach syrup and orange peels for garnishing…'

Anu talked so fast, giving out little details of every cocktail recipe learnt during her very informal but practical sessions.

'Wow! That's fabulous! Tell me more about some other recipes,' Moni demanded, visibly impressed.

'Well… There are virtually thousands of them… All you need is a sense of taste and flavour and a bit of innovative spirit! For example, you can mix vodka and apple juice and lemon juice to create another kind of flavor… Vodka is the most versatile ingredient in creating flavours of cocktails… Cocktails are like Indian gravies, you can churn out unlimited variations from a family of, say, 20 basic recipes… Nowadays… Energy drinks like Red bull are also mixed with vodka or whiskey to create another brand of cocktails… For example the Jager Bomb which is a mix between Jagermeister and Red Bull…' Anu informed.

'Well... Melvin taught you all that in such a small span of time?' Moni asked.

'Not all he taught, literally... I watched him closely working on blenders and ready mixes... I monitored his every move with all attention and whenever I had any doubt, I just raised my finger and he would just come to me to describe me as hurriedly as possible, the recipes...' Anu said.

'With the pace you're currently in, you could learn at least hundred recipes in a week!' Moni exclaimed at her Anu's extraordinary agility and eagerness to learn mixology.

'No dear.... Only learning the recipes will not do...you need to practice the art to perfection... I've just started... And I know I have miles to go, before I become a true mixologist... and then I would ...' Anu stopped short.

'Then what? Will you open up a pub of your own?' Moni probed.

'Exactly! I will open up a pub... Where not only will I serve customers or connoisseurs of wine, but where, I will forever experiment with mixology... The pub would be my laboratory as well as business venture... How does that sound?' Anu asked with dreams in open eyes.

'Nice... Very nice and inspiring,' Moni said.

'Don't you have any such dream?' Anu asked Moni suddenly.

'Yes... I also have. Though, a more humble one. Not any business venture... But to become a poet...' Moni replied hesitatingly.

'Oh! That you are already! You write poems every day... on every occasion... I know that...' Anu said.

'No… Not that kind of thing… I wish to write a long poem… A very long poem… Like, say, an epic written in pure verse…' Moni tried to explain.

'O… Now I get it… You want to be a John Milton, writing *Paradise Lost* in several books…' Anu nodded as she spoke, as if she was seriously trying to get into the idea of writing poetry herself.

'Ya… Sort of…' Moni said as she began thinking.'Tell me, as you're quite an expert in that field, how does it feel when one is having sex?' Moni asked after a brief silence.

'Sex? Hey look who's talking! Sex? You want to know about that?' Anu asked visibly surprised.

'Yeah… I have no experience of it…' Moni said, somewhat sad as if she was ruing the fact that she had not so far experienced that thing.

'Well… I don't know why you are willing to know about that, all of a sudden… It may be you want to experience it… Or it may be… You're curious to know my stories… Anyway… I find it a pleasant thing… It is full of thrills and once you go through it, you feel spent up… Exhausted, but this exhaustion is quite good—it makes you believe that there is happiness in the world—and no cares,' Anu said, playing with her own fingers.

'You mean to say, good sex brings in blessedness?' Moni asked.

'Yes… It does, if your partner is equally sensitive and not too animalistic… Because sex is primarily an animal thing… It can only be transformed into an art if people involved in the act are artistic… If they are emotionally vulnerable,' Anu said and sighed at once.

'Talk about the blessedness…' Moni wanted to know more.

'I think I am not the right person to talk about that because in my case, sex is mostly animalistic… Full of energy and high voltage sparks… But I can understand that people with a kind of sensitivity and emotional attachment can make it a sublime thing, a poetry… That I learnt from books, from various films… but tell me why are you so interested in knowing about sex? I always thought you're a saint who looks upon it as a kind of taboo!' Anu said candidly.

'There are reasons… Throughout my life I've found men to be too predatory towards a woman's body… The way they look at beautiful women is very much akin to how a tiger looks at his prey… To devour it… To kill it…' Moni spoke sternly.

'Hey! That's true as well… I know beauty attracts the beast…' Anu supported.

'Yes… You've said it right… I've never found anyone who would not malign me or my beauty but appreciate it in the right manner… As if, he has come to beautify me, my soul, my body… By his gentle touches… By his caring voice, by his sensitive eyes which missed nothing, even my slightest grief would make him morose… He would be pained by my grief and happy seeing me happy,' Moni spoke dreamily.

'Oh! You're so romantic! But don't you think you're becoming too idealistic… Can you really find idealism in human beings? Are we all not sinners?' Anu asked.

'Yes we are… Or maybe we are not… For instance, I've never committed any major crime… But I know, I've been party to duplicity sometimes… Especially in my workplace, where I have to wear a mask of pretension… And I have to compromise every moment with injustice and anomalies… But that's life… Surviving the cruel, mad, bad world.' Moni confessed.

'I think you're in love with someone… And if I know the person, I will definitely try my best to get you involved in a relationship… That's vital… That's needed… That is part of life… I mean, I find it quite awkward to move on without relationships…' Anu said.

'Look Anu… You've expressed your ideas about my love life in more concrete terms like leaving a long letter on my computer… Like talking about Ved and me… I… I think… You're making a mistake.' Moni said, finally going straight to the issue of dispute, which she had so far deliberately avoided.

'Ha ha ha… Still remember that? O I was just an envious child then! Believe me… Okay I confess… I was too envious, probably I was too selfish… But believe me, now I am changed! I'm not the same Anu… After that midnight adventure, I've learnt a lot of things… And most importantly I've learnt to respect people… Had I not gone through all those adventures, I would not have learned the thing that all men are not the same… There is still enough goodness left in the world… There are still men who do not look upon women as mere sex toys… And when you encounter one of those men, you realise how mean you have been…' Anu said, thinking.

'Hey! Now I feel you're in love,' Moni quipped.

'Yes! I was, almost! But I've also learnt that love is just a passion… It could be linked to anyone or anything… And life, if lived passionately, could be equally disastrous and beautiful… It is all up to you to choose the way… Passionately heading towards destruction, or passionately moving towards sublimity,' Anu said.

'You're right dear! I think I am really talking to a different Anu... An Anu who has just got redemption,' Moni said.

'Yeah! I also feel the same... And I know who's responsible for that...' Anu said.

'Who? Ved?' Moni asked.

Anu just smiled a curious smile which was very much akin to her infamous grass-induced smiles.

'So, was it he who respected you?' Moni asked.

'Hey! Are we having an *Open-your-soul-night*?' Anu asked in a lighter vein after all those serious talks.

'Look Anu... I'm not particularly curious about your ways of life, though I feel surprised too often by your whimsical, lackadaisical, hyperactive ways... But I firmly believe that it is your life after all, and you have every right to choose the ways, as you have just mentioned... Now, coming back to me, I am actually mulling over a long poem, as I've told you, involving two characters... And the poem's principal theme will be the communion of souls, and communion of souls between a man and woman requires some kind of physical union, I guess... So...' Moni stopped, thinking she had clarified her position quite well to Anu.

'Why not experience it yourself? I mean, second hand info will not help you as a writer in a big way... Isn't it?' Anu asked, smiling her wicked smile.

'Hey! Are you trying to say that every writer, whatever he or she is trying to write, is a part of his or her real experience?' Moni countered.

'No... Not always,' Anu contemplated.

'Writers usually have that intuition... That powerful imagination which enables them to understand things better. It is all about a state of mind... Without prejudices, presumptions and inhibitions...' Moni murmured self-absorbed.

Anu remained silent for a while, brooding, and then broke the silence of the night saying, 'I agree... Sometimes, I feel that the major part of our life is spent in our mind... For example, now that I'm trying to attain some kind of perfection in the art of mixology... I'm actually storing up in my memory each and every bit of the flavour, taste and colour of the liquors...'

'Yeah! That's what I was talking about!' Moni spoke with exaltation, as if she was finding it quite pleasing to make someone understand her point. But her exaltation was brief, as she turned seriously sad when she tried to further explain, 'You know Anu... I find you more free than me... You've lesser mental blocks than me in certain things... Like you love mixing with people, with men... Which actually establishes the fact that you've got less inhibitions about men than me... While I... Kind of wall myself up in front of men... Tell me Anu, am I becoming a frigid kind of a woman?'

Hearing this, Anu looked at Moni, trying to understand her words by observing the little movements of her eyelids and pupils. Then she sighed and said, 'I think... It is probably because you're more beautiful than me... And as someone said beauty attracts the beast... Probably you've only seen bestiality in men... In my case, relationships with men are physical to a great extent because I've no poetry like you... But I've got a big bump... And heavy bosom... To be pressed...'

Anu laughed as if she loved the way she projected herself.

Moni saw a sudden spurt of pain shoot to Anu's eyes and quickly she put her hand on Anu's head and patting her sweet cheek said, 'I understand you fully... Your mind... Your ways... And you will find it strange that sometimes I want to be someone like you... Believe me... Bold, whimsical, reckless...Only as I've said, I've got inhibitions... Some very strong ones, because of my... Well... My ways of life... Maybe I am a coward... Or naïve...'

Moni stammered, looking very much pained by something she could not let out in the open as if there was a thorn stuck in her bosom which caused bleeding, a type of bleeding that was seeping through, almost imperceptibly and that could never be stopped.

Anu looked at Moni for a while, trying to understand her mate's words fully, but she could not get to the bottom of it. Moni's words, definitely, were lugubrious but the cause of that sudden agony was not known to Anu and so she thought it was better not to probe, as she had already caused a flutter in her mind and soul by overdoing certain things. So, she yawned and turned her back, preparing to sleep.

'Good night dear! I'll have to be at Big Ben tomorrow... Melvin thinks that handling Sunday crowd in a pub is a great learning experience...' Anu said, thinking that there would surely be another time when Moni herself would let things out to her if there were any such cause of hard and deep pain.

'Good night and sweet dreams,' Moni reverted.

But Moni could not sleep. She could not have sweet dreams either.

Beauty attracts the beast...

Moni was suddenly reminded of narrow filthy looking fingers running all over her digging into her. She was reminded of her cousin brother's betel stained teeth. She was reminded of fingers groping…

It was a black stormy night. Her uncle and aunt had been out to attend a wedding or something. Her cousin brother, who was almost of her age, came towards her, while she was sleeping on the floor with a mosquito net around her. He removed the net and dashed onto her. She woke up in terrible horror with her heart thumping. She had thought she had seen a ghost. But the betel stains on the teeth reminded her that the ghost was real. It was her cousin brother for whom she cooked food everyday and whose laundry she had done all those years. She felt his long filthy fingers touching her belly, her bosom, and her thighs. Those fingers were monstrous. But she had even more monstrous rage and pain wringing within her. So she just threw her legs to that bastard's scrotum and punched a full blooded hit on his eyes and got rid of him.

A few hours later her uncle and aunt had returned. They just came and slept off. They had never asked why from that night onwards she had preferred to sleep outside the room, on the small verandah of that dingy house, alone, bearing the mosquito bites and the rain and the storm and the bitter cold. Her cousin kept on intimidating her with dire consequences if she told anyone. He continued threatening her with his ugly smiles in front of uncle, aunt or other people and by his hushed and sombre voice, showing his betel stained teeth, whenever he had got her alone. She, like a cowed girl, put up with all that and somehow managed to graduate. She had been afraid all the while, of being left alone with her cousin, even in broad daylight.

There was, luckily, no repetition of that dastardly act. Her cousin did not show any remorse either. Had he shown any slight remorse even, she could have pardoned him, thinking it to be a spur of the moment thing. But the threats continued till she got the job and left uncle's home forever. She did not even tell her uncle her new address for she feared that her nightmares would come back to her again in another form or shape.

After that sudden recollection of the events of past life, Moni felt terribly hot as if her blood pressure was rising. She could not understand why all those unhappy and shocking and closely guarded secrets came back to her suddenly. Was it because she talked a lot about sex with Anu tonight? She felt her head was spinning and she wanted to vomit. She got out of the bed but her head began spinning at once. She sat down mumbling:

'Oh God! Wipe those unholy pictures from my mind... Delete those days of living with a pervert brother... Oh god! Tell me that I'm good... Tell me I have done nothing wrong...'

Then she stood up and walked to the bathroom. She undressed and switching on the geyser, stood under the water jet looking up to the shower nozzle... She wanted to get purged, to get cleansed... But those pictures so carefully tucked away somewhere in her mind kept coming back like worst nightmares. She was getting tired of storing those pictures in her mind... Those evil pictures... Those nasty pictures... Those filthy pictures...

Fuck you! You bastard! You ruined my mind! You corrupted my normal self!

Moni cried as she got drenched in the shower struggling hard to shake off, and wash off the memory of those filthy fingers of her cousin brother lurking on her body.

As long as I will have to bear this I will suffer... *I'll have to recover from thinking about evil... I want to live life peacefully...* I'll have to... For I've got rid of all those evils... After a long struggle... I've made it... I've become independent... Maybe I'm not enjoying my job... But I'm independent... I earn my living... I am surviving... In this real world... Moni tried to calm her agitated soul, mumbling to herself.

Hey! I'm good... I've got good people around me... Like Anu... Like Sonai, Ved... Ved... Ved? Ved!

O my god! Am I deceiving myself? O God! Am I in love with him?

36

'Hey! Look at those clouds in the eastern sky!'

Sonai drew Ved's attention as they both stood on the terrace. It was six thirty in the morning. Sonai had, for strange reasons, woken up early and forced Ved out of his bed to accompany her to the terrace. So the father-daughter duo stood on the terrace and watched the sun rise. Sonai brushed her teeth not leaving the terrace. Ved had to run downstairs twice to bring Sonai's toothbrush and towel and then to bring her a hot cup of Bournvita.

Now looking at the cloudlets floating in the sky, Sonai gushed. Ved had been actually enjoying this sudden change of Sonai's likes and dislikes. She had not touched her computer even once over the last few days. She had turned to pen and paper instead to scribble her thoughts. Her sense of observation had also undergone a sea change. Was it because she was repentant of her little online prank? Or was it that she was just trying to teach her father a lesson by not doing things which she usually did earlier? Ved wondered, as he followed Sonai's gaze at the pink sun-drenched clouds.

'I think I can see a candy man there selling pink sweet candies…' Sonai said.

Ved stared. The clouds looked like pink candies no doubt. But where was the candy man?

'Shift your eyes towards the north eastern part of the sky…' Sonai said, realising at once that her father was at a loss in finding the candy man in the sky.

Ved followed Sonai's instructions and he was genuinely surprised to see a cloud looking like a human, floating in the north eastern end of the sky.

'That's your candy man?' Ved asked pointing his fingers.

'Yes! Now guess who his buyers are?' Sonai asked.

'Na… Can't…' Ved mumbled.

'Well… Those who are coming… Look!' Sonai directed Ved to a flock of birds flying across the sky from West to East.

Ved was amused. He laughed.

The beautiful white clouds looked like cotton balls spread across the blue dome. They were wayward in their movement. Only the all powerful wind had foreknowledge of the destination of those cotton balls…

Ved thought as he observed the joyous movement of the clouds and felt the breeze from the north sweeping the city in the morning haze.

I love winter… Ved murmured and turning his head towards Sonai standing by his side he asked:

'Do you love winter dear?'

'Yes… I love it…' Sonai answered.

'Can you tell me the reasons?' Ved asked.

'For winter brings a lot of things… The smell of flowers at bloom in our garden, the smell of body lotions and moisturisers and olive oils and glycerin soaps on people… The long queues at the gates of zoos, parks, museums, movie halls… Badminton rackets and shuttlecocks… And… The taste of pickles…'

Sonai could have continued further with her long list of winter specific things, had Ved not laughed aloud and patted her back to appreciate her close sense of detail and listing powers.

'Hey! The way you put things together and stitched them into a long monologue, reminded me of an ad jingle of a cream.' Ved said.

'Boroline?' Sonai asked.

'Yeah! Right!' Ved nodded and smiled.

'Why do you love winter?' Sonai got back to her dad.

'Well… In my case… The list is shorter than yours…the blue sky, the bright sunshine and wonderful natural conditions in general for photographic expeditions,' Ved said.

'In that case, you should exploit the time to the fullest…' Sonai said.

'Meaning?' Ved asked.

'Meaning you should start your photographic expeditions… Winter is short…' Sonai reverted.

'But how can I leave you and go out?' Ved asked.

'You can take me along… I'm grown up now to go with you… I can take care of myself,' Sonai said.

'But you've got your school and I've got my university… and I can't take leave now,' Ved replied sadly.

'Why not go for a photographic exploration in the city and its suburbs then? I've seen foreigners take pictures of our city, of our streets and pavements, of our bridges, of our monuments and temples,' Sonai asked.

'Yeah they do, probably all these things are new to them and they want to take those pictures as mementos,' Ved said.

'But isn't the sunrise over the river beautiful or the bridge decked up in lights in the evening grand to look at?' Sonai asked.

'Yeah... They are... I think there are still a lot of things to be photographed in the city itself... Photography is an art and art forms are everywhere... Yes! You're right!' Ved exclaimed with a sudden rise of enthusiasm.

'Then? Why not today we go out?' Sonai asked, her widening with excitement.

'But... The cells... I need cells... For the camera... And the lens needs cleansing.' Ved became hesitant.

'Buy the cells... Clean the lens... We'll go out today itself!' Sonai shouted.

'Let's see,' Ved was doubtful and lethargic.

'Come'n dad! Be a sport!' Sonai egged her father on.

Ved pulled the car over at the gate of the Botanical gardens. It was one fifteen. Together they chose the gardens because it was the nearest place that Sonai had never visited.

The bicentenary gate with a black plaque engraved with the date and occasion. Ved read the plaque. July 15, 1994 was the day on which the bicentenary gate was inaugurated by a Central Minister.

'That means the garden was made way back in 1794, by the British perhaps,' Ved thought. The thought of standing in an ancient place, with a lot of ancient trees around, brought a sense of wonder in Ved. He had visited the garden only once earlier, when he was a school boy. But then there was no plaque mentioning its age. The black plaque was placed on a red brick wall, and in front of the wall were red pots and vases and tubs of flowers. The garden looked peaceful, serene. There was, of course, the Sunday public in picnic spirit, loitering around. But the garden was vast, with a lot of trees, and the crowd looked sparse in comparison. Walking down the path Ved and Sonai first came to a group of trees which looked like big reptiles lying on the ground. Sonai was so curious that she just ran towards those trees and reaching them, started to look at them with wide eyes.

'Hey Dad! Aren't they wonderful?' Sonai shouted.

Ved had already brought out his camera and standing a few yards away from the cluster of trees lying on the ground like reptiles, he was setting his focus right. The trees were really fascinating. They were a kind of palm trees but they got bent from their roots touching the ground and again they rose up, like reptiles looking up to the sky.

Sonai stood looking down at the roots for some time. Then she gradually went nearer and touched the trunk of the trees.

Sans flash, Ved set the focal length at 2.8 and ISO at 200. Holding steady, suppressing his breath, he pressed the shutter and almost at once, realised that he done a wonderful thing. He had moved on, leaving aside all his indolence and mental blocks. He realised he had once again started treading the path he liked the most. This realisation gave him great joy. Seeing Sonai climbing the trunk of the trees with excitement all over her face and the sun falling on her hair and the pink hat that she wore and the trees and the green grass, Ved felt the joy of breaking free from all shackles of morbidity and hopelessness that crept into him after Mayurika's death. He felt he had started to reclaim his life.

Joie de vivre! Ved shouted and ran towards the girl.

'Everything is derived from joy, is nourished in joy and finally returns to joy…' Ved recalled the lines suddenly, from the *Upanishad*, as he took his baby in his arms and kissed her.

37

'Are you serious about your mixology lessons?' Moni asked, as she saw Anu munching her bread too quickly. It was only nine thirty in the morning and it was Sunday. Anu had dressed up in black chinos and a white shirt. She had bathed and had combed and tied her hair neatly.

'Any doubts?' Anu asked as she continued gorging.

'Doubts? No... Got worries,' Moni replied returning to the newspaper.

'Leave worries to the wind,' Anu said.

'I could if you were not the impulsive kind,' Moni retorted without looking up from the newspaper which partially blocked her face from full view.

'Oh dear! Haven't I told you I'm on a detour of life?' Anu said, standing up from the table, taking her plate in hand, purportedly to dump it into the sink.

'That is a real mystery for me... You said you had a dream... And in that dream you had that realisation to change your path... Then you spent almost a day with Ved... Then, that guy Melvin, enters from nowhere and starts acting as your mentor… All those leave me wary.'

Moni said as she moved her face from the newspaper and looked at Anu, with all implied seriousness.

'Ha ha ha! Why are you thinking so much about me? I'm perfectly aware of what I'm doing… And as far the dream is concerned… Well… I myself have thought a lot about it, trying every time to understand really what it meant, or why it occurred to me that night… But believe me, every time I thought about it, I felt a kind of ecstasy… A kind of happiness, as if I'd found out the real self, as if I'd made a self discovery… And I should also acknowledge here, professor VPB's contribution… He has made me realise that in life, it is never late to find your goal and run after it if you've got the passion… So here, I'm running after my goal, though it is a bit strange one, apparently… But when you see your customers showing you thumbs up after taking a sip of the cocktail you've prepared with all your passion… You feel elated… And that elation can only move you forward… Is it not?' Anu asked, talking at a stretch, to explain her mind.

Moni looked at Anu for some time, before nodding.

'Even I can go to the extreme of saying that preparing a cocktail, say, for example, a Mojito 39 or O Sole Mio… Is as good as writing a poem as you often do… Both are creative… and so both require an imagination, a perfect imagination…' Anu claimed, with all seriousness, linking two different things, in a fashion, which only she could do.

Moni nodded again, thinking and trying to decipher what Anu had said. 'Perhaps you're right… And I'm wrong… Perhaps… I have become too old to understand all these…' Moni said looking sad.

'Hey! Moni! Why are you so sad? You're damn good looking and you're not old… You have a good job and I feel, the only thing needed in your life is a damn sexy man who'll just sweep you off your feet… Come'n, don't be a moron!' Anu said as she hurriedly washed her face and came to Moni.

Moni smiled.

'It's okay… Just a passing thought… Now I shouldn't be holding you up by these inane talks… Got ready to go?' Moni asked, shrugging off her unhappy state of mind.

'Will you not go to office today?' Anu asked.

'I don't feel like… But I think I'll have to go in any case… Job is a compulsion, isn't it?' Moni asked rhetorically.

'Ya… It is… Jobs are dream killers… I've heard somewhere…' Anu said and she rushed to the shoe cabinet.

'Take care… Have your meals properly… Taken the keys?' Moni asked.

'Yes dear! Love ya,' said Anu blowing her a kiss and going out, slamming the door behind her.

Soon after Anu left, Moni stood up and walked towards her room. She just lay down on the bed and looked up to the ceiling.

You need a damn sexy man who'll just sweep you off your feet…

Moni tried to imagine who would be a damn sexy man in her eyes.

She was reminded of Ved. She figured out that Ved was the only man she could think of as her companion, but this thought was quite disturbing for her and she wanted to fight it. She felt it was just her admiration for a nice looking widower, who had been very helpful. Then she started thinking about whatever Ved had done so far. She thought of her online chats with *SA* and felt that she missed *SA*.

Who's better? SA or Ved? Online avatar of Ved can never be better than his offline or real identity, because as Ved, he had done a lot of things like, searching for Anu in the middle of a desolate night, finding her, almost retrieving her… And it is the real entity that matters, not the online projection… But why had he been so helpful? Had he also been feeling a pull towards her? Why he had done so much for Anu? Why?

Why not call him? I can always call him to know how Sonai is doing. Haven't I got that little privilege to call him to ask about Sonai? No! I shouldn't call them… They might take me for a woman with a long poky nose… Sonai? Can't she call me? Hasn't she told me that she loves me? Has she forgotten me?

Moni thought restlessly. She felt sad and lonely.

No! I need to move out of this bad state of mind, at any cost… It is not helping me in any way… I'm losing my self-confidence… But why? Anu said jobs are dream killers… Do all jobs kill dreams? Does everyone engaged in any kind of routine work feel the same… Or is it that I dislike the job because I'm not fit for it? But I've done a lot for Blitz… Managed it through ups and downs… Haven't I? Then what? Why am I so morbid? Why can't I pull myself up? Why am I feeling so lethargic suddenly?

Moni got up from bed.

I need a bath… A long bath… Indulging myself… Thinking that, Moni entered the bathroom and flung open her night dress. She could see her naked self in the mirror. She looked at her bosom. *They are not saggy…*

Moni looked at her pelvic region. *It is curved and handsomely flabby…*

Moni looked further to see the tiny curls. She looked at the triangular patch of pubic hair for some time. Then, she moved round. *My bum is okay…*

She took up the soap and the shampoo and standing before the mirror she wanted to become narcissistic.

Suddenly, like the return of a forgotten thought, the image of a woman came to her mind. Moni turned the silver shower knob to the fullest rung. The water jet grew sharper and faster as if it would blind her eyes. She could not keep her eyes open. The jet was hurting her body. So she closed her eyes and put her mind to absorbing the feeling of being poked by sharp needles of water. She thought she saw herself sitting under a sky that was curiously pink in colour, she was dressed in heavy jewelry and adorned like a bride.

Pink is the colour of a new bride… Moni thought.

She tried to concentrate on the picture in her mind's eye. A virtual thing, no doubt, but it was there like a real one. Moni could feel that she was traversing the long distance between the virtual and the real. She knew that she was in her bathroom, for sure, standing naked, under the water jets but still she felt a pull towards that image of a new bride dressed in heavy gold jewellery and all the adornments of a bride. She delved deep into the image trying to forget the reality, for she wanted the unreal badly. So she stood and thought she was the bride, sitting under the pinkish sky. She thought she could see herself as a bride and the more she thought, the more she became the bride in her mind.

She started perceiving the face of the bride, fully, with red vermillion on the middle of her hair and turmeric smell emanating from her body, and the sandalwood paste decoration on her forehead. She looked at the virtual image with all her mind. She could see the red Banarasi saree worn by the bride and her pinkish face with tiny droplets of sweat accumulating on her nose. She could see the palms of the bride with henna on them. And there was the red liquid Alta on her feet.

Hey Anu! See! I've crossed the line of marriage, at last!

Moni thought she shouted and the next moment she felt her eyes turning salty. She felt she was crying like a child, profusely, as if she would be crying forever.

Moni opened her eyes and touched her cheek. There was water everywhere and she could not differentiate between her tears and the water from the shower. She rubbed her face. She turned the shower knob off. The water jet stopped. She looked at her reflection on the mirror which appeared blurred by the warm vapour of the jet. She wiped a portion of the mirror by the back of her palm and tried to look at her own reflection again. Her eyes were red. Her face was pinkish. Her palms were reddish.

Moni picked up the towel to rinse her wet hair. She wanted to turn to the real events of life. But looking at her wet self in the mirror, she thought she had a query. She felt she needed to resolve an issue before wrapping up the flight of her mind for the day. So, she asked herself, looking at the mirror:

Which one is better? Moni in real? Or the Candletree?

She asked herself this question because she recollected that she had actually tried a similar question about someone.

She remembered that then she had found the real one better than the virtual one. She had preferred Ved over *SA* But in her own case, she thought *CT* the better alternative.

'Why?' Moni asked her inner self.

Cause you are afraid of the reality... Her mind answered.

'What am I actually afraid of?' Moni asked again.

Because you are afraid of facing realities... The inner self answered.

'And what are those realities?' Moni asked the mirror image as she felt somehow that her inner self had come out and taken a suitable position on the mirror, looking at her, with its fixed eyes.

'That you are afraid of males, and yet you are desperate to find someone to fall in love with...' The image seemed to answer.

'Have I fallen in love with Ved?' Moni asked.

'Yes you have...' The inner self answered.

But how do I know whether he loves me or not? Moni asked.

'Why are you so selfish?' The image of the true self asked.

'Am I selfish if I want to know someone's feelings about me?' Moni asked, puzzled.

'Of course, you are... For you want someone's love for your own good... Instead try to spread yourself out... Into everybody and everything around you... Love them and you will be flooded by love,' said the reflection.

But... Didn't Ved chat with me for hours telling me that he missed me... Reminding me that he would be pissed off if I ever discontinue the chat with him... Didn't he follow me? Both online and offline? Moni asked shivering with angst.

'How can I know about someone else's mind? I can only talk about you...' The image answered.

Moni became thoughtful.

'I'm disappointed... I thought you're omniscient,' Moni said.

I could have been the wisest, if you were God! the image replied.

'So can't you say anything about Ved?' Moni asked, seemingly desperate to break the jinx of the image's piercing calm eyes that stared on her like a blade of a sword pointed towards her and getting her worked up.

'I can... Only when you'll make some kind of union with that person,' the image answered.

'What kind of a union?' Moni asked.

'A union which your heart yearns for...' the image replied.

'What do you think? Does my love demand physical union?' Moni asked, looking at her perfect body, which had not received the male appreciation, in true and real terms.

'Body? What's the use of it if you cannot spread your mind?' the image asked and smiled at her.

'What do you mean? You are just a fanciful image! How can you understand and grasp the full meaning of physical union? How can you feel the agonies and ecstasies of sex?' Moni asked, feeling dejected by the answers of her inner self.

'I am your mind and being what I am, I have the knowledge of everything around you... I have all the packets of information about every gesture you make, every move you wish to take, your past, your present, your future... I am the Mind which governs you... And without me you're just an inanimate object... I am the master of your mind... I am the captain of your soul,' The image stated.

'Hey! You've just quoted from a poem... I know it... I've read it somewhere,' Moni exclaimed, hearing the last piece of statement from her Self.

'Of course you've read it... I'm your mind... I know precisely when you read it and why... Under which precise circumstance... Want to know?' the self asked.

'Yes... I want to know,' Moni said.

'You read the poem when you were doing your graduation... Not in a book but in a magazine which you lent from a friend of yours who used to live near your uncle's house at Howrah... The name of the poem is Invictus... *You read it several times and you became so excited reading it, that the next day, even before you reached your college gate you had recited it the millionth time... You read it and it touched your mind... so I had kept it within, for I knew you would love to recollect it,'* the self answered.

Moni was amused by the supreme potential of her alter self. She just looked at her mirror image. She did not know what to say. She felt she should quiz the self more.

'So... You know everything?' Moni asked dreamily.

'Yes... Each and every single thing connected to you, to your experience, to your body and soul,' the Self answered.

'Then tell me, what I am thinking all these things...why did I just imagine myself to be a bride? Why?' Moni asked desperately.

'Oh that's all hormonal... You're thirty and your body wants a male mate... Mating is necessary for certain hormones... Hormones are devised that way,' the Self replied.

'So it's hormonal only?' Moni asked, astonished.

'The pining for physical union is... Anything physical and animalistic is hormonal... The physical urge to eat, drink, sex,' the Self stated.

'Can anyone live without eating or drinking?' Moni asked.

'Yes... One can... When one's body is no longer there... When it becomes the mind itself... When one is totally suspended into the void of the universe,' the Self said.

'That's death!' Moni reverted excitedly.

'Yes… So all bodies perish… When they gain all the experience of their lives… That's natural… That's salvation… That's the liberation of mind from the physical constraints… Some wise people do it deliberately… They are called the ascetics… The saints… But most of the beings die without choosing it… They run the normal course towards death, unless of course, they die by accidents.'

Moni shook her head. She pulled her hair. She was feeling wrecked and restless at the same time.

Okay! I think I've had enough… Of your philosophical gibberish… Cut that out! I'm fine! Do you hear me? Moni shouted and putting the hands on the mirror shook it violently, as if she would pull the thing off the wall.

Leave me, for god's sake!

Moni yelled, as she banged her head on the mirror. It did not break, but there were hairline cracks on it which rendered Moni's reflection somewhat clumsily as the image of an old lady with scars and wrinkles all over her face and body.

The scared face still spoke, for the last time though:

'Go for the union… Only then you'll be free from your wrath… and then you'll figure out everything…'

Moni looked at the reflection and noticed a red patch of blood on her forehead that looked, quite curiously, like a bindi.

Will you revisit me? Moni asked the face on the broken mirror which was fading.

'If I deem it right… And before I go, I have two bits of advice for you—just unite with the person you are in love with and try to finish off the task you've undertaken,' the face said and disappeared.

Moni looked at the mirror and felt she had witnessed a dream. But as she touched the mirror, she felt the cracks on it and could not simply rubbish the whole thing away as just a dream. Even if it had been a dream, it was very real. Moni thought as she walked out of the bathroom.

'I should go to office today, otherwise, I would be maddened by these strange thoughts,' Moni thought, as she walked into her room.

38

'Dad! Can't we print these?' Sonai asked as she saw the slide show of the pictures taken by Ved, on the camera display, sitting by her father in the car.

It was four fifteen and the father and the daughter called it a day as far as their short visit to the Botanical garden was concerned.

'Want to eat something?' Ved asked as he turned the car towards the flyover.

'Surely… And would love to get some books… For myself,' Sonai said looking at the pictures on the camera display. She saw pictures of trees of various shapes and sizes and those of swans. But the most fascinating one was of the shot of a pool full of water lilies.

'Wow Dad! What a shot! Wish I could turn it into a big wall mount board!' Sonai gushed watching the picture of water lilies, thousands of them, on a green pool.

Ved smiled.

'Are you serious about printing them?' Ved asked.

'Yeah! Of course!' Sonai replied.

'Well... In that case, I know a place that suits the bill in every sense... There you can buy books, have something to eat and order the photos for printing...' Ved remarked.

'What are you waiting for, then? Take me there, if there is a place to do all those things... I mean... If you can have all those under one roof...' Sonai stated.

'I think so if they had not turned things topsy-turvy...' Ved said as he wheeled towards the Hooghly Bridge.

He knew that a bookstore at Sarat Bose road has a cafeteria and mini photo studio.

Ved asked Sonai to get down from the car at the gate of the three-storied books and gifts store on Sarat Bose road and parked the car under a tree. Sonai went inside, holding on to her father's arms. They climbed the stairs to the second floor. Sonai was perplexed seeing so many books placed on shelves, neatly arranged. There were gift items at one corner of the big hall.

'Where's the children's section?' Sonai asked a teenage boy dressed in a black tee with an ID card hanging from his neck. The boy showed her one corner. Sonai rushed.

Ved smiled as he walked towards his section of books—the lifestyle and photography section.

After a while, Sonai came with a basket full of books.

'Don't want to eat?' Ved asked.

'Yes!' Sonai said looking down at her carry basket. Ved glanced at the books chosen by Sonai. Enid Blyton, Ruskin Bond, Tintin, Adventures of Robin Hood, A book of poems... all were there in the heap.

'Let's go to the second floor then,' Ved said.

On the second floor, facing the road, there was a cafeteria called Aqua Java.

'You've been to this shop before? Haven't you?' Sonai asked, as Ved started walking towards a particular section of the floor which was separated from the rest of the floor by a wooden cubicle.

Sonai looked at the big LCD hung on the wall near that section which was showing different snapshots continuously. That's the studio, for sure, Sonai thought.

It was. Ved brought out the memory card of the camera and handed it to one of the employees of the studio who immediately put the thing into a card reader and the photos captured at the garden were displayed on the LCD. On a big screen like that, they looked wonderfully fascinating. Not only Ved and Sonai, but all the employees of the studio wearing yellow tees with the word ZOOMIN written on them, looked at the display with admiration in their eyes.

'They are really wonderful Sir!' said the man to whom Ved handed over the memory card.

Ved asked Sonai to select those that were to be printed. Sonai kept on uttering her choices while the man took out a notepad and started writing down the serial numbers of the snaps.

After they were duly noted, Ved gave instructions of the dimensions of the prints and their print types, like matte or glossy finish etc. Having done that, Ved took Sonai to Aqua Java.

Sonai sat comfortably on a chair beside the huge glass window facing the street below. A man in a red tee came forward with a smile on his face, extending his hand.

'Hello Priyanko! How's life?' Ved said as soon as he saw the man and shook his hands.

'Two java special cold coffees and chicken sandwiches four each in two...' Ved ordered.

The man smiled and by waving his hand called another man in a red tee who took the order.

'You've come after a long gap... Not buying books nowadays?' The man, presumably Priyanko asked Ved.

'Been a tad busier,' Ved said.

As soon as Priyanko and the other man left the table Sonai looked at Ved with eyes full of mock anger and asked: 'So you're hanging around without your daughter nowadays?'

'Oh no! Came here probably twice before but made a rapport with these folks... They are fine... Last time when I came... It was late evening... And...' Ved stopped as if he was recollecting something and then suddenly he smiled.

'And then?' Sonai asked.

'Nothing...' Ved said.

'Nothing? No... You're hiding something... You're here with someone?' Sonai asked as if she had suspicions.

'No... Not really... Actually I bought a few books on photography from here the last time I chanced upon coming here... Those books were wonderful...' Ved did not say that the last time he came there, he actually met Moni for the first time in person, though quite curiously he had never known then that the woman who collided with him on that evening was *CT*.

'Curious coincidence! Ved thought. She also did not know then that he was *SA*... And both of us never knew that all those things would happen afterwards... That they would meet again at the Alclove... That they would be staying awake whole night and searching for Anu... That they would eventually cease chatting online... That their realities of life would be bogging them down... Many days have passed I haven't chatted with *CT*... Our online entities are no longer relevant... We just met by chance as life revolves around accidents and incidents... Ved kept on thinking.

The coffee glass was there in front of him lying unattended.

'Hey! Won't you drink?' Sonai asked seeing her father sitting plunged into some thoughts which made him completely oblivious of the place.

✦ ✦ ✦

39

'What the hell are you talking about! Whatever I've done was in accordance with the instructions I received from Mr. Bhatia from Bangalore!' Moni fumed at the man in the silk black suit, sitting before her in her cabin, leafing through the sales document and stock reports.

'You've got mails from him? Show me their copies then…' the man stated without any outward show of emotion, robotically.

'I can't… For they were verbal… Bhatia called me and asked me specifically not to put those woollens on display and keep them dumped in the stock room till fresh things arrive, so I dumped them… There…' Moni tried to explain, though she was angered by every move made by the inventory official from Bangalore, so far.

The man arrived at Blitz at 4:00 p.m. without any prior intimation. He came with a group of three men. They showed their ids and got straight down to an inventory of the mall, not missing a single item. Now this man, some Sanyal or something, had come to Moni's cabin and started quizzing her all of a sudden about the woollens dumped in the stock room at the basement.

'You dumped them, and they were bitten by bugs... They're moth eaten... How can you get away with such severe negligence to duty, Madam, by putting forward all those inane things?' Sanyal asked, screwing up his eyes.

Moni watched Sanyal. He was a middle aged man with a speck of hair on his chin that had not grown out into a full fledged beard.

'They came moth eaten! I reported so to Bhatia as soon as I received them... But he asked me to just dump them till fresh stocks arrived and he even proposed to mix them up with the new ones and put them on display at an opportune moment!' Moni exclaimed, feeling helpless and terribly annoyed.

'Tone down, Madam... There's no use saying all those things which have no truth in them... Do you think we have come all the way from Bangalore without knowledge of marketing people like Mr. Bhatia? In fact, we've got specific allegations about the way the mall is being driven to a state of sickness by you... Do you understand? By you!' Sanyal shouted furiously.

'What! By me! Hey wait a minute, Mr. Sanyal! I have got all my stock room staff to testify before you... Ask them... And I'm calling Bhatia right now, okay?' Moni fumed and took out her cellphone.

'Put it on loudspeaker, Madam,' Sanyal said smiling, seeing Moni press the buttons of her phone.

'Surely. Let me connect first...' Moni said.

Bhatia's cell rang for few minutes before he picked up.

'Hello!'

'Hello Sir! I'm Moni from Kolkata... We've got an inventory team from Bangalore here... There's someone called Mr. Sanyal who's asking me why I dumped those woollens and he's alleging that by dumping them, I caused them to be eaten by moths... Can you believe it?' Moni asked.

'No I can't,' Bhatia said.

'See? Have you heard that?' Moni turned to Sanyal with fiery eyes.

'Monideepa,' Bhatia was trying to say something.

'Yes Sir,' Moni said.

'I can't understand why really you've dumped them, if they are really dumped in the dark stock room,' Bhatia said.

'We've photographed them lying there Sir!' Sanyal burst out suddenly, with sufficient loudness so that his words could reach all the way to Bangalore from Moni's cell.

'What you guys are up to eh?' Moni asked, bemused by Bhatia's statement and that of Sanyal's.

'It's not fair... Moni... I had great expectations from you... you've let me down...' Bhatia chuckled over the phone.

'Mr. Bhatia! You're lying... You've instructed me to dump them and now you're backtracking like a chameleon, changing your colours... That's hypocrisy... That's pretence... That's an evil ploy to malign me... But I'll see to it that I meet the VP. Sales and have a talk with him... Do you understand?' Moni cried out. But the line at the other end went dead.

And Sanyal was there smiling wickedly at Moni, as if he was relishing every bit of Moni's helplessness, her humiliation.

'Okay ma'am... We'll be going soon... But we'll be coming back next week... I feel whatever you've done was not right... And the way you've dealt with Bhatia Sir over the phone was also quite unbecoming of a mere manager of a sick outlet…' Sanyal said, clenching his teeth. His fingers were folded into two fists joined together with anger.

Moni looked at Sanyal's fingers for the first time. They weren't long. They had no nails with thin dark dirt lines. They were clean, unmistakably clean. This perplexed Moni. She had expected his fingers to be creepy. Then Moni looked at Sanyal's face. It was long, as if the chin had dropped unnaturally from its designated position. Sanyal's teeth, however, were stained. At once, her rage multiplied.

'You're all part of the ploy, aren't you?' Moni barked, and noticed for the first time that half of her staff was standing around her cabin, a bunch of curious onlookers, watching a climactic scene of some engaging play unfolding before them courtesy professional artistes.

Soon after the inventory team left, Moni picked up her bag and went out, without saying anything to anyone. She simply could not show her face or talk to anyone, after being humiliated so badly before her subordinates. She was enraged, and hapless. She knew why it had happened to her. Bhatia was surely pulling the strings from Bangalore, to teach her a lesson, for she had once tried to talk straight. Probably, she had overdone this by asking too many questions about those woollens.

Moni just kept on walking down the pavement. She did not even look up to see the streets being decorated with lights for Christmas, and the happy crowd moving to and fro with bags full of Christmas gifts. She did not even sense that the evening was cold. She thought that she needed to get home to have a warm bath and unclog her mind.

But it had all started with the nightmarish image on the mirror at the bathroom! I've broken the mirror... And keeping a broken mirror is a curse... I need to replace it... Moni thought as she walked.

Why am I getting so superstitious? Am I losing self belief? Why am I giving so much weight to those delirious images? Why am I getting delirious in the first place? *Am I losing sanity?* Moni thought.

Body and Soul... Those two were intertwined... Psychosomatic disposition... Moni thought and walked the footpath. The chill was cutting her shoulders. She felt her hair, sloppy. She tugged at the two front ends of her kurti as if she was trying to stretch its length by an inch or two.

A few blocks away, on the pavement, some people lighted up a fire and they were sitting around it, trying to keep them warm. Moni caught a glimpse of the golden fire and the white smoke. The smoke rose up like a column, unattended by any kind of wind. The light from the street lamppost filtered through the column of smoke. Moni looked at the column of smoke resembling an eerie figure under the light. She thought she was staring up at a colossal figure standing motionless on the pavement with hands wide open, to embrace her: the streets, the cars, the people, the buildings, and the whole city perhaps.

40

'I'm sorry… It was impossible to dictate things to you while working… Today the crowd was really big…' Melvin flashed a hurt smile to Anu.

Anu nodded.

'Yeah… I can understand… It's really absurd to teach someone while working… Besides, I think I'm lucky that so far no one has raised questions about me sitting on the high stool every day, at the counter and spending so little money… I might be demanding too much from you… I think I should apologise to you instead, for hatching such a bizarre idea of getting to know about mixology at your workplace… Whatever you have done so far for me, is beyond expectation… I'm really indebted to you,' Anu said putting her right palm on Melvin's.

Melvin clasped her palm and flashed a smile.

They were standing under a banyan tree that had withstood the dust and the smoke and all the hostilities of the city. Melvin had ordered two glasses of malai tea from the Punjabi dhaba set right at the foot of the giant tree, a few meters away from the Kenilworth hotel and the pub. Anu looked at the old man sitting at the counter of the dhaba. He had a long white beard and his turban was saffron which made him look more like a sage than a dhaba owner. Anu was at once reminded of the old man she had met at Babughat the morning after her nocturnal adventure in the city.

'You know,' Anu started, looking at Melvin's hand that held her palm, 'I have always been erratic to the point of being eccentric… I find myself always at strange twists and turns in life… For example, one fine morning, I realised that I should learn the art of mixology… And so I went to Big Ben because that was the only authentic English pub I had visited before… And met you there… Seeing you give instructions to others and helping out the boys with so much grace and agility, I thought you would be the right person to show me the way… And you did whatever you could do, without even questioning me once,' Anu broke off, finding it difficult to talk more.

Melvin ran his fingers on Anu's palm for a while and then let go of it to hold the tea glass handed to him.

'I was amused to see the spark of eagerness in your eyes… the way you introduced yourself to me without feigning anything… I felt you really wanted to learn it… And so I just gave out some small details… And I was surprised to see someone coming to a pub really with pen and paper to note down things… It was incredible, absurd and yet very much convincing,' said Melvin, sipping from the tea glass.

Anu sipped from hers.

'And you never asked anything in return from me…' Anu said, looking at Melvin.

'What can I really ask from you? Money? For petty little tips on bartending? We the Goanese people are essentially candid... And I'm proud of being a Goanese, you see,' Melvin said, smiling.

'Yes... You're candid. But you can name a price,' Anu replied.

'Money dear... Is a bad habit... If you go on asking for money for everything you do, you will end up asking for it from yourself one day,' Melvin answered thoughtfully.

'Well said!' Anu smiled and returned the glasses.

'I understand, it is not a very feasible idea to come to Big Ben every day to learn the art from you though it was the best possible way to learn. But I cannot let you go. I've something more to learn. And I don't know how this teaching-learning process between you and me could be continued,' Anu stated.

Melvin looked at his watch.

'Look it is nine twenty only... We can go to my place and there you can ask your questions... I can answer them... Of course, if you're willing...' Melvin said hesitantly.

'Who all are there at your place?' Anu asked.

'No one... I live alone... My parents are in Margoan...' Melvin replied.

'You're single?' Anu asked.

'Yes... But not in the strictest sense of the term right now,' Melvin said with a wicked smile.

'So you want me to take me to your place so you can deliver a lecture on mixology? Right?' Anu asked smiling.

'Yeah! If you're willing...' Melvin said.

'That's the price?' Anu asked. Her eyes were fixed on Melvin's and she played with the buttons of her shirt.

'What? No! No! I'm a gentleman and I don't believe in playing with someone's modesty...' Melvin replied shrugging his shoulders, visibly angry.

'Come'n... Don't be chivalric!' Anu said hopping into the front seat of the car.

Melvin started the engine.

'Are you going to take tuitions even here, in the car?' Melvin asked as he noticed Anu bringing out pen and paper from her handbag. She had placed the bunch of papers on her knees, pushing against the dash board.

'Yeah... Just answer me while driving... You need not look at what I am doing... I noticed today that you used dashes of Angostura Bitters in Adonis and Grenadine in Zombie... What are they, actually?' Anu asked. Her eyes were on the papers kept on her knees.

Melvin chuckled.

'Are you serious?' He asked.

'Yeah! I'm! Now please tell me about them... I've noticed the bottles but one can't use them unless one is aware of their contents...' Anu stated, impatiently. Melvin cast a look at Anu's fingers holding the pen with its nib open, ready for dictation.

'Okay... I'm amazed by your devotion and determination, I must admit... Angostura Bitters was invented by someone called Johann Gottlieb Benjamin way back in the 1824. It is actually a unique blend of herbs containing 44.7% alcohol and vegetable extracts... It is widely used in cocktails... *Grenadine* is like good mixers. We use mixers or syrups like them too often in preparing cocktails... It is pomegranate juice, red in colour... So to make something red... We use it... Then we have another syrup called the *Orgeat*... It is a sweet syrup made from almonds, sugar and rosewater... Then there is another ingredient called *Vermouth*... It comes in two forms—red and white...'

Anu was scribbling down whatever Melvin was saying, on a notepad. Her pen was running frantically and every time the car came to a halt or sped up, her script twisted downwards. Noticing this, Melvin chuckled.

'You can't write like this... Let's go home first... Besides, what's the use of writing things down unless you lay your hands on the real things... And taste them on your tongue and get a smell of them through your nose or perceive their colour through your own eyes... Real life experience is important, isn't it?'

Melvin tried to dissuade Anu by saying all these. But Anu paid no attention to him. She just penned ideas like an avid student who does not want to miss out on a thing from her teacher's lecture.

'Carry on... Life's short, you know... This opportunity might never come...' Anu stated casually, as she sighed, looking at Melvin.

'You're crazy...' Melvin said.

The mist had already settled on car windows, dropping a translucent curtain on them, through which the sights of the outside world blurred, as if painted on a canvas with watercolour strokes.

'I know that.' Anu said. Her notepad was there on her lap and the pen was held in her fingers.

'Where do you want to go from here?' Melvin asked, suddenly breaking the brief silence.

Anu turned her eyes to Melvin who had turned the car towards right from the Hazra crossing.

'What happened?' Melvin asked seeing Anu look at him in a strange manner. She said nothing, just kept on looking at him with eyes that wore all the sadness of the world.

'Nothing... I want to go home... Drop me there if you can,' said Anu.

'What happened dear? I'm sorry if I've hurt you in any way,' Melvin said.

'No! You've given me more than I expected... I'm crazy... That's my fault,' Anu spoke with gentle graveness.

'Come on! I just wanted to know your plans... Okay, I'll drop you home but before that I want you to have a little talk with me... I think I can push you somewhere, especially if you're this devoted to the task,' Melvin said, taking the car through the gate of a white building.

Alipore Heights was the name of the building which stood like a white tower on the right hand side of the road. The other adjoining buildings looked less grand compared to Alipore Heights.

'Is it always necessary to go with certain plans, Melvin?' Anu asked standing on the sixth floor balcony of Melvin's flat, overlooking the road on which plied tiny cars and buses that looked like those so often seen in toy shops.

'I think it is... Desired, if not necessary...' Melvin said.

'Desired? What are the much desired things Melvin, in one's life, which is transient?' Anu asked in the same philosophical vein with which she posed her previous query.

Melvin smiled. 'You've got traits of a philosopher, I guess,' he said as he came and stood beside Anu on the balcony, turning his back to the iron rails, to face Anu, directly. 'A philosophiser mixologist!' he chuckled.

'Not really... But sometimes, I feel, what's the point of living a life which is short and uncertain?' Anu asked rhetorically.

'As it is uncertain, we should try to make the most of it... Isn't it?' offered Melvin, looking at Anu, who was looking at the street.

'That I'm trying to do actually, but... All the people put so many epithets to describe my ways, calling it so many names... whimsical, erratic, senseless, drastic... But you know, to me it always appears that no matter what you do, life will take its own course... *Que sera sera... Whatever will be, will be...*' Anu sighed.

'What others feel about you or your dealings with life should have the least bearing on you if you're certain about yourself,' Melvin said.

'Yeah,' Anu nodded.

'How certain are you about learning the art of mixology?' Melvin asked.

'Very much... I've put, I think, myself at stake, for it,' Anu answered thoughtfully.

'Yes that I understood, the way you've asked for paying the price...' Melvin said. His eyes sparkled suddenly with mischief. His smile had the wickedness. Anu could feel his eyes hovering over her. She slid towards Melvin impetuous as ever in getting physical to any man.

'Yeah... I'm willing to pay the price, dear...' Anu placed her arms around Melvin's shoulder and pressed herself against him.

'Are you really?' Melvin asked, joyfully and visibly excited.

'Yes! I've no such scruples about the body... But, how far can you take me?' Anu asked, coyly.

'Oh! To the point of your orgasm!' Melvin said as he clasped Anu tightly with his arms.

'You silly! I'm talking about the art I'm learning!' Anu demanded, assuming a role of mock command.

'Sure! You'll be given enough of wine to play with while I play the way I like most!' Melvin said as he lurched forwards and very slightly, bit Anu's lips, before turning it into a fascinating lip lock.

'Ummm... I'll see...' Anu hissed through her teeth, running her fingers all over Melvin's chest, demonstrating complete knowledge of the rules of this game she often played.

'Remember, you started it, not me,' Melvin said, kissing Anu's ears.

'Remember, you promised me *something more*,' Anu said relishing every bit of the hot air exhaled into her ears by Melvin.

'Trust me...' Melvin said, as he pulled Anu towards him and into the bedroom.

41

After cleaning out the shards of glass from the bathroom floor, Moni went to the basin to wash her hands. The space taken up by the mirror on her wall, looked strangely vacant. The iron peg, from which a mirror originally hung, was the only thing that remained of her mirror. Moni looked at the peg and the thin outline of dust on the wall and felt sorry for the mirror. *How many times have I stood before it, naked, in my truest self.* She thought before going near the basin to wash her hands. She put her palms under the nozzle of the tap as water ran over her palms.

Then suddenly she felt a pain somewhere in her right palm. She squeezed her eyes to closely examine her palm. There it was—a small mark of a cut with blood oozing out. Moni pressed the area to let the blood out for a while, placing the palm right under the tap. Water being mixed with blood fell into the basin cave like a red stream of liquid.

Moni looked at the flow of the red liquid moving inevitably to the hole in the middle of the basin covered by a glistening steel cap. Moni rinsed the area of the cut. A small cut, it was almost microscopic. Soon the blood stopped. The stream again became colourless as it should be.

Relieved, Moni went to the kitchen and started thinking about what could be cooked for the night. She remembered that she had forgotten to buy green groceries. She thought for a while before deciding to settle for egg curry and rice.

While cooking, her mind wandered a number of times, though she was not thinking about anything in particular. At one point of time, when the curry was boiling, she thought about shooting a resignation letter to the V.P. Then she drifted away from that, realising she could not just risk her daily bread and butter by doing something in haste. She thought that the option of resigning would always be there but she should stick around to see what Bhatia and Sanyal were upto.

Then, she thought about Sonai and Ved. She felt an urge to talk to Sonai but restrained herself from calling her, as she thought if they were not interested to talk to her, why should she call them. *Wouldn't that make me a poky person?* Thinking about Sonai and Ved gave her some kind of joy and helped her a bit to get rid of the insecurity that had gripped her ever since she left the office.

Her train of thoughts was interceded by a strong burning smell and then, she realised the egg curry had almost steamed out. The pan had become black almost and the curry was nowhere. It had been vapourised!

'Curse me!' Moni shouted, trying to somehow salvage the half burnt eggs and potato pieces from the darkened pan.

She put out the burner and putting the burnt eggs and potatoes on a separate dish, almost ran out of the kitchen.

'I'm so worthless!' Moni murmured and felt the darkness of hopelessness coming back to her with more sting. Just then, she thought she heard the faint sound of a whistle of a train, piercing through the misty air of the night, coming straight to her room, from some location afar.

No! No! I'll have to get rid of this feeling! Moni shook her head and opened the computer flap.

She felt she had a surge of emotions and she knew there was only one way out of the turmoil—to scribble and write away. So, she started typing on her blog page, initially slowly, but within seconds her fingers picked up speed as she tried to cope up with her fresh outpourings.

I have been floating on a boat of cloud since last night,
And Methought, the dense, impregnable darkness of the sky
Like the secrets of the knowledge of Time,
Would be revealed to me;

The voice of the Time
Coming to me, piercing the curtain of memories,
Was trembling, spreading its wings;
With the object of touching my dreams,
I made a desperate call;
The call of mine went high up to the northern sky,
Till it met its destiny, the Pole Star;
And I tried to invoke the star through the art of magic
Learnt by my lonely heart;
The Pole Star said:
'The Northern sky is my room,
If I get drifted away,

Who will show the light to the ships?
You go away, and weave songs,
And let those songs come to me by the wings of clouds;'

So, I searched for a speck of white cloud in the sky,
To send my songs to the Star;
But alas! I couldn't find a bit of cloud, white and pure,
To be my messenger to the Star;
Only the black demonic Nimbus
Came down laughing,
Encircling the periphery of my existence;
Methought, I have no way to unravel the mystery of darkness...

Just then, as if by some providence,
Removing the rain-drenched curtain of the Nimbus
And piercing the bosom of moist smells,
Like the deflected truth, the whistle of a train told me—
Leaving behind the riverside life,
I have almost reached the desert;
And at that particular moment,
An unknown bird, swooping down straight
From the visage of clouds,
Threw to me a heap of sarcasm from her wings
Before she flew away to the meet
The call of the horizon...

And I discovered all my newborn poems
grappling for breathing space
in their prosaic existence,
Trying to reach for the Sun,

As if they are trying to know
The history of their origin;

Despite knowing the name of their father,
I just left them afloat on the uncertain waves of my tears,
As I was desperate to save my grace;
And I noticed
The drops of water falling incessantly
From the captive Sun
On weary, dry leaves of my poems—
Left grappling for breath,
And Methought, they looked blessed...

Having written this much, Moni stopped for a while, and felt there was still something left to be expressed, as if she had collected in her palms, water from a flowing stream, and the water was dripping continuously and even by closing in her palms she could not prevent her liquid emotion from seeping.

So she looked at the shiny keys of the keyboard and like a possessed woman, she typed on, forgetting everything around her, like the smell of the burnt egg curry which lingered on to the enclosed air of the flat or the sight of the blood oozing out of a tiny cut on her palm caused by shards of the broken mirror.

She could have written a few more lines, had the cellphone not rung. Moni looked at the screen of the phone which had an unknown number on it.

'Who can that be? Bengaluru people?' Moni thought and was hesitant to pick up the cell.

What would I tell them if they kept on pressing me?

Moni had heard about management honchos making life unbearable for many with their iron-fisted volley of words over phone calls and emails, especially when they found lack of cooperation or respect of seniors in staff.

'Hello,' Moni uttered, as meekly as possible, clouds of doubt and suspicion hanging loosely over her voice.

'Hello,' cracked a female voice at the other end of the line. Moni thought the person at the other end to be in an even more dubious state of mind than hers.

'Yes?' Moni said, gaining some kind of authoritative posture, brushing mentally aside her fears about getting a call from the management higher-ups.

'Hello… I'm Laksmi… Laksmi Agarwal… Mother of Anoushka… Anu stays with you… But I can't make any contact with her… Her phone is switched off… I've been trying since seven this evening…' the cracked voice came through in broken English, struggling for expression in a language less familiar.

'O… Yes Aunty! I know you… I mean I've heard of you too, from Anu… Tell me, is there any particular worry?' Moni asked, earnestly.

'Yes… Actually, I think, I need her help… Living almost alone for the last one day… Her father… He had gone missing… He just went out of the house yesterday evening around seven and he had not turned up home so far… *kal sham saat baje se woh ghar nahi lauten hain*… I don't know… His mobile is off,' Laksmi Agarwal spoke, haltingly, still struggling to let go of her feelings and heightened emotional stress.

'Okay… Have you tried to make any search? I mean, have you tried to contact those people and places with whom and where he usually hangs around?' Moni asked, worried.

'I don't know much about this place, the people here and their business... *Mujhe is jagah ya yahan ke logo ke bare mein kuch nahi pata*... I sent one of our servants to the places where he usually goes... He is not found anywhere... Since last night I've been waiting for him... And... He hasn't turned up yet... I'm afraid... I'm feeling helpless... I've been praying to God... praying, dear, with all my heart and soul,' Laksmi Agarwal muttered as her voice cracked further.

'Don't you worry Aunty; I am going to tell everything to Anu and can possibly make her go back to you as soon as possible,' Moni said assuring and at the same time she became very thoughtful.

Laksmi Aggarwal became silent as if she had been waiting all her life with an inexhaustible amount of patience to get help from people, as if she was habituated, almost conditioned, to seek help from others.

Moni did not know what to do. She said finally, with worked-up cheerfulness,'Don't just worry... I'm trying to contact Anu... I'm going to send her to you at the earliest...'

As soon as Laksmi Aggarwal hung up, Moni called Anu. It didn't even ring.

'What to do?'Moni thought, tapping on her knuckles.

Should I go out in search of her? But where could she be at this time of the night? At a nightclub? Is she with Melvin?

Moni felt uncomfortable. She got down from bed, looked at the clock. It showed ten to twelve.

My goodness! It was so late already?

Moni called Anu again. It did ring this time for a few minutes before Anu picked it and replied in a huff, 'At the gate... Keep the door unlocked...' and snapped the line.

After exactly eight minutes, in came Anu. As she unstrapped her shoes, she kind of went off balance, and fell clumsily on the floor, by the shoe stand. Moni stood and watched her fumble dizzily with her purse and cellphone as she struggled to get up and struggled further to flash a smile with embarrassment and self-castigation intertwined.

'So... You come home tipsy... Bah!' Moni wreaked of sarcasm as she tried to hide her angst within.

'Why? It's my life!' Anu barked suddenly, more to save her grace than to mean anything to Moni. At least Moni felt that.

'Go freshen up...Your mom called me all the way from Siliguri... She needs you to return home by the first flight in the morning... Your dad has gone missing...' Moni said crisply and without even bothering to look back at Anu, she strolled towards her room.

Had Moni chanced to look behind, she would have noticed how the slightest sign of intoxication vanished from her as soon as Moni's words hit her. She now stood erect and started frantically keying into her cellphone.

'Hello, *ma*! What happened?'

'Oh! Anu dear? I've been calling you since seven this evening...'

42

'Wow! This pic is brilliant! When did you take that?' Sonai asked, looking at one particular snap of two palms crossing each other in a strange fashion as if they were two hands of some kind of a giant.

Ved had brought home prints of his shots taken at the botanical garden a few days back. Sonai had spread them all over her bed and took a close look at each of them, passing remarks on almost each one. Ved, having sat on the chair beside the bed, was actually staring at his daughter's face and secretly enjoying each and every remark and reaction of his daughter. It gave him the kind of pleasure which probably a father of a daughter, whose mom was no longer there, could feel. It had its own significance and uniqueness. It was a kind of unique emotional bonding which, people thrust by fate or providence, feel.

Ved just kept on looking at his daughter, his only offspring, trying every moment to realise that his situation was not the worst. Life could still be lived with hope and love. Perhaps, Ved got carried away thinking all this on a wintry night, from his cosy warm bedroom.

'Dad! What are you looking at? Are you thinking something?' Sonai asked aloud, thinking her dad was distracted by something, for he had not answered her query.

'What?' Ved asked, suddenly becoming conscious.

'I asked, are you thinking hard about something?' Sonai asked pausing after each and every word, teasing him and suppressing her smile.

Ved squinted in the distance.

'I love youuuuuuu!' Sonai cried aloud and pounced on Ved, almost sending him off balance.

'It is Okay... Okay... Now cool off,' Ved said smiling and started collecting the photos strewn on the bed.

Sonai joined him.

'Have you seen *Sleepless in Seattle*?' Sonai asked, collecting the snaps and handing them over to Ved.

'Nope! Why?' Ved asked, absentmindedly.

'Devakshi saw it the other day and told me the story of the movie...'

'Really?'

'Yes... It was an interesting one... With the climax taking place in the Empire State Building...' Sonai mumbled in a very calm tone as if she was in a dream.

'Really?' Ved asked, this time casting his full attention on Sonai. He noticed Sonai's sombre yet dreamy eyes. 'May I know the story?' Ved prodded.

Sonai kept silent for a moment or two and then murmured, weakly again,'Yes... But another day... I'm feeling sleepy...'

'Oh! Then let's go downstairs.'

Ved got down from the bed and extended his arms to let Sonai hop onto them, which she did, immediately.

Post dinner, Ved took Sonai to her bedroom and made her sleep. Sonai slept off, without her usual quibbles about little things like a doll being broken, accidentally, by Padma-di's carelessness etc., she just put her head on the pillow and turned one leg upon the bolster and went straight, seemingly, to the kingdom of sleep, which, by itself, was quite surprising.

Ved stared at his sleeping child for a while before going out and pulling the door closed from outside.

Coming out, Ved went straight to his room and sat before his computer. He googled for *Sleepless in Seattle* and found soon a site in which he could watch the full movie online. Half an hour into the movie, Ved realised why Sonai appeared so engrossed with the story of *Sleepless in Seattle*. Ved thought he and Sonai were living a life similar to the one lived by Sam and Jonah in the movie.

But characteristically, Ved thought, could he ever be Sam, or for that matter, Sonai could be Jonah… And could someone like Moni be Maggie? Thinking about Moni, led Ved to visit the blog page of *CT*. 'Haven't seen her page for long…' Ved thought as he typed the address on the address bar and entered the virtual space.

'I have been floating on a boat of cloud since last night…'

Ved read the first line of the poem that was posted a few hours back. After reading the first few lines, Ved felt he had come across a kind of a postmodernist abstract poem. But as he kept on reading further, he felt the initial abstract ideas became concrete, as images of the Sun the rain and the train came rushing. He also felt that the poetess was actually getting a bit psychological as she had presented the image of the sun as the father of her poems and left sufficient hints that painted herself as the mother of the same.

Ved reread the poem and felt like reading it several times, not only to grasp the underlying meanings, but also to get to grips with the numerous and varied images it presented. From this thought, he got deviated slightly when he suddenly discovered how poems actually present the mindset of the poetess or the poet. He also contemplated the fact that the mind was the only thing virtual and all other things are pretty real.

The poems are real, the blog page is real, the poetess is real but only the minds of the poetess and her readers are virtual. Ved thought.

On the comment box, just beneath the poem, Ved typed:

'Hope you will find the right path while wandering the zigzag patterns of life… And the poetry within you will then never be left grappling—SA'

While he was typing, Ved silently hummed a song from a TV soap of many years ago, when television screens in the country were all black and white and the TV cabinets were made of wood with strange circular knobs, placed on a right hand side front panel to control the volume and change channels, much like radios in those days.

The name of the soap was called *Imtihan,* meaning tests or trials in Hindi.

'Chalte huye payega tu manzil, gam se na dar… hogi khushi haasil.'

(As you walk you will attain destiny, do not fear sorrow, happiness will be won)

Ved hummed this Hindi song softly within. He went *online*, this time mentally.

43

Moni kept on watching Anu pack her bags. It was almost three in the morning. Anu spoke with her mom on the phone all night, until two thirty in the morning. Moni continued overhearing Anu's conversation on the phone, and from the one-sided responses, had understood something very serious and puzzling had happened back in Siliguri.

Ramakant Agarwal had fled from the town and gone into hiding, to evade some police and anti-fraud officials. Though it was not possible for Moni to make out exactly what Mr. Agarwal had done, it was becoming increasingly clear to her that her friend's father had become involved in some kind of murky bank deal. He had made payments to some people through bank drafts but the cash he deposited to the bank to get those drafts, was not at par with the amount given away through the drafts. In connivance with the bank officers, he had actually robbed money from the bank through drafts, by making underpayments in cash.

The procedure seemed complicated and it also seemed that the difference between cash deposited and drafts prepared and sent out amounted to several lakh of rupees. It was all that Moni understood from Anu's queries to her mom and her responses to her mom's responses.

'So… You have to rush back to Siliguri? Right?' Moni finally asked, feeling terribly tired and anxious within, watching the sleepless, reddened eyes of Anoushka.

Anu just nodded and kept on packing her bag, without even looking at Moni. She just nodded and Moni could see beads of sweat over her eyebrows accumulating, expressing strong signs of her distress and anxiety, even in wee hours of the winter morning of the twenty-third of December.

Moni felt she should hold Anu's hands and ask her if she needed any kind of help, but she lacked the courage, for the first time in all those years, to come near Anu or to hold her hand, for Anu's face was sombre and tensed. Anu looked grave and fatally serious, as if she had grown mature within these few hours. She already looked older than the girl she used to be, drinking happily and living life casually.

'Should I accompany you?' Moni asked, hesitantly.

At this, Anu looked up and gave a blank stare conveying helplessness and maybe, doom. Then she flashed her weakest smile which made her look even more pitiable.

'No Moni… You stay here… You work and carry on with your life… My life… Has always been… A kind of…messed up, you see…' Anu said, struggling.

Moni could say nothing. Big dollops of tears fell from her eyes. Anu, seeing the drops of tears in Moni's eyes, stopped and came near Moni, putting her hands on her shoulders, and shrugged them saying, in a soft and philosophic tone:

'Don't you worry dear… I'll be okay… It is time… For a person like me to payback… *Penance*… You know… *Que sera sera*… Whatever will be… Will be… You or I can't just change' em…'

'So… This Christmas… You would be not with me… For the first time since you came to stay with me…' Moni murmured, almost inaudibly, and foolishly, as if she had not yet come to proper terms with reality.

Anu said nothing. She combed her hair, splashed water over her eyes, and checked her bag and purse, in a businesslike manner, hard and mechanical.

Moni kept on looking at Anu. She looked at Anu's green kurti and blue jeans and she remembered exactly the day when they went out together, a few months back to buy those clothes for Anu. Anu always kept that kurti and pair of jeans aside, claiming every time that they were special, for Moni gave them to her.

'Would you not add moisturiser to your face and hands?' Moni said as she came back from her room with two tubes, one a moisturiser and another a lip balm.

Anu smiled seeing those new tubes.

She stretched her palms forward. Moni pressed out the semi liquid substance from the tubes on Anu's palms. Anu applied the substance quite hurriedly on her face and lips which appeared dry.

'Keep 'em…' Moni said as she handed the tubes over to Anu and went back again to her room. She came back though, within a few seconds, with something wrapped in a plastic bag and tied by rubber bands.

'What's this?' Anu asked as Moni took her right hand and placed the thing on her palm.

'Keep them... They might come in handy... And... Please don't open the bag till you reach home... And keep it safe...' Moni mumbled. Her eyes had a kind of piety that Anu observed for a while before she started packing again.

When Moni and Anu got down to the street, it was still awfully dark outside, as if the night would never turn into morning and the darkness would permeate their souls. Anu looked like a traveler with her green kurti and blue jeans with sneakers. Moni looked at Anu's moist face and strongly tied hair. She felt a terrible urge within to cry and embrace Anu, but somehow felt restricted by Anu's face, which had become stony. She had grown sombre and uncommunicative. Surely, she was stressed out overtly, and covertly.

O, how I wish to hold her back.

Moni thought and just muttered clumsily:

'Dear... Can you allow me to accompany you?'

Anu's eyes which were busy searching for any vehicle that could take her to airport, turned straight from the dark and misty and vacant road, to Moni.

Her eyebrows were raised. She looked puzzled.

'What? You said you want to accompany me all the way to Siliguri?' Anu asked, with eyebrows raised.

Moni nodded like a child, and added, 'Is Melvin going with you?'

Anu laughed out loud. Her laugh almost reverberated, breaking the deathly silence of the mist-filled, indistinct morning. Moni just stood there teary eyed. Anu slowly came and embraced her. Moni felt she would cry out aloud, but in reality she just groaned.

'Never thought you were so impulsive... No... No one is accompanying me... Now stop crying like a child...' Anu whispered as she held on loosely to the embrace.

Moni said nothing. She just stood closeted in Anu's arms, as if she had submitted herself to Anu.

'I wish... I could take you... But one has to clear up one's own debts... You know... I'll be in touch... Don't you worry... Besides I've that packet with me that you gave me... Though I don't know what you've given me in that packet... As you asked me not to open it before I reach Siliguri... I'll abide by your request...' Anu whispered with some heaviness and sadness.

'The radio cab should be here... I called the service half an hour earlier...' Moni said as she let go Anu from the embrace.

'You called the radio taxi? That's great!' Anu said, looking at Moni with eyes which were full of love—a newly discovered one. Just then, Moni got a call on her cell.

'Madam... Kolkata cab *se... Main* Dilip... *Kaha par hain aap?* I'm Dilip from Kolkata Cab, where are you?'

'Oh... Please be at Bardhaman Road... Near the Talwar's... We're actually on the road... Waiting for you...' Moni replied in haste.

Moni stood on the road till she could actually perceive the back of the white radio cab. The red backlight of the cab shone like the only thing visible on the road still foggy and vacant. Moni watched the tail lamps become blurred as the cab moved away and finally turned at the bend of the road. A few seconds even after the disappearance of the cab, Moni stood on the road, as if the image of the tail lamps was lingering on to her mind.

✦ ✦ ✦

44

If one could climb up the ribbon like path, going up the forest of pine and deodar and eucalyptus, one could actually reach a wooden cottage, partly obscured by trees and the undulated landscape around. The place had remained uninhabited for long and the possibility of human settlement in the near future in this remotest corner of North Bengal, is pretty uncertain. The cottage, sitting atop a cliff, looked dilapidated for several years. Only recently, someone had actually bought it and renovated it. But then the renovation was not the kind that would turn it into something very grand or beautiful. It was a kind of repair work that had been carried out quite hastily, leaving sufficient room for further improvements. Whoever had done that, had done it with a purpose.

The local Lepcha people were definitely curious, but, interestingly, their curiosity never made them abandon their daily fight for bread and butter and scout for information about the person who bought the place all of a sudden from a local timber dealer. They only heard that someone from the plains below had bought the cottage, paying up the legitimate price.

They heard that the man from the plains was a businessman. Now, businessmen buying up plots of land or old cottages on hills, is nothing new to them, for they have seen herds of them doing that in the past. They found this behaviour of the people from the plains quite interesting—especially the way they cause the price hike of land which always appeared to them as uselessly functional sometimes or sometimes functionally useless. They, from their own experience, found these people, ignorant of the ways of hill-life. In most cases, they turned these places into hotels or tourist destinations and earn money. Because, to buy a dilapidated two-room cottage on a top of a cliff with no approaching road but only a narrow stretch of rocks flattened by nature, is very idiotic for any kind of business.

Tourists from the plains love to trek sometimes, but that is a rarity in this region because other than hills and cliffs and forests, there is nothing to see or visit—no temple or holy shrine or any kind of mountaineering milestone. There is not even a medium-sized market nearby to satisfy tourist demands. The place was wild, with a deep gorge just opposite the cliff. In fact, the place is full of bad omens as at least on three occasions in recent years, people jumped from the cliff right into the gorge, committing suicide. To stay at a suicide point and to run a tourist business from there is quite unholy and illogical. So thinking all these, the local people only thought that the person who actually bought the cottage is not going to stay there or run business. They have taken the whole thing as a wild whim of someone rich.

So, after a few days of the repair work, the man himself appeared one day, just after dawn, with two people. The man who looked like the owner was heavy built with a big moustache and clean shaven face. He was at least six feet tall and weighed at least ninety kilos. He walked straight but always kept his eyes covered under the shade of glasses. He was always shadowed by two other people of medium height but strong build. They conversed in chaste Hindi, unlike the people from plains. They stayed mostly indoors. Only at seven in the evening, one of the two medium height accomplices of the owner would come down the cliff and go straight down at least four and half kilometers to a particular roadside cheap eatery in which the local woodcutters eat half burnt rotis and momos of different kinds—chicken, pork, veg. etc., with a lot of chilli soup.

Presently, the new owner could be seen sitting on the small verandah of the wooden cottage, overlooking the gorge from a cane chair. The time was almost seven in the evening. The mist being dense all around had created a kind of haze… A kind of whiteness which shut everything out. Visibility beyond two feet was miserably poor. The tall pine trees and the deodars looked like some blurry dark images as if an unknown but gifted painter had accidentally splashed water on his freshly painted canvas, smudging every object.

The man was just sitting on the cane chair, wrapped up in a woollen shawl. His face could not be seen properly as the yellow solitary bulb hanging overhead provided little to prevent the whitish clumsy state of fog and mist from enveloping the space around the man. The legs of the man, covered up to ankles by woollen trousers, were put indolently on a cane tea table. A bottle of liquor was surely there on the table too, for the man poured the liquid from the bottle, time to time, in a glass tumbler and drank it. Every time he drank from the tumbler, he made a kind of grimace and shook his head. As if he did not like the taste of the liquor but he could not help drinking it.

At least twice, in an inebriated stupor, the man mumbled, trying to call names of some persons. He just tried to call aloud:

'Laxmi...Laxmi... Can't you hear? I want my dinner!'

Next time around, he called out, quite softly, as if he was crying like a child:

'Anu dear... Please come back... I need you... I know... I've done wrong all through my life... but... but...' the man could not finish the sentence for he was overcome by intoxication.

The man just dozed off on the chair. His head, covered partly by the shawl, bent sideways gradually. The shawl which so far covered his head fell, revealing the man's face for the first time in that evening, as the bulb still shone overhead. The man was no other than Ramakant Agarwal.

Soon after, one of the accomplices appeared on the verandah from nowhere, as if he had been waiting for the man to doze off. He called someone, in a hushed manner and another person appeared, in a fashion similar to the other accomplice. Both of them lifted the heavy load of the sleeping giant, with a lot of difficulty and carried him slowly indoors, before shutting the front door and switching off the solitary yellow bulb. No sooner had the bulb been switched off than the darkness enveloped the whole cottage. It was getting sombre, dark and silent. The hilltop reached its climax of eeriness with the darkness, mist, fog, ghostly trees, wild smell of grass and weeds all contributing. The cottage looked like a dark botch from distance, indistinct and yet visible. The only thing that lent a tinge of light somewhere near, was the faint ray of light emanating from a lamp post standing a few feet down the cliff, like the last brave man standing against all odds.

For Anu, her place of birth was almost the same as the last time she came here a few years back. Only some brand new buildings appeared on her sight abruptly with their glass façade, making the town a bit glitzy and providing sweet contrast to the distant hills.

It would not be apt to call the town just another hill town with a lot of timber work around. Siliguri, a transit point linked the north east and north of the country with other parts, was destined to prosper, albeit in dubiously. Anu looked at changes happening in her birthplace, and thought of them to be a natural part of the town so fluid and cosmopolitan and pluralistic in every possible way. However, after spending a few years in Kolkata with new associations, seeking almost a spiritual refuge there, Anu felt terribly distressed to return to the very city that gave her family a dubious name and that too because of her father. To return to search for her absconding dad was never her objective.

She returned putting her post-graduation studies and the experiment with Melvin to pursue her dreams in literal terms, in jeopardy, because she felt she was needed by her mom, Laxmi… The woman with no worldly views, the woman who spent her life so far in a cage and who has no knowledge of her imprisonment even! She chose to be by the side of that woman because she had only suffered, much more than her and yet never really complained, as if to cavil was beyond her thoughts… As if to be free, would mean a kind of disaster for her… As if she had long resigned herself to the proposition of being cooped!

To return to the homeland, changed every day, by the concrete piling every passing moment, is like returning to the land of the dead... To return to the evil name brought upon the family by the family headman, is like returning to the inescapable agony... And to one's eternal submission to filth...

Anu thought and felt like crying out aloud. She felt she would better be keeping all these nonsensical thoughts at bay. She thought she would try her best to fly out of the place with her mom the first thing, leaving her moneyed, dubiously rich, monstrous, father forever to penance... *But has he got any sense of penance?*

Thinking all this, Anu became unmindful of the fact that the cab had entered through the known rusty iron gate of the walled compound, so familiar to her. The two storied white house appeared kind of sombre and silent, with the shabby exterior.

She got down from the cab, with the bag on her shoulder and kept looking at every nook and corner of the front portion of the compound. The deodar trees just beside the main gate were still standing tall and fresh.

'Kitna hua... How much?' Anu asked the cabbie. Now cabs here at hills would never become typical cabs of the plains, say, of Kolkata. Cabs here had always been vans, SUVs, jeeps turned into commercial vehicles with yellow streaks painted on their roofs. In this case, it was a van. So the van driver yawned and claimed two hundred rupees.

Anu's heart was throbbing unusually fast when she stood at the brown front door and pressed the bell. The doorbell yielded a kind of music, though indistinct enough to be fully comprehensible from outside. It ran for sometime before coming to an abrupt stop. As if, someone had stopped the music. Anu waited. She was now feeling terribly tired and groggy. She felt a momentary impulse to bang the door.

Then, the door was opened and there stood a woman who appeared just like someone coming straight from a temple after some kind of religious ceremony, for her forehead bore marks of orange tilak and she smelt like incense sticks. Anu looked for a while at that woman, trying to judge her... Her very futility at being so inclined to religion.

The woman, Laxmi Agarwal, just smiled, faintly and stretched her hand to get something from Anu. Anu at once realised that her mom was asking for the bag on her shoulders. She dropped the bag on the floor, and embraced her mom.

Laxmi remained calm as ever. She just stood there, with impassivity, only allowing Anu to embrace her. She just stood and cried silently, much like the silent rain that falls incessantly on the ground to make the ground fertile.

45

The night on Christmas Eve, like every other festive night, was boisterous, smoky and chaotic. Kolkata, being a city of people, processions, festivals and rallies, Christmas Eve night in Kolkata is always full of light… Dazzling, blinding light and nerve racking noise.

The time was eleven thirty. And it would take only thirty minutes more to make the crowd on the streets go haywire.

A particular flat in a particular apartment on Bardhaman Road, in the city of the joy, was unusually dark. Not fully dark though, considering the presence of the low watt night lamp shining in one room.

In that room, on the bed, could be seen sitting a woman with a glass of wine. A laptop was kept open on the bed too. If we keep a closer look on the screen we would definitely be getting a glimpse of an email addressed to someone called Monideepa Banerjee.

The email was short and crisp. It said:

We are sorry to let you know that your service to the company as manager of a retail outlet is put on suspension as per the decision arrived at the company's board meeting no 14/12/c. Please find the necessary documents of charges brought against you by the shareholders of the company enclosed herewith. You are also requested to tender your fittest defense in writing, on or before the last day of this month.

The woman sitting on the bed, was delirious. And, we all know who she was, don't we?

Moni, our dear Moni... She was mumbling. *'Fuck you all assholes... Sanyal... You'll die soon... Curse you all...'* After a long marathon of rambles and rants, Moni drank the poison from the glass to empty it. Then she poured into the glass a brown liquid from a medium sized bottle and drank the thing at once, grimacing all the way. Then her anger dissipated a bit but gradually the contours of her face took shapes resembling the face of someone crying within all the time, crying hard... pitiably hard.

The mumblings got less harsh but were still audible:

'O god! Help me out from this dungeon...don't leave me this way... without the job...without Anu... Without dreams... Without hopes... Let me die... Let me die with honour and pride at least!'

At that very moment, there came into her mail inbox, a mail. In spite of being fully inebriated, Moni somehow got the idea that a mail had got into her account and she fumbled in the dark for the mouse pad.

This was an auto generated mail from her blogger account. Someone has made a comment or something underneath one of her worthless poems. For an instant, she thought she should delete the junk and mark it as spam, but before doing that, she would take a look at the mail notification at least.

And she read the mail which stated clearly and as unequivocally as all email notifications do, that someone called *SA* had posted a comment beneath her latest poem and the comment thread could be fully visible if she could click on the designated yellow box. Moni clicked on the box and found the comment just in front of her eyes. She naturally started reading it. She was kind of amazed reading the last part of the comment: '*... and the poetry within you will then never be left grappling—SA*'

She reread and found immediately the ever expansive idea embedded into the commentary.

'*But...*' Moni started mumbling again, for the third time probably in the night:

'*But... How can I actually dear... How can I be able to pursue seriously my dream if there is as serious an impediment as the uncertainty over the basic survival support system... Added to that... Added to that, can a person with poetic mindset find happiness in the ambience which is primarily governed by things diametrically opposite to poetry... Can really?*'

Moni brooded seriously and her brooding temporarily stopped her upsurge of tears.

She was reminded of Anu's remarks about her being a kind of a misfit. 'But Anu herself was a misfit... With all her sex-plays... And pranks... And marijuana induced fits...'

Suddenly, Moni felt worried about Anu. She had not called her. No... No... She probably had called her after reaching home, in the afternoon... I should call her now... Moni thought and picked up the phone. It rang but no one picked up.

Just then, a lot of crackers started bursting in the apartment complex. Moni, being curious, shoved aside the curtain and for the first time realised that while the whole world was busy celebrating Christmas, she had just been crying and cursing herself and her life.

46

'How's the dinner?' Ved asked Sonai, the first thing after coming out of the restaurant and getting into the car.

'Great! Muuuuah!' Sonai exclaimed fully animated, though, concentrating on the white truffle cake box in her hand.

'Good... Good...' Ved said and turned the ignition on.

'Which song dear? Christmas carols?' Ved asked, taking the flyover towards the second Hooghly Bridge.

'No... No... Hindi film songs.' Sonai opined.

'Hey! You're listening to Hindi film songs?'

'We listen to film songs. Devakshi actually sings for us during tiffin-breaks!'

'Really? Teachers don't scold you?' Ved asked amazed.

'No... Actually, we listen in the lowest volume...' Sonai giggled, putting her right palm on her mouth.

'Devakshi? She's your best friend?' Ved asked, looking at the driver's looking glass, trying to gauge the cars behind theirs, as he was about to turn the car right.

'Yes! She is! She told me the story of *Sleepless in Seattle*'

'Really? What did she tell you about the movie?' Ved asked, getting curious.

'Well... She told me to watch the film actually saying that the movie actually has a character of a motherless child and his obstinate father...' Sonai blurted, effortlessly. But soon after blurting, she understood she had probably made a mistake in using the word *obstinate*.

Ved got a severe jolt not only from the words spoken but also from the way in which they were delivered. He could not talk. He just kept silent.

Sonai remained silent for a while and then she became restless, knowing that she had hurt her dad.

'I'm sorry dad...' Sonai said, turning her head towards her father.

Still, Ved could not speak. His head was jarring. He just thought, *'My goodness... Little kids think so much? My god! They are so advanced in analysing situations? They are so smart?'*

'Dad? I'm sorry... I never meant to hurt you...'

'No... No... It is okay... Today is Christmas... We go home and we will have some gaming sessions at the computer... How's that?' Ved asked, gearing up.

But Sonai did not appear too elated with the suggestion.

She just smiled. Even a few days back, Sonai actually jumped, whenever she heard suggestions like that.

'Not happy?' Ved asked as he tailed the SUV into the toll plaza.

'Happy of course... But...' Sonai's voice trailed.

'But... What?' Ved asked, as his curiosity was slowly turning into something seriously probing.

'Well... I donno why... But I feel I am not liking the games anymore...'

'That's good!' Ved said, nodding and paying up at the toll-plaza.

'Play the song…' Sonai said, looking out of the window, absentmindedly.

'Which song, dear?' Ved asked.

The bridge was adorned with festive lights. The decked up bridge on the river looked like a bride. The water below glimmered in the moonlight. Crackers burst in every direction. The bridge was full, with a two way stream of vehicles. Some cars carried young, wild party animals, hooting, cheering, and greeting 'Merry Christmas' to every passing car.

'Have you heard the song *der lagi lekin maine ab hai jina seekh liya?'* Sonai asked, softly as if she was trying to say something, standing far away from her dad.

'No… Dear… From which film?' Ved asked, intently.

'It is from the latest Bollywood flick… ZNMD…' Sonai quipped.

'ZNMD? What's that?'

'*Zindagi na milegi dobara*'

'Really? Sing it for me…' Ved said, staring through the windshield, the long road lying still in front of them like a long idle path of unmoving vehicles.

'You want to listen… Really?' Sonai asked, looking at her father, who stared back at her.

Der lagi lekin, maine ab hai jina seekh liya…

(It took a long time, but I've learnt finally to live)

Ved kept on looking at Sonai's face, for a while, though he could not do that for long as he had to pay attention to the long road as well.

But a single glance, told him clearly that Sonai's little eyes were watery. A single look at her face told him emphatically that she was feeling terribly lonely, much like him, now that the whole world was celebrating love and care as propagated by *Jesus*.

'I'm going to download the song and listen to it as soon as I get home…' Ved thought silently.

Sonai, however, kept on singing the whole song. She kept on singing… In her own childish manner, overcome by a kind of deep pathos and loneliness. She just kept humming. She said nothing. She just sang on quietly, softly, which made Ved sad no doubt, terribly sad and agonised.

And the Christmas spirit of being happy, with which they went out, evaporated into nostalgia for Mayurika, for days spent happily together… Reminding the father-daughter duo of the incurable sadness left behind by the dead.

'Is my spiritual inclination fake? Is my belief in *Gita*, just a cushion? Am I reading all these texts just to turn me away from the real hard world… Is my happiness just pretence and only skin deep? Or am I getting too emotional, forgetting the simple truth that we are all mere mortals… We all die… But memories… They are so real and hard to forget… They are so painful…' Ved thought.

'Dad! Watch out!' Sonai shouted out suddenly.

And Ved saw a truck in front of their car, carrying logs, stopping suddenly. Ved pressed hard on the brakes. The car screeched but stopped without sliding fast because of the built in anti-braking system.

'HOOOH!' Ved gasped, releasing some tension.

'Dad! You… You're getting absentminded… Come'n… We're on the road! You could've collided with the truck! Come'n! dad!' Sonai shouted with surprise and irritation.

'I'm so sorry dear...' Ved murmured pulling over to the left, switching off the engine.

'Will you mind if I get down and have a smoke before we finally take the canal road and reach home... I mean, it is not so late... Only ten forty... And we'll surely reach home in five minutes hardly,' said Ved embarrassed, and still kind of nervous, for his heart was thumping hard, and he felt he needed to smoke to pacify his tensed self and bring himself back to the real world.

Hearing this, Sonai, screwed her little eyes for a while, before smiling her best and nodding.

Ved got down, clutching the pack of cigarettes and the matchbox in his hand. He then walked over to the side where Sonai was sitting and leaned on the door and lit up the fag.

Sonai rolled down the window and peeped out.

'Dad... Are you ok?'

Ved turned back and put his hand on Sonai's head, sort of playing with her hair and smiled, nodding.

'Can I have the coke?'

'Yes... It is in the glove compartment,' Ved said and took the second puff.

Sonai took the can and the moment she opened the tin, the coke fuzzed, bubbling over.

'Hey!' Ved rescued the can put it out of the car window and held it till the liquid fizzed out and wiped the can clean with his handkerchief.

'Now... Drink ... But slowly...' Ved cautioned, taking the third puff.

Sonai smiled, gratefully. 'Dad... Can I ask you for a Christmas gift?' Sonai asked after, taking her first sip from the can.

'Sure!'

'Can we go to Blitz tum'ro?'

'Blitz? Why Blitz?'

'Because I wish to go there,' declared Sonai before her second sip.

'Come'n! You're far too influenced by *Sleepless in Seattle*!' Ved said, throwing the fag and turning back to the window to get a full glimpse of his daughter's face which just then shone brightly with the headlights of a passing vehicle.

'You watched it?' asked Sonai.

'Yes... Look Sonai... You're not Jonah... And there's no Maggie!' Ved said, raising his voice a bit.

At this, Sonai kept silent for a while, not sipping from the can. She just sat there on the seat, hanging her head low, lost in thought.

Ved kept on looking at her intently.

'She was just like magic... The moment I touched her I knew that... It was like coming home...' Sonai murmured.

Ved was dumbfounded to hear the lines quoted exactly, so exactly from the movie.

'She?... Meaning Moni?' Ved asked, thinking and looking at Sonai's face, hanging low down still.

Sonai moved her head up and down, asserting, very softly... As if she was thinking and dreaming about Moni and Maggie... As if she was mixing up the two in her head.

'It is not anything like living in dreams dad... It is like discovering mom in someone... Cause I know the best... I know exactly who could be like me... My best friend...' Sonai uttered, slowly.

Ved's head was spinning. He never expected such a revelation from his daughter. He thought he had rediscovered Sonai. He now thought all his education on human psychology was bullshit. He had just been handed a lesson on human development by his own daughter.

47

The cottage on the hilltop, surrounded by trees looked different in the morning. Instead of being sombre, it looked wondrous... Just like a picture perfect wooden cottage on the hill. The dew drops accumulated on the leaves fell every passing moment, making a kind of soothing sound, as if there was a mild drizzle. The mist was white and pure. The sun had probably risen but failed to penetrate the thick cover of fog and mist. The ribbon like path up to the cottage looked shiny, as if someone had washed it clean so early in the morning. The solitary concrete slab overlooking the gorge, looked like an altar.

Ramakant Agarwal woke up early. Living in this place outside of his home was really uncomfortable. He was not feeling at home without the comforts of a soft bed, expensive wine, beautiful prostitutes, a submissive wife, and cigarettes aplenty. Living here sans all the known familiar comforts, was like living abandoned, insecure, and lonely. So last night, no sooner had his intoxication subsided than he fell sleepless on the wooden, moth-eaten tiny bed, with an old smelly quilt.

He just kept on looking at the sooty ceiling and felt bad for himself.

Why I am here? Why am I living like a fugitive, absconding wretch?

The more he thought, the more he was reminded of all the people he had sinned against. The more he thought the more he felt sorry for himself and he longed to see his daughter. He was reminded of his little daughter and cuddly wife of yesteryears.

He was reminded of those days when there was no money but peace and sanity. He remembered when and how exactly he first deviated. He remembered:

> How, soon after gathering a contract of teaks and deodars in the forest, he had started living without his family… His wife… He used to stay away at least once every week, in the forest, with labourers and their families… And how on one monsoon night he was lured by the feminine mystique… And almost like an animal driven by instincts, brought Mohini to his hut… Mohini… The wife of Ajay… A labourer… It was raining hard… Ajay was sleeping like a dead man after the day's toil… And he just entered the shanty wearing an overcoat and carrying a knife in his pocket… He saw Mohini lying on the bed… Awake… And the moment he peeped into, she jumped out of bed and tried to raise a hue and cry… But was he not a devil? Didn't he bring out the steel, sharp and manly, to intimidate her with the dire consequences?
>
> And Mohini… Became silent… She remained silent for the rest of the episode, barring a few groans…

And even after that… Till she committed suicide a few days later… And then after the issue died down… He brought another… A widow… This time the middle-aged widow was a bit condescending… For he lured her with his money… He continued to enjoy the pleasure… He continued… But never loved that woman… So when the woman tried to seek emotional refuge… He just threw her away… Like people throw away half eaten food into the dustbin… He just flung her out of existence… And by that time his money had multiplied… And power… He was enjoying the power of being the devil… Despite an outward show of gentility… He had already started investing money in smuggling goods across the border through Sikkim… He bought local politicians… Henchmen… However, his money, unwittingly, did not help him to buy his wife and daughter… Laxmi… His wife… Gradually grew alienated from him… Seeking her refuge in the deities and goddesses… His daughter… Grew up and one fine morning told him that she passed graduation… He was amazed and happy… For he never knew his daughter had grown so big and educated… That gave him pride… But he was quite irritated when he learnt that Anu, dear Anu… Was actually planning to go away from home… Then one day, she told him that she applied and got selected to pursue her further studies… Somewhere in Kolkata… He was angry… He shouted… Laxmi remained silent as ever… Her silence was also terribly exasperating… He got infuriated… And threw expletives at her for being so timid... And suspected that her silence was actually helping Anu with a kind of tacit support... That night he did not eat at home and went straight to a bar... And drank a bellyful... And returned the next morning... After spending the rest of the night in a lodge... Anu, however, remained resolute... And she was preparing to go to Kolkata... Then he gave money to Laxmi and asked her to make arrangements for her stay at Kolkata... Laxmi remained silent then as well... But probably she was happy inside... God knows... She was happy... For she never wanted Anu to reconcile with him... Soon after Anu left for Kolkata.

He all the more detested his wife... And home... He started living outside... Almost permanently... He bought a villa just outside the town... And made it his den... He drank, enjoyed sex, devised plans of murder, rape, smuggling... He got so many friends... He got acquainted with politicians, robbers, thieves, lawyers, henchmen, car owners, bar owners, hoteliers... Then one evening, he and a local manager of a bank thought of a plan to dupe the bank by siphoning off money from the bank through bank drafts and overdrafts... The manager assured him complete secrecy and safeguards...Saying he knew the banking business too well... He relied on them, for he wanted money... Money the sweet honey... The plan succeeded initially, giving confidence... They started thinking bigger... They devised new plans to siphon off money from other banks by conspiring with other similar friends in other banks... Now this plan... Failed... The news

> got leaked to some source… And a warrant was issued first against the bank manager… And then against him… The bank manager got caught… And he is still absconding… But he knows… He cannot evade this ordeal for long… In fact, he could have saved himself by fleeing to another part of the country… But he is losing the very urge… He has only one urge now… To drink liquor raw… Bellyful…

All these thoughts, his journey down memory lane, made him so lugubrious that he actually jumped out of his cot in the dark and began searching for his magic potion… Bottle of liquor… He found several, but they were all empty… He got frustrated. Out of frustration, he came out of the dark room, opened the wooden door with a mild push and stood on the verandah only to see light. The mist, the fog, the chill in the air, all came rushing onto him, as if they would embrace him. He felt numbed. But this numbness soothed him in a strange manner. He just looked at nature so wild, and the sun coming out in the softest manner possible. He thought after coming to that place, he, for the first time, realised the beauty of the place. He gradually descended from the verandah and strolled across the undulated land to reach the concrete slab. The slab looked shiny and wet.

Ramakant coughed and spat, before he chose to sit on the slab. He sat down facing the gorge and the distant clumsy hills. He was blank. The silence of the place enveloped him. He could even hear the rustle of leaves quite distinctly. He could hear dewdrops falling. He could even hear the sombre sounds of gongs emanating from some distant monastery. He sat. He was not thinking anything, for thinking about himself and his life spent made him restless. He just wanted to sit that way as long as he could. Only one image, however, came to his mind. The image of a little girl playing in his lap... Peeing, pooping, puking... A little baby... Soft, gentle eyed... The image of his little Anu.

Suddenly Ramakant Agarwal felt like vomiting. His throat suddenly became heavy as if something was trying to get out of his body system. He tried to hold it back. But he could not. He vomited. He vomited the bad smell of liquor and pork. Soon after the vomit, he felt deeply weary. He felt sleepy. But the vomit... It smelled bad. He suddenly realised that by vomiting he had made the place so clean, consecrated dirty. So, he thought he should cleanse his own vomit. Now this thought was completely new to him. This thought was so new and strange and comforting that he was himself amazed by the mere thought. He got up and walked speedily to the cottage, brought out two buckets straight from the bathroom and poured the water. He felt he needed a kind of broom to cleanse the place spic and span. So he went in again and rummaging the storeroom, found a small broom. He ran the broom across the slab and poured more water and swept until his heavy body shook from heat and sweat. He also realised he was not so physically fit, for he was panting. He felt he had grown fat all over his body. He felt his heart was thumping way too fast. His legs were weak and his head was spinning. He fell.

48

The city of joy looked really joyous on the twenty-fifth of December, as it should. Sonai was super excited when she got into the car, wearing her favourite white frock and white-strapped shoes. Ved looked at her for a while, smiling. He felt he was looking at an angel.

'I just want to make you happy dear... I just want to be happy forever,' Ved murmured as he looked at his angel.

Last night, had been a revelation for him. He had seen Sonai's pent-up agony unfold before them. He realised, despite his providing everything to his daughter, there was still a space left unfilled. Sonai, in fact, told him last night, how she had learnt her first poetry lesson from Moni.

'You never know dad! How Moni helped me to write the first poem in my life, just by giving me some clues, while working in her kitchen... And that poem got all the appreciation... At school by my teacher and friends... You never know dad...' Sonai actually told Ved last night while talking about Moni and her brief stay at her flat and how she deftly managed everything before taking her to the school, straight from her flat, the night after Anoushka disappeared.

Last night, Ved told his mother Debjani that he would be taking Sonai to Blitz, where Moni works. He told her matter-of-factly, as if he was assigned with the task informing her of the next day's schedule. But Debjani smiled. Her smile carried motherly indulgence. Her smile carried a peace of mind she felt as soon as she heard about Blitz and Moni. Debjani's face looked so similar to Dr. Ramani's… Like the all knowing face of the mother.

It was afternoon. Ved's car had hit the canal road. If one drives straight down the road for four and a half kilometers, one would come to the spot where it intersects the Bombay road. From the intersection, one would have to turn left to catch the approach-way to the second Hooghly Bridge. The soft sun was still visible. The streets were comparatively empty in Howrah. Cars and buses, carrying men, women and children, passed by, noisily.

Picnic spirit… Gaily clad humanity in motion…

The air was mild and joyous.

'What will you buy from Blitz?' Ved asked casually, trying his best to keep his own thoughts at bay.

'O… Ho… Hmmm… I'll but… A lot… A doll… A big doll… With pink dress… A pair of Capri… A pair of sports shoes… And a handmade paper scrapbook and a fountain pen,' Sonai said, thinking, as if she was just reminding herself of things she stored away in her memory for long.

Ved smiled.

'Your list is good… I would add a few things more to the list for your granny and grandpa… But fountain pen… It would not be suitable for you…'

Sonai said nothing. She just leaned a bit to press on the car stereo and put a USB drive into the relevant port, to play a particular song *'der lagi lekin...'*

Ved had downloaded the song last evening soon after reaching home and listened to it at least thrice. On Sonai's insistence, he had copied the track into a USB flash drive. Sonai, before going out, this afternoon, urged Ved to take the USB stick along, that had several songs stored into it.

Sonai looked excited, as if she was anticipating something. All the way, she jabbered a lot. She talked about lots of things like the games they played at school... And how one teacher particularly behaved whenever she caught anyone smiling at her... And how Padma-di pronounced the word 'rickshaw' as '*rishka*' and 'box' as '*basko*'... And how one day her grandpa, tried to play 'Roadrash' on computer and finished the score as the second last racer, fumbling all the way with mouse and keys... And how her granny mistook sugar for salt when making her a salted health drink... And so on, so forth.

But whatever she said, her candid childish smile always showed up, pasted on her lips. She smiled and giggled as if she was full of laughter and fun. She looked like a true angel in her white dress and smiling face. She was so happy and blessed.

Ved noticed everything. Ved noticed her happy state of mind and thought that now that he had already begun their journey to Moni, he should not be troubled by any consequence, for he realised last night that he had to take the road to Moni, in any case.

The streets of the city were as gay as the face of Sonai... Happy happy faces... Smiling faces... Giggling faces... As if there were no cares in the world... As if all were destined only to be a part of the happiness, eternal.

Ved remembered the path he chose after Mayurika's death and thought that whatever he was doing actually conformed to that path, because the path of love actually meant devotion, and devotion without expectation was the truest path. However, the road to Blitz was full of temptation and expectation.

Then he looked at Sonai's face and felt pained, for he was afraid that her expectations could possibly get a great jolt... Her dreams based on Sleepless in Seattle could be shattered...

Finally, they reached the mall. The setting sun had lent a pinkish aura to the façade of the building which was decorated by papier-mâché lanterns, stars, and big Santas all over. Sonai jumped out of the car, staring at the façade. Ved locked the doors and walked to the spot on the pavement where exactly Sonai stood. He put his hands on her shoulders and asked:

'Are we not going in?'

'Of course!' Sonai said, coming into her restless, animated self again.

And they entered the mall. The ground floor was still to be peopled. It was five. The staff were busy arranging things. A big Christmas tree was placed strategically the centre of the ground floor. Just in front of the tree, a big bowl was placed with lots of chocolate goodies. The hall looked tidy.

Entering the mall, Sonai started walking towards the right side flank as if she knew exactly where she would find her desired object.

She was walking briskly. Ved followed her, not knowing where his angel was heading. Sonai stopped in front of the manager's cabin. Ved also stopped.

A man wearing a deep blue coat was working on the computer, inside the cabin. The glass door was shut. The man was working so hard that he did not notice that a father and daughter were standing there at the door. Sonai pushed the door open suddenly, leaving Ved on tenterhooks, for Ved was not sure how his daughter would react if she would get any harsh treatment. He just followed in.

'Sir! Sorry for disturbing you… For I see you are busy…' Sonai started the conversation in the most genteel manner, surprising Ved even.

The man looked up. Now Ved could see the face of the young man with an I.D. card hanging from his neck.

'No not at all,' the man called Kevin, smiled happily.

'Well… Where can I find Monideepa Banerjee?' Sonai asked.

'Are you from her family?'

The man appeared less jovial as soon as he heard Moni's name.

'Well…' Sonai fumbled.

'We're her family friends…'Ved came in to help Sonai.

Sonai nodded, asserting.

'She's not working here anymore…' The man replied sternly and started typing something.

Sonai did not say anything. She was too shocked.

'Thanks…' Ved said and almost pulled Sonai out.

Coming out of the room, Sonai started walking towards the exit straightaway. Ved followed her, calling, 'Sonai! Aren't you going to buy anything?'

But she just did not pay heed to anything. She just walked out of the mall, without even bothering to look back at her dad, following her hurriedly.

✦ ✦ ✦

49

It was three in the afternoon, when Anu set out from her home, leaving her wailing mother alone in the care of one of their servants. She had to, for she knew her mom would never be able to stand the journey in such an emotionally disturbed state. She told her before leaving home, that she would call her as soon as she met dad. She was not carrying her cellphone. She had just left it switched off upon reaching Siliguri. She had wanted it to be silent—she wanted herself detached from Moni and Melvin and her friends of the university.

A man called Mathur arrived at their home at about two, just after she and her mom had had their meager meal to take her by car. Mathur carried the news that her dad had fallen ill, in fact, he was found unconscious, near a gorge, just opposite the cottage somewhere at Lava, where he and Mathur and another of his trusted aides had been staying for the last few days.

Anu could have started early. She could have set out as soon as she had heard the news. But she felt great conflict within. She thought at one point that she should leave that monster to death. But her mom was crying bitterly and profusely. She just begged her to go. But Anu was still thinking then, as she was informed by Mathur that Ramakant had regained consciousness and wanted to see her. (Somehow that monster had found out about her arrival!)

'I don't want to see him!' Anu had exclaimed, all her pent-up angst erupting like a volcano.

But Laxmi, the woman with extraordinary kindness and love and devotion, kept on pleading. Anu finally agreed to go all the way… thinking such a confrontation needed no further delay. She had called Ramakant over the phone, at the number given to her by Mathur. She told him that she would be on her way soon.

Now that the car was moving uphill, following the snake-like shiny road twisting and turning, and tall pines and deodars lining the misty road, Anu became a bit nostalgic. She remembered exactly how in her early teens, sometimes her dad would come home all excited, bring out his red bike and would take her for a ride down the Sevoke road. Dad was pretty different then. He was more human. Anu thought, sadly.

Then she started thinking of how money came in to their family all of a sudden and how it brought in all the evils. Initially, the feeling was terribly good. Money brought in all the happiness, *feel-good factor*. But as dad got more involved with his money making, he took lesser care of home… Of her… Of her mom. *He kind of drifted away. He just drifted away….*

Anu thought with a loud, heavy sigh.

Suddenly she saw two Lepcha girls, returning from school in their blue frocks and white blouse. They were busy talking, and walking the winding road. As Mathur's car whizzed past them, they almost leaned on the mountain slope, looking with curious eyes. Probably because, few tourists came to Lava during winter and fewer cars ran up the road during late evenings, as the visibility got poor.

Looking at the girls, Anu was suddenly reminded of Moni. She thought how it would have been if Moni had been by her side, this winter afternoon, like a true companion for a journey to face-off destiny. She thought it would have been really gratifying and comfortable for both of them, perhaps.

Then suddenly she felt like crying for Moni, for she was reminded of the packet that Moni had given her when she was leaving their Bardhaman Road flat, so early in the morning. She had been specifically asked by Moni not to open the packet, before reaching Siliguri. She, god knows why, complied fully, for she thought she should not cause the breach of faith that Moni, the goddess, bestowed upon her. So she never opened the packet before reaching home. But as soon as she opened the packet, she could not control her tears, for Moni had given away her two newly bought solid gold bangles, from every bit of her hard earned money. The very sight of those bangles reminded her of the evening Moni returned home late, drenched, from a wet monsoon evening. She remembered how animated Moni had been, having finally bought some gold ornaments for her. Maybe, she had thought of her own marriage and had started arranging things bit by bit. Anu knew how important and precious those bangles were for Moni, for it cost her blood and toil. The more she thought about it, the more she felt morbid.

She thought herself to be most erratic and irresponsible. She thought about her lustful ventures. She thought about her whimsical eccentricities, which in retrospect, looked too selfish.

She thought how she had given pain to both Moni and Ved, to her mother, Laxmi, to Sandy, to Melvin. She thought she had given only pain to all who loved her best. She just cried silently as the car rode on the road, which was getting darker as the evening set in. She cried like a little child, causing Mathur, to look back from the front seat of the van. She still could not stop her tears rolling down her cheeks, almost irresistibly. She knew the driver was watching her through the mirror and Mathur was watching her too. But still she felt it hardly mattered.

At precisely seven, the car stopped in front of a forested cliff. Mathur got down from the car hastily and opened the door for Anu, who lumbered out, slowly taking in the dark surroundings. Only a faint ray of yellow bulb could be traced to a distance, at the top of the cliff.

'*Chaliye*... Let's go, madam...' Mathur said, as he started walking towards the forest, bringing out a small torch, leading the way.

The steps made of flattened rocks, were not visible, and mostly covered by grass and weeds. Anu treaded on the steps, closely observing them. She tried to grope her way up, as the light of the torch was too faint to be of any real help. It only made the darkness around, more prominent.

Mathur led the way. He was not struggling like Anu, for he had the torch and was well-acquainted with the steps. Still, he stopped sometimes to give light to Anu. After a few minutes of walking up the steps and navigating the mossy layer of grass and weeds, they reached a cottage. A yellow bulb hung in the verandah. Before the cottage, was an even piece of land. A few small shrubs were arranged in lines as if someone had tried to create a garden on the flat land. But it was more like an unkempt garden.

Mathur walked up the wooden stairs of the cottage. Anu followed. In the verandah, a bulb lit up the whole place, and Anu tried to fully analyse the cottage. It looked old, with planks coming off here and there. The wooden floor was moist and dark, screeching every time someone stepped on it with a bit of force.

'Andar aiye... Please come in...' Mathur motioned, opening the wooden door for Anu.

Anu walked in. She could feel her heart beating fast. She could feel her nervousness clubbed between angst and anxiety, making her feel weak. For the final time, once and for all, she buckled up strength to meet her destiny. The door opened to a fairly big room, lit up by a single white tube light.

In one corner, was a couch full of clothes. Just beside it, was a cot with someone lying on it, covered to his chin, with a faded, dirty quilt. Beside the bed, was a man sitting on a chair, who sprang to his feet the second Anu entered the room.

Anu walked to the cot, towards the sleeping man. The man's face, sent up a flurry of hot conflicting emotions in her. On the one hand, she felt like attacking, shaking him violently awake, to land on his face with all her force, a mighty blow. On the other hand, she felt like caressing his rough bearded cheeks and run her fingers through the wet and clumsy man's uncouth, uncombed hair.

'He has shrunk... At least horizontally... If not vertically... And he appears unfed, weak and ill...' Anu thought as she sized up the sleeping man in bed.

For, there lay the man, the monster, Ramakant Agarwal, her dad... There lay the ugly progenitor... Her origin and truth...

'When will he wake up?' Anu asked, about him.

'*Pata nahin*... I don't know... We somehow brought him here... We splashed water on his face... He woke up and tried to say something... And then again, dozed off...' The man, who was standing beside the chair, said haltingly.

At this, Anu rushed to touch the forehead of her dad. It had normal temperature. Then she removed the quilt to check the pulse. It was running slow and erratic.

'God! He should be taken to doctor!' Anu gushed.

'A doctor, here?' Mathur asked, surprised.

'What do you mean? We'll have to take him to a doctor or any kind of hospital!' Anu almost barked.

'But ...' Mathur tried to oppose.

Anu turned to Mathur and said sternly, 'If you don't, I will! He is my dad! You understand?'

'But... That would mean very trouble... Your dad and even you... Police looking for us...' Mathur uttered in broken English.

The other man in the room, nodded in agreement.

'I don't care!' Anu said and asked the other man to arrange for the car and driver again.

Within twenty minutes, Anu was back on her way to Siliguri again, where a local quack diagnosed Ramakant's health to be deteriorating severely, fast. Mathur hadn't come, nor did the other man. They had just stayed back.

Anu called her mom from a pay phone booth and asked her to call their local home physician, narrating in brief Ramakant's condition.

She kept sitting by the window, with her dad's head on her lap. All the way, she had cried and her tears fell on the face of the man, but he still did not wake up. It had grown completely dark and the environment was misty. Anu, time and again, tried to get the pulse and sometimes she just could not get it. Then she would just lean on her father's bosom, putting one ear to hear his faint heartbeat. She kept on praying to God. She cried, sobbed, panted, cursed herself, her mother, her fate… All the way she was very nervous. It was a long winding road, downhill. There were times when she felt the road was too long and kept on asking the driver how long it would take to reach Siliguri.

The driver, a Nepalese, was also trying to console her, saying everything would be all right and there would be no worry once they reached town. And Anu, the helpless, lonely daughter of a dying man, repeatedly begged the driver to speed up, promising him a hefty gift. The driver nodded and sped, aware of the danger lurking at every turn. Anu was desperate. She did not think of the risk involved in overspeeding through darkness and mist. *But wasn't time runing out? Wasn't her dad dying?*

50

'Why don't you understand, Sonai! It would be quite foolish for us to go all the way to Moni's place... Today is Christmas! She might not be at home! She might've gone away to some other place... And she's not picking up the phone... She might be in some party' Ved tried reasoning with his adamant daughter, for the thirteenth time, that day. But each time, Sonai only started crying—unlike behaviour, he thought, from such a mature, calm and brooding child.

Ved was particularly baffled by Sonai's insistence on not buying anything for Christmas. 'I have to meet her first before I buy anything,' Sonai kept on insisting, obstinately.

This irritated Ved, who also thought that if he rebuked her on Christmas Day, the situation might worsen for Sonai and she may not even eat anything and probably would go home straightaway. That would complicate situations further at home with the larger family bearing witness to their mutual awkwardness.

Besides, he also was curious to know what happened to Moni, given that she had lost her job and been writing poems that were sad and grief stricken.

He also thought that once they reached Moni's place and did not find her there, it would become easier for him to convince his daughter that Moni had no real feelings for her, and then probably her movie-induced state of mind of getting a stepmom as a Christmas present, would die permanently.

With these thoughts, Ved drove to the Bardhaman Road apartment. The road was quiet compared to other streets and roads in the city. Though the cars were fairly large in number on the road and even honking and blaring music. The festive appearance was not amiss nor out-of-place.

The apartment was decorated with tiny yellow lights. Ved drove through the gate. The doorman came up to the window.

'Visitor to flat no. 3/c,' Sonai quipped, even before Ved could say something.

The doorman showed Ved the place to park his car and he complied. As soon as their elevator reached the designated floor, Ved and Sonai stepped out, almost deafened by loud party music coming out from some place.

The corridor was decorated with Christmas trees and balloons and lights of different hues. The track emanating from a location unrevealed to the father and daughter was a very good dance number... *Welcome to New York city...*

'Hey! It's Ricky Martin, Dad!' Sonai gushed and nodded her head to the beat of the track, coming instantly into a party mood, quite childishly, as if... *Life is a big party...*

Ved laughed and pulled her to the door which both of them had the desire to open and peep through. Perhaps more than just peep through. Get into someone's life with a lot of love, unconditional love.

But the door was locked. Ved rang the bell thrice. Sonai knocked on the knocker. But still, the door remained closed. No one opened it. The father and daughter just stood there foolishly at the door.

'*Hola!* What do you want?' someone called out from the other end of the corridor.

Both Ved and Sonai turned to find the exact source of the gay voice. They found an old man, probably in his late sixties, in a cotton half-pant and floral print Caribbean beach shirt, strolling towards them lazily and somewhat unsteadily. He was holding a glass wrapped in a paper napkin. He was drunk and happy. His face, as he came near Ved and Sonai, looked happy and robust. As if his motto in life was, get drunk be happy.

'*Hola!* Me Rudranarayan… Ex army… Neighbour of the two beautiful darlings! One is erratic and the other… Well… poetic!' The man jabbered, transferring his napkin-clad wine glass to his left hand and stretching out his right hand to shake hands with Ved. Ved reciprocated, smiling curiously.

'How are you dear? Merry Christmas!' Rudranarayan, ex army and the neighbour of Moni, said as he cuddled Sonai, pressing her cheeks.

'Merry Christmas to you and family, as well!' Sonai replied cheerfully and a bit formally.

'Family? I've got no family… I live alone here… My wife left me… Divorced… I am living here alone…' Rudranarayan uttered, replacing his gaiety and twinkling eyes for a moment, perhaps suddenly sent back to a past which had never been too happy.

Sonai remained silent.

The music track changed to *Last Christmas.*

'George Michael…' Ved murmured, inadvertently.

Rudranarayan gently shook his heavy legs, rocking to the rhythm of the song.

He behaved as if he was no more interested in their talk. He brought out his trembling right hand once more. Ved shook his hands. Sonai sensed that if the man, Moni's neighbour slipped away, then she would not get the info about Moni's whereabouts. So, with a sudden rise of desperation, she asked:

'Hey! Can you let us know where Moni is? Or, where is Anoushka?'

The man in cotton shorts and floral printed beach shirt who had already started drifting away, stopped and turned sharply, to look straight down at Sonai. Then, gave a tired smile, saying:

'Well… I found Moni standing long in her balcony last night, when I went up to my balcony to sit there and have my third glass of beer… I noticed her to be without proper winter clothing, but not shivering at all… She was smoking… Smoking and coughing… I didn't find Anu… I also found Moni going out a few minutes back, dressed in a black kameez and white pants… She looked distracted when she came out of the room and locked the door… And she was not at all looking happy.'

'Do you know where she went?' Sonai asked, as if she was an investigator or something.

Rudranarayan shrugged his shoulders and probably tried to remember something, screwing his thick brows.

'O… I remember… I was then trying to help some kids to hang the lanterns and paper balls in the corridor… I found her coming out of the flat… Locking it… She gave us a glare… For the kids were shouting gaily… Then looking at me and finding me help the kids decorate the corridor… She smiled, faintly… I also smiled back… Then she greeted us Merry Christmas… to which I and the kids reciprocated… I asked her, "where are you going darling?" as I always do when I find anyone in the apartment going out… That's the way I am… Talking to everyone… Interacting… Jabbering… Being inexplicably garrulous… But god knows why… Everyone puts up with my talkative behavior and informal deportment.'

Rudranarayan stopped to take a long swig from the glass, as if he needed that swig to carry on further, still standing in the corridor where the music played loudly.

'Then what happened?' Sonai asked, trying like a detective to extract exact information.

Ved said nothing. He was just watching Rudranarayan, trying to understand fully the man, his jabbering, his ways of life.

'Oh yes… Sorry… I drifted off… Moni said she was going out to get the air… The Christmas air… She had joked…. And we all laughed… But I find it unusual… For she in all those years had never gone out so improperly dressed… I mean… Moni always dressed to perfection.'

'When, exactly, did Moni go out?' Sonai asked, with curiosity in her eyes, looking at Rudranarayan.

Ved felt Sonai had become Diana again, at least for the time being.

Rudranarayan smiled and pressed Sonai's cheeks once more.

'You love her, *na*?' Rudranarayan said, smiling, looking at Sonai and then turning his gaze to Ved.

'O yes… I do…' Sonai said, without fumbling, but pausing a bit.

Then Rudranarayan looked at Ved.

Ved did not know what to say. He just felt, he had been given this look by his mom and dad, Debjani and Biswanath, and from people like Dr. Ramani. He thought he recalled the writing on the billboard, he remembered noticing a few months ago, near the Alipore zoo and National library crossing:

Marriages are made in Heaven, with a little help from us…

Thinking all these thoughts, Ved just stood there, dumb and idiotic. He felt he should talk about his ways, but Rudranarayan, seemed absentminded. He was standing there, looking at his empty glass.

'Hey! Come'n! Where has she gone and when did she actually go out?' Sonai asked, getting impatient.

She could not understand this elderly habit of stopping and stumbling and fumbling and breaking off amidst a serious investigation. Ved patted Sonai's shoulders, signaling her not to press Rudranarayan harder. Rudranarayan shed his absentmindedness. He smiled again, but his eyes were moist. He finally uttered, looking at Sonai, 'I saw you dear, staying over one night with Moni… Later I learnt somehow that your dad had found that jaywalker Anu from somewhere… Your dad seems good… You're young and so naturally good… Moni is poetic… Moni is good… She, unlike Anu, is not a jaywalker… So if she has gone out on the Christmas evening at around five, with her hair not tied and wearing white pants crumpled… That actually means she is in some trouble…'

'What kind of trouble?' Ved asked impromptu, for he was reminded of a line of Moni's blog which he had chanced upon, almost inadvertently… *Caught in the middle… Of a riddle…*

'I don't know dear…' Rudranarayan shrugged his shoulders and smiled again, with moist eyes, looking at Ved, straight.

Ved kept on looking at Rudranarayan's face for a while and he realised only goodness and emotion pure. So he smiled back, candidly and brought out his hands to hold the ex-army's hands.

Rudranarayan's eyes were now full of tears which could drop at any moment. He somehow managed to regain composure, probably because he was ex-army. He coughed, and spoke distinctly this time:

'Have you got her cell number? Try it… She shouldn't have gone far with Anu not at home… She must have gone to the bazaar… Or to… Well… Any less crowded place… Nearby.'

'Well… We called actually!' Sonai snapped.

'Then call again… Keep on calling… She might respond…' Saying this Rudranarayan, the ex-army, smiled for the last time in the evening, and opened the door of his flat and went in. Ved and Sonai, stood there, like statues, immobilized.

Before shutting the door, Rudranarayan looked at the father and the daughter. This time his eyes were full of pleasure… kind of a joy. He seemed pleased by his own act perhaps.

'Dad! Give me your cell please!' Sonai said soon after the door of the ex-army man was closed, almost upon their face, but in a very gentle manner, as if the process of closing the door was something inevitable.

Ved brought out his cell, as he watched Sonai closely who by then, had started pressing a number.

'Hello,' Sonai uttered, with doubt, after someone picked up the line after it rang for some time.

'Hi… Sonai? Merry Christmas!' The known female voice uttered, with a soft tone as if the call was always expected.

'Yes! I called you earlier... You didn't even care to pick up then... Anyway, me and dad are at your door... Where are you?'

'O really? I'm coming... Stay there... Five minutes... Okay?' Moni spoke hastily, as if in a terrible hurry.

'Yea... Hippie! Hippie! She is coming home!' Sonai almost danced in joy, holding the cell in one hand. Ved thought she might drop the cell, but he just allowed his heart's joy to dance, teary-eyed.

Five minutes felt like five long hours. Every time there was a sound in the elevator, Sonai would go and check it. Finally, exactly after seven minutes of waiting, the elevator door opened and out came Moni, looking very exhausted but happy. She was carrying a packet in her hand, which, Ved thought contained a bottle of a beer.

Sonai didn't notice anything. She just ran towards Moni with all speed and pounced on her to embrace her. Moni laughed. Sonai giggled.

Ved looked at the scene and thought he might have to give both Moni and Sonai a bit more allowance.

'Merry Christmas!' Sonai shouted.

'Same to both of you... Come in...' Moni said in a choked up voice.

Ved was looking at Sonai, his dear Sonai, hopping and dancing, holding onto Moni's hands. Seeing this, while entering the flat, Ved felt pleased, but at the same time his mind was ruminating...

Possession is part of any kind of love... Love, which is material and pinpointed... Love which might be deep but is terribly narrow... Love which is blind and not wide... Love which has not gone beyond self... Love which is primarily guided by one's own self-gratification... Love, which is a kind of give and take...'I give because I want to take' and not with the feeling that I give because by giving away I live... I give because in this short life, I am supposed to give away my all, without thinking of what I actually get.

'You know... I planned to gift you something... We went to Blitz... But you were not there... So we came straight here... How's that?' Sonai asked, in an animated voice.

'Very good dear! But how can I play the perfect hostess for you on Christmas, dear! I haven't arranged for anything... You see... I'm... I never expected that you would come calling,' Moni stammered, not knowing how to put her exact feelings into words—the feeling of being surprised, overwhelmed and pained at the same time...

'We can go out for dinner! Can't we dad?' Sonai asked hyper excited.

Ved felt uneasy. He said nothing. He just waited for Moni's reaction.

Moni seemed uncomfortable. She just stood, with a helpless look as if she did not know what to say; as if, she had she been provided with the opportunity, she would have left the room and gone somewhere else to put to rest her inner turmoil. She felt she should just hide her face.

Ved looked at Moni's eyes for a while and thought he should somehow try to dissuade Sonai from pressing Moni hard to go out to dine.

'Sonai... Moni Aunty must be very tired... Let's not press her too much... You can always come another day and spend quality time with her... Right?'

Moni nodded, but her eyes were soft, dimmed, as if she wanted desperately to go out with Sonai, but she could not for something very repressive was working on her, hindering her.

Sonai came close to Moni.

'Are you? Are you so tired? Really?'

'Yes dear! I am so... Tired... Sleepy...'Moni mumbled.

'Okay then! You sleep... We go...' Sonai smiled and said, somewhat dejectedly.

'Just a minute...' Moni went towards her room.

Just then Ved noticed that Anu's room was closed.

Moni came back with a scrapbook and a pen.

'These are for you dear... My Christmas Gift... You just write... Whatever strikes your mind... Though neither the scrapbook nor the pen is new... They are old... The scrapbook has been used once by me... But the page on which I once scribbled my gibberish, has been torn off... So... I think...' Moni stammered, embarrassed.

'Hey! Don't worry! I am so happy! Whatever you've given me... They are good! I actually wanted to buy a scrapbook and a fountain pen for you!' Sonai exclaimed and ran to Moni to hug her and plant a kiss on her cheek.

Moni just stood, looking weary...

Sonai held Moni's hands in her hands and slowly murmured, 'Merry Christmas... Don't worry... I'm with you... for I love you...'

'I know dear... I know...' Moni said, hugging Sonai tightly.

Ved just stood there, like a bystander… And he thought he should ask something of Moni to make the situation less emotionally charged. He thought he should divert both Moni and Sonai to some other realities of life. So he coughed and found his words, 'Moni… Where is Anu?'

Had it been known to Ved that any query about Anu would make the situation even more emotionally charged, he wouldn't have done that, for sure. He only thought Anu had gone to some night club or disc, so the question was a bit casual with the objective of creating a diversion.

But to his dismay, Moni touched hysterics.

'Anu… O God! She's so depressed… She's so tested and tried by the god! O Anu…' Moni started crying bitterly which made both Sonai and Ved curiously surprised.

'What happened to Anu?' Ved asked, reminded of Anu's nocturnal misadventure and its consequences, including her wayward demeanour and uncontrolled lust thanks to her psychosomatic indisposition, as witnessed by him.

'Her dad… He went missing for some days… Her mother called… She went home… Probably more to provide emotional support to her mom, than to really search for her dad… With whom she had a long standing relationship full of hatred and spite,' Anu said, stopping, starting, panting and weeping, all the way.

'Okay… Okay… Now cool off… Did she call on reaching home?' Ved asked.

'Yes… But after that one call she is not picking up the phone. I called her mom. She is also not picking up…' Moni said, anxiety and grief lacing each other on her beautiful face.

'Don't worry... Give me her cell number... I'll call her and let you know if she ever picks up... You're overwrought,' Ved said with finality.

Moni looked up. For a brief moment, her eyes probed him gently, they looked grief-stricken.

But Ved smiled, with complete ingenuity of his intent.

Moni stared still at Ved and then looked at his hands. Then she suddenly asked coldly, 'What time is it by your watch?'

'Well... It is almost eight... Why?' Ved asked back, after looking at his watch.

'You've got a beautiful watch... May I have a closer look?' Saying this, Moni came quite close to Ved, staring down at his wrist and then, hand as if it carried something very obscure in design, something very rare and of terrible importance.

'Of course!' Ved said, and flipped open his silver watch.

Moni took the watch in her hands, but she was still looking at Ved's hand, his fingers, his palm. She was scrutinising them like some kind of palmist.

Sonai and Ved watched her, puzzled.

'Chronograph! That's great!' Moni exclaimed, but not appearing to compliment the watch. She appeared to have found something very pleasing in Ved's hand. She felt satisfied by some signs, apparently, in Ved's hand.

'Can you give me Anu's cell number?' Ved asked.

'I can... But as you see... Anu has confided details about her father going missing only to me... So...' Moni was hesitant to give the number.

'Okay, I understand... Well... You seem tired... We're leaving... Sonai... Shouldn't we leave and let Moni take rest?' Ved said this to Moni first, before turning to Sonai.

'Yes... Yes... Bye Moni... And Merry Christmas!' Sonai said as she walked towards Ved.

'Same to you dear,' Moni said, her face darkening.

'Bye... But before I go, may I be allowed to ask you something?' Ved asked, gently, looking straight at Moni.

Moni half nodded.

'What is your plan?' Ved asked.

'What?' Moni asked back, preoccupied in her own thoughts.

'About your life... Job...'

'Well... Not yet decided... Jobs... Are like dream killers...I feel sometimes,' Moni uttered, haltingly.

'Yes... They are... I think, if I may be allowed to suggest something: try to get a job... And try harder to write more... You write well... You've got that within you... Keep on,' Ved said, before waving adieu.

'Just a minute,' Moni shot him a serious look, then turned to Sonai, 'Can you please go to my room, for I have something to discuss with your dad,' she said softly.

Sonai obeyed like a meek, obedient pupil.

Ved smiled and waited, thinking that all these were always expected. In fact, he anticipated this move by Moni.

'Mr. Bhattacharya,' Moni began gravely, 'Can you... In your capacity, please tell me... Why you're always trying to help out me or Anu? I mean, we met by chance... In the case of Anu, she was your student... But do you actually go out all the way to help all of your students?'

Ved smiled.

Moni continued, 'Now... Now... Don't flash that smile... I almost demand the answer... It is important for me... For Anu also, I think.'

'Well... You have any other queries?' asked Ved.

'Only these for the time being...' she snapped, mechanically.

'Well... To start the discussion on a serious issue like this... I need to be a bit explanatory... So it might take a few minutes... But I only need one assurance from you... And that is you'll allow me to talk... And not interrupt me... Is that a very usual and common precondition which is okay for you?' Ved asked, gently.

Moni nodded, with her eyes being fixed on Ved.

'Yes... That's good! Well... As you know I am a widower... and my daughter is a bit emotional and innocent as all children usually are... Now, I feel that child rearing for a single parent is a difficult and unhealthy proposition,' Ved said like he was lecturing on single parenthood.

'So... You mean... You're on the look out?' Moni asked.

'Though you said, you would not interrupt me, I allow you... Because it might actually help us both to understand each other better... No, I am not actually on the look out for a *"stepmom"* for my daughter. I feel that somehow both of you need each other... Because both you and Sonai are pretty close... In case of Sonai... I fully understand and appreciate her position... She is helplessly alone... She needs someone to give motherly support, despite me doing everything possible to compensate for her motherlessness,' Ved stopped.

'May I smoke?' Ved asked, looking at Moni.

Moni half nodded, probably because her brain and heart were busy analysing Ved's each and every word.

Ved lit up a fag and exhaled a cloud before resuming. 'I am not sure, however, how much you actually need Sonai's company. Because you're the best judge of that... As far as

Anu is concerned, well... I'm bothered... Terribly bothered by her eccentricities... Not only because she is my student, but because I find her to be a very bright student with a lot of potential... And as a teacher, I think, my role is to ignite the minds of my students... So whatever I've done for her is absolutely justified... And I can assure you if ever I come across students like her... Bright and intelligent, going astray, I will, god willing, jump and try my best to salvage the student and put him or her into the right perspective...'

Ved spoke with a lot of conviction and tirelessly.

Moni still looked at Ved, gauging him.

'I understand and appreciate your views about *"salvaging Anu"*... But I have another question... Can I put that forward?' Moni asked, a bit relieved.

'Sure...' Ved said, as he took another puff.

'Should I take your views as if you had no personal wishes... You do whatever you do for others... For example, as you yourself clarified... You are always helpful to anyone... Anu or any of your students... You are trying to keep your daughter happy...' Moni asked, more like a statement.

'Yes... You're partially right... I do love helping others... I do care for strangers even if ever I come in contact with strangers with whom I can easily relate,' Ved answered.

'Now... I understand... You're a philanthropic... You love being that... It is your ego... It is your choice of self gratification...' Moni said, this time her tone was a bit serious.

'Partially true again... Self gratification should be replaced by a better word I think... Self emancipation,' Ved added, thoughtfully.

'Hey! Are you trying to say you're a Swami? A Vivekananda? Jesus? A saviour?' Moni smiled sarcastically.

Ved shook his head vehemently.

'No no… I'm not a saint… I know that… I have full knowledge of that… But I believe I am trying… To be good, to be happy, by making others happy.'

'That's good!' Moni said, looking pleased this time, but soon her brows contorted again, 'Well… I have another question for you.'

'Sure! Shoot!' said Ved.

'Well… Are you trying to say that you've reached a mental level from where you can actually look down on other mere mortals, considering yourself superior… At least mentally or spiritually?'

Ved smiled.

By this time, Sonai has come back and curled up beside Moni on the couch, looking at her dad.

'Hello dear… Not wanting to write anything on the computer?' Moni asked Sonai.

'No… I thought I should be here with you people,' Sonai said, looking curious and interested.

'Well,' Ved started in the same vein as he was actually carrying his voice and his whole being so far in the interrogation process initiated by Moni, 'I don't think it is my ego which is actually prompting or instigating me to do all these… It is something else… It is something very pure and divine… though I understand I am just another human… And I have no such problems with my instincts as a mortal, as far as I am not infringing on others' rights or privileges…'

Moni said nothing. She just looked at Ved.

'Now as I have answered all your queries… I think I need to ask you only one thing,' Ved said.

'Sure!' Moni nodded.

'Do you feel a kind of attachment to my daughter? Is it a serious attachment? Or is it an attachment that can possibly happen with you every time you meet a kid?' Ved asked, smiling.

'Well…' Moni started, turning and looking at Sonai who smiled at her, eagerly.

'Well… I have spent almost a whole day with her… I liked her… Her innocence… Her intelligence… Her poetic mind… Her candidness… Her familiarity… Her good upbringing… Her taste… Almost her everything…'

'That's good… But still…' Ved added and paused, to let Moni continue.

'Yes. I understand that all kids are actually lovable… They are primarily innocent… But the fact is, I've never in my life mixed so deeply with any kid other than Sonai… Not because I didn't get the chance or opportunity… For, in our apartment there are so many kids… I don't know how to put it… Sonai seemed good to me… She seemed too good,' saying this, Moni hugged Sonai. Sonai was always waiting for this hug. She just closed her eyes in happiness.

51

'When one dies one is acquitted of all sins, so don't worry...But other people like Mathur and Sultan Singh are alive. They will be hunted down and booked. I will come down to your place after the funeral. To ask you and your mother some routine questions. And to offer my heartfelt condolences...' added the Inspector, patting Anu's shoulders, at the hospital, before going away.

Anu was sitting speechless, tired, lonely, on the wooden bench of the lobby of the government hospital at Siliguri. Only one scene kept on repeating in her head in a cyclical manner, as if it was being played in auto-repeat mode:

> Suddenly Ramakant opened his eyes... It was so sudden that Anu who carried his head on her lap, all the way, as he lay motionless and still, on the backseat of the van, got a terrible jolt... As if he had awakened from the dungeon of death... His eyes looked still... No batting of lids... Nothing... As if a dead man was watching her... Then she shook him hard... Shook him

as if she wanted him to sit up and talk to her, thinking him to be cured of his brief unconsciousness and comatose state... Then, she shook him again, causing him to groan, be indistinct, inaudible... Anu dropped her ears to his mouth... So that she could hear what he was trying to say... He groaned for the second and last time... This time it was a bit prominent... Anu thought she heard the word—'*Shukriya*...thanks'

'Shukriya...'

That was probably the last word spoken by him last, late evening, as the van sped down the winding road, cutting through mist and fog and darkness.

'Shukriya...'

That was the last word uttered by the man who provided the seed to her mother so that she could be born.

That was too hard a word for her to come to proper terms with. When a dying father expresses thanks to his daughter, with his head on the daughter's lap, it is hard for the daughter to accept that impassively. So Anu cried more, shaking her dad, mumbling incoherently:

'Why? Dad? Why? It is okay... Look I'm here... To take you to the hospital... Look dad... Look!'

But the man, closed his eyes soon after that, as if he woke up only to say that. His face had no signs of pain. In fact, it looked as though he had gone into a very peaceful sleep.

That's how the seed thanked the plant. That's how probably all seeds thank their plants, seeing the plants full grown, mature, with branches spread out, standing tall, on their own, facing the challenges of life.

'Hello... Sorry to disturb you... Here are the official papers... Postmortem has been evaded as per your earnest request and the police intervention... Medically speaking he had died of cerebral hemorrhage...' A man in mid-thirties wearing a white V neck sweater and black trousers declared to Anu, cutting through her dense thoughts.

'I'm the doctor... Arunava Pal Chowdhury...' The man then said, half smiling.

Anu looked up. She felt she should stand up, but did not gain enough strength. She was feeling tired, lonely, morbid and void. Void was her mind and her eyes. Void was her existence; at least, it seemed like, then.

The doctor gave her the papers and went away before asking her to collect the death certificate from the office after two hours.

Anu thought she should call home and tell her mother the news. She did not know how she should put it across.

Earlier, instead of taking her dad home, she had taken him straight to the hospital, because she had thought that was the best thing to do. She herself also informed the local police, just after admitting him to the hospital, thinking that the police would come to know of Ramakant's hospitalisation anyway, as they were looking for him. She called her mother once the admission procedure was over. She called her from the phone booth at the hospital campus, requesting her not to worry.

Now with the man gone forever, leaving behind memories, she thought she should become mindful of the tasks ahead. She thought she should call her mom. She thought she should call the hearse service. She thought she should give a call to Moni, thanking her for bangles which provided her with quick money that she got hold of by selling them, before going to Lava. She did not bother her mom about money, because she knew she had nothing. Laxmi did not even know if there were any fixed deposits at the bank under her name. Rummaging through the almirahs and the single iron chest at home, she found a few bank notes not more than a few hundred rupees. So she had to barter the bangles, only one of the two, though to get hold of fifteen thousand in cash, instantly. She thought she should call Moni to assure her that the bangle would soon be hers, for she would salvage it somehow, at any cost.

So she stood up and walked lethargically to the cabin where Ramakant was kept wrapped, in white cover, to the chin.

Anu slowly moved towards the bed. She looked at the face.

The face looked peaceful. Only the beard unshaven, a thick scatter of salt pepper, made it look sickly. Otherwise, it was fine, as if a man was sleeping, without care. Taking a long sleep after a lot of trouble… After a lifetime of hassles and worries… As if, a soldier was taking rest after a long-drawn battle that had ended, and that his role of soldier had also ended with it…

Anu thought looking at the face. Then she came out and started walking towards the main exit of the building. She thought she would have to make a few calls.

It was almost nine in the morning… Twenty-sixth day of December… Marks of last night's revelry were still there on the streets… Confetti lay strewn… Balloons still hung from the shop windows.

In case of Bardhaman Road, Kolkata, the confetti and balloons strewn across bearing the marks of revelry were much more prominent, quite naturally. Festive colours are always more conspicuous in big cities and towns, compared to the smaller towns and the reasons are always decipherable—more money, more influx of people, more options of entertainment, more freedom, lesser social restrictions... And a few more reasons.

At nine on the twenty-sixth of December, the apartment on the road in which Moni stayed, looked sleepy. Distinctly sleepy, like the rest of the city, perhaps, with the main iron gate closed and all cars parked neatly as if they would not be going out anytime soon. The courtyard, which normally buzzed with activities, like maintenance staff sweeping and washing, fell vacant. Only, just beside the gate, in the designated cramped gate office, one of the security personnel could be seen sitting on a wooden stool, with his eyes half closed, relaxed, as if he was having an off-day at the office, with no visitors coming in or residents going out.

Moni, waking up at eight, also felt kind of aimless, as if she had nothing to do and nowhere to go. She felt she was yet to come to proper terms with her joblessness, which she hoped would be a brief stint of idleness, for last night on, she had begun thinking a bit positively about everything about her life, her job, her poems... Even about Anu. She had given it a hard thought and realised to some extent that she had to move on, for stagnation would mean death. She felt she still possessed all the qualities to break away from her brief stagnation. She felt the world had not been broken apart. More than anything else, she felt that there was still love in this mundane world full of crooks like Sanyal or Bhatia or Kevin. She also realised how much she had been egged on by the mere presence of Sonai and her beautiful, smiling face. She felt she should work even harder as she had a little girl relying so much on her. She felt, finally, she had something to live for.

Moni started thinking about Sonai and Ved and the constant flow of positive vibes emanating from them towards her:

How could a little girl, Sonai, carry so much conviction in love? Was it because she missed her mom and found something in Moni? What had she found in her? A mother? A friend? A poet? And was Ved really a helpless father? Moni thought quietly, 'He's good... He's principled... He's clean... He's not what he appears... He's not a fashion icon a *la Antonio Banderas*... He is more than that... A thinker... A deep thinker... A man with certain artistic ingenuity... A man, despite being a very youngish widower, not getting drifted away to ways of the modern world... Why you people are so good to me? Tell me? Tell me please,' she looked heavenwards.

Moni thought sadly that she did not deserve all the attention or love she was getting. She felt she was being showered with more love and care than she had received from anyone so far, besides Anu, and felt it all was so unwarranted.

Thinking about Anu, she strolled across the living to open Anu's door. It had remained closed since she had left it. The door was unlocked. It opened to reveal a clumsy bed. The pillows were stacked in the middle and the bed spread was crumpled. Moni thought she should clean the room and make it tidy. She thought, by doing that, she could while away some of her unlimited time in hand with nothing to do and nowhere to go.

Just then she heard her cell ringing somewhere. She remembered she had left it on the table at the living. She went out. The call was coming from a landline number. Moni looked at the glowing screen. She thought the number was familiar to her, though she could not exactly recall whose number it could be. I'm suffering from amnesia, for sure... Moni thought as she picked the phone up.

'Hello...' Moni said, pressing the green button.

'Hello... Good morning!' A sweet voice of a girl could be heard.

'Sonai?' Moni was surprised.

'Where from are you calling dear? From home? So early in the morning?' Moni jabbered, not knowing how to hide her surprise.

She also heard a soft and sombre song playing at the background.

'Hey! Opened the scrapbook given by you and thought to write something on the first page... Any suggestions?' Sonai asked.

Moni felt she heard the rumble of the cascading river.

'That's good! Really good! Well... Write something on the blue sky and the morning breaking out after a night of revelry... how's that?' Moni replied, playfully, though she herself was surprised by her own playful voice. She was surprised by her own change of mind, caused so suddenly by only a phone call.

'Great! Okay... I'm hanging up,' Sonai seemed to be in a hurry.

'Okay... But... Before you hang up can you please tell me what the song is?' Moni asked, as she still heard the soft and sombre music over phone.

'O! That's George Michael's *Jesus to a child*... My dad is listening to it... He usually listened to songs like that... Even instrumental music, especially early in the morning... Okay... I need to hang up... I'll call you as soon as I write something, okay?' Sonai said, hurriedly, as if she was terribly occupied with a lot of work.

'Okay… Have a good day!' Moni said, smiling.

No sooner had Moni hung up than the cell rang.

This time the number on the display, appeared quite unfamiliar, with STD code pasted upfront.

'Hello,' Moni uttered.

'Hi… Good Morning… Sorry to disturb you so early…'

'Hey! Are you Anu? Anu? Aren't you?' Moni almost screamed, recognising the familiar voice, being super excited.

'Yes… Dear…' Anu seemed tired, so tired that she could hardly speak.

'What happened?' Moni asked, anxious.

'Well… I just called to express *Shukriya* to you… to you all dear…' Anu's voice trailed, as if she was suppressing something and by doing that she was getting choked up.

'Anu! Come'n! What happened? I called you so many times, you know! But your cell was switched off… So was your mom's number… What happened dear?' Moni asked, a bit loudly, getting impatient.

'Well… My dad… He died this morning… At hospital… From cerebral hemorrhage…' Anu spoke finally up, with all her sadness overwhelming.

'What? How?' Moni asked even before she realised that her queries had been answered actually, in proper medical terms.

Moni fell silent. She felt helpless. She felt shocked.

Anu was also silent for a while. Then she started:

'Well… He died on my lap… So I know fully that when he died he was at peace with himself and with the world… He died as if he had chosen to die... Or to sleep permanently,' Anu spoke, as if she was in a trance.

'*Shukriya*, Moni... For your great help... You're so good...' Anu was choking up again, close to tears.

'It's okay dear... It's okay...' Moni said, overcome by helplessness.

'No... Let me speak for a while... You know, without your bangles... I wouldn't have paid up the hospital charges and other charges... I bartered one of them though... But be rest assured, you'll get'em back... As soon as I return... Don't you worry,' Anu said, choking still.

'Come'n! How's your mom? Is she okay? Should I go there?' Moni asked.

'You? O how you can possibly do that? You've got your job... With festive season on... Besides... The cremation will be over within a few hours,' Anu was hesitant.

'No no... I'll just catch a flight somehow and reach there within afternoon... You can go ahead with the funeral process... I just think I should be by your side... You also think that, don't you?' Moni asked, wiping her cheek by the back of her left palm, for tears rained down them, unknowingly almost.

'O... It would have been the best thing... For me... I'm not sure... You'll have to take a lot of trouble for that... Travelling such a long distance... Only for me...' Anu said, a bit cheerfully, but hesitant still.

'Don't worry! I'm trying to reach you... As quickly as I can...' Moni rushed through and hung up.

After hanging up, Moni stood still for a while, trying hard to process how she could get a flight seat booked. She could go to the travel agency's office down the road, a few metres away from their apartment. But will they have opened it, so early?

Moni looked at the watch. It was nine forty five in the morning. She thought she should get dressed up for the street, quickly. The cell started ringing again. Moni looked at the screen. Landline number from which Sonai called a few minutes back could be seen. Moni's first reaction was not to pick the phone up. But then she thought she must attend to the girl who loves her so dearly.

'Hello...' Moni said, sluggishly.

'Hi... I've written something... Can I recite the poem to you?' Sonai asked.

'Well... Will it be okay if I call you afterwards to listen to it... Actually, I am kind of busy... I need to arrange for an air ticket immediately,' Moni fumbled and soon realised that she had made a mistake. She blurted out too many.

'Air ticket? Why? Where are you going? Without me knowing?' Sonai probed, in a rhythmic manner though.

'Well... Anu... Her dad died this morning in Siliguri... And I need to get there today itself...' Moni replied, finding no escape route.

'I see! Just a minute... Dad!' Sonai shouted, holding the line, calling her dad.

This act of Sonai, of calling her dad, holding Moni on the line, was so sudden that Moni could not even realise what she could possibly do. Should she hang up?

'Hello... Good morning!' Ved picked up the line.

Moni's heart throbbed faster. She thought she should somehow hang up. But the voice of the man was so gentle and caring. Moni started crying even before she properly started talking to Ved.

She felt something within her collapse fast... As if floodgates were opening up and tears and wails and sobs were gushing with all force and she could no longer hold back. She could no longer control her inner turmoil, as if she had to let go. She felt time had come to finally release all her pent-up emotions, cooped tight for too long, in her dual existence—online and offline, both in reality and in her dreams. Now she felt truly freed in both worlds-in the physical world and also in psychological clouds.

52

Thirty first December.
Ratnarishi Bihar Buddhist Gumpha, Lava, Darjeeling district.

Sitting on the green grassy and mossy slope, overlooking the main red and yellow building of the Gumpha, and the eight white and golden bordered stupas standing like minarets just in front of him, Ved adjusted the focus of his camera. The surrounding was calm as ever, only distant cries of Sonai could be heard, reverberating across the whole courtyard of the Gumpha. Moni and Sonai were running round the sprawling campus of the Gumpha, through the mist and the fog that kept things less visible. The fog was like a translucent curtain, spread across the Gumpha and across the green hills.

Today they would be boarding the flight to Kolkata.

They meant him, Sonai and Moni. Anu would stay back for a while before taking her mother along. Anu would preferably sell their house here, at least that she opined that strongly on the day after the funeral of her father, in front of Ved and Moni and Sonai and some of their relatives. Her mother remained silent.

It seemed that she was not as eager as Anu to sell everything and go to the city of Kolkata, but she had few options left, as her daughter seemed hellbent to move away from Siliguri.

Ved adjusted and checked the light meter and felt that ISO settings should be fine tuned. He looked at the display with all his discerning eyes, checking the minutest details of the frame.

'So… Prof. Banderas? You are here? Capturing Moni from such a distance, with your camera, ha?

Anu's voice could be heard from behind. Ved turned back to see Anu standing a few yards up, on the slope, beside the white and red flags which fluttered in the chilling breeze. Ved looked at the flags, Anu and the green slope. Anu's red pullover served as a bright and colourful contrast to the green and lucid ambience, but not as something too flashy to outshine everything, but as something which enriched the beauty of the place. Ved turned the lens towards Anu.

'Hey! That's not fair! Moni might get hurt,' Anu said, in a tone of mock-seriousness, pulling Ved's legs.

'It seems you have more problems with Moni than I do … Miss Cruise,' Ved replied calmly as he adjusted the focal length again.

(This game of calling each other names had started very recently among the four, after Ved, Moni and Sonai arrived in Siliguri on twenty sixth evening.)

Sonai was now being called *angel* by Ved, Moni and Anu. Ved was called *Banderas* by Moni and Anu. Sonai called him dad as usual. Moni was called the *poetess* by Ved and Anu. Sonai however, calls her Moni. Anu was called *Miss Cruise* by Ved, Sonai and Moni. Anu *Miss Cruise,* because when she came to Lava, she drank a lot and jabbered intoxicated, repeatedly about how perfectly Tom Cruise played the part of a sommelier in the Hollywood movie *Cocktail*.

Anu, soon after the funeral of her dad, hatched a plan to go to someplace together and Lava was selected unanimously as it was near Siliguri and a serene place. Laxmi stayed back at Siliguri with some of her relatives for company.

This plan of going to a place after the funeral of one's father, appeared pretty awkward to everyone. Ved, however, agreed to the plan almost instantly and even played a significant role in convincing Laxmi Agarwal. He did not have to push her through, as she was already greatly impressed by the way Ved and Moni had arranged for everything soon after their arrival in Siliguri. They had sent out invitations for the *Shradh*—the act of offering water, food etc to the priests in honour of ancestors, in consultation with Anu. They did shopping.

They arranged for the priests and the evening prayer on twenty seventh. They stood by Anu like real older siblings, shouldering each and every responsibility. The few relatives of Laxmi and Anu, who somehow put up a poor show so far, after the death of Ramakant, initially tried to create a kind of disquiet, but both Anu and Laxmi, allowed and almost indulged in Ved's and Moni's company and support. Sonai, being a beautiful girl with a lovely face, won the heart of Laxmi, by her sheer smile and talk. She needed to do nothing extra. She could win anyone's heart.

So when Ved asked Laxmi's permission to allow Anu for a brief stay away from home, at Lava, with him, Sonai and Moni, she nodded, involuntarily. She even put her hands on Ved's head and murmured,'*Aap jaisi santaan sabko miley*...May everyone be blessed with a son like you'.

'Well… Shot it … Now you can move,' Ved said, after clicking two consecutive shots of Anu, standing by the flagposts, on the slope, in a red pullover, looking grimly gay.

'So … I'm just a model for your photo shoots, right?' Anu said as she started coming down the slope, to be near Ved.

'Ha ha… Miss Cruise, not only you … Everyone and everything around can be objects of photography… A photographer needs eyes that can spot the unusual in the usual…' Ved murmured, as he looked at the display running slide show of his photographs.

'Good! Can you tell me what "unusual" did you find in Moni? A poetess?' Anu almost retaliated, as she sat beside Ved. Ved turned his eyes from the LCD display of the camera, to Anu. He looked straight into her eyes. He wanted to decipher her mind.

'Anu… Dear… Are you getting jealous of Moni … Now that she appears happy?' Ved asked, baffled.

'No… No… Believe me… Not a bit… Only…' Anu stammered, pitifully.

Ved coughed to clear his voice and started:

'Anu, dear … You know that I am not attracted by her physical charms … But to understand and realise how much she is getting attached to Sonai is itself a rewarding experience for me … Sonai must have found something in her… She and Sonai. Look at them… fooling around this beautiful campus… with the fog and the mist covering them…. Look at the place dear … the trees … the flag posts … the stupas ahead… the sombre silence here enveloping us …. Don't you feel Anu, we are so tiny … And our life is so temporary? Don't you feel that the moment we are living together is only the moment of truth and beauty? Tell me … Anu … tell me. Now that your dad gone forever … don't you feel a void within? I felt the same all those years … More so because of Sonai … She appeared so lonely… So whimsical… Now I can find a change happening to her … She is scribbling her mind on paper… She's becoming creative … And I am certain it happened because of Moni … Now I can feel that Sonai, little Sonai needs someone motherly… to be her female confidante … as she is growing up fast… Moni is fitting into that role brilliantly and that role is also making her happy… Don't you see that?'

Ved kept on talking, in a grave but soft, almost inaudible voice.

Anu sat silently, listening to Ved, her head bent, looking at the green grass and the mossy slope that eventually met the eight white stupas with golden borderlines, glistening from dew and mist.

'Anu dear … I love you … In fact, I love all my students… I love all your batch mates… But as a teacher I feel you needed that light… You needed that path… So, I tried to show you that… You had narrated your dream of becoming a sommelier… That's important … That is more important than anything else in the world … I can help you to get to STIR academy and work as an apprentice under Shatbhi … I can actually support and guide you as a teacher.' Ved stopped briefly, looking tired, as if he had gone out of breath.

'Sorry… Prof. I didn't mean that… I got tremendous respect and love for Moni… Living with her all these years at Kolkata … She is an angel … She can perfectly act as Sonai's mom … Yes … And I also understand that I am feeling lonely … Because of my dad's death and because of the fact that Moni might be spending more time with Sonai ... With you ... But I also appreciate the fact that you, Moni and Sonai had come all the way to extend your help to me in my hours of distress ... But I never sought your help, did I?' Anu asked, with furrowed brows.

'No... Dear... I know you're self-dependent... You want to move independently... But I also feel you need a guide... friends ... To show you the path, with love ... You're lovesick... you need support ... I came here because you don't know how much Moni wanted to come here, to be beside you... She has got a golden heart ... And Sonai insisted that we should also come here, for Sonai wanted to spend more time with Moni in this vacation ... Moni, after initial resistance, finally budged ... So we are here ... Have we done wrong by coming here? Is something amiss? Tell me ... Speak your mind Anu ... Don't hide your genuine feelings ... Are you bothered that Moni is giving almost all her attention to Sonai? To me? Well ... Make no mistake Anu ... We're not going to get married as soon as we get back to Kolkata ... In fact, we never talked about that ... Probably, she needs our company and we do need the same ... we all need company ... Friends ... Confidantes ... Soul mates ... Because, that is the only way to make this short sojourn of mortal life ... Peaceful, blessed and joyous ... *Joie de vivre* ... light?' Ved said as he put his hand on Anu's shoulder, heaving a sigh.

'No ... No ... I didn't mean to hurt you or Sonai or Moni ... Believe me ... Please ...' Anu shook her head vehemently, looking sad.

'Good girl ... And you know how much Moni need our support. Your support? She has lost her job at Blitz. She's probably in financial distress … But she's not resorting to any cavil about that. She is bearing that pain within, all by herself,' Ved said, shrugging his shoulders.

'Is it so? Oh my god! Now I understand why she's getting absentminded, now and then. And feeling pained deeply within. A bit too frequently. Well … I assure you, I'll do something on that front … Don't worry,' Anu smiled.

Ved felt he had seen light in Anu finally.

The sun had also broken the dense curtain of fog and mist, to some extent, making the surroundings distinct. The eight stupas glistened more with new light of the day falling on them. Ved looked at the stupas and focused the camera on them.

'What are you people doing here?' Sonai said as she started climbing the white flight of stairs to come nearer to the slope where Ved and Anu were sitting. Moni was following her huffing and puffing.

'Sonai … Don't run on the steps, dear … You might fall!' Moni cried as she tried to match the fast happy feet of Sonai.

'We are taking photos … Come join us!' Ved cried back.

'Anu is your model?' Sonai asked, hopping and jumping on the steps as she came even closer to the slope.

'Yes! You too can be a model for me… Call Moni as well…' Ved said, holding onto his camera upright, working on the focus and aperture settings again, getting ready for another long spell of snapshots.

'No… No… You people stand…' Moni said, as she reached the last step of the flight of marble white steps.

'Come'n!' Sonai said.

Anu looked at Moni and uttered slowly but clearly, 'Moni dear, my poetess! Come'n! For my sake! Please!'

Moni looked at Anu and smiled and like an obedient pupil, followed suit.

The three women of different dresses, of different ages and height stood on the slope like Russian dolls.

'No... You people sit ... Side by side, on the slope... Putting your arms over each other. Like buddies,' Ved said, as he started slipping down the slope to get the proper frame.

He stopped near the stupas, eight in number, shining distinctly now, in the blazing sun.

53

Two years later: Twentieth day of October
River bank, Howrah.

The sun had set, taking the shape of a small red tennis ball.

Ved could be seen sitting on a ghat beside the flowing river, silently staring at the water.

Moni and Sonai were lighting candles nearby, under a tree. Earlier, they had placed candles in the crematorium. Today, being the twentieth of October, Ved had to come to the river bank. For the first time, after Mayurika's death, Sonai had come with him. Laxmi too called from the Bardhaman Road flat, where she and Moni had been staying together, for the last two years, to express her willingness to come to the bank. Moni did not call Ved. She came all by herself, straight from her office at Space Circle, on E.M. Bypass, to the riverside with candles and incense sticks. Moni had arrived even before Sonai and Ved could reach.

After lighting up the candles, Sonai and Moni came and sat beside Ved. The three just sat there silently, looking at the lush, silken river.

'Dad,' said Sonai, a bit grown up, and looking even more mature, called Ved finally.

Moni looked at Ved for a while before typing something on her smart phone. 'Yes dear,' she said.

'Are you not happy… Now that we've got so many people around us?' Sonai asked, heaving a sigh and looking at the cropped hair of her dad, tinges of white sprouting like hay in between his black hair.

'Sure! Dear! Why not?' Ved said and looked over his shoulder to catch Moni's eyes.

Moni was staring at him, with a faint smile on her lips. Ved noticed the beauty of Moni's face glowing in the weak white rays of her smart phone, held in her palm.

The silence of the place was only interrupted by the lashing waves of the river on the cemented ghat steps.

Suddenly, Ved's cellphone rang. Ved dished out the phone from his shirt pocket. Sonai leaned over closer, to glance at the caller.

Anu was calling, all the way from Mumbai. She had gone there, for a two years' course on mixology at STIR Academy.

'Hi Banderas! My deepest regret for not being able to be at the river bank with you,' Anu spoke, emotionally charged as ever.

'Where are you? At hostel?' Ved asked, smiling.

'No. Can't you hear the sound of waves? At the beach … Sitting on boulders … alone … and not drinking … but thinking of you … Moni, Sonai and my mom,' Anu shouted almost, for her voice was overcome by the sound of waves of the Arabian Sea.

'That's good ... Now get up and go back to hostel ... It is late already ... Don't sit there alone for long ...' Ved said, a tad seriously, concerned.

'Okay ... Okay Banderas! I'm fine! Don't you worry ... By the way, have you seen *CT's* blog page this evening?'

'No ... didn't scrape out time. Tell me ... any new poem from her?' Ved asked as he looked over his shoulder again to catch a glimpse of Moni's face. But she was not there. Moni had gone down to the last step of the ghat, to dip her feet in the cool water.

Sonai was also with her. He could them both at a distance, standing adjacent to each other. Sonai was holding Moni with her right hand. Ved looked at the silhouettes, on the ghat.

'What has she written?' Ved whispered.

'Well,' Anu said, 'it would be better if you read it yourself.'

'Come'n dear! Tell me.' Ved almost implored.

'Well... I'm reading it... Listen up...!'

I agree that we are not provided with the exact knowledge of our birth, but our genes carry all the codes that we inherit from our progenitors. In other words, our birth is controlled, governed by many factors not in our hands.... But that doesn't make our births unpredictable! As soon as we are born, the unpredictability of our birth is resolved... As long as we are alive, the unpredictability of life is to be taken as a constant... taken for granted.... In case of death, the same idea gets automatically applied ... doubtlessly. But that is not the focal issue. We should not be bothered by the constant ... as we can never change it (Even if we try, we are actually taking life into our hands, unnecessarily!). Instead, we should work on the variables ... cause they could actually take us to our heights in every sense.... Ain't it?'

Anu paused after reading the lines from Moni's blog page.

'Got anything Banderas?' Anu asked, after gathering her breath.

'Got that... Our poetess is becoming a philosopher,' Ved said.

'Now it is time you people get married ... otherwise the poetess will become a Socrates and leave you forever ... in her quest for the unknown,' Anu chuckled.

'That's a real cause of worry. Okay I will think hard on the issue and revert to you at the earliest,' Ved said, jokingly.

'Do it fast! I mean ... think of marriage... propose to her. Let me know your plans ... I've got four bangles to be made ... Gold bangles,' Anu said, full of concern.

'Bangles? What for?' Ved asked surprised.

'It is not your business, Banderas! Go ahead! Just tell Moni that she would get four gold bangles from me ... As a gift! Understood?' Anu asked with all seriousness.

'Okay okay ... but I am thinking right now of an exciting plan... How about going somewhere together? You, me, Sonai, Moni, Laxmi Aunty, and my parents. Hey! What about taking a sabbatical?' Ved asked, with sudden enthusiasm.

'A sabbatical? Where will we be going?' Anu asked.

'You're coming home *na*, this winter?' Ved asked.

'Yes ... Of course! I'm dying for the winter vacation, to be with you all!' Anu gushed.

'Well ... I'm making arrangements for a holiday trip to Simla. How's that? For us all?' Ved asked.

'Thank god! You haven't chosen a temple or monastery or a church! Good!' Anu said.

'Hey! Still talking to Anu?' Sonai asked as she came near Ved.

Moni was standing behind Sonai with her hands on Sonai's shoulders, looking at Ved.

'Oh dear! We've finished jabbering … want to talk to her?' Ved said as he extended the cell to Sonai who grabbed it instantly and started talking, slowly moving away from Ved and Moni.

'Got a new pair of low-waist? That's mischievous Anu!'

Ved heard Sonai exclaiming over phone. Moni stood there. She was looking at Ved.

Ved thought he should stand up and go near Moni, to embrace her and plant a kiss on her shiny forehead. He thought it was time for him to walk the little distance.

Life … could never be a tragedy … because that would make everything meaningless. It could never be a comedy even, for that would make life utterly ridiculous … Life, is only a journey which is true … both online and offline … both in real terms and the unreal ones … in dreams and non-dreams.

Ved thought of all this, as he strolled that little distance between him and Moni. Moni was, however, standing there, as if she had been made to wait exactly there throughout her life, teary eyed and smiling.

Life … to most people … is just like an Archimedean spiral … You can always move at a uniform angular velocity from the point of your origin … like a pebble tied to that point with an ever expanding string … You always circle that point …

You can keep moving away from the centre, as the string is expandable, elastic ... But you simply can't cut the string off ... You just keep on moving in ever expanding circles ... Knowing perfectly well that the strength of the string—like love—pins you to the point of your origin.